"Wonderful, mesmerizing. A finely written and deeply considered SF novel that deserves to stand with the classics in the field. It reads like Arthur C. Clarke channeling Einstein channeling Thomas Aquinas—and that's only the beginning. This book should be garlanded with awards, but more important, it should be in your hands, and you should be reading it."

—Robert Charles Wilson

"Flynn takes us deeply into two marvelous worlds: a medieval village in Germany where rationalism and folk beliefs are forced to deal with an alien intruder, and our modern world, where a scientific historian and a theoretical physicist, because they happen to live together, are able to cross the boundaries between disciplines and make some vital discoveries together. . . . It is refreshing to see Flynn pop up with a deeply researched and well-thought-out novel that moves us and makes us smarter just for having read it. How often do we get to read a novel that makes us think, 'This guy knows what he's talking about'? By the end, I found myself halfway believing the story of aliens arriving in Germany in the fourteenth century. . . . I wanted it to be true, in a weird, semi-tragic way."

—Orson Scott Card

"For fans of . . . brainy first-contact tales (Carl Sagan meets Umberto Eco). Lowdown: Bursting with pungent historical detail and big theme musings, this dense, provocative novel offers big rewards to patient readers."

—*Entertainment Weekly*

"With a sure grasp of both speculative science and medieval history, Flynn compellingly weaves past and present together in a dialog of faith and science. With neat turns of plot and intriguing medieval and modern characters, this book, parts of which were previously published as a novella, belongs in even small libraries. Highly recommended."

—*Library Journal* (starred review)

"Flynn's combination of science fiction, historical fact, and logical deduction makes for a fascinating and addictive read."

—*Rocky Mountain News*

"In Flynn's masterful hand, even the most fateful conversations take delightful turns as human and alien discuss the heavens and how to return to them. *Eifelheim* is both speculative fiction and morality tale."

—*Sunday Free Press* (four out of four stars)

"Marvelous. Wonderful. A tour de force. Choose your superlative. Flynn uses physics, theology, logic, and extraterrestrials to explore the subtleties of the human heart and mind while telling a page-turner of a tale filled with vivid characterizations of time and place. Highly recommended."

—*Starlog*

"*Eifelheim* is a truly impressive and enjoyable novel."

—Stanley Schmidt

"*Eifelheim* is one of those very occasional novels that you know early on you will never forget. A powerhouse."

—Jack McDevitt

"Michael Flynn's *Eifelheim* is a gripping multilayered masterpiece, that pulls off the extraordinary feat of imagining a convincing first contact with aliens that might have taken place in 1348, and adds an equally convincing account of the manner in which the event might be rediscovered by a twenty-first century historian. The intricate detective story is supplemented by a heartfelt moral commentary on the manner in which the contact was negotiated and the crucial significance it retains, in spite of having been forgotten for nearly seven hundred years."

—Brian Stableford

EIFELHEIM

ALSO BY MICHAEL FLYNN

*In the Country of the Blind**

The Nanotech Chronicles

Fallen Angels (with Larry Niven and Jerry Pournelle)

*Firestar**

*The Forest of Time and Other Stories**

*Lodestar**

*Rogue Star**

*Falling Stars**

*The Wreck of the River of Stars**

*denotes a Tor book

EIFELHEIM

Michael Flynn

A Tom Doherty Associates Book
New York

This is a work of fiction. All of the characters, organizations, and events portrayed in this novel are either products of the author's imagination or are used fictitiously.

EIFELHEIM

Edited by David G. Hartwell

Map by Ellisa Mitchell

A Tor Book
Published by Tom Doherty Associates, LLC
175 Fifth Avenue
New York, NY 10010

www.tor.com

Library of Congress Cataloging-in-Publication Data

Flynn, Michael (Michael F.)
Eifelheim / Michael Flynn.
p. cm.
"A Tom Doherty Associates book."
ISBN-13: 978-0-7653-1910-4
ISBN-10: 0-7653-1910-1
1. Germany—History—1273–1517—Fiction. 2. Black Death—Fiction. 3. Fourteenth century—Fiction. 4. Priests—Fiction. 5. Historians—Fiction. 6. Women physicists—Fiction. 7. Human-alien encounters—Fiction. I. Title.

PS3556.L89E35 2006
813'.54—dc22

2006005468

First Hardcover Edition: October 2006
First Trade Paperback Edition: November 2007

Printed in the United States of America

0 9 8 7 6 5 4 3 2 1

JEAN BURIDAN DE BETHUNE

the Paris Master

ACKNOWLEDGMENTS

I would like to thank especially Dr. Mohsen Janatpour, now of the College of San Matteo, for his help in creating Janatpour space for the original novella, back in 1986. Variable light speed using Kaluza-Klein dimensions, three-dimensional time, and quantized time seemed pretty far-out in those days. Still does, come to think of it.

Vielen Dank, too, to the staff at the Fürstenfeld Museum for background data on Ludwig der Bayer, William of Ockham, and German art and culture of that era; also to Fr. William Seifert for background on pre-Tridentine liturgical developments.

I would also like to thank Stan Schmidt, editor of *Analog Science Fiction* magazine, for publishing the novella from which the "Now" portions of this book derive, and Eleanor Wood, my agent, for pestering me into writing the medieval portions of the book. Finally, also, to Tor editor David Hartwell, who helped me chop the unwieldy first draft into shape.

NOTE ON THE CALENDAR. Although the civil year *III Caroli, rex germanorum,* began on 1 January, the Year of the Lord *(Anno Domini)* did not begin in some places until 25 March, the Feast of the Incarnation. Thus the first three months of what we would call "1349" were still "1348" in some parts of Europe. Other regions counted the years of the Lord from the Nativity rather than the Incarnation, and still others used the civil year. The Greeks used a different system. A merchant caravan could thus travel from year to year as easily as from place to place!

CONTENTS

LIST OF CHARACTERS

Sharon Nagy. A cosmologist and longtime domestic partner of Tom
Tom Schwoerin. A cliologist (mathematical historian) and longtime domestic partner of Sharon
Judy Cao. A librarian, later Tom's research assistant
Jackson Welles. Sharon's chairman
Hernando Kelly. Post-doc in nucleonic engineering; shares an office with Sharon
Anton Zaengle. An historian at the Albert-Louis University in Freiburg and colleague of Tom
Monsignor Heinrich Lurm. An official of the Diocese of Freiburg and an amateur archeologist
Gus Mauer and Sepp Fischer. Workmen from Freiburg

GEMEINDE OBERHOCHWALD

Pastor Dietrich. The *doctor seclusus.* Onetime student of Jean Buridan de Bethune, now pastor of St. Catherine's Church in Oberhochwald
Brother Joachim von Herbholzheim. A Spiritual Franciscan waiting out a quarrel in the Strassburg friary
Theresia Gresch. Herb woman and healer; Dietrich's onetime ward
Gregor Mauer. Stone mason in Oberhochwald
Lorenz and Wanda Schmidt. Blacksmith in Oberhochwald and his wife
Klaus Müller. *Maier* of the village. Operates the Herr's mill
Hildegarde Müller. The miller's wife
Volkmar Bauer. A strong farmer holding several manses
Seppl Bauer. Bauer's son; betrothed to Ulrike Ackermann
Felix and Ilse Ackermann. A farmer in Oberhochwald and his wife
Maria Ackermann. Ackermann's younger daughter
Ulrike Ackermann. Ackermann's older daughter; betrothed to Seppl Bauer
Heinrich Altenbach. A homesteader near Oberhochwald
Herwyg One-eye. Farms Dietrich's tithe lands
Trude Metzger. Widow. Holds the strips abutting Herwyg. Her sons are Melchior and Peter
Nickel Langermann. A gärtner
Walpurga Honig. Beekeeper and ale-wife
Oliver Becker. Son of Jakob the baker
Bertram Unterbaum. Owes "handservice" as herald to the Herr. Oliver's rival for Anna Kohlmann

Anna Kohlmann. Kohlmann's daughter
Geirech Jaeger. A hunter

BURG HOCHWALD

Herr Manfred von Hochwald. Lord of the High Woods. A widower
Kunigund. Manfred's older daughter, fiancée to Eugen
Irmgard. Manfred's younger daughter
Eugen. Manfred's junker (der junge Herr)
Thierry von Hinterwaldkopf. One of Manfred's vassals. A Ritter (knight)
Max Schweitzer. Sergeant at arms. Has charge of Manfred's garrison
Peter von Rheinhausen. Manfred's minnesinger
Fr. Rudolf. Manfred's chaplain
Everard Steward. Manfred's steward, responsible for the sallands and the serfs

THE KRENKEN

The Herr Gschert. Steward of the vessel, later called Baron Grosswald
The Kratzer. Senior scientist of the charter group
Shepherd. *Maier* of the pilgrims
Johann (Hans). Servant of the talking head
Gottfried. Servant of the electronic essence
Arnold. Chirurgeon
Ulf and Heloïse. Labtechs

OTHERS

Philip von Falkenstein. A robber baron
Malachai ben Shlomo. A factor for the Seneor family, based in Regensburg
Tarkhan Hazar ben Bek. Malachai's servant
Einhardt and Rosamund. An imperial knight and his wife. Holds a fief near Oberhochwald
A Freiburg fishwife and her son.
Archdeacon Willi Jarlsberg. Onetime classmate of Dietrich's. Holds Freiburg for the Bishop of Strassburg
A Savoyard Chirurgeon.
William of Ockham. The *venerabilis inceptor.* Widely known philosopher, at Kaiser Ludwig's court
Imre. A peddler from Hungary

Oberhochwald and Vicinity
1348 ~ 1349
To Bear Valley
Krenkish Camp
Charcoal Kiln
The Great Woods
To Stag's Leap
fallow
Common
Pasture
To Altenbach's Farm
Spring Planting
To St. Wilhelm
Autumn Planting
Mill Pond
Gärtner's huts
Meadows
Church of St Catherine of Alexandria
Smithy
Stone-yard
Church Hill
Schloss Hochwald
The Lesser Wood
Hof Hochwald
Castle Hill
To Oberreid
Ellisa Mitchell 2006

For God is deaf nowadays and will not hear us,
And for our guilt he grinds good men to dust.

—WILLIAM LANGLAND,
Piers Ploughman

C'est le chemin qu'on appelle le Val d' Enfer. Que votre Altesse
me pardonne l'expression; je ne suis pas diable pour y passer.

—MARSHAL VILLARS,
regarding the Höllenthal, 1702

EIFELHEIM

· PREFACE ·

Anton

I KNOW where the path to the stars lies. The gate opened once, a long time ago and in a far and unlikely place. And then it closed. This is the story of how it opened and of how it closed and perhaps of what hinged upon it.

You see, Sharon Nagy was a physicist and Tom Schwoerin was a cliologist. That was the heart of the business right there. That was the beginning of it and the end of it and most of what happened in between.

Or perhaps you don't, for the seeing was not easy. Medieval settlement patterns and multiple brane theory seem worlds apart. Indeed, they *are* worlds apart, tangent only in that small apartment in Philadelphia that Tom and Sharon shared. But at such close quarters they could not avoid learning a little of each other's work, and that was the fulcrum on which they turned the world.

But I was into the affair last and least of all, and perhaps it would be best to let the story tell itself.

· I ·

AUGUST, 1348

At Matins, The Commemoration of Sixtus II and His Companions

DIETRICH AWOKE with an uneasy feeling in his heart, like a bass voice chanting from a darkened choir loft. His eyes flew open and darted about the room. A night candle guttering in its sconce cast capers over table and basin, prie-dieu and psalter, and caused the figure upon the crucifix to writhe as if trying to tear itself down. In the corners and angles of the room, shadows swelled enormous with their secrets. Through the east window, a dull red glow, thin as a knife across a throat, limned the crest of the Katerinaberg.

He took a long, stilling breath. The candle told Matins anyway; so, throwing the blanket aside, he exchanged nightshirt for cassock. Goose bumps puckered his skin and the short hairs rose on his neck. Dietrich shivered and hugged himself. *Something will happen today.*

By the window stood a small wooden table with a bowl and aquamanile upon it. The aquamanile was of chased copper and had the form of a rooster, with the feathers worked into it by a coppersmith's clever awl. When he tipped it, the water ran from the beak over his hands into the bowl. "Lord, wash away my iniquities," he murmured. Then he dipped his hands into the bowl and splashed the cold water onto his face. A good dousing would scatter the night fears. He broke a piece of soap off the cake and rubbed it on his hands and face. Something will happen today. Ach, there was prophecy! He smiled a little at his fear.

Through the window he noticed a light moving about at the base of the hill. It would appear, move a short space, then disappear, only to rematerialize after a moment and repeat the dance. He frowned, not quite knowing what it was. A salamander?

No. A blacksmith. Dietrich became aware of his tension only in the moment of its release. The forge lay at the bottom of the hill and the smith's cottage beside it. The light was a candle moving to and fro before an open window: Lorenz, pacing like a caged beast.

So. The smith—or his wife—was awake also, and evidently in a nervous state.

Dietrich reached for the aquamanile to rinse the soap off and a needle stabbed him in the palm. "Sancta Katherina!" He stepped back, knocking bowl and water pitcher to the floor, where the soapy water fanned across the flagstones. He searched his hand for wounds and found none. Then, after a moment's hesitation, he knelt and retrieved the aquamanile, handling it gingerly, as if it might bite him once again. "You are a froward rooster," he told the pitcher, "to peck me like that." The rooster, unmoved by the admonition, was returned to his place.

When he wiped his hands on a towel he noticed that his hairs stood away, as a dog's fur might bristle before a fight. Curiosity wrestled with dread. He pulled the sleeve of his cassock back and saw how his arm hairs rose also. It reminded him of something, long ago, but the memory wouldn't come clear.

Recalling his duties, he dismissed the puzzle and crossed to the prie-dieu, where the dying candle sputtered. He knelt, crossed himself and, pressing his hands together, gazed at the iron cross upon the wall. Lorenz, that very smith who prowled at the base of the hill, had fashioned the sacramental from an assortment of nails and spikes and, although it did not look much like a man upon a cross, it seemed as if it might, if only one looked deeply enough. Retrieving his breviary from the shelf of the prie-dieu, he opened it to where he had marked his morning office with a ribbon the day before.

"The hairs of your head are all numbered," he read from the prayer for Matins. "Do not be afraid. You are of more value than many sparrows . . ." And why *that* prayer on this particular day? It was too appropriate by far. He glanced again at the hairs on the back of his hand. A sign? But if so, of what? "The saints will exult in glory," he continued. "They will rejoice upon their couches. Give us the joy of communion with Sixtus and his companions in eternal beatitude. This we ask of Thee through our Lord, Jesus Christ. Amen."

Of course. Today was the feast day of Pope Sixtus II, and so the prayer for martyrs was called for. He knelt in silent meditation upon the steadfastness of that man, even in the face of death. A man so good as to be remembered eleven centuries after his murder—beheaded at the very celebration of the Mass. Above the tomb of Sixtus, which Dietrich himself had seen in the cemetery of Callistus, Pope Damasus had later inscribed a poem; and while the verses were not so good a poem as Sixtus had been a man, they told his story well enough.

We had better popes in those days, Dietrich thought and then immediately chastised himself. Who was he to judge another? The Church today, if not overtly persecuted by kings themselves nominally Christian, had become a plaything of the French crown. Subordination was a more subtle persecution, and so perhaps a more subtle courage was called for. The French had not cut Boniface down as the Romans had Sixtus—but the Pope had died from the manhandling.

Boniface had been an arrogant, contemptuous man with not a friend in the world; and yet, was he not also a martyr? But Boniface had died less for proclaiming the Gospel than for proclaiming *Unam sanctum,* to the great displeasure of King Philip and his court, whereas Sixtus had been a Godly man in an ungodly age.

Dietrich glanced suddenly over his shoulder, then chided himself for the start. Did he suppose that they would come for him, too? It was not beyond reason that they might. But what cause had the Markgraf Friedrich to seize him?

Or rather, what cause that Friedrich might know of?

Do not be afraid, the day's prayer had commanded, the most frequent command from the Lord's mouth. He thought again of Sixtus. If the ancients had not quailed even at death, why should his own heart, instructed by modern wisdom, harbor fear for no sound reason?

He studied the vagrant hairs on the back of his hand, brushed them flat, and watched them rise up again. How would Buridan have approached this problem, or Albrecht? He marked his place in the book for Lauds; then he placed a fresh hour-candle in the candlestick, trimmed the wick, and lit it with a taper from the stub of the old.

Albrecht had written, *Experimentum solum certificat in talibus.* Experiment is the only safe guide.

He silhouetted the woolen sleeve of his gown before the candle flame, and a smile slowly creased his lips. He felt that curious satisfaction that always enveloped him when he had reasoned his way to a question and then coaxed an answer from the world.

The woolen fibers of his sleeve stood also upright. *Ergo,* he thought, the impetus impressed upon his hair was both external and material, as a woolen cassock had no ghostly part to be frightened. So, the nameless dread that troubled him was no more than a reflection of that material impression upon his soul.

But the knowledge, however satisfying to the intellect, did not quiet the will.

LATER, AS Dietrich crossed to the church to pray the morning Mass, a whine drew his gaze to the shadowed corner beside the church steps and, in the flickering light from his torch, he saw a black and yellow dog cowering with its front paws crossed over its muzzle. The spots on its fur blended into the shadows so that it looked like some mad creature, half-dog and half–swiss cheese. The cur followed Dietrich with hopeful eyes.

From the crest of Church Hill, Dietrich saw that a lustrous glow, like the pale cast that bleached the morning skies, suffused the Great Woods on the far side of the valley. But it was too early—and in the wrong sky. Atop the church spire, blue-flamed corposants swirled around the cross. Had even those asleep in the cemetery been aroused by the dread? But *that* sign was not promised until the last days of the world.

He uttered a hasty prayer against occult danger and turned his back on the strange manifestations, facing the church walls, seeking comfort in their familiarity.

My wooden cathedral, Dietrich had sometimes called it, for above its stone foundation St. Catherine's oak walls and posts and doors had been whittled by generations of earnest woodsmen into a wild congeries of saints and beasts and mythic creatures.

Beside the door, the sinuous figure of St. Catherine herself rested her hand upon the wheel whereon they had thought to break her. *Who has triumphed?* her wan smile asked. *Those who turned the wheel are gone, but I abide.* Upon the doorposts, lion, eagle, man, and ox twisted upward toward the tympanum, in which the *Last Supper* had been carved.

Elsewhere: Gargoyles leered from the roof 's edge, fantastic in horns and wings. In spring, their gaping mouths disgorged the flow of melting snows from the steep-pitched tiles of the roof. Under the eaves, kobolds hammered. On lintels and window jambs, in panels and columns, yet more fantastic creatures were relieved from the wood. Basilisks glared, griffins and wyverns reared. Centaurs leaped; panthers exuded their sweet, alluring breath. Here, a dragon fled from Amaling knights; there, a *sciopod* stood on his single enormous foot. Headless *blemyae* stared back from eyes affixed to their bellies.

The oaken corner-posts of the building had been carved into the images of mountain giants upholding the roof. Grim and Hilde and Sigenot and Ecke, the villagers called them; and Ecke, at least, seemed a proper name for a corner-post. Someone with a sense of humor had worked the pedestal of each column into the form of a weary and irritable dwarf upholding the giant and glaring with resignation at passersby.

The wonderful riot of figures, emerging from the wood but never entirely separate, seemed indeed to be a living part of it. *Somewhere,* he thought, *there are creatures like these.*

When the wind blew hard or the snow lay heavy upon the roof, the menagerie would whisper and groan. It was only the shifting and bending of joists and rafters, yet it often seemed as if Sigenot rumbled and dwarfish Alberich squeaked and St. Catherine hummed a small tune to herself. On most days, the murmuring walls amused him, but not today. With the unease that lay upon him, Dietrich feared that the Four Giants would suddenly unburden themselves and bring the whole edifice down upon him.

More than one cottage below the hill now showed a flicker of candlelight behind its windows, and atop Manfred's keep on the other side of the little valley, the night watch paced in unwonted alertness, peering first one way then another for the approach of some unseen enemy.

A figure stumbled toward him from the village, recovered, slipped in the dirt, and a thin sob carried in the early morning air. Dietrich raised his torch and waited. Was the heralded menace even now slouching brazenly toward him?

But even before it fell to its knees breathlessly before him, the figure had resolved itself into Hildegarde, the miller's wife, barefooted and with her hair a tangle, a hasty cloak thrown over her night smock. Dietrich's torchlight glimmered on an unwashed face. A menace she may have been, but of another and long-familiar sort.

"Ach, pastor!" she cried. "God has discovered my sins."

God, Dietrich reflected, had not had far to look. He raised the woman to her feet. "God has known all our sins from the beginnings of time."

"Then why has he awakened me today with such fear? You must shrive me."

EAGER TO put walls between himself and the foreboding miasma, Dietrich led Hilde into the church; and was disappointed, if not surprised, to find his anxiety undiminished. Holy ground might hold the supernatural at bay until the end of time, but the merely natural intruded where it would.

In the stillness Dietrich heard a soft whisper, as of a small wind or a running brook. Shading his eyes against the brightness of his torch, Dietrich discerned a smaller shadow crouched before the main altar. Joachim the Minorite hunched there, his hurried ejaculations rushing over themselves like a fleeing crowd, so that the words blended into an indistinct susurration.

The prayers cut off, and Joachim turned, rising in a quick, lithe movement. He wore a tattered, brown habit of long employment, carefully and repeatedly mended. The cowl shadowed sharply chiseled features: a small dark man with heavy brows and deep brooding eyes. He wet his lips with a quick motion of his tongue.

"Dietrich . . . ?" the Minorite said, and the word quavered a little at the end.

"Don't be afraid, Joachim. We all feel it. The beasts, too. It is some natural thing, a disturbance in the air, like silent thunder."

Joachim shook his head and a curl of black hair fell across his brow. "*Silent* thunder?"

"I can think of no better way to describe it. It is like the bass pipe of a great organ that makes the glass shiver." He told Joachim his reasoning with the wool.

The Minorite glanced at Hildegarde, who had lingered at the rear of the church. He rubbed both his arms under his robe and looked side to side. "No, this dread is God's voice calling us to repentance. It is too terrible to be anything else!" He cried this in his preaching voice, so that the words came back from the statues that watched from their niches.

Joachim's preaching favored gestures and colorful stories, while Dietrich's own closely reasoned sermons often had a soporific effect on his flock. Sometimes he envied the monk his ability to stir men's hearts; but only sometimes. Stirred, a heart could be a terrible thing.

"God may call," he instructed the younger man, "by wholly material means." He turned the young man with a gentle pressure on his shoulder. "Go, vest the altar. The Mass 'Clamavérunt.' The rubrics call for red today."

A hard man to deal with, Dietrich thought as Joachim left, and a harder one to know. The young monk wore his rags with greater pride than the pope in Avignon his gilded crown. The Spirituals preached the poverty of Jesus and His Apostles and railed against the wealth of the clergy; but the Lord had blessed not the poor, but the poor *in spirit*—"Beati pauperes spritu." A clever distinction. As Augustine and Aquinas had noted, mere poverty was too easily attained to merit such a prize as Heaven.

"Why is he here?" Hildegarde asked. "All he does is sit in the street and beg and rant."

Dietrich made no answer. There were reasons. Reasons that wore golden tiaras and iron crowns. He wished that Joachim had never come, for he could accomplish little else but draw attention. But the Lord had said, "I was a stranger, and you took me in," and He had never mentioned any exceptions. *Forget the great events of the world beyond the woods,* he reminded himself. *They concern you no longer.* But whether the world beyond the woods would forget him was another, and less comforting, thought.

IN THE confessional, Hildegarde Müller confessed to one small and petty act after another. She had damped the flour on the bags of grain brought to her husband for milling, the second worst-kept secret in Oberhochwald. She had envied the brooch worn by Bauer's wife. She had neglected her aged father in Niederhochwald. She seemed determined to work her way through the entire Decalogue.

Yet, two years past, this same woman had sheltered a ragged pilgrim on his way to the Church of St. Sepulcher in Jerusalem. Brian O'Flainn had walked all the way from Hibernia, at the very edge of the world, through a land in turmoil—for that year the English king had slaughtered the chivalry of France—only to be robbed of everything by the lord of Falcon Rock. Hilde Müller had taken this man into her house, nursed his sores and blisters; had given him new raiment from her scowling husband's garderobe, and had sent him on his way refreshed and hale. Against the theft and the jealousy and the covetousness, weight that in the pan, as well.

Sin lay not in the concrete act, but in the will. Behind the woman's recitation lay the cardinal sin of which these mean transgressions were but the visible signs. One could return a brooch or visit a parent; but unless the inner flaw were healed, repentance—however sincere the moment—would shrivel like the seed upon the bad ground.

"And I have taken pleasure with men who were not my lawful husband."

That being the worst-kept secret in Oberhochwald. Hildegarde Müller stalked men with the same cool deliberation with which Herr Manfred stalked the stags and boars that adorned the walls of Hof Hochwald. Dietrich had a sudden and disconcerting vision of what might dangle from Hildegarde's trophy wall.

Trophies? Ach! *That* was the inner sin. Pride, not lust. Long after the fleshly pleasures must have palled, the stalking and capture of men remained an affirmation that she could have whatever she desired whenever she desired it. Her kindness to the Irish pilgrim, too—not paradox but confirmation. She had done it for show, so that others could admire her generosity. Even her endless recitation of venial sins was a prideful thing. She was bragging.

For every weakness, a strength; and so for pride, humility. Her penance, he decided, would require the usual restitutions. Return the brooch, restore the flour, visit her father. Have no other man than her husband. Treat *any* distressed pilgrim, however mean his station, with the same charity as she had shown the Irish lordling. But she must also, as a lesson in humility, scrub the flagstone floor of the church nave.

And this must be done in secret, lest she take pride even in her penances.

AFTERWARD, ROBING in the sacristy for the morning Mass, Dietrich paused with his cincture half tied. There was a sound, like that of a bumblebee, at the edge of his hearing. Drawn toward the window, he saw in the distance woodleafsingers and acorn-jays flying in mad gyres above the place where earlier had glowed the pale luminescence. The glow had either faded or was now insensible against the brightening sky. But the vista seemed odd in some indefinable manner. There was a pinchedness to the outlook, as if the forest had been creased and folded on itself.

At the base of Church Hill, a knot of people milled as witlessly as the birds above. Gregor and Theresia stood by the smithy in agitated conversation with Lorenz. Their hair was wild and unkempt, sticking out from their heads, and their clothing clung to them as if wet. Others were about as well, but the usual morning work had come to a standstill. The smithy's fire was unlit and the sheep bleated in their pen, the sheepboys nowhere in sight. The pall of smoke that usually marked the charcoal kiln deep in the forest was absent.

The humming grew distinctly louder as Dietrich approached the window. Touching the glass lightly with a fingernail, he felt a vibration. Startled, he pulled away.

Dietrich passed a hand through his locks, only to feel his hair writhe like a nest of snakes. The cause of these curiosities was waxing in strength, as the sound and size of a galloping horse grew with its approach—which analogy would argue that the source of the impetus was drawing nearer. *There can be no motion in a body,* Buridan had argued, *unless an actor impresses an impetus.* Dietrich frowned, finding the thought disturbing. *Something* was approaching.

He turned from the window to resume vesting and paused with one hand on the red chasuble.

Amber!

Dietrich remembered. Amber—*elektron,* as the Greeks called it—when rubbed against fur impressed an impetus to the fur that caused it to move in much the same way as his hair. Buridan had demonstrated it at Paris while Dietrich had been in studies. The master had found such delight in instruction that he had foregone the doctorate—and had become from his fees that great anomaly: a scholar never in want. Dietrich saw him now in memory, rubbing the amber vigorously against the cat's skin, his mouth pulled back in an unconscious grin.

Dietrich studied his own image in the window. *God was rubbing amber against the world.* Somehow, the thought excited him, as if he were on the verge of uncovering a form previously occult. A dizzy feeling, like standing atop the belfry. Of course, God was not rubbing the world. But something was happening that was *like* rubbing the world with amber.

Dietrich stepped to the sacristy door and looked into the sanctuary, where the Minorite was finishing the altar preparations. Joachim had thrown his cowl back, and the tight black curls ringing his tonsure danced to the same unseen impetus. He moved with that lithe grace that betokened gentle birth. Joachim had never known the villein's hut or the liberties of the free-towns. The greater wonder when such a man, heir to important fiefs, dedicated his life to poverty. Joachim turned slightly, and the light from the clerestory highlighted fine, almost womanly features, set incongruously beneath shaggy brows that grew together over the nose. Among those who measured the beauty of men, Joachim might be accounted beautiful.

Joachim and Dietrich locked gazes for a moment, before the monk turned to the credence table to fetch two candlesticks used for the *missa lecta.* As the Minorite's hands approached the copper prickets, sparks arced forth to dance on his fingertips.

Joachim jerked and reared his arm. "God's curse on this wealth!"

Dietrich stepped forward and seized the arm. "Be reasonable, Joachim. I have had these prickets since many years and never have they bitten anyone before. If God is displeased with them, why wait until now?"

"Because God has finally lost patience with a Church in love with Mammon."

"Mammon?" Dietrich gestured around the wooden church. From beams and rafters wild faces looked down on them. In the lancet windows, narrow saints in colored glass scowled or smiled or raised a hand in blessing. "This is hardly Avignon."

He stooped to squint at the chased metalwork of the candlesticks: the chi-rho emblazoned on the Mother Pelican. He stretched a tentative forefinger toward the candlestick. When it came within a thumb's-length of the base there was a snap, and a spark appeared in the air between fingertip and candlestick. Though he had known what would happen, he pulled away as quickly as had Joachim. His fingertip felt as if pierced by a hot needle. He stuck the digit in his mouth to soothe it and turned to Joachim.

"Hngh." He took the finger out and inspected it. "A small hurt," he announced, "seeming greater only through surprise." It had felt much like with the aquamanile, only stronger. Further argument that the mover was drawing nearer. "But it is entirely material. A moment ago, I recalled a trick with amber and fur that creates a similar effect."

"But, the small lightnings . . ."

"Lightning," said Dietrich. A new thought had struck him. He rubbed his finger absently. "Joachim! Could this essence be of the same species as the lightning itself?" He grinned broadly and touched the candlestick again, drawing another arc from it. Fire from earth! He laughed and the Minorite drew away from him. "Imagine a waterwheel rimmed with fur," he told the monk, "rubbing against amber plates. We might generate this essence, this *elektronikos* and, could we but learn to control it, we could command the very lightning!"

The lightning struck without warning!

Dietrich felt fire run through his entire being. Beside him, the Minorite arched his back, his eyes bulging wide and his lips pulling back from his teeth. Sparks leapt between the two candlesticks.

A great burst of light washed through the stained-glass lancets in the north wall of the church, casting rainbows. Saints and prophets blazed in glory: Mary, Leonard, Catherine, Margaret of Antioch, bright as the sun. Radiances streamed through their images and played across the dim interior, speckling the statues and columns with gold and yellow and red and white so that they seemed almost to move. Joachim fell to his knees and bowed, covering his face against the radiant windows. Dietrich knelt also, but looked everywhere at once, trying to take it all in.

An avalanche of thunder followed upon the flash; and the bells in the tower pealed a mad, arrhythmic clanging. The timbers of the church creaked and moaned and wind rushed through the vises and passageways under the roof, howling like a beast. Griffins and wyverns growled. Carven dwarfs groaned. Window glass shrieked and cracked into spiderwebs.

And then, as abruptly as it had begun, the light dimmed and the thunder and the wind faded. Dietrich waited, but nothing more happened. He took a deep breath and found that the feeling of dread had left him as well. Whispering a brief prayer of thanksgiving, he rose to his feet. He glanced at Joachim, who had curled on the flagstone paving with his arms wrapped around his head, then he turned to the credence table and touched the candlestick.

Nothing happened.

He looked at the cracked windows. Whatever had been approaching had arrived.

· 1 ·

NOW
Sharon

DURING SUMMER sessions, Sharon and Tom both did their research from home. That is easy enough today, when the world lies literally at our very fingertips; but it can be a trap, too, for what we need may lie just beyond the tips of our fingers. There is Tom hunched over the computer by the window, tracking down obscure references over the Net. He has his back to the room, which means to Sharon.

Sharon lounges on the pillow sofa on the other side of the room, notebook open, surrounded by wadded-up balls of paper and half-finished cups of herbal tea, thinking about whatever it is that theoretical physicists think about. She gazes in Tom's direction, but she is looking on some inner vision, so in a way she too has her back turned. Sharon uses a computer, too, but it's an organic one that she keeps between her ears. It may not be networked to the wider world, but Sharon Nagy creates her own worlds, strange and inaccessible, among which lies one at the very edges of cosmology.

It is not a beautiful thing, this world of hers. The geodesics are warped and twisted things. Space and time spiral off in curious, fractal vortices, in directions that have no name. Dimensions are quicksilver slippy—looked at sideways, they would vanish.

And yet . . .

AND YET, she sensed a pattern lurking beneath the chaos and she stalked it as a cat might—in stealthy half-steps and never quite straightforward. Perhaps it lacked only the right beholding to fall into beauty. Consider Quasimodo, or Beauty's Beast.

"Damn!"

An alien voice intruded into her world. She heard Tom smack his PC terminal and she screwed her eyes shut, trying not to listen. Almost, she could see it clearly. The equations hinted at multiple rotation groups connected by a meta-algebra. But . . .

"Durák! Bünözö! Jáki!"

. . . But the world shattered into a kaleidoscope, and for a moment she sat overwhelmed by a sense of infinite loss. She threw her pen at the coffee table, where it clattered against white bone-china teacups. Evidently God did not intend for her to solve the geometry of Janatpour space quite yet. She glared at Tom, who muttered over his keyboard.

There is something true about Sharon Nagy in that one half-missed detail: that she uses a pen and not a pencil. It betokens a sort of hubris.

"All right," she demanded. "What is it? You've been cursing in tongues all day. Something is bugging you. I can't work; and *that's* bugging *me.*"

Tom spun in his swivel chair and faced her. "CLIO won't give me the right answer!"

She made a pout with her lips. "Well, I hope you were able to beat it out of her."

He opened his mouth and closed it again and had the grace to look embarrassed, because there was something true about him also. If there are two sorts of people in the world, Tom Schwoerin is of the other sort. Few thoughts of his failed to reach his lips. He was an audible sort of man, which means that he was fundamentally sound.

He scowled now and crossed his arms. "I'm frustrated, is all."

Small doubt of that. Sharon regarded his verbal popcorn much as a miser does a spendthrift. She was the sort of person for whom the expression, *That goes without saying,* really does induce silence. In any event, Tom's frustration was only a symptom. "*Why* are you frustrated?"

"Eifelheim won't go away!"

"And *why* should it go away?"

He threw his arms out wildly. "Because it's not there!"

Sharon, who had had another *why* ready in wait, massaged the bridge of her nose. Be patient, and eventually he would make sense.

"Okay, okay," he admitted. "It sounds silly; but . . . look, Eifelheim was a village in the Black Forest that was abandoned and never resettled."

"So . . . ?"

"So, it *should* have been. I've run two-score simulations of the Schwarzwald settlement grid and the site gets resettled *every time.*"

She had no patience for his problems. An historian, Tom did not create worlds, he only discovered them; so he really was that other sort of person. Sharon yearned for her geodesics. They had almost made sense. Tom wasn't even close. "A simulation?" she snapped. "Then change the freaking model. You've got multicollinearity in the terms, or something."

Emotion, especially deep emotion, always caught Tom short. His own were brief squalls. Sharon could erupt like a volcano. Half the time, he could not figure out why she was angry with him; and the other half of the time he was wrong. He goggled at her for a moment before rolling his eyes. "Sure. Throw out Rosen-Zipf-Christaller theory. One of the cornerstones of cliology!"

"Why not?" she said, "In the *real* sciences, theory has to fit the facts; not vice versa."

Tom's face went red, for she had touched (as she had known she would) upon one of his hot buttons. "Does it, *a cuisla*? Does it really? Wasn't it Dirac who said that it was more important that the equations be beautiful than that they fit the experiment? I read somewhere that measurements of light speed have been getting lower over the years. Why not throw out the *theory* that light speed is constant?"

She frowned. "Don't be silly." She had her own hot buttons. Tom did not know what they were, but he managed to hit them all the same.

"Silly, hell!" He slammed his hand down sharply on the terminal and she jumped a little. Then he turned his back and faced the screen once more. Silence fell, continuing the quarrel.

Now, Sharon had that peculiar ability to stand outside herself, which is a valuable skill, so long as one comes back inside now and then. They were *both* being silly. She was angry at having her train of thought derailed, and Tom was angry because some simulation of his wouldn't work out. She glanced at her own work and thought, *I'm not helping me by not helping him,* which might be a poor reason for charity, but it beats having none at all.

"I'm sorry."

They spoke in counterpoint. She looked up, and he turned 'round, and they stared at each other for a moment and ratified a tacit armistice. The geodesic to peace and quiet was to hear him out; so Sharon crossed the room and perched on the corner of his desk.

"All right," she said. "Explain. What's this Zip-whatever theory?"

In answer, he turned to his keyboard, entered commands with the flourish of a pianist, and rolled his chair aside for her. "Tell me what you see."

Sharon sighed a little and stood behind him with her arms folded and her head cocked. The screen displayed a grid of hexagons, each containing a single dot. Some dots were brighter than others. "A honeycomb," she told him. "A honeycomb with fireflies."

Tom grunted. "And they say physicists make lousy poets. Notice anything?"

She read the names beside the dots. *Omaha. Des Moines. Ottumwa* . . . "The brighter the dot, the bigger the city. Right?"

"Vice versa, actually; but, right. What else?"

Why couldn't he just tell her? He had to make it a guessing game. His students, waiting beak-open for his lectures, often felt the same disquiet. Sharon concentrated on the screen, seeking the obvious. She did not regard cliology as an especially deep science, or much of a science at all. "Okay. The big cities form a partial ring. Around Chicago."

Tom grinned. "*Ganz bestimmt, Schatz.* There should be six of them, but Lake Michigan gets in the way, so the ring's incomplete. Now, what surrounds each of the big cities?"

"A ring of not-so-big cities. How fractal! But the pattern isn't perfect . . ."

"Life's not perfect," he answered. "Microgeography and boundary conditions distort the pattern, but I correct for that by transforming the coordinates to an equivalent, infinite plain."

"A manifold. Cute," she said. "What's your transformation?"

"*Effective* distance is a function of the time and energy needed to travel between two points. Non-Abelian, which complicates matters."

"Non-Abelian? But then—."

"B can be farther from A than A is from B. Sure, why not? The Portuguese found it easier to sail down the coast of Africa than to sail back up. Or, take our own dry cleaners? The streets are one-way, so it takes three times longer to drive there than it does to drive back."

But Sharon wasn't listening any longer. *Non-Abelian! Of course, of course! How could I have been so stupid?* Oh, the happy, unquestioning life of an Abelian, Euclidean, Hausdorff peasant! Could Janatpour space be nonisotropic? Could distance in one direction differ from distance in another? *It's always faster coming home.* But how? How?

His voice shattered her reverie once more. ". . . oxcarts or automobiles. So, the map is always in transition from one equilibrium to another. Now watch."

If she didn't hold his hand while he complained, she would never get her own work done. "Watch what?" she asked, perhaps in a harsher voice than she had intended, because he cast her a wounded glance before bending again over the keyboard. While he did, she slipped across the room and retrieved her notebook so she could capture her butterfly thought.

"Christaller's original survey," said Tom, who had not noticed her sortie. "*Land* Württemberg, nineteenth century."

Sharon spared the screen a cursory glance. "All right—" Then, almost against her will, she leaned toward the computer. "Another honeycomb," she said. "Is that a common pattern?"

He didn't answer. Instead he showed her a series of maps. Johnson's study of Late Uruk settlements around Warka. Alden's reconstruction of Toltec polities in the Valley of Mexico. Skinner's analysis of Szechuan villages. Smith's anomalous study of western Guatemala that found *two* grids, Indio and Ladino, superimposed on each other like parallel universes.

"Now check out this map. Verified sites of ancient Sumerian and Elamite pueblos."

To her own annoyance, she found herself intrigued. One such map might be an oddity; two or three, a coincidence; but not this many. "Why is that dot red?" she asked.

Tom regarded the screen with indulgence. "My claim to fame. There was no known pueblo at that site. But ancient writings are full of references to places we've never pinned down. So, I sent old Hotchkiss an e-mail, telling him to move his dig. That made him mad—he's an old-school microhistorian. But what really ticked him off was when he finally found the ruins, two years later, right where I'd told him they would be."

So his patterns had predictive value, too. Patterns were interesting. They could lead, like astrology, to real science. "There has to be a cause," she said.

He gave her a satisfied nod. "*Ochen khoroshó.*"

"Okay, I'll bite. What is it?"

He tapped a fingernail against the display. "Each locus provides some degree of biopsychological reinforcement to its inhabitants. Rich bottomlands, a vein of silver, a plentiful supply of guano, anything. *Andere Länder, andere Sitten.* The intensity of that reinforcement defines a potential function over the landscape, and the gradient of that potential is a force we call affinity."

Sharon withheld comment. She had never considered Tom's "forces of history" as anything more than a metaphor. She was a physicist, and physicists dealt in real forces.

"If affinity were the only force," Tom continued, "the entire population would be sucked into the local maximum. But population density itself creates a second potential because, *cæteris paribus,* people prefer wide open spaces to getting someone's elbow in their ear. So there's a countertendency for the population to spread out evenly across the landscape in a kind of cultural heat death. The interaction between these two forces generates the differential equations for a reaction-diffusion process. Population accumulates at the equilibrium sites, with settlement sizes distributed according to Zipf 's rank-size law. Each settlement generates a cultural potential field whose strength is proportional to its wealth and population and which diminishes with the square of the distance. Geographically, these settlements and their hinterlands form hexagonal patterns called Christaller grids. *Ert, Nagy kisasszony?*"

"*Ertek jol, Schwoerin ur,*" she answered. Sharon wasn't entirely convinced, but if she argued the point, they'd be up all night, settle nothing, and she'd never get back to Janatpour space. Besides, the model did account for that remarkable consistency of settlement patterns. She pursed her lips. If she wasn't careful, she'd get sucked into solving *his* problem instead of her own. "So, where does this Eifelheim of yours fit in?"

Tom flipped his hands up. "It doesn't." He called another map onto the screen. "Here's the Black Forest. Notice anything odd?"

After all those maps, the empty cell fairly jumped out at her. Sharon touched the screen, her finger dancing from village to village. Bärental, Oberreid, Hinterzarten, St. Wilhelm . . . The roads all twisted around the blank spot, some doubling back on themselves to avoid it. She frowned. Tom was right. There *should* be a village there.

"That," he announced sourly, "is Eifelheim."

"The little town that wasn't there," she murmured. "But how can a town that isn't there have a name?"

"The same way that the Elamite pueblo had a name. Enough references in various sources to triangulate its location. *Attendez.*" Another command entered. "The same region in the Early Middle Ages, reconstructed from LANDSAT photos." He cocked his head. "*C'est drôle, ma chérie.* Up close, you wouldn't see a damned thing; yet from miles above, the ghosts of vanished villages stand out clearly." He looked at the screen and pointed. "There's Eifelheim."

The little dot stared back at her from the previously empty hex. "Then I don't get it. You've discovered another 'lost city,' like in Sumeria."

But Tom shook his head. "No," he said sadly, gazing at the screen. "Settlements are abandoned because their affinity drops, or technology changes the effective distances. The silver mines play out, or an interstate runs through. That's not the case here. Affinity should have caused a successor-village to coalesce within a generation *somewhere* inside that hex. Look at the way Baghdad followed Seleucia, Babylon, and Akkad in the same hex in Mesopotamia."

"Do your satellite photos tell when this Eifelheim disappeared?"

"Based on the pattern of stripping—the 'furlongs'—I'd guess the Late Middle Ages, probably during the Black Death. Land usage patterns changed after that."

"Weren't a lot of places depopulated then? I read somewhere that a third of Europe died." She actually thought she had explained something. She actually thought she had seen something that Tom had overlooked. No field of knowledge is so transparently simple as another's.

Tom was deaf to her triumph. "Yeah," he said off-handedly, "and the Middle East, too. Ibn Khaldûn wrote . . . Well, it took two hundred years for the population to rebound to medieval levels, but every other abandoned village was eventually either reoccupied or replaced by a new settlement nearby. *Você accredita agora?* People lived there for over four hundred years, and then—no one ever lived there again."

She shivered. The way he said it, it did sound unnatural.

"The place became *tabu,*" he continued. "In 1702, Marshal Villars refused to march his army past the place to join his Bavarian allies." Tom opened a slim manila folder on his desk and read from a sheet of paper. "This is what he wrote to the Elector: '*Cette vallée de Neustadt que vous me proposez. C'est le chemin qu'on appelle le Val d'Enfer. Que votre Altesse me pardonne l'expression; je ne suis pas diable pour y passer.*' This was the route he rejected, up the Höllenthal—Hell Valley." His finger traced a path on the map screen, running northeast from Falkenstein past Eifelheim, below the Feldberg. "There wasn't even a road through that tanglewood until the Austrians built one in 1770—so Marie Antoinette could travel to France in comfort, which also turned out to be a bad idea. Even after the road was put in, it was a bad place to travel through. Moreau's Retreat down the valley was such a feat that, when he finally reached the lower end, he was nearly hailed a victor. Then here . . ." He rummaged again in his folder. ". . . I have a copy of a letter by an English traveler named Hughes, who writes in 1900: 'I pressed on to Himmelreich, lest darkness catch me on the malign ground of Eifelheim.' He's being a little tongue-in-cheek—a snooty Edwardian Englishman winking at 'quaint' German folktales—but you notice he didn't stay the night. And Anton Zaengle—you remember Anton—he sent me a newspaper clipping that . . . Here, read it yourself." He handed her the manila folder. "Go ahead. It's right on top."

If a cosmologist learned anything, it was that the shortest route was *not* always a straight line. Opening the folder, Sharon found a clipping from the *Freiburger Wochenbericht* with an English translation stapled to it.

DRACULA CULT FINDS NEW GRAVE

(Freiburg i/ Br.) Although officials discount it as superstition, some US soldiers on maneuvers here believe they have found the tomb of Count Dracula, hundreds of miles from Transylvania. A spokesperson for the US Third Infantry Division acknowledged that something between a cult and a fad had emerged among the soldiers over an obscure medieval headstone decorated with the carving of a demonic face.

The grave lies in a region of the Black Forest called Eifelheim.

The region is heavily forested and the soldiers refuse to divulge the precise location, claiming that curious tourists would offend the grave's inhabitant. This suits nearby farmers, who have a superstitious dread of the place.

Monsignor Heinrich Lurm, a spokesman for the Diocese of Freiburg-im-Breisgau, is concerned about possible desecration of the cemetery by curiosity-seekers, even though it is centuries old. "I suppose you can't stop these young fellows from believing what they want," he said. "Facts are much less exciting than fables."

The monsignor also downplayed the possible connection between the carving the soldiers have described and local folktales of flying monsters, called the Krenkl. "After a few hundred years of wind and rain," he said, "my own face would not look so good, either. If modern American soldiers can make up stories about a carving, so can medieval German peasants."

Sharon returned the clipping. "There's your answer. Krenkl. They've got their own version of the Jersey Devil flying around."

He gave her a look of pity. "Sharon, *this is the Black Forest.* There are more demons, ghosts, and witches per square mile than anywhere on the face of the earth. These 'Flying Krenkl of Eifelheim' sit on the shelf next to the 'Feldberg Demon' and the 'Devil's Pulpit' and the witches' covens on the Kandel and Tannhäusser's secret cave and all the rest. No, *Schatzi.* History happens because of material forces, not mystic beliefs. The abandonment caused the stories, not the other way around. People don't wake up one morning and suddenly decide that the place they've lived in for four centuries is suddenly *verboten. Das ist Unsinn.*"

"Well . . . The Black Death . . ."

Tom shrugged. "But the Death was a 'common cause.' It affected *all* the villages. Whatever the answer is, it has to explain not only why Eifelheim was abandoned forever, but why *only* Eifelheim was abandoned forever." He rubbed his eyes. "Trouble is, there's no data. *Nada. Nichts. Nichto. Nincs.* A few secondary sources, nothing at all contemporary to the events. The *earliest* reference I found was a theological treatise on meditation, written three generations later. That's it there." He jabbed a finger at the folder.

Sharon saw a scanned image of a Latin manuscript. Most of the page was occupied by an ornate capital D supported by a trellis of vines twisted into a complex pattern that broke out here and there into leaves and berries, odd triangles and other geometric figures. A vague feeling of *déjà vu* stole over her as she studied it. "Not very pretty," she said.

"Positively ugly," said Tom. "And the contents are worse. It's called 'The Attainment of the Other World by Searching Within.' *Gottes Himmel,* I'm not kidding. Mystical drivel about a 'trinity of trinities' and how God can be in all places at all times 'including times and places we cannot know save by looking inside ourselves.' But . . . !" Tom held his index finger up. "The author credits the ideas to—and I quote—'old mason Seybke, whose father knew personally the last pastor at the place we call Eifelheim.' Unquote." He crossed his arms. "How's that for first-hand data?"

"What a curious way to phrase it: 'the place we call Eifelheim'." Sharon thought Tom was bragging as much as complaining, as if he had come to love the brick wall against which he was butting his head. Fair enough. Both were made of similar material. She was reminded of her mother's endless litanies of medical complaints. Not that her mother had enjoyed being sick, but she had taken not a little pride in the insurmountable nature of her illnesses.

Sharon flipped idly through the printouts, wondering if there were some way to get Tom out of the apartment. He was spinning his wheels and making her life miserable. She handed him back the folder. "You need more data."

"*Bozhe moi.* Sharon. *Ya nye durák!* Tell me something I *don't* know! I've looked and I've looked. CLIO's chased down every reference to Eifelheim in the entire Net."

"Well, not everything's *in* the Net," she snapped back. "Aren't there musty old papers in archives and the back rooms of libraries that no one's ever *read,* let alone *scanned*? I thought that's what you historians used to do before you got computers—root around in dusty shelves, blowing off cobwebs."

"Well . . . ," he said doubtfully. "Anything off-line can be scanned in by request . . ."

"That's if you know the document exists. What about uncatalogued stuff?"

Tom pursed his lips and looked at her. He nodded slowly. "There were a few marginal items," he admitted. "They didn't sound too promising at the time; but now . . . Well, like they say: *Cantabit vaceus coram latrone viator.*" He grinned at her. "A penniless man sings before the robber," he explained. "Like me, what can he lose?" He leaned back in his chair and stared at the ceiling, pulling absently on his lower lip. Sharon smiled to herself. She knew that habit. Tom was okay, but he was like an old motorcycle. You had to kick hard to get him started.

LATER, AFTER Tom had gone to the library, Sharon noticed CLIO's screen still lit and sighed in exasperation. Why did Tom always go off and leave things running? Computers, electric lights, stereos, televisions. He left a trail of perking appliances behind him wherever he went.

She crossed the room to turn his PC off, but paused with her finger over the track pad while she stared at the empty cell. Eifelheim . . . A sinister black hole surrounded by a constellation of living villages. Something horrible must have happened there once. Something so wicked that seven centuries later people shunned it and had forgotten why.

Abruptly, she cleared the machine. *Don't be silly,* she told herself. But that made her think of something Tom had said. And that made her wonder, What if . . . ? And nothing was ever the same again.

· II ·

AUGUST, 1348
At Primes, The Commemoration of Sixtus II and His Companions

DIETRICH STEPPED from the church to find Oberhochwald in turmoil: thatch roofs blown askew; shutters loose on their hinges; sheep milling and bleating in the pen by the meadow gate. Women shrieked, or hugged crying children. Men milled about arguing and pointing. Lorenz Schmidt stood in the doorway of his smithy, a hammer tight in his grip, eyes searching for an enemy to strike.

Dietrich inhaled the dusty, urgent scent of smoke. From the portico's edge, whence he could spy the village's farther end, he saw thatch roofs ablaze. Farther off, across the common meadow, black clouds churned and roiled above the Great Wood where the lustrous glow had been.

Gregor Mauer, atop the carving table in his yard, shouted and pointed toward the mill pond. His sons, Gregerl and Seybke, hurried past with buckets hanging from their thick arms. Theresia Gresch ran from house to house, sending people to the stream. Across the Oberreid road, the portcullis of Manfred's castle rose with a clatter of chains, and a squad of armsmen dog-trotted down from Castle Hill.

"It's the wrath of hell," said Joachim. Dietrich turned to see the younger man sagging against the doorpost. The eagle of St. John hovered in the wood beside him, beak and talons poised. Joachim's eyes were wide with fear and satisfaction.

"It's the lightning," said Dietrich. "It has set some cottages on fire."

"Lightning? With no cloud in the sky? Where is your reason, now?"

"Then it was that wind, toppling lamps and candles!" Dietrich, having no more patience, seized Joachim's arm and sent him stumbling down the hillside toward the village. "Quickly," he said. "If the flames spread, the village burns." Dietrich tied the skirts of his alb up to his knees and joined the throng heading toward the millpond.

The Minorite had fallen halfway down the path. "That fire is unnatural," he said as Dietrich passed. Then he turned and scrambled back toward the church.

THE GÄRTNERS' huts, mean dwellings at best, were engulfed in flames and folk had given up any thought of saving them. Max Schweitzer, the sergeant from the castle, organized bucket lines to pass water from the millpond to the burning freeholder cottages. Dispossessed animals barked and snorted and ran in panic. One billy scampered toward the high road, chased by Nickel Langermann. Schweitzer held a wand in his right hand and pointed here or pointed there, directing the effort. More buckets to Feldmann's cottage! More buckets! He slapped the wand against his leather hose, and twisted Langermann by the shoulder to direct him back to the fires.

Seppl Bauer, straddling the roof beam of Ackermann's cottage, dropped an empty bucket and Dietrich snatched it up.

Dietrich made his way through the rushes and cattails that bordered the millpond to the head of the bucket line, where he found Gregor and Lorenz knee-deep in the water, filling the buckets and handing them ashore. Gregor paused and wiped an arm across his brow, leaving a muddy streak. Dietrich handed him the empty bucket. The mason filled it and gave it back. Dietrich passed it on to the next man as the line made space for him.

Gregor whispered softly as he drew another bucket through the water, "This is no natural fire." Beside him, Lorenz showed with a glance that he had heard; but the smith kept his peace.

Others nearby also cast furtive glances in his direction. Sacred priest, annointed with holy oil. He would know the answers. Call down anathemas on the flames! Wave a shinbone of St. Catherine at them! For an instant Dietrich was angry, and longed for the cool, scholastic rationalism of Paris. "Why do you say that, Gregor?" he said mildly.

"I have never seen such things in my life."

"Have you ever seen a Turk?"

"No . . ."

"Are Turks then supernatural?"

Gregor scowled, sensing a flaw in the argument but unable to root it out. Dietrich passed his bucket along, then turned back to Gregor, hands outstretched and waiting. "I can create a smaller version of the same lightning with only cat's fur and amber," he told him, and the mason grunted, not understanding the explanation, but taking comfort in an explanation's existence.

Dietrich fell into the swaying rhythm of the work. The buckets were heavy and the rope handles rubbed his palms raw, but the fear of the morning's occult events was smothered under the natural fear of fire and the homely, urgent task of fighting it. The wind turned and he coughed as the smoke momentarily enveloped him.

An endless procession of buckets passed through his hands, and he began to imagine himself as a cog in a complex water pump comprised of human muscle. Yet artisans could free men of such mind-numbing labor. There were cams, and the new-fangled cranks. If mills could be driven by waterwheels and wind, why not a bucket line? If only one could . . .

"The fires are out, pastor."

"What?"

"The fires are out," said Gregor.

"Oh." Dietrich shook himself from his trance. Up and down the line, men and women sank to their knees. Lorenz Schmidt raised the last bucket and poured the water over his head.

"What damage?" Dietrich asked. He sank to his haunches in the reeds along the millpond's edge, too tired to climb up the embankment and see for himself.

The mason's height gave him an advantage. He shaded his eyes against the sun and studied the scene. "The huts are lost," he said. "Bauer's roof will want replacement. Ackermann has lost his house entirely. The two Feldmanns, as well. I count . . . five dwellings destroyed, perhaps twice that many damaged. And outbuildings, as well."

"Were any hurt?"

"A few burns, so far as I can see," said Gregor. Then he laughed. "And young Seppl has scorched the seat from his trousers."

"Then we have much to be thankful for." Dietrich closed his eyes and crossed himself. *O God, who suffers not that any who hope in Thee should be overmuch afflicted, but listens kindly to their prayers, we thank Thee for having heard our requests and granted our desires. Amen.*

When he opened his eyes, he saw that everyone had gathered at the pond. Some were wading in the water, and the younger children—not comprehending the close brush with disaster—had seized the opportunity to go swimming.

"I have a thought, Gregor." Dietrich examined his hands. He would have to mix a salve when he was back in his quarters, else there would be blisters. Theresia made such ointments, but she would likely run short today, and Dietrich had read from Galen in Paris.

The mason sat beside him. He rubbed his hands slowly back and forth, palm to palm, scowling at them, as if searching for signs and portents among the scars and swollen knuckles. The little finger of the left hand was missing, crushed off in a long-ago accident. He shook his head. "What?"

"Affix the buckets to a belt moved by Klaus Müller's wheel. It wants only Herr Manfred's grace and the services of a skilled cam master. No. Not a belt. A bellows. And a pump, like the one used at Joachimstal."

Gregor frowned and turned his head so he could see Klaus Müller's waterwheel downstream from the millpond. The mason pulled a reed from the earth and held it dangling at arm's length. "Müller's wheel is out of plumb," he said, sighting along the reed. "From that strange wind, do you think?"

"Have you ever seen a water pump?" Dietrich asked him. "The mine at Joachimstal is at the top of the hill, but the miners have fashioned a latticework of wooden spars extending up the hillside from the stream. It takes its power from a waterwheel, but a cam translates the wheel's circular motion into the latticework's to-and-fro." He moved his hands in the air, trying to show Gregor the motions he meant. "And that to-and-fro works the pumps up at the mine."

Gregor wrapped his arms around his knees. "I like it when you weave these fancies of yours, pastor. You should write fables."

Dietrich grunted. "These are not fables, but fact. Would paper be so plentiful without water mills to pound the pulp? Twenty-five years ago, a cam was fashioned to run a bellows; and I have lately heard that an artisan at Liège has joined the bellows to the hearth and created a new kind of iron furnace—one that uses a blast of air. For now eight years it has been smelting steel in the north."

"These are wondrous times," Gregor acknowledged. "But what of your bucket line?"

"Simple! Equip the bellows to throw water instead of air and attach it to a pump, as at Joachimstal. A few men holding such a siphon could direct a continual stream of water at the fire. There would be no need for bucket lines or—"

Gregor laughed. "If such a thing were possible, someone would have built one by now. No one has built one, so it must be impossible." Gregor stuck his tongue in his cheek and looked thoughtful. "There. That was a logic, wasn't it?"

"*Modus tollens,*" Dietrich agreed. "But your major premise is faulty."

"Is it? I'd not make a good scholar. These things are all a mystery to me. Which is the major premise?"

"The first."

"How is that faulty? The Romans and the Greeks were clever men. And the Saracens, heathen though they are. You told me yourself. What was that you called it? The one where they do the numbers."

"*Al-jabr.* The cipher."

"Algebra. That's the one. And then that Genoese fellow when I was apprenticed down in Freiburg who claimed he walked to Cathay and back. Didn't he describe arts that he had seen there? Well, what I mean is, with all these clever people, Christian, infidel and pagan, ancient and modern, inventing things since the beginning of the world, how could they have overlooked something as simple as you say?"

"There would be difficulties in the details. But mark me. One day, all work will be done by clever machines and people will be free to contemplate God and philosophy and the arts."

Gregor waved a hand. "Or free to contemplate trouble. Well. I suppose anything is possible if we ignore the details. Didn't you tell me that someone had promised a fleet of wind-driven war chariots to the king of France?"

"Yes, Guido da Vigevano told the king that wagons rigged with sails like a ship—"

"And did the French king use them in this new war with the English he's gotten?"

"Not that I have heard."

"Because of the details, I suppose. What of the talking heads? Who was that?"

"Roger Bacon, but it was only a *sufflator.*"

"That's right. I remember the name, now. If anyone actually did fashion that talking head, Everard would use it to keep better accounts of our rents and duties. Then the whole village would be mad at you."

"At me?"

"Well, Bacon is dead."

Dietrich laughed. "Gregor, every year sees a new art. Only twenty years past, men discovered the art of reading-spectacles. I even spoke with the man who invented them."

"Did you? What sort of mage was he?"

"No mage. Only a man, like you or I. One who tired of squinting at his psalter."

"A man like you, then," Gregor allowed.

"He was a Franciscan."

"Oh." Gregor nodded, as if that explained everything.

THE VILLAGERS dragged their buckets and rakes home, or picked through the charred poles and smoking thatch to salvage what they could from the ruins. Langermann and the other gärtners did not bother. There had been little enough in their huts to make their ashes worth sifting. Langermann had however recovered his goat. The cows in the cattle pen, unmilked since morning, complained without comprehension.

Dietrich saw Fra Joachim, smudged black by smoke and gripping a bucket and hurried after him. "Joachim, wait." He caught up in a few steps. "We will say a Mass in thanksgiving. '*Spiritus Dómini,*' since the altar is vested already in red. But let us delay until vespers, so everyone can rest from the labor."

Joachim's sooty face showed no emotion. "Vespers, then." He turned away; and again Dietrich caught his sleeve.

"Joachim." He hesitated. "Earlier. I thought you had run off."

The Minorite gave him a stiff look. "I went back for this," he said, rapping the bucket.

"The bucket?"

He handed it to Dietrich. "The holy water. In case the flames proved diabolical."

Dietrich looked inside. A residuum of water lay in the bottom. He gave the bucket back to the monk. "And since the flames proved material, after all?"

"Why then, one more bucket of water to fight them."

Dietrich laughed and gave Joachim a slap on the shoulder. Sometimes the intense young man surprised him. "There, see? You do know something of logic."

Joachim pointed. "And who does logic tell you hauled the buckets that put out the fires in the Great Woods?" A thin, gray pall lingered over the forest.

At that, he resumed his progress toward the church, and this time Dietrich let him go. God had sent Joachim for a reason. A trial of some sort. There were times when he envied the Minorite his ecstasies, the cries of joy he wrang from God's presence. Dietrich's own delight in reason seemed bloodless by comparison.

DIETRICH SPOKE with those who had lost their homes. Felix and Ilse Ackermann only stared back dumbly. Everything they had salvaged from the ruin of their home they had wrapped into two small sacks, which Felix and his daughter Ulrike carried across their backs. The child, Maria, clutched a wooden doll, blackened and covered with a rag of scorched fabric. It looked like one of those African men that the Saracens sold at slave markets around the Mediterranean. Dietrich squatted beside Maria.

"No worries, little one. You will stay with your uncle Lorenz until the village can help your father build a new home."

"But who will make Anna better?" Maria asked, holding the doll up.

"I will take her to the church and see what I can do." He tried to take the doll gently from the girl's grasp, but found he had to pry her fingers away.

"All right, you worthless sons of faithless wives! Back to the castle with you. Don't straggle there! You've had yourselves a break in the routine *and* a bath in the millpond—and high time, too!—but there's still work wanting to be done!"

Dietrich stepped aside and let the men-at-arms pass. "God bless you and your men, Sergeant Schweitzer," he said.

The sergeant crossed himself. "Good day to you, pastor." He gestured toward the castle with a toss of his head. "Everard sent us down to help fight the fires." Maximilian Schweitzer was a short, thick-shouldered man who, in disposition, reminded Dietrich of a tree stump. He had wandered down from the Alpine country a few years before to sell his sword, and Herr Manfred had hired him to take his foot soldiers in charge and act against outlaws in the high woods.

"Pastor, what . . ." The sergeant frowned suddenly and glared at his men. "No one told you to listen. Do you need me to hold your hands? There's only the one street through the village. The castle is at one end and you're at the other. Can you figure the rest out yourselves?"

Andreas, the corporal, bawled at them and they moved on in a rough line. Schweitzer watched them go. "They're good lads," he told Dietrich, "but they want for discipline." He tugged at his leather jerkin to straighten it. "Pastor, what happened today? All morning I felt like . . . Like I knew there was an ambush laid for me, but not when or where. There was a fight in the guardroom, and young Hertl broke down in sobs in the common room for no reason at all. And when we laid hand to knife or helm—to anything metal—there would be a short, stabbing pain that—"

"Were any hurt?"

"By such a small dart? Not in the body, but who knows what damage was done to the soul? Some of the lads from back up in the forest, they said it was elf-shot."

"Elf-shot?"

"Small arrows, invisible, fired by the elves. What?"

"Well, the hypothesis 'saves the appearances,' as Buridan requires, but you are multiplying entities without need."

Schweitzer scowled. "If that is mockery . . ."

"No, sergeant. I was but recalling a friend of mine from Paris. He said that when we try to explain something occult, we should not suggest new entities to do so."

"Well . . . elves are not *new* entities," Schweitzer insisted. "They've been around since the forest was young. Andreas comes from the Murg Valley and he says it might have been the Gnurr playing tricks on us. And Franzl Long-nose said it was the *Aschenmännlein* out of Siegmanns Woods."

"The Swabian imagination is a wonderful thing," Dietrich said. "Sergeant, the supernatural lies always in small things. In a piece of bread. In a stranger's kindness. And the devil shows himself in mean and shabby dealings. All that shaking this morning and the booming wind and burst of light—all that was too dramatic. Only Nature is so theatrical."

"But what caused it?"

"The causes are occult, but they are surely material."

"How can you be so—" Max froze and stepped onto the wooden footbridge that spanned the stream below the mill, peering toward the woods.

"What is it?" asked Dietrich.

The sergeant tossed his head. "That flock of acorn-jays took sudden flight from the copse on the edge of the woods. Something's moving about in there."

Dietrich shaded his eyes and looked where the Swiss had pointed. Smoke hung lazily in the air, like streamers of teased wool. The trees at the edge of the wood cast dark shadows that the climbing sun failed to dispel. Within the motley of black and white, Dietrich spied movement, though at this distance, he could make out no details. Light winked, as one sometimes sees when the sun glints off metal.

Dietrich shaded his eyes. "Is that armor?"

Max scowled. "In the Herr's woods? That would be bold-faced, even for von Falkenstein."

"Would it? Falkenstein's ancestor sold his soul to the Devil to escape a Saracen prison. He has despoiled nuns and holy pilgrims. He badly wants a reining-in."

"When the Markgraf grows irritated enough," Max agreed. "But the gorge is too hard a passage. Why would Philip send his henchmen up here? Not for profit, surely."

"Might von Scharfenstein?" He gestured vaguely toward the southeast, where another robber baron had his nest.

"Burg Scharfenstein's taken. Hadn't you heard? Its lord seized a Basler merchant for ransom, and that proved his undoing. The man's nephew disguised himself as a notorious freelance they'd heard tale of and went to them with word of easy spoils a little ways down the Wiesen valley. Well, greed dulls people's wits, so they followed him—and rode into an ambush laid by the Basler militia."

"There's a lesson there."

Max grinned like a wolf. " 'Do not vex the Swiss.' "

Dietrich studied the woods once more. "If not robber knights, then only landless men, forced to poach in the forest."

"Maybe," Max allowed. "But that's the Herr's lands."

"What then? Will you go in and chase them off?"

The Swiss shrugged. "Or Everard will hire them for the grain harvest. Why hunt trouble? The Herr will be back in a few days. He's had his fill of France, or so the messenger said. I'll ask his will." He stared a while longer at the woods. "There was a strange glow there, before dawn. Then the smoke. I suppose you'll tell me that was 'Nature,' too." He turned and left, touching his cap as he passed Hildegarde Müller.

Dietrich saw no more movement among the trees. Perhaps he had seen nothing earlier, only the swaying of saplings within the forest.

· III ·

AUGUST, 1348
At Compline, The Vigil of St. Laurence

"DISPÉRSIT," SAID Dietrich. "Dédit paupéribus; justítia éjus mánet in saéculum saéculi: córnu éjus exaltábitur in Glória."

Joachim answered him. "Beátus vir, qui tímet Dóminum; in mandátes éjus cúpit nímis."

"Glória pátri et Fílio et Spirítui Sáncti."

"Amen." That they said in unison, but with no echo from the church save that of Theresia Gresch, who knelt solitary on the flagstones of the nave in the flickering candlelight. But Theresia was a fixture, like the statues that lurked in the niches in the wall.

There were only two sorts of women so perfervid in their devotions: madwomen and saints, nor were the two species entirely distinct. One must be a little mad to be a saint, at least as the world measured madness.

Theresia had the soft, round face of a maiden, though Dietrich knew her for twenty. She had never to Dietrich's certain knowledge gone with a man, and indeed, still spoke with simplicity and innocence. At times, Dietrich knew jealousy on her account, for the Lord had opened Heaven to those who became as little children.

". . . from the oppression of the flame which surrounded me," Joachim read from the Book of Wisdom, "and in the midst of the fire I was not burnt . . ." Dietrich gave silent thanks for their deliverance from the fires three days before. Only Rudolf Pforzheimer had died. His aged heart had stopped when the *elektronik* essence had been at its thickest.

Dietrich shifted the book to the other side of the altar and read from the Gospel of Matthew, concluding, "If any man will come after me, let him take what he has and give it to the poor."

Joachim cried, "Amen."

"Na, Theresia," he said as he closed the book, and she sat back on her heels to listen with a guileless smile. "Only a few feasts possess a Vigil-Night. Why is St. Laurence among them?" Theresia shook her head, which meant she did remember, but preferred that Dietrich tell her.

"A few days since, we remembered Pope Sixtus II, who was killed by the Romans while praying Mass in the catacombs. Sixtus had seven deacons. Four were killed at the Mass with him and two others were hunted down and killed the same day. That is why we say, 'Sixtus and his companions.' Laurence was the last of the deacons, and eluded capture for several days. Sixtus had given him the possessions of the Church for safekeeping—including, so they say, the cup from which Our Lord drank at the Last Supper and which the Popes had used at Mass until then. These he had distributed to the poor. When the Romans found him and ordered him to hand over 'all the wealth of the Church,' Laurence took them into the hovels of the city and showed them the poor, declaring—"

"*There* is the wealth of the Church!" Theresia cried and clapped her hands together. "Oh, I love that story!"

"Would that more Popes and bishops," Joachim murmured, "loved it as much." Then, seeing himself heard, he continued more forcefully: "Remember what Matthew wrote of the camel and the needle's eye! Someday, O woman, artisans may fashion a singularly large needle. Somewhere in far Arabia may live an exceedingly small camel. Yet if we take the Master's words at their least meaning, it is this: Wealthy lords and bishops—those who dine at groaning tables, who sit their asses on satin pillows—are not our moral guides. Look to the simple carpenter! And look to Laurence, who knew where true treasure lay—where thief cannot steal nor mice consume. Blessed are the poor! Blessed are the poor!"

Ejaculations like that had put Joachim's order in deep disfavor. The Conventuals had disavowed their brothers in the face of it, but the Spirituals would not hold their tongues. Some had burned; some had fled to the Kaiser for protection. How much better, Dietrich thought, to escape notice entirely. He raised his eyes to heaven, and something seemed to move among the candle-sent shadows in the rafters and vises in the clerestory. A bird, perhaps.

"But poverty is not merit enough," Dietrich cautioned Theresia. "Many a gärtner in his hut loves riches more than does a generous and open-handed lord. It is the desire and not the possession that diverts us from the straight path. There is good and ill in any besitting." Before Joachim could dispute the point, he added, "Ja, the rich man finds it more difficult to see Christ because the glitter of the gold dazzles his eyes; but never forget that it is the man that sins and not the gold."

He returned to the altar to finish the Mass, and Joachim took the bread and wine from the credence table and followed him. Theresia handed him a basket of herbs and roots that she had gathered and Joachim brought those to the altar, too. Then, since he had received only the lesser orders, the Minorite stood aside. Dietrich spread his arms wide and recited a prayer for the offerings. "Orátio mea . . ."

Theresia took all in with the same simplicity with which she accepted everything else in life. This was a good woman, Dietrich thought. She would never be placed on the calendar of saints, never be remembered for centuries like Laurence and Sixtus; yet she owned their generosity of spirit. Christ lived in her because she lived in Christ. Irresistably, he compared her to the wanton Hildegarde Müller.

Councils had proposed that the priest should turn his back on his flock, and not face them across the altar as had been done since the earliest times. The argument was that priest and people should face God together, the celebrant standing at the fore as the commander of an army leads his lances into battle. Some of the great cathedrals had already reversed their altars, and Dietrich expected the practice to become soon universal. And yet, how sad if he could not gaze upon the Theresias of the world.

AFTER THE vigil, as they returned by torchlight to the parsonage, Joachim said to Dietrich, "That was a fine thing you said. I had not looked to you for it."

Dietrich had been watching Theresia make her way down the hillside with her basket of herbs, now blessed and therefore meet for preparing salves and unguents. "What did I say?" He had not expected praise from Joachim, and the compliment of the first utterance pleased him more than the implicit criticism of the second nettled.

"When you said that the rich man cannot see Christ because the gold dazzles his eyes. I liked that. I would like to use it myself."

"I said it was *more* difficult. It's never easy for anyone. And don't forget the glitter. Gold itself is a useful thing. It is the glitter that is the blinding illusion."

"You could have been a Franciscan yourself."

"And burn with the rest of you? I'm a simple priest of the diocese. Thank you, but I will stay out of it. Kaisers and Popes are like the upper and nether millstones in Klaus's mill. Between them is a bad place to lie."

"I never read of Christ praising luxury and wealth."

Dietrich lifted his torch the better to see his companion. "I never heard of him leading bands of armed peasants to the sacking of a manor house, either!"

Joachim shrank from the vehemence he heard. "No!" the Minorite said. "We don't preach that. The Way of Francis is—"

"Where were you when the *Armleder* went about the Rhineland hanging the rich men and burning their houses?"

Joachim stared at him. "The Armleder? Why, I was a child in my father's house. The Armleder never came there."

"Be thankful they never did."

A strange look passed across the monk's features. Fear, but something else. Then the face closed up once more. "It is vain to discuss what might have been."

Dietrich grunted, suddenly tired of baiting the young man, who might have been eight or nine when the mobs rampaged. "Be wary," he said, "of unlocking such passions as envy."

Joachim stalked away from him, but turned after a few paces. "It was still a good thing to say." He left, and Dietrich gave thanks that the younger man had not asked the same question of him. *Where were you, Dietrich, when the Armleder passed through?*

A motion to his right drew his attention, but his eyes were dazed by the torch and he could make out nothing but a shape that leapt from behind the church. Dietrich ran to the crest of the hill and held his torch high to illuminate the rocky slope behind, but he saw only the rustle of a wild raspberry bush and a stone that clattered down the hill.

Another movement, this one behind him. He whirled suddenly, caught a glimpse of great glowing eyes, then the torch was knocked from his grasp, and he was tripped to the ground. He cried out over the snapping of twigs and the rustling of leaves as the second intruder fled.

In moments, Joachim and Theresia were at his side. Dietrich assured his rescuers that he was unhurt, but Theresia explored his skull and arms for injuries anyway. When her fingers reached the back of his head, he winced. "Ach!"

Theresia said, "You'll have a lump there in the morning, but the bone is not fractured."

Joachim had retrieved Dietrich's torch and held it so Theresia could see what she was doing. "Are you a chirurgeon, then?" he asked.

"Father taught me herbs and medicines and bone-setting from his books," Theresia told him. "Put something cold against it, father," she added to Dietrich. "If you have a headache, take some ground peony root with oil of roses. I'll blend a compound tonight and bring it to you."

When she had gone, Joachim said, "She called you 'father.' "

"Many do," Dietrich answered dryly.

"I thought she meant . . . something more."

"Did you? Well, she was my ward, if you must know. I brought her here when she was ten."

"Ach. Were you then her uncle? What befell her parents?"

Dietrich took the torch from him. "The Armleder killed them. They burned the house down with everyone in it. Only Theresia escaped. I taught her what I had learned of healing in Paris, and when she turned twelve and became a woman, Herr Manfred granted her the right to practice the craft on his manor."

"I had always thought . . ."

"What?"

"I had always thought they had a just grievance. The Armleder, I mean, against the wealthy."

Dietrich looked into the flames of the torch. "So they had; but *summum ius, iniuria summa.*"

ON MONDAY, Dietrich and Max set out for the Great Woods to look after Josef the charcoal-burner and his apprentice, neither of whom had been seen since the Sixtusday fires. The day broke hot, and Dietrich was sodden with his own sweat before they had walked half the distance. A thin haze mitigated the sun's intensity, but it was small dispensation. In the spring fields, where the harvest army labored on the lord's salland, Oliver Becker idled in the speckled shade of a broad oak, unmindful of the scowls of his peers.

"The gof," Max said when Dietrich pointed him out. "Grows his hair long as if he were a young Herr. Sits on his ass all day and watches everyone else do the work because he can pay the shirking-fine. In the Swiss, everyone works."

"It must be a wonderful country, then, the Swiss."

Max cast him a suspicious glance. "It is. We have no 'mine Herrs.' When a matter needs settling, we gather all the fighting men and take a show of hands, with no need for lords."

"I thought the Swiss lands were Hapsburg fiefs."

Schweitzer waved a hand. "I expect Duke Albrecht thinks so, too; but we mountain folk have a different opinion. . . . You look pensive, pastor. What is it?"

"I fear the hands of all those neighbors, raised together, may impose one day a tyranny weightier than the hand of a single lord. With a lord, at least you know who to bring to account, but when a mob raises its many hands, which holds the blame?"

Max snorted. "Bring a lord to account?"

"Four years since, the village brought suit against the steward when Manfred enclosed the common greenway."

"Well, Everard . . ."

"The lord must save his honor. It's a legal fiction, but a useful one. Like that quillon of yours. One thumb longer, and it would be a sword, which would be above your station."

"We Swiss like them," he said, laying a hand on the pommel and grinning.

"What I mean is, Manfred could then chastise his steward for doing what he had told him to do, and everyone pretends to believe it."

Max made a curt gesture. "Moorgarten rendered a more vigorous verdict. We brought the Hapsburg Duke to account there, I tell you."

Dietrich looked at him. "Anything too vigorous ends with peasants dangling from trees. That's a fruit I'd not see harvested again."

"In the Swiss, the peasants won."

"And yet here you are, serving the Hochwald Herr, who serves both the Baden Markgraf *and* the Hapsburg Duke." To this, Max made no response.

THEY CROSSED over the millbrook bridge and took the road toward Bear Valley. The fallow fields lay on the left and the autumn fields on the right, the ground swelling higher and edging into the dirt track, pinching it until it seemed more trench than road. Hedgerows and briar bushes, meant to keep cows and sheep from wandering into the croplands, provided a bit of inadvertent shade to the walkers—and seemed veritable trees by reason of the height of the land from which they sprouted. The road, muddy through this stretch from a rivulet tributary to the millbrook, meandered first this way, then that, as slope and pitch dictated. Dietrich had wondered at times what sort of place Bear Valley might be that travelers seemed disinclined to go straight there.

Near the common pasture, the road shed its subterranean aspect and emerged onto the shoulder of the hill, a gentle swell of land that marked the first pitch into the Katerinaberg. The sun was more unremittingly present here, with even the small shade of the hedgerows gone. Someone had opened the gate between the commons and the autumn fields so that the village cows could graze on the stubble and deposit their manure for the fall planting.

From the higher ground of the meadow, yellow with goose-blooms, they spied Heinrich Altenbach's homestead on the track to Stag's Leap. Altenbach had left the manor several years since to drain some marshland. Being waste, the marsh had been claimed for no lord's manor, and Altenbach had built on it a cottage so he would not have to walk each day to his fields.

"I suppose every man would rather live on his own land," Max suggested when Dietrich had remarked the farmhouse. "*If* he owned his own plow and beasts, *and* had no wish to share them with his neighbor. But it is a far run to the castle should an army pass this way, and those neighbors might not open the gate to him."

On the far side of the meadow, the forest glowered softly black. Thin streamers of white smoke twisted among the birch and pine and oak. Dietrich and Max paused under a solitary oak to drink from their water-skins. Dietrich had some chestnuts in his scrip, which he shared with the sergeant. The latter, for his part, studied the plumes of smoke with great attention, juggling the nuts in his hand like a set of knucklebones.

"Easy to get lost in there," Dietrich commented.

"Stay to the game trails," Max said, half-distracted. "Don't hare off into the brush." He popped the meat from a chestnut and threw it into his mouth.

THE FOREST was cooler than the open meadow. Sunlight penetrated only in shattered fragments, dappling the hazel bushes and bluebells underneath the canopy. A few strides and Dietrich was swallowed up. The harvest sounds grew distant, then muffled, then ceased entirely to argue with the silence. He and Max passed among the oaks and larches and black spruce on grumbling carpets of last year's leaves. Dietrich soon lost all sense of direction and stayed close by the sergeant.

The air reeked of stale smoke and ashes and, overlaying it, a sharp smell, like salt and urine and sulfur all mixed together. They came soon to burnt land. There, hot wood glowered within split trunks, awaiting only a blast of air to unravel again into flames. The seared corpses of small animals lay tangled in the brush.

"Holzbrenner's kiln is deeper in, I think," Dietrich said. "That way." Max said nothing. He was trying to look everywhere at once. "The charcoal burner is a solitary man," Dietrich continued. "He would have made a fine contemplative." But Max was not listening. "It was only lightning," Dietrich said, and the sergeant flinched, turned at last to look at him.

"How did you—?"

"You were thinking too loudly. I would not have asked you to accompany me, but Josef has not been seen since the fires and Lorenz fears for him and his apprentice."

Max grunted. "The smith fears running short of charcoal. Klaus tells me that this Josef only comes into the village when he has charcoal to sell or duties to pay the Herr, and then he nearly always sends the boy. That supernatural wind toppled his kiln and set the woods on fire, and he's been digging a new one. That's why we've not seen his smoke."

"The wind was not supernatural," Dietrich insisted, but with no great conviction.

THE RUIN grew more extensive the farther they walked. They saw trees broken off, uprooted, toppled, leaning one upon the other. Sunlight poured through holes in the canopy. "A giant has played at jack-straws," said Dietrich.

"I've seen destruction like this," Max said.

"Like this? Where?"

Max shook his head. "Only not so vast. Look how the trees lie here and how they lie over there, as if they have all fallen outward from some center."

Dietrich gave him a look. "Why?"

"At the siege of Cividale down in the Friuli, nearly—oh, near twenty years ago, I think. Christ, I was young and stupid, running off that way. To help the Austrians fight the Venetians? What quarrel was that of mine? Two of the German knights brought a *pot-de-fer* with the black powder. Well, it helped us carry the city, but one of the barrels burst while they were mixing the powder—they always do the mixing in the field, and I can see why. There was a crack like thunder and the wind blast scattered men and equipment all about." He looked again at the fallen trees. "Like those."

"How large must a barrel of the black powder be to do so much damage?" Dietrich asked.

Max did not answer. A chittering sound, like the buzzing of locusts, filled the air—though it was the wrong year for locusts. Dietrich looked at the fallen trees and thought, *The impetus came from* that *direction.*

Finally, the sergeant blew his breath out. "Right, then. This way." He turned away to follow the trail toward the kiln.

THE CLEARING was a shallow pit fifty paces across and floored with a layer of ash and beaten earth. In the flattened center stood the kiln itself: a mound of earth and sod five long paces in diameter. But the earthen seal had been ripped away on one side, exposing the wood inside and allowing the wind to blast the fire. The sparks had been scattered into the woods, setting the fires whose remnants they had lately passed.

The Sixtus' Day wind had rung the church bells on the far side of the valley. Here, it must have blown a hundred times stronger—harrowing the trees that surrounded the clearing, scattering the windbreaks that regulated the airflow into the kiln, peeling the earth from the kiln, gouging a channel through the forest like a river in flood. Only the strongest trees remained upright, and many of those were shattered and bent.

Dietrich stepped around the ruined kiln. A fan of burnt timbers and thatch marked where the charcoal-maker's cottage had once stood. At the end of that spray, against the sagging trees on the far side of the clearing, Dietrich found Josef and his apprentice.

Their charred torsos lacked arms and legs and, in the lad's case, a head. Dietrich searched his memory for the boy's name, but it would not come. Both bodies had been smashed and broken, as if they had fallen from a great cliff, and both were skewered with splinters of wood. Yet, what wind could be so strong? Farther off, he saw a leg wedged in the fork of a cracked beech. He searched no further, but put his back to the terrible sight.

"They're dead, aren't they?" Max asked from the other side of the kiln. Dietrich nodded and, bowing his head, recited a short prayer in his heart. When he crossed himself, Max did the same.

"We'll need a horse," the sergeant said, "to carry the bodies out. Meanwhile, the kiln will serve for a crypt."

It took only a few minutes, in the course of which Dietrich found the boy's head. The hair had been burned off and the eyes had melted, and Dietrich wept over the charred remnant of the lad's beauty. Anton. He remembered the name now. A comely lad, with much promise in his eyes. Josef had loved him greatly, as the son his solitary life had never granted.

When they had finished, they arranged the loose sod around the opening to provide as much protection as they could from animals.

Schweitzer jerked suddenly about and took a step toward the smoky woods behind him. A snapping of twigs faded rapidly in the distance. "We are watched," he said.

"It didn't sound like footsteps," Dietrich suggested. "It sounded more like a deer, or a rabbit."

The sergeant shook his head. "A soldier knows when he's being watched."

"Then, whoever these people are, they're timid," Dietrich told Max.

"I don't think so," Max answered without turning. "I think they are sentries. They run to take word back or to remain unseen. It's what I would do."

"Outlaw knights?"

"I doubt it." He tapped the pommel of his Burgundian quillon. "France has employment enough. They needn't live like poachers in a place like this." After a few more minutes, he said, "He's gone, at any rate. The Herr will be back on the morrow. We'll see what his wishes are."

· IV ·

AUGUST, 1348
The Feast of St. Clare of Assisi

IN THE shimmering heat of an August afternoon, the Herr Manfred von Hochwald danced his *palefridus* up the Oberreid road to the amazement and delight of the peasants bent over the grain. First, came Wolfram the herald, astride a white jennet, bearing the banner with the Hochwald arms and crying the lord's return to the harvest army. There followed a troop of men-at-arms, with their pikes resting upon their shoulders and their helmets glinting like the sun off the tumbling mill stream. Then came the captains and the knights, then chaplain Rudolf and Eugen the jungherr, then the Herr himself: tall and splendid, well-seated, gorgeous in his surcoat, with his helm crooked in his arm and his hand raised in beneficent greeting.

In spring-sown fields now sagging with wheat, the women unbent from the reaping, sickles dangling from their numbed hands, and the men turned from sheaves half-bound to gape at the procession. They paused, mopped brows with kerchief or cap, traded uncertain looks, questions, guesses, exclamations, until all—villein and free, man and woman and child—drifted in one accord toward the road, gathering speed as they went, excitement building upon itself, splashing through the brook that bordered the fields, voices swelling from murmur to shout. Behind, atop the wagons, the wardens of autumn seethed over the lost afternoon, for the grain would ripen with or without the sickle. But the wardens, too, waved their caps at the noble procession, before tugging them firmly back into place.

The party crossed the valley. Feet and hooves drummed the brook bridge; armsmen shouted greetings to sweethearts and wives long unswyved (as they hoped). Fathers called to sons happily returned (and grown unaccountably older) amid wails for husbands, sons, brothers missing from the ranks. Hounds gave tongue and chased alongside the file of men. Glitter in the air as Eugen tossed small coins to the throng. Booty taken from dead English knights, or ransomed off live ones. Men and women scrabbled for coppers in the dirt, praising their lord for his generosity, and biting the coins.

The procession trudged up Church Hill, where Dietrich, Joachim, and Theresia awaited. Dietrich had vested for the occasion in a gold chasuble, but the Minorite wore the same patched robe as always and watched the approaching lord with a mixture of wariness and contempt. More of the former and less of the latter, Dietrich thought, might serve the man better. Beside them, less quiet, more uncertain, the Herr's daughters chattered with their nurse. Irmgard, the younger, alternated smiles with apprehension. Her father was coming! But two years is forever in the life of a child, and he was that long estranged. Everard chewed his moustache with the unease of a man left two years in charge of his master's estate. Klaus, who was *maier* for the village, stood beside him with an indifference that betokened either an innocent heart or one more confident in its misappropriations.

Max had drawn the castle guard up in two lines, and sixteen men presented their arms in a shout and a clash of metal as their lord rode between them. Even Dietrich, who had seen more splendid displays than this in towns and cities far more grand, was stirred by the spectacle.

The herald dismounted and planted the Hochwald banner—*vert, a boar passant below an oak tree, all proper.* Manfred reined in before it and his horse reared and pawed the air. The harvesters, who had rambled up the hillside, cheered the horsemanship, but Theresia whispered, "Oh, the poor beast, ridden hard."

If the horse had been ridden hard, so had the men. Dietrich noted the signs of a forced march beneath the brave show. Weary eyes; tattered livery. There were fewer than had marched forth, and some strange faces had been added—the discards and left-behinds of some battlefield, hungry for a lord to feed them. Hungry enough, indeed, to leave their homelands behind.

Eugen, the jung-herr, dropped to the ground, staggered, and grabbed hold of the snaffle rein to steady himself. The horse shied and pawed the ground, tossing up a clot with his foot. Then Eugen stepped smartly to his lord's stirrup and held it while the Herr dismounted.

Manfred touched knee to ground before Dietrich, and the pastor placed his left hand on the Herr's brow and drew the sign of the cross over him with his right, announcing public thanks for the troop's safe return. Everyone crossed themselves, and Manfred kissed his fingers. Rising, he said to Dietrich, "I would pray a while in private."

Dietrich could see creases around the eyes that hadn't been there before, a greater and more pallid gray in the hair. The long, lean face framed sorrow. *These men,* he thought, *have come a long, hard way.*

Passing to the church, the lord clasped hands with his steward and with Klaus and told them both to come in the evening to the manor house for the accounts. His two daughters, he embraced with much feeling, removing his gauntlets to stroke their hair. Kunigund, the older, giggled with delight. Each one he greeted—priest, steward, maier, daughter—the Herr studied with deep concern; and yet it had been Manfred absent and unheard from these two years.

The Herr paused at the church door. "Good old Saint Catherine," he said, running a hand along the curve of the saint's figure and touching a finger to her sad smile. "There were times, Dietrich, when I thought I would never see her again." After a curious glance at Joachim, he strode inside. What he told God, what boon he asked or thanks he gave, he never afterward said.

THE *HERRENHOF,* the lord's manor house, sat within its curial lands atop a hill across the valley from the church, so that lord and priest oversaw the land from their separate perches and warded the folk between them, body and soul. There were other symbolisms behind the separation, playing—in miniature—dramas that elsewhere had shaken thrones and cathedrals.

Upon the crest, Burg Hochwald warded the Oberreid road. The outer wall was a small affair, embracing *curia* as well as castle; but it and the moat were meant only to keep wild animals out and domestic ones in and so was of no military significance. The inner wall, the *Schildmauer,* was prouder and of more warlike intent. Rearing behind the shield-wall was the tower of the *Bergfried,* the redoubt which had anciently housed the lords of the high woods when Saracen and Viking had roamed at will and each dawn might see a Magyar horde lining the horizon. The castle was a machine designed for defense and could be held, like most, by only a small garrison; but it had been tested only once, and then not to the limit. No army had marched from the Breisgau since Ludwig the Bavarian had bested Friedrich the Fair at Mühldorf; so the drawbridge was down and the portcullis up and the guards none too vigilant.

The *curia* spread across an acre and a half around the manor house, crowning the hill with dairy, dovecote, sheepfold, malting house, a kitchen and bakery, a great timber barn of twelve bays to store the grain harvest from the lord's salland; a stable grunting with cows, horses, oxen. To the rear, more noisome, the curial privy. Elsewhere, an apple orchard, a vineyard, a pound for stray animals that had wandered innocently onto the salland. In generations past, the manor had produced for itself everything needful; but much now lay abandoned. Why weave homespun when finer cloth could be had in the Freiburg market? In the modern age, pack peddlers trekked from the Breisgau, braving for the sake of profit the chance of von Falkenstein's regard.

No serfs were about. By long custom, the harvest day ended with the meal served in the fields and the lord could demand no work afterward. No monastic sexton, appraising his water clock to mark the canonical hours, ever gauged time so finely as a manorial serf. Matters differed among the freeholders. Dietrich had noted much late activity in shed and garden and within walls by candlelight in his passage through the village. But a man who labored on his own account did not watch the sun as closely as one who labored for another's.

Dietrich's entry into the curial grounds was met with much indignation by the resident geese, who harried and chivvied the priest as he made his way to the Hof. "Next Martinmas," Dietrich scolded the birds, "you will grace the Herr's table." But the chastisement had no effect and they escorted him to the doors of the hall, announcing his arrival. Franz Ambach's cow, impounded for trespass on the salland, watched placidly while she awaited her ransom.

GUNTHER, THE *maier domo,* conducted Dietrich to a small scriptorium at the far end of the hall, where the Herr Manfred sat at a writing table below a slit window. Through the window drifted the woodsmoke of evening meals, the cries of hawks circling the tower battlement, the clanging of the smithy, the slow toll of Joachim at the Angelus bell on the other side of the valley, and the amber remains of the afternoon light. The sky was deepening to indigo rimmed by bright orange on the underside of the clouds. Manfred sat in a curule chair fashioned of gracefully curved rosewood whose slats ended in the heads of beasts. His pen scratched across a sheet of paper.

He glanced up at Dietrich's appearance, bent once more to his writing, then put quill aside and passed the sheet to Max, who stood a little to the side. "Have Wilimer make fair copies of this and see it sent to each of my knights." Manfred waited until Max had gone before turning to Dietrich. His lips twitched into a brief smile. "Dietrich, you are prompt. I've always admired that in you." He meant "obedient to a summons," but Dietrich forbore from pointing it out. It might not even be true, but neither of them had tested it as yet.

Manfred indicated a straight-backed chair before the desk and waited until Dietrich had seated himself. "What's this?" he asked when the priest placed a pfennig before him.

"The fine for Ambach's cow," he said.

Manfred picked up the coin and regarded Dietrich for a moment before placing it in a corner of his desk. "I'll tell Everard. You know if you always pay their fines for them, they'll lose their dread of delinquency." Dietrich said nothing, and Manfred turned to his coffer and removed a bundle of parchments wrapped in oiled skin and tied up in string. "Here. These are the latest tractates from the Paris scholars. I had them copied by the stationers while we idled in Picardy. Most of them are direct from the masters' copies, but there were a few from the Merton calculators, who interest you so much. Those are from secondary copies, of course, brought over by English scholars."

Dietrich paged through the bundle. Buridan's *On the Heaven.* His *Questions on the Eight Books of Physics.* A slim volume *On Money,* by a student named Oresme. Swineshead's *Book of Calculations.* The very titles conjured up a swarm of memories and Dietrich recalled for a blinding moment of unbearable longing lost student days in Paris. Buridan and Ockham and he arguing the dialectic over tankards of ale. Peter Aureoli scowling and interrupting with the petulance of age. The free-for-all quodlibets, with the master determing on questions thrown up by the crowd. Sometimes in the rustle of the spruces that surrounded Oberhochwald, Dietrich thought he could hear the disputations of doctors, masters, inceptors, bachelors, and wondered if peace and seclusion had been too high a price to pay.

He found his voice with difficulty. "Mine Herr, I hardly know what . . ." He felt himself as one of Buridan's famous asses, uncertain which manuscript to read first.

"You know the price. Commentaries, if you think 'em useful. Suitable for a 'kettlehead' like me. You must have your own tractate—"

"Compendium."

"Compendium, then. When it is finished, I will have it sent to Paris, to your old master."

"Jean Buridan," Dietrich said reflexively. "At the school called Sorbonne." But did he really want to remind Paris where he was?

"So." Manfred steepled his hands under his chin. "I see we have a Franciscan about."

Dietrich had been expecting the inquiry. He laid the manuscripts aside. "His name is Joachim of Herbholzheim, from the Strassburg friary, living here now since three months."

He waited for Manfred to ask why the Minorite was staying in a backwoods parish rather than in the bustling cathedral town of the Elsass, but instead the lord cocked his head and placed a finger alongside his cheek. "A von Herbholz? I may know his father."

"His uncle, that would be. His father's the younger brother. But Joachim forswore his inheritance when he took the vow of poverty."

Manfred's lip quirked on one side. "I wonder if he gave it up faster than his uncle cut him off. He won't give me any trouble, will he? The boy, I mean; not the uncle."

"Only the usual denunciations of wealth and display."

Manfred snorted. "Let him protect the high woods without the means to support a troop of armsmen."

Dietrich knew all the counterarguments and saw in the lord's quickly narrowed gaze that Manfred remembered that he did. The rents and services from the peasantry supported more than armsmen. They supported fine clothing and banquet-feasts and clowns and minnesingers. Manfred kept a household suited to his station and was lavish in its maintenance; and if protection was needed, it lay at the lower end of the valley, at Falcon Rock, far nearer than Mühldorf or Crécy. "I will keep him on a check-rein, sire," he assured the Herr before old matters could be resurrected.

"See that you do. The last thing I want is an *exploratore* asking questions and distressing people." Again, he paused and gave Dietrich a significant look. "Nor you, I should think."

Dietrich chose to misunderstand the resurrection. "I try not to distress people, but I cannot help asking questions now and then."

Manfred stared a moment, then he reared his head and laughed, smacking the table with his palm. "By my honor, I've missed your wit these past two years." He sobered instantly and his eyes seemed to look somewhere else without actually turning. "By God, if I have not," he said more quietly.

"It was bad, then, the war?"

"The war? No worse than others, save that Blind John died a fool's death. I suppose you've heard that tale by now."

"Charged into the melee roped to his twelve paladins. Who hasn't heard? An imprudent act for a blind man, I would say."

"Prudence was never his particular strength. All those Luxemburgers are mad."

"His son is German King, now."

"Yes, and Roman Kaiser, too. We were still in Picardy when the news reached us. Well, half the Electors had voted Karl anti-king while Ludwig was still alive, so I don't suppose they were seized by any great hesitation once he was dead. Poor old Ludwig—to survive all those wars with Hapsburg, and then fall off his horse while hunting. I suppose old Graf Rudolf—no, it's Friedrich now, I've heard—and Duke Albrecht have sworn their oaths, so that settles matters for me. Do you know why Karl did not die with John at Crécy?"

"Were I to guess," Dietrich said, "I would say he had no ties to his father."

Manfred snorted. "Or a rope uncommonly long. When the French chivalry charged the English longbows, Karl von Luxemburg charged in the other direction."

"Then he was a wise man, or a coward."

"Wise men often are." The Herr's lips twitched. "It's all that reading that does it, Dietrich. It takes a man out of the world and pushes him inside his own head, and there is nothing there but spooks. I hear Karl is a learned man, which is the one sin that Ludwig never committed."

Dietrich made no reply. Kaisers, like Popes, came in diverse sorts. He wondered what would happen now to those Franciscans who had fled to Munich.

Manfred rose and walked to the lance window and stared out. Dietrich watched him brush idly at the grit of the window stone. The evening sun bathed the lord's face, giving his skin a ruddy cast. After a silence, he said, "You haven't asked why it's taken me two years to return."

"I imagined you had difficulties," Dietrich said with care.

"You imagined I was dead." Manfred turned away from the window. "Assumption's natural when you think how thick the dead lie between here and Picardy. Night's coming on," he added, inclining his head toward the sky outside. "You'll want a torch to see you safely back." Dietrich made no response, and after another moment, Manfred continued.

"The French-Reich is in chaos. The King was wounded; his brother killed. The Count of Flanders, the Duke of Lorraine, the King of Majorca . . . And the fool King of Bohemia, as I've said . . . All dead. The Estates have met and scolded Philip handsomely for losing the battle—and four thousand knights with it. They voted him new monies, of course, but fifteen *deniers* will not buy what three once did. It was a close thing, our returning. Knights are selling their lances to whoever will hire them. It was . . . a temptation, to throw off all responsibility and seize whatever a strong right arm might seize. When princes flee battle, and knights turn freelance, and barons rob pilgrims, what value has honor?"

"Why, all the more, seeing how rare it has become."

Manfred laughed without humor, then resumed his study of the sunset. "The pest reached Paris this past June," he said quietly.

Dietrich started. "The pest!"

"Yes." Manfred crossed his arms and seemed to become smaller. "They say half the city lies dead, and I think it but plain fact. We saw . . . things no man should see. Corpses left to rot in the street. Strangers denied hospice. Bishops and lords in flight, leaving Paris to fend for herself. And the church bells tolling funeral upon funeral until the town council bade them stop. Worst, I think, were the children—abandoned by their parents, dying alone and uncomprehending."

Dietrich crossed himself three times. "Dear God have mercy on them. As bad as Italy, then? Did they wall up families into their houses, as the Visconti did in Milan? No? Then some shred of charity remained."

"Ja. I was told the sisters in the Hospital stayed at their posts. They died, but so fast as they died, others took up their place."

"A miracle!"

Manfred grunted. "You have a grim taste in miracles, my friend. The English fare no better in Bordeaux. And it reached Avignon in May, though the worst was over by the time we passed there. Don't worry, Dietrich. Your Pope survived. His Jew physicians bade him sit between two fires and he never even fell sick." The Herr paused. "I met a brave man there. Perhaps the bravest man I shall ever meet. Guy de Chauliac. Do you know him?"

"Only by reputation. He is said to be the greatest physician in Christendom."

"That may be. He is a large man with the hands of a peasant and a slow, deliberate way of speaking. I would not have marked him a physician had I found him in the fields. After Clement left the city for his country house, de Chauliac remained—'to avoid the infamy,' he told me, though there is no shame in fleeing such an enemy. He fell ill himself of the pest. And all the while he lay abed, wracked with fever and pain, he described his symptoms and treated himself in divers ways. He wrote everything down, so that any who came after him would know the course of the disease. He lanced his own pustules, and recorded the effect. He was . . . He was like a knight who stands his ground against his enemy, whatever wounds he has received. Would I had six men with such courage by my side in battle."

"De Chauliac is dead, then?"

"No, he lived, praise God, though it is hard to say which treatment saved him—if indeed it was anything more than the whim of God."

Dietrich could not understand how sickness could travel such distances. Plagues had broken out before—inside town walls or castles, among besieging armies—but never since the time of Eusebius had it consumed whole nations. Some invisible, malevolent creature seemed to stalk the land. But it was bad air, all the doctors were agreed. A *mal odour*—malady.

An alignment of the planets had caused deep earthquakes in Italy, and the chasms had exuded a vast body of stiff, bad air, which the winds then drove from place to place. None knew how wide the malady was, nor how far it would travel before it finally broke up. Folk in sundry towns had tried to sunder it with loud noises, church bells and the like, but to no avail. Travelers had marked its progress up the Italian peninsula and along the coast to Marseilles. Now it had gone to Avignon, and so to Paris and Bordeaux.

"It has passed us by!" he cried. "The pest has gone west and north!" Dietrich knew shameful joy. He did not rejoice that Paris had suffered, but that Oberhochwald had been spared.

Manfred gave him a bleak look. "No sign among the Swiss, then? Max said not, but there is more than one road out of Italy since they hung that bridge across St. Gotthard's Pass. It worried us on the march that we would find you all dead, that it had passed through here before reaching Avignon."

"We may be too high for the malady to reach," Dietrich told him.

Manfred made a dismissive wave. "I am only a simple knight, and leave such notions as malady to scholars. But in France, I bespoke a knight of St. John, lately come from Rhodes, and he said that the pest came out of Cathay, and the story is that the dead *there* lie without number. It struck Alexandria, he told me, and his brotherhood at first deemed it God's judgment on the Saracens."

"God has not such poor aim," Dietrich said, "as to lay Christendom waste while smiting the infidel."

"They've been burning Jews over it, all the way from the Mediterranean north—save in Avignon, where your Pope protects them."

"Jews? That makes nonsense. Jews die also of the pest."

"So said Clement. I have a copy of his Bull that I obtained in Avignon. Yet Jews travel all about Europe; as also does the pest. The story is that the kabbalists among them have been poisoning the wells, so it may be that the good Jews themselves know nothing about it."

Dietrich shook his head. "It is bad air, not bad water."

Manfred shrugged. "De Chauliac said the same, though in his delerium, he wrote that rats brought the pest."

"Rats!" Dietrich shook his head. "No, that cannot be. Rats have been always about, and this pest is a new thing on earth."

"As may be," said Manfred. "But this past May, King Peter put down a pogrom in Barcelona. I had the news from Don Pero himself, who had come north looking for glory in the French war. The Catalans ran wild, but the burger militia protected the Jewish quarter. Queen Joanna sought likewise in Provence, but the folk rose up and expelled the Neapolitans. And last month Count Henri ordered all the Jews in the Dauphine brought into custody. To protect them from the mob, I think; but Henri's a coward and the mob may ride him." Manfred curled his right hand into a fist. "So you see that it was no such simple thing as a war that kept me at bay these past two years."

Dietrich did not want to believe it true. "Pilgrim tales . . ."

". . . may grow in the telling. Ja, ja. Maybe only two Jews have been burned and only twenty Cathayans died; but I know what I saw in Paris, and I would as soon not see it here. Max tells me there are poachers in my woods. If they bring the pest with them, I want them kept away."

"But people do not carry bad air with them," Dietrich said.

"There must be a reason why it spreads so far and wide. Some towns, Pisa and Lucca among them, have reported good fortune by blockading travelers, so travelers may well spread it. Perhaps the malady clings to their clothing. Perhaps they really do poison the wells."

"The Lord commanded we show hospitality to the sick. Would you have Max chase them off, to the peril of our souls?"

Manfred grimaced. His fingers drummed restless on the tabletop. "Find out, then," he said. "If they are hale, the wardens may use them in the grain harvest. One pfennig the day plus the evening meal and I overlook any trapping or fishing they may have done in the meantime. Two pfennig if they forego the meal. However, if they need hospitality, that is your affair. Set up a hospital in my woods, but none may enter onto my manor or into the village."

IN THE morning, Max and Dietrich went in search of the poachers. Dietrich had prepared two perfumed kerchiefs with which to filter the malady, should they encounter it, but he did not think much of Manfred's theory that clothing could carry bad air with it. There was nothing in Galen; nor had Avicenna written of it. All that clothing customarily carried were fleas and lice.

When they came to the place where the trees lay toppled like mown hay, Max hunkered down and sighted along a trunk. "The sentry ran off in that direction," he said, holding his arm out. "Past that white beech. I noted its location at the time."

Dietrich saw a great many white beeches, all alike. Trusting, he followed the soldier.

But Max had walked only a few arm-lengths into the brush when he stopped by the flat stump of a great oak. "So. What is this?" A bundle sat upon the stump. "Food stolen from the boon," the sergeant said opening the kerchief. "These are the loaves that Becker makes for the harvest meal—see how much longer they are than the normal loaf? And turnips and, what's this?" He sniffed. "Ah. Soured cabbage. And a pot of cheese." Max turned, brandishing a loaf big enough to feed three men. "Eating well, I think, for landless men."

"Why would they abandon it?" Dietrich wondered.

Max glanced about. "We frightened them off. Hush!" He held an arm out to Dietrich to still him while his eyes searched the surrounding brush. "Let's be on our way," he said more loudly, and turned as if to proceed deeper into the woods, but at the sudden snap of a twig behind them, he whirled and in two leaps grabbed hold of an arm.

"Got you, you rubbish!"

The figure yanked from concealment squealed like a yearling pig. Dietrich glimpsed a brocaded coverslut and two long, flying, yellow braids. "Hilde!" he said.

The miller's wife swung on Max, who had turned at Dietrich's cry, and struck him on the nose. Max howled and slapped her with his free hand, spinning her so that he could pull her other arm up high behind her back, nearly to her shoulder blade. "Max, stop!" Dietrich cried. "Let her go! It's Klaus's wife!"

Max gave the arm another twist, then shoved the woman away. Hilde staggered a step or two, then turned. "I thought you were robbers, come to steal the food I laid out for the poor."

Dietrich regarded the bread and cheese on the tree stump. "Ach . . . You are bringing the poachers food from the harvest meal? Since how long?" Dietrich wondered that Hilde should have done so. There was nothing of pride in the act.

"Since Sixtus Day. I leave it here on this stump just before sunset, after the harvest work. My husband never lacks for meal, and this is as good a use for it as any. I paid the baker's son to make loaves for me."

"So that is how the fellow bought himself free of the boon-work. But, why?"

Hilde drew herself up and stood straight. "It is my penance before God."

Max snorted. "You should not have come here alone."

"You said there were landless men here. I heard you."

Dietrich said, "Landless men can be dangerous."

"More dangerous than *this* doodle?" Hilde jerked her head toward Max. "They're timid folk. They wait until I leave before they take the offering."

"So you thought to hide and have a look at them?" the sergeant said. "Womanly thinking. If they're serfs off their manor, they'll not wish to be seen."

She turned and wagged a finger at Schweitzer. "Wait until I tell my Klaus, *the maier*, how you handled me!"

Max grinned. "Will that be *after* you tell him how you go into the woods to feed poachers? Tell me, do you bite and scratch as well as you punch?"

"Come closer and learn."

Max smiled and took a step forward to Hilde's step back. Then, his gaze traveled past her, and the smile froze. "God's wounds!"

Dietrich glimpsed a stealthy figure darting into the woods with the food bundled up into the kerchief. He was a spindly sort—arms and legs too long for his body, joints too far down his limbs. He wore a belt of some shining material, but wore it too high to mark a waist. That much, and grayish skin through strips of colorful cloth, was all that Dietrich saw before the figure had disappeared into the brush. Hazel twigs rustled; an acorn-jay complained. Then all was still.

"Did you see him?" Max demanded.

"That pallor . . ." said Dietrich. "I think he must be a leper."

"His face . . ."

"What about it?"

"He had no face."

"Ah. That oft happens in the last stages, when the nose and ears rot off."

They stood irresolute, until Hildegarde Müller stepped into the brush. "Where are you going, you ignorant slattern?" Max cried.

Hilde cast a bleak look on Dietrich. "You said they were landless men," she said in a voice like an overtuned lute string. "You said it!" Then she took two more steps into the hazelwood, stopped, and looked about.

Max closed his eyes and let out a breath. Then he pulled his quillon from its sheath and set after the miller's wife. "Max," said Dietrich, "you said we should stay on the game trails."

The sergeant hacked an angry blaze into a tree. "The game has better sense. Stand still, you silly woman! You'll get yourself lost. God save us." He squatted and ran some branches from a raspberry bush through his hand. "Broken," he said. "That way." Then he set off without looking to see if the others followed.

Every few steps, Max would stoop and examine the ground or a branch. "Long steps," he muttered at one point. "See where the shoe has come down in the mud? Its fellow was back there."

"Leaping," Dietrich guessed.

"On deformed feet? Mark the shape. When have you ever heard of cripples leaping?"

"Acts," said Dietrich. "Chapter three, verse eight."

Max grunted, stood, and brushed his knees. "This way," he said.

He led them by stages deeper into the forest, blazing at times a tree or arranging rocks upon the ground as a sign for which way they had come. They pushed past thickets and brambles, stepped over felled trees that had buried their heels in their path, stumbled down sudden ravines. "Lover-God!" said Max when he had found the footprints once more. "He leapt from one bank to the other!"

The trees grew taller and farther apart, their branches arching overhead like the vaulting of a cathedral. Dietrich saw what Max had meant about the game trails. Here, protected by a ridge, no trees had fallen to the blast and every direction looked the same. Bushes and smaller trees had abandoned the field to their triumphant seniors. A mat of leaf-fall, years thick, softened their footsteps. Nor was there cue from the sun. Light was present only in shafts that, arrow-like, pierced the foliage above. When Max hacked a tree, muffled echoes spoke from every direction, so that Dietrich thought that sound itself had gotten lost. Hilde began to say something, but her voice, too, whispered from the stillness and she quieted immediately and thereafter followed the Schweitzer more closely.

In a small clearing where a brook chattered through the forest, they stopped to rest among the ferns. Dietrich sat on a mossy stone beside a pool. Max tested the water, then cupped his hands and drank from it. "Cold," he said as he refilled his water-skin. "It must run down from the Katerinaberg."

Hilde looked about and shivered. "Woods are frightnening places. Wolves live here, and witches."

Max laughed at her. "Villager tales. My parents were foresters. Did I ever tell you that, pastor? We cut wood and sold it to the charcoal burners. We bought our grain from the valley folk, but fruits and meat we took from the forest. It was a quiet life, peaceful, and nobody bothered us much, except once when a troop of Savoy's men came through on some quarrel." He thought silently for a time, then rammed the stopper into his water-skin. "That's when I left. You know what young men are like. I wondered if there was a world outside the forest, and the Savoyards needed a guide. So I went with them until I had shown them the way to—to somewhere. I've forgotten. They had a quarrel there with the Visconti over some worthless patch of the Piedmont. But I stayed with them and carried arms and fought the Milanese." He took Dietrich's water-skin and refilled it as well. "I found I liked it," he said as he handed it back. "I don't think you can understand that, pastor. The overcoming joy when your opponent falls. It's like . . . It's like having a woman, and I guess you don't understand that, either. Mind you, I never killed a man who did not have his sword bared for me. I'm no murderer. But now you know why I can never go back. To live in the Alps after what I've seen, to live in a place like this," and he swept his arm around him.

Hilde stared at the sergeant with a peculiar intensity. "What sort of man *enjoys* killing?"

"A living one."

That utterance was greeted by silence from both the priest and the miller's wife; and in that silence they heard through the continuo of chittering locusts, the sound of distant hammers. Max craned his neck. "That way. Close. Move quietly. Sound carries in a forest."

NEARING THE source, Dietrich heard a chorus in an arrhythmic but not unpleasing mix. Drums, perhaps. Or rattles. Beneath it all, rasping and clicking. One sound, he could identify: the chunk of ax on tree, followed by the peculiar crackling rush of a toppling fir. "Now," said Max, "we can't have that. Those are the Herr's trees." He waved the others back and crept forward on cat feet to the edge of the screen of trees that marked the top of the ridge. There, he stiffened and Dietrich, who had come up behind him, whispered, "What is it?"

Max turned and cried, "Run, for your soul's sake!"

Dietrich instead grabbed the sergeant and said, "What . . . ," before he too saw what lay below.

A great, circular swathe had been cut out of the forest, as if a giant had swung a scythe through it. Trees lay broken in all directions. In the center of the fall was a white building, as large as an abbot's tithe barn, with doors along its side lying open. A dozen figures in suspended activity stared up the ridge at Max and Dietrich.

They were not landless men, at all, Dietrich saw.

They were not men.

Spindly, gangly, misjointed. Bodies festooned with ragged strips of cloth. Gray skin suffused with blots of pale green. Long, hairless torsos surmounted by expressionless faces lacking nose and ear, but dominated by huge, golden, globular eyes, faceted like diamonds, that looked nowhere but saw everything. Antennae waved from their brows like summer's wheat.

Only their mouths showed expression: working softly, or hanging half-open, or shut into firm lines. Soft, moist lips parted two ways at either end, so that they seemed to smile and scowl at once. Twin strips of some horny substance lay in the folds at either end of the lips and a broken sound lifted from them as of distant locusts.

One creature was supported by two of its fellows. It opened its mouth as if to speak; but what issued forth was not words, but a yellow pus that dribbled down its chin. Dietrich tried to shriek, but his throat was choked with fear. Nightmares arose from childhood of the great stone gargoyles of the Köln Minster come alive in the night to steal him away from his mother's bed. He turned, flight in mind, only to find that two more of the creatures had come up behind him. He smelled the sharp tang of urine and his heart pounded like the Schmidmühlen trip-hammers. Were *these* monsters the folk that spread the pest?

Max whispered, "Holy Mary, Mother of God," over and over. Otherwise, all was hushed. Birds silent, only the low susurrus of the wind. The forest beckoned, its bracken and recesses a lie of safety. If he ran, he would become lost—but was that not better than to stay and be lost for all eternity?

Yet he was all that stood between these apparitions and his two companions, for only he had been consecrated with the power to cast out demons. From the corners of his eyes he saw Max's fingers frozen on the hilt of his quillon.

Dietrich's right hand inched up his chest and gripped his pectoral, holding the Crucified One before him like a shield. A demon responded by reaching slowly toward a scrip that hung from his belt—only to have his hand stayed by his companion. The hand had six fingers, Dietrich noticed, not a comforting number. He tried to speak the words of exorcism—*I, a priest of Jesus Christ, do abjure you unclean spirits . . .* —but his throat was spitless.

A shrill buzz pierced the air, and every head turned toward the barn, from which another creature had emerged, this one dwarfish and with an oversized head. It ran toward them and one of the taller demons let out a clacking ululation and charged after it. To do what? *To rip their souls from their very bodies?*

At that, the tableau broke.

Dietrich cried out.

Max drew his quillon.

The demon behind them pulled a strange, shiny tube from his pouch and pointed it at them.

And Hildegarde Müller staggered down the ridge toward the demons below.

She stopped once and looked back, locking gazes with Dietrich. Her mouth parted as if to speak; then she set her shoulders and continued forward. Oddly, they drew back from her.

Dietrich seized his fear and watched the unfolding drama with dreadful concentration. *God, grant me the grace to understand!* He felt that much depended on his understanding.

Hildegarde halted before the demon spewing pus from his mouth and she extended both hands to him. The hands clenched, drew back, opened again. And the demon fell into her arms and collapsed against her.

With a thin, high cry, she went to her knees in the dust and ashes and wood chips and cradled the creature on her lap. The greenish-yellow ichor stained her clothing and gave forth a sweetish, sickly odor. "Welc—" She stopped, swallowed, and began again. "Welcome, pilgrims, to the hospitality of my home. It pleases—It pleases me that you might abide with us." She stroked the thing's head gently, looking much like the Sorrowful Mother in those *Vesperbilder* that had lately grown popular, save that her eyes were squeezed shut and she would not look on what she comforted.

Everything came clear for Dietrich in a sudden, dizzying rush. The monster cradled by the miller's wife was badly injured. The effluvium that issued from him was a humor of some sort. The strips of cloth the demons wore were the torn and burnt remnants of clothing employed as bandages around limbs and torsos. Their bodies and faces were smoke-smudged and the motley of their skin signified dull-green bruises and scratches. *And do hellish creatures suffer earthly torments?* As for the smaller creature who had charged them buzzing like an angry hornet . . .

A child, Dietrich knew. And demons had no children; nor did they run and snatch them up into their arms as did the second creature racing close behind.

"Pastor?" said Max. His voice trembled. He was on the point of breaking, and with his hand on a knife. "What manner of demons are these?"

"Not demons, sergeant." Dietrich had seized hold of Max's wrist. He glanced at Hildegarde and the injured one. "Men, I think."

"Men!"

Dietrich held fast. "Think, sergeant! Are there not centaurs, half-man and half-horse? And what of the *blemyae* of which Pliny wrote—men with their eyes in their torsos? Honorius Augustodenensis described and sketched dozens of such." The words tumbled and fought each other, as if they fled from his own tongue. "Stranger beings than these grace the very walls of our church!"

"Creatures more talked of than seen!" Yet Dietrich felt the man untense, and so released his knife arm. The sergeant backed away a step, and then another. *One more step and he runs,* Dietrich thought.

Then would tales run through the village and down the mountainside to pool in the ears of Freiburg; and a commotion would ensue in this quiet fleck of earth. Preachers would find God or Devil in the hearing and announce new heresies. Ecstatics would claim these creatures in visions; philosophers gravely question their existence. Some would in hidden rooms burn incense and pray to their images; others would ready the stake for those who did. Questions would be asked; inquisition would be made. Old matters would be remembered; old names recalled.

A woodleafsinger trilled from the treetop and Dietrich noticed how the monsters shrank from an innocent bird.

"Max," he said. "Hurry to the parsonage and fetch my bag of salves and my copy of Galen. It's bound in dark brown leather and has a drawing of a man's body on the cover." He doubted Galen had much to say on injuries to demons, but he could not let anyone vomit his life into the dirt without some attempt to save him. "And, Max," he said, calling after the man. "*Tell no one* what we have seen. We want no panic. If anyone asks, say that . . . that these strangers may carry the pest."

Max gave him a serious look. "You'd warn them of the pest to *stay* a panic?"

"Then tell them something else. Leprosy. *Only keep them away.* We have need of cool heads. Now hurry—and bring my salves."

Dietrich slid down the face of the ridge to where the creatures stood, now in a compact mob. Some held axes and mallets at the ready, but others bore no arms at all and shrank from him. A stack of logs had been placed to the side of the strange white building, and Dietrich realized that they had been clearing the broken trees from around it. Yet how could such a large building have been erected in the midst of the forest without a clearance to begin with?

He knelt beside the creature that Hilde comforted and moistened his fingers with spit. "On the condition that you have led a just and good life, I baptize you in the Name of the Father, and of the Son, and of the Holy Spirit. Amen." He traced a cross on the thing's brow. "Amen," said Hildegarde.

Dietrich rose and brushed his habit off, wondering whether he had committed sacrilege. Held Heaven a place for such creatures? Maybe, had they souls. He could make nothing of the injured one's featureless gaze; could not, indeed, know if it was gazing or not, as there were no lids to the faceted hemispheres. The others had not turned a head while he gave their fellow a conditional baptism. Yet he had the uneasy feeling that they were all looking directly at him. Their strange, bulging eyes did not move. *Could* not move, he guessed.

Discovered now, what would these creatures do? That they had sought to remain hidden boded well, for their unnatural presence, demonic or not, must remain secret. Yet, they had built themselves a house on the Herr's land, so it seemed that they meant to stay, and no secret could keep forever.

· 2 ·

NOW
Tom

TOM SCHWOERIN was no hermit. He was the sort of man who liked company and, while hardly boisterous, he enjoyed a song and a drink, and there were clubs in town where he had once been a Known Man.

That was before he met Sharon, of course. It would not be fair to call Sharon a wet blanket, but she did put a damper on things. This is not entirely bad. Carbon rods are dampers, too, and to good purpose. There had been something frivolous about Tom before she took him in hand. A grown man ought not wear so much grease paint. Sharon put a stop to that, mostly, and some of her seriousness had rubbed off on him.

So Tom, when on the scent, could give a credible imitation of a hermit—albeit one with a more chatty disposition than most. He liked to make his ideas real, and this meant talking about them aloud. Sharon usually played the unwilling role of Ear—often very unwilling, as on that particular evening—but it was the talking that mattered, not the hearing. Tom would have talked to himself in a pinch, and sometimes did.

He knew quite well that he had been thrown out of the apartment. He was not especially alert to the subtle cues of human relationships, but it was hard to miss the old heave-ho, and a man need not be particularly sensitive to feel a little vexed over the matter. Visiting the archives really was the sensible thing to do when seen from the clear, cold heights of logic; but logic wasn't in it.

THE MEDIEVAL collection in the Teliow Memorial Library had started with a small art collection, housed in a gallery decorated to resemble a medieval hall. There were some fine pieces there: triptychs, altar fronts, and the like. There followed: bibles, psalters and other incunabula, pipe rolls and cartularies, registers and estate papers, ledgers and accounts—the raw materials of history. Primary sources bought at auctions or found in troves or bestowed by tax-weary donors; never edited, never published, grouped loosely by source into folders, tied in stacks between pieces of heavy cardboard, and hidden away to await a scholar sufficiently desperate to wade through them. They had been lying in wait for Tom and had caught him fair.

Tom had prepared a list. He was not the methodical sort, but even he knew better than to dive headfirst into uncharted waters. He didn't know what he was looking for, but he did know what *sort* of thing he was looking for, and that was half the battle. So he scrutinized the contents of each carton, setting aside certain documents for more careful perusal. Along the way, he acquired stray bits of the trivium and the quadrivium, for he was the sort of man who cannot look up one thing without in the process finding half a dozen other things. In this manner, the sun grew long, and passed into evening.

AMIDST THE chaff already winnowed lay by that time but a single grain of wheat: A note in a seventeenth century index of episcopal court cases that, "*de rerum Eifelheimensis,* the matter of the baptism of one Johannes Sterne, wayfarer, had been mooted by the death through pestilence of all the principals." This index had been compiled in part from an earlier fifteenth century index, based in turn on long-lost fourteenth-century originals.

Not exactly hot on the trail.

He closed his eyes and rubbed his forehead and contemplated surrender. He might have packed it in then, had it not been for a nudge from an unlikely direction.

"You know, Dr. Schwoerin," said the nudge, "we don't get many live ones in here."

Paul on the Damascus highway could not have been more startled apprehending a sudden voice. The librarian, who had dutifully shopped cartons for him all night in silent obscurity, stood by the table with the carton he had just finished braced against her hip. She was a fine-featured woman, decked with a long print dress and adorned by large, plain glasses. Her hair met behind her in a tight bun.

Lieber Gott, Tom thought. *An archetype!* Aloud, he said, "I beg your pardon?"

The librarian flushed. "Usually researchers phone their requests in. One of the staff scans it into the computer, charges the cost against the appropriate grant, and that's that. It can be terribly lonely, especially at night, when all we do is wait for requests from overseas. I try to read everything I scan, and there's my own research of course. That helps some."

That was the nexus. A lonely librarian wanted a human conversation, and a lonely cliologist needed a break from his fruitless hunt. Otherwise, no words at all might have passed between the two of them that whole night.

"I needed to get out of the apartment for a while," Tom said.

"Oh," the young woman told him, "I'm glad you came. I've been following your researches."

Historians do not normally acquire groupies. "Why on earth would you do that?" Tom said in surprise.

"I majored in analytical history under Dr. LaBret at Massachusetts, but differential topology was too tough for me; so I switched to narrative history instead."

Tom felt much as a molecular biologist might upon encountering a "natural philosopher." Narrative history wasn't science; it was literature. "I remember my own problems with Thom's catastrophe surfaces," he ventured. "Sit down, please. You're making me nervous."

She remained standing hipshot, with the carton. "I don't mean to keep you from your work. I only wanted to ask you . . ." She hesitated. "Oh, it's probably obvious."

"What is?"

"Well, you're researching a village called Eifelheim."

"Yes. The site is an unexplained void in the Christaller grid." That was a deliberate test on Tom's part. He wanted to see what she would make of it.

She raised her eyebrows. "Abandoned and never resettled?" Tom nodded confirmation. "And yet," she mused, "the locus must have had affinity or it would never have been occupied in the first place. Perhaps a nearby site. . . . No? That *is* odd. Perhaps their mines were depleted? Their water dried up?"

Tom smiled, delighted at her perception, as much as her interest. He'd had a difficult time convincing Sharon that there even was a problem, and all she'd come up with was a common cause, like the Black Death. This young woman at least knew enough to suggest local causes.

After he explained his problem, the librarian frowned. "Why haven't you searched for information from *before* the village's disappearance? Whatever caused its abandonment must have occurred earlier."

He swatted the carton. "That's why I'm here! Don't teach your grandmother to suck eggs."

She ducked her head to the storm. "But, you've never referenced Oberhochwald, so I . . ."

"Oberhochwald?" He shook his head in irritation. "Why Oberhochwald?"

"That was Eifelheim's original name."

"What!" He stood sharply, knocking the heavy reading chair backward. It hit the floor with a bang and the librarian dropped her carton, folders skittering across the floor. She clapped a hand to her mouth, then stooped to gather them up.

Tom darted around the table. "Never mind those now," he said. "It was my fault. I'll pick them up. Just tell me how you know that about Oberhochwald." Lifting her to her feet, he was surprised at how short she was. Sitting, he had thought her taller.

She pried her arm from his grasp. "We'll both pick them up," she told him. She set the carton on the floor and dropped to her hands and knees. Tom knelt beside her, handed her a folder. "Are you certain about this Oberhochwald place?"

She stacked three folders into the carton and looked at him and he noticed that her eyes were large and brown. "You mean you *didn't know*? I learned only by accident, but I thought you . . . Well, it was a month ago, I think. A brother in the theology school asked me to find a rare manuscript for him and scan it into the database. The name *Eifelheim* caught my eye because I had already scanned several items for you. It was a marginal gloss on the name Oberhochwald."

Tom paused with several more folders in his hand. "What was the context?"

"I don't know. I read Latin, but this was in German. Oh, if I'd only known, I would have sent you an e-mail about it. But I thought—"

Tom placed a hand on her arm. "You didn't do anything wrong. Do you have it here? The manuscript the brother asked for. I need to see it."

"The original is at Yale—"

"A copy is fine."

"Yes. I was about to ask you that. We kept a copy of the pdf scan in our own database, and df_imaging comes in once a month and organizes the archives for us. I can call it up."

"Could you do that for me? *Bitte sehr?* I mean, pretty please? I'll finish this."

He reached under the table to retrieve another wayward folder. Hot damn! Another blow struck for serendipity! He piled two more folders atop the ones he had. No wonder he hadn't found any contemporary references to Eifelheim. *It hadn't been called Eifelheim yet.* He glanced at the librarian, busy at the keyboard in her office.

"*Entschuldigung,*" he called. She paused and turned. "I haven't even asked your name."

"Judy," she told him. "Judy Cao."

"Thank you, Judy Cao."

IT WAS a slim lead, a loose thread dangling from an old tangle of facts. At some unspecified time in the fourteenth century a wandering Minorite named Fra Joachim had evidently preached a sermon on "the sorcerers at Oberhochwald." The text of the sermon had not survived the centuries, but Brother Joachim's oratorical fame had, and a commentary on the sermon had been included in a treatise on homiletics against witchcraft and devil worship. A later reader—sixteenth century to judge by the calligraphy—had added a marginal gloss: *Dieses Dorp heißt jetzt Eifelheim.* This village is now called Eifelhiem.

And that meant . . .

Tom groaned and laid the printout on the table.

Judy Cao laid a hand on his arm. "What's wrong, Dr. Schwoerin?"

Tom batted the sheet. "I've to go back through all these files." He ran his hand through his hair. "Oh well. *Povtorenia—mat' uchenia.*" He pulled the carton closer to him.

Judy Cao took a folder from the carton and, eyes cast down, turned it over and over in her hands. "I could help," she suggested.

"Oh . . ." He shook his head distractedly. "I can't ask you to do that."

"No, I'm serious." She looked up. "I volunteer. There's always a lull on the server after eight P.M. The hits from California drop off and the early morning hits from Warsaw or Vienna don't pick up until later. The math, I can't do, but research and documentation . . . I'll have to check these cartons in real time, of course; but I can also mouse around the Net."

"I can run a search engine," Tom said.

"No offence, Dr. Schwoerin, but no one can mouse the Net like a master librarian. There is so much information out there, so poorly organized—and so bogus—that knowing how to find it is a science in itself."

Tom grunted. "Tell me about it. I run a search and I get thousands of hits, most of it *Klimbim,* which I'm damned if I can figure out how they made the list."

"Most sites aren't worth the paper they're not written on," Judy said. "Half of them are set up by cranks or amateur enthusiasts. You need to boole your search-string. I can write a worm to sniff out not only citations of Oberhochwald, but citations of any key words associated with the place. Like . . ."

"Like Johannes Sterne? Or the Trinity of Trinities?"

"Or anything. The worm can be taught to screen for context—that's the hard part—and ignore items that aren't relevant."

"All right," Tom said. "You've convinced me. I'll pay you a stipend from my grant money. It won't be much, but it'll give you a title. Research Assistant. And your name will go on the paper after mine." He straightened his chair. "I'll key you a special access code for CLIODEINOS so you can dump into my files whenever you find anything. Meanwhile, we . . . What's wrong?"

Judy pulled back from the table. "Nothing." She looked away briefly. "I thought we might meet here periodically. To coordinate our activities."

Tom waved his hand. "We can do that easier over the Net. All you need is a smart phone and a modem."

"I have a smart phone," she told him, tugging on the string that bound the folder she held. "My phone is smarter than some people."

Tom laughed, not yet getting the joke.

THE TWO cartons they already had on the table were as good a place as any to start, so Tom took one and gave Judy the other and they went through them, folder by folder. Tom was reading the same items for the second time that night, so he forced himself to concentrate on the words. Searching for "Oberhochwald," his eyes were snagged by any word starting with an "O"—or even a "Q" or a "C." The manuscripts were penned in a disheartening variety of hands; mostly Latin, but some Middle High German, a few French or Italian. A motley assortment, with nothing in common but their donors.

Three hours later, and two hours after Judy's shift on the help desk had ended, his eyes red and his brain muzzy, Tom came up for air clutching a single manuscript page.

Judy was still there, and she had found one, too.

THAT JUDY could read Latin surprised Tom. He found it curious that a Southeast Asian should be interested in the culture and history of Europe, although the converse would not have puzzled him in the least. So while Tom learned little about Eifelheim that night, you could not say he learned nothing. In fact, he was a little mistaken about Judy Cao's interests.

"*Moriuntur amici mei . . .*"

While Judy read, Tom listened with his eyes closed. This was a trick of his whenever he wanted to concentrate on what he heard. By shutting down one information channel, he thought to heighten his attention on the other. However, he was never known to put his fingers in his ears when he wanted to see something especially clearly.

Tom once told me that we Germans keep our verbs in our pockets, so that the meaning does not "until the end of the sentence appear." Latin can scatter words like candy at *Fasching*, trusting to its suffixes to maintain discipline. Fortunately, the medievals had imposed a word order on Latin—one reason the humanists detested them—and Tom had a bent for language.

> *"My friends are dying despite all that we do. They eat, but take no nourishment from their food, so the end draws ever closer. I pray daily that they not succumb to despair, Oberhochwald being so far from their homes, but face their Creator with hope and faith in their hearts.*
>
> *"Two more have taken Christ in their last days, which pleases Hans no less than me. Nor do they place blame with those of us that took them in, knowing well that our time, too, is coming. Rumors fly swift as arrows, and with as much harm, that the pestilence that gutted the southlands in the past year even now lays waste the Swiss. Oh, let this be some lesser ill that has come upon us! Let this cup pass us by."*

That was all. Just a fragment of a journal. No author. No date. "Sometime between 1348 and 1350," Tom guessed, but Judy pinned it down more closely.

"Mid-to-late 1349. The Plague reached Switzerland in May of 1349 and Strassburg in July, which puts it at the edge of the Black Forest."

Tom, reflecting that narrative history did have its points, handed her a second sheet. "I found this in the other carton. A petition for redress from a smith in Freiburg to the Herr Manfred von Hochwald. He complains that a copper ingot, left by Pastor Dietrich of Oberhochwald as payment for drawing some fine copper wire, had been stolen."

"Dated 1349, Vigil of the Feast of the Virgin." She handed the page back.

Tom made a face. "Like that pins it down . . . Half the medieval year was taken up by Marian feasts." He made another note in his palmtop, tugged on his lip. There was something about the letter that bothered him, but he couldn't put his finger on it. "Well . . ." He gathered the hard copies together, stuffed them into his briefcase, and snapped it shut. "The exact date doesn't matter. I'm trying to learn why the place was abandoned, not whether its priest stiffed a local artisan. But, *alles gefällt,* I've learned the one thing that's made this whole trip worthwhile."

Judy closed one of the cartons and initialed the log printed on its lid. She gave him a brief glance. "Oh? What was that?"

"I may not be exactly hot on the trail; but at least I know that there *is* a trail."

HE LEFT the library to find the night far advanced and the campus deserted and quiet. The classroom buildings blocked the traffic noises from Olney and the only sound was the soft rustling of the branches overhead. Their shadows writhed in the moonlight. Tom hunched his shoulders against the insistent breeze and headed for the campus gate. So, Oberhochwald had changed its name to Eifelheim . . . *Why Eifelheim?* He wondered idly.

He was halfway across the quadrangle when it suddenly hit him. According to the *Moriuntur* document, the village had been called Oberhochwald right up until the Black Death swept through and wiped it from the Earth.

Why would a village that no longer existed change its name at all?

· V ·

AUGUST, 1348

The Feast of St. Joachim

SEPPL BAUER delivered the goose-tithe on St. Mary's Day: two dozen birds, short and tall, white and dun and dappled, heads at all inquisitive angles, complaining and strutting with the unfeigned arrogance of the goose-clan. Ulrike, with her longish neck and undershot chin looking not unlike a goose herself, ran ahead of the flock and held the gate open while Otto the goose-hound chivvied the birds into the yard.

"Five-and-twenty birds," Seppl announced while Ulrike latched the gate. "Franz Ambach added an extra bird as a love-gift because you ransomed his cow from the Herr."

"Give him my thanks," said Dietrich with grave formality, "and to the others too for their generosity." The levy on the goose-flock was fixed by custom and not by generosity, yet Dietrich always treated it after the manner of a gift. While he did much gardening of his own and owned a *milch* cow which he farmed to Theresia, his priestly duties precluded him from devoting his time to raising food; and so the villagers tithed of their own sustenance to maintain him. The remainder of his benefice came from archdeacon Willi in Freiburg and from Herr Manfred, in whose gift it lay. He pulled a pfennig from his scrip and placed it in Seppl's palm. This, too, was a customary duty, which was why the young men of the village jostled for the privilege of delivering the tithe payments.

"I'll put this against my second furlong," the boy announced, dropping the coin into his own scrip, "and not use it to buy myself out of my duties, like *some* I could name."

"You're a frugal lad," Dietrich said. Ulrike had joined them and stood now holding hands with the boy while Otto panted and his gaze darted from boy to girl with puzzled jealousy. "So, Ulrike," Dietrich said, "you are prepared for the wedding?"

The girl bobbed. "Yes, father." She would be twelve the next month, a grown woman, and the union of the Bauers and Ackermanns had been long in the planning.

Through arrangements comprehensible only to an ambitious peasant, Volkmar Bauer had organized a swap involving three other villagers, several furlongs, some livestock, and a bag of copper pfennigs, so as to settle the manse named "Unterbach" on his son. The trades had enabled both the Bauers and the Ackermanns to bring their plots together in a more compact arrangement. *Fewer turnings of the plowteam,* Felix Ackermann had explained with grave satisfaction.

Dietrich, watching the young couple depart, hoped the union would prove as loving for the couple as it promised to be advantageous for their kin. The minnesingers extolled the virtues of affection over calculation, and peasants ever mimicked the manners of their betters; yet men had a way of loving that which might prove profitable. Love stopped no king from shopping his sons or daughters. The daughter of

England, Manfred had said, was resting in Bordeaux on her way to wed the son of Castile, and for no better reason than that the union would discomfit France. Likely, love stopped no peasant, either, however long and narrow his kingdom.

At least Seppl and Ulrike were no strangers to each other, as Prince Pedro and Princess Joan were. Their parents had arranged that, too, cultivating the affections between their offspring with the same patience with which they pruned their grapevines in hopes of a future vintage.

Dietrich entered his yard, to the displeasure of the goose-tithe, and took a billet and a knife from the shed in the rear. He passed a greeting with Theresia, who was tending the beans in his garden, and, stunning a goose from the flock with the billet, he took it to the shed and tied it securely by the legs to a hook there. He slit the throat, being careful not to sever the spine lest the muscles contract and make the plucking more difficult. "I am sorry, brother goose," he told the carcass, "that my hospitality—and yourself—has been so short-lived, but I know of some pilgrims who might be grateful for your flesh." Then he hung the goose to bleed out.

THE NEXT day, the goose now plucked, butchered, and safely wrapped in a leather game-bag, Dietrich crossed to Burg Hochwald, where Max Schweitzer awaited with two jennets harnessed and ready. "Sweet enough riding for a priest," the sergeant promised, offering him one of the horses. "The nag is as fat as a monk—and will stop to eat at every chance, so the resemblance is no happenstance. A good kick in the ribs will start her if she does." He gave Dietrich a leg up and waited until the priest was settled in the saddle. "Do you know the way by now?"

"You're not coming this time?"

"No. The Herr desires I attend to certain duties. Tell me you know the way."

"I know the way. The kiln trail to the wind-fall, then I follow the blazes as before."

Schweitzer looked doubtful. "When you see . . . *them,* try to buy one of those tubes they keep in their scrips. They pointed one at us that first time."

"I remember. You suppose it a weapon?"

"Ja. Some demons kept their hands near their scrips while we are about. A wary man's hand would hover near his scabbard in just such a way."

"Mine would hover near my crucifix."

"I think it may be a sling of some sort. A miniature *pot-de-fer.*"

"Can they be made so small? But it would sling such a mean bullet that it cannot be much of a weapon."

"So said Goliath. Offer them my Burgundian quillon, if you think they may trade for it." He had unfastened his belt and held it up to Dietrich, scabbard and all. Dietrich hefted it. "You want this sling of theirs so much? Well, that leaves only the question of how I may tell them so."

"Surely demons know Latin!"

Dietrich did not argue terms. "They lack the lips and tongues for it. But I will do what I can. Max, who is the second horse for?"

Before the soldier could answer, Dietrich heard the approaching voice of Herr Manfred and a moment later, the lord passed through the gate in the outer wall with Hilde Müller on his arm. He was smiling down at her, covering her hand with his where it gripped his left elbow. Dietrich waited while a manservant placed a stool and lifted Hilde into the saddle.

"Dietrich, a word?" said Herr Manfred. He took the mare by the rein and stroked its muzzle, speaking a few words of endearment to the beast. When the servant had gone past earshot, he said in a low voice, "I understand that we have demons in our woods."

Dietrich gave Max a sharp glance, but the soldier only shrugged. "They're not demons," Dietrich told the Herr, "but distressed pilgrims of a strange and foreign mien."

"*Very* strange and foreign, if my sergeant can be believed. Dietrich, I do not want demons in my woods." He held up a hand. "No, nor 'pilgrims of a strange and foreign mien.' Exorcise them—or send them on their way—whichever seems appropriate."

"My lord, you and I are of one accord on that."

Manfred stopped petting the beast. "I would be grieved to know otherwise. Come tonight, after your return."

He released the horse, and Dietrich jerked the jennet's head toward the road. "Move, horse," he said. "You'll find more to nibble yonder."

THE HORSES plodded their way past the fields, where the harvesters still labored. The salland having been gleaned, the villagers now worked their own manses. The serfs had retired to the curial barn to thresh the lord's grain. The peasants labored in common, moving from strip to strip according to some intricate schedule that the maier, the schultheiss, and the wardens had brokered long before.

A fistfight had broken out in Zur Holzbrücke, a manse belonging to Gertrude Metzger. Dietrich stood in his stirrups to watch, and saw that the wardens already had matters in hand. "What is it?" Hilde asked as she came abreast of him on the road.

"Someone was stuffing grain in his blouse to steal it and Trude's nephew raised the hue and cry against him on her behalf."

Hilde sniffed. "Trude should remarry and let a man work her land."

Dietrich, who saw no connection between one's widowhood and another's theft, remained silent. They resumed their progress toward the wood. Shortly, he said, "A word of caution?"

"Regarding?"

"The Herr. He is a man of appetites. It would be well not to feed them. His wife has been dead now these two years."

The miller's wife said nothing for a space. Then she tossed her head and said, "What would you know of appetites?"

"Am I not a man?"

Hilde looked at him sidewise. "A fair question. If you'd pay the fine 'under the linden,' you could prove it to me. But the fine is double if the woman's married."

The heat rose in Dietrich's neck and he watched her for a while as their horses plodded steadily onward. The Frau Müller rode with the inelegance of the peasant, flat against the saddle, bouncing against it with each step. Dietrich looked away before his thoughts could travel much further. He had tasted from that table and had found its pleasures overrated. By God's grace, women held little appeal for him.

It was not until they had entered the forest that Hilde spoke again. "I went to pray him food and drink for those awful *things* in the woods. That was all. He gave me the sacks you see here, tied behind the saddle. If he thought a price for the favor, he did not name it."

"Ah. I had thought . . ."

"I know what you thought. Try not to think about it so much." And with that remark, she kicked heels to her horse and trotted ahead of him down the path, her legs splaying artlessly at every jounce.

REACHING THE charcoal kiln, Dietrich reined his mount in and spoke a short prayer for the souls of Anton and Josef. Shortly, the horse whickered and shied and Dietrich looked up to see two of the strange creatures watching from the edge of the clearing. He froze for a moment at the sight. Would he ever grow accustomed to their appearance? Images, however grotesque, were one thing when carved of wood or stone; quite another thing when formed of flesh.

Hilde did not turn. "It's them," she said, "isn't it? I could tell by the way you started." Dietrich nodded dumbly, and Hilde heaved a breath. "I gag at their smell," she said. "My skin crawls at their touch."

One of the sentries swung its arm in a passable imitation of a human gesture and leapt into the woods, where it paused for Dietrich and Hilde to follow.

Dietrich's horse balked, so he kicked until the beast followed, with notable reluctance. The sentry moved in long, gliding lopes, pausing now and then to repeat the beckoning arm gesture. It wore a harness on its head, Dietrich saw, although the bit stood free before its mouth. From time to time it chittered or seemed to listen.

At the edge of the clearing where the creatures had erected their strange barn, the mare tried to bolt. Dietrich called upon half-forgotten skills and fought the beast, turning it away from the sight, shielding its eyes with his broad-brimmed traveling hat. "Stay back!" he told Hilde, who had lagged behind. "The horses fear these beings."

Hilde jerked hard on the reins. "Then they show better sense." She and Dietrich dismounted out of sight of the strangers. After picketing the horses, they carried the food sacks to the camp, where several of the creatures awaited them. One snatched the sacks and, using an instrument of some sort, cut small pieces from the foods inside. These, it placed into small glass phials. Dietrich watched the creature sniff at the mouth of one phial and hold it up to the light, and it suddenly occurred to him that it was an alchemist. Perhaps these folk had never seen goose or turnips or apples and so were wary of eating them.

The sentry touched Dietrich on the arm—it was like being brushed with dry sticks. He tried to fix the creature's uniqueness in his memory, but there was nothing that his mind could seize on. Its height—taller than many. Its coloring—a darker gray. The yellow streak that showed through the gap of its shirt—a scar? But whatever idiosyncrasies there may have been were drowned in a wild impression of yellow faceted eyes and horny lips and too-long limbs.

He followed the sentry to the barn. The wall had a subtle and slippery feel, unlike any material he had ever encountered, likely a mixed body combining the elements of earth and water. Inside, he discovered that the barn was in fact an *insula* like the Romans used to build, for the interior was divided into apartments, meaner in size than even a gärtner's hut. These strange folk must be remarkably poor to boast such cramped quarters.

The sentry led him to an apartment where three others awaited, then departed, leaving Dietrich curiously bereft. He studied his hosts.

The first sat directly before him, behind a table holding a number of curious objects of varied shapes and colors. A thin rectangular frame held a painting of a flowered meadow against distant trees. It was not a bas-relief, and yet it had depth!

The artist had evidently solved the problem of rendering distance on a flat surface. Ach, what might Simone Martini, dead now but a handful of years, have given to study the craft! Dietrich peered closer.

There was something wrong about the shapes, something off about the colors. These were not quite flowers and not quite trees and had too much blue in their green. The blooms bore six petals of intense gold, arranged in three opposed pairs. The grass was the pale yellow of straw. A scene of the homeland from which these beings had come? It must be far, he thought, to possess such strange blossoms.

The iconography in the arrangement, the symbolism that informed a picture and called upon the painter's true skills, eluded Dietrich. Meaning lay in the placement of particular saints or beasts, or in the relative sizes of the figures, or in their gestures or accouterments; but *no living creatures occupied the scene,* which was perhaps the strangest feature of all. It was as if the painting had been intended only as a simple reproduction of a vista! Yet, why essay such bald realism when the eye could behold as much unaided?

The second creature sat at a smaller table to the right side of the apartment. This wore a harness on its head and sat half-turned to face the wall. Dietrich took the harness as a mark of servitude. Like any such intent upon his duties, it took no notice of Dietrich's entrance, but its fingers danced over another painting—an array of colored squares bearing various sigils. Then the servant touched one and—the image changed!

Dietrich gasped and stumbled backward, and the third creature, the one who leaned against the left-hand wall with its long arms entwined upon themselves like vines, spread its mouth wide and flapped its upper and lower lips together, making a sound like a babe learning to talk. "Wa-bwa-bwa-bwa."

Was it a greeting? This one was tall, perhaps taller than Dietrich himself, and adorned with more colorful garb than the others: a buttonless vest such as the Moors favored, loose trousers of three-quarter's length, a belt with a variety of tokens dependent upon it, a sash of bright yellow. Such finery marked a man of rank. Dietrich, having recovered his aplomb, bowed from the shoulders. "Wabwabwabwa," he said, repeating the greeting as closely as he could.

In response, the creature dealt Dietrich a sharp blow.

Dietrich rubbed the stinging cheek. "You must not strike a priest of Jesus Christ," he warned. "I will call you Herr Gschert." The easy resort to blows had confirmed his surmise that this was one gently born.

The first creature, dressed as plainly as the servant but withal possessing an air of command, smacked the table with its forearm. A chittering arose and both it and Gschert waved their arms. Dietrich could see now that the sounds were made by the horny sides of the creatures' mouths clicking rapidly together like the twin blades of a scissors-pair. He thought it must be speech but, despite his most intent concentration, it seemed only the noise of insects.

Whatever discussion obtained between the two reached a crescendo. The seated one raised both bare forearms and rasped one against the other. There were callused ridges along them and the gesture made a sound like ripping cloth. Herr Gschert made a move as if to strike, and the seated one stood as if prepared to return the blow. From the other side of the apartment, the servant looked on, as servants are wont to do when their betters quarrel.

But the Herr checked its swing and made another gesture entirely, a tossing motion that Dietrich had no difficulty interpreting as a dismissal, conceding whatever point had been in contention. The other creature tilted its head back and spread its arms and Herr Gschert clicked its side-jaws once, sharply, whereupon the other resumed its seat.

Dietrich could not conjugate precisely what had just happened. There had been an argument, he thought. The first creature had challenged its lord—and had in some fashion triumphed. What then was the status of the seated one? To raise a challenge implied that the party had honor, which a commoner could not possess. So. A priest, perhaps? A powerful vassal? Or the man of another lord whom Gschert wished not to offend? Dietrich decided to call this one the Kratzer, because of the gesture it had made with its arms.

Gschert leaned back against the wall and the Kratzer resumed his seat. Then, facing Dietrich, it began clicking its horned side-lips. In the midst of the insect buzz, a voice said, "Greet God."

Dietrich started and looked to see whether somone else had entered the room.

The voice said again, "Greet God." It issued undisputedly from within a small box on the table! Through the loose weave of a cloth stretched tightly across its face, Dietrich could discern a drum head. Did the creatures have a *Heinzelmännchen* trapped within? He tried to look through the curtain—he had never actually seen a brownie—but the voice said, "Sit thee."

The command was so unexpected that Dietrich could think of no other response but to comply. There was something like a chair nearby, and he fit himself—badly—into it. The seat was uncomfortable, shaped to fit a different ass than his.

Now, a third time, the voice spoke. "Greet God." This time, Dietrich merely answered. "Greet God. How goes it by you, friend *Heinzelmännchen*?"

"It goes well. What means this word *Heinzelmännchen*?" The words were toneless and fell like the beat of a pendulum. Did the sprite make fun? The little people were wont to pranks, and while some, like the brownies, were reputedly playful, others, like the Gnurr, could be petty and malicious. "A *Heinzelmännchen* is one like yourself," Dietrich said, wondering where this dialogue was going.

"Know you then others like myself?"

"You are the first I have met," Dietrich admitted.

"Then, how know you that I be a *Heinzelmännchen*?"

Oh, clever! Dietrich could see that a battle of wits was about. Had the creatures captured a brownie and required now Dietrich's offices to speak with it? "Who else," he reasoned, "could fit inside a very small box but a very small man?"

This time there was a pause in the reply, and Herr Gschert made wa-wa sounds again, to which the Kratzer, who had been staring at Dietrich throughout, made the dismissive toss-gesture. It clicked its lips together—and the sprite said, "There is no small man. The box himself speaks."

Dietrich laughed. "How can that be," he asked, "when you have no tongue?"

"What means 'tongue'?"

Amused, Dietrich stuck his tongue out.

The Kratzer reached its long arm out and touched the picture frame, and the picture changed to a portrait of Dietrich himself, fully rendered in depth in the act of sticking his tongue out. In some manner, the tongue in the portrait glowed. Dietrich wondered if he had been wrong about the demonic nature of these beings. "Is this tongue?" the *Heinzelmännchen* asked.

"Yes, that is *doch* the tongue."

"Many thanks."

"IT WAS when it thanked me," Dietrich told Manfred later that evening, "that I began to suspect that it was a machine."

"A machine . . ." Manfred thought about that. "You mean like Müller's camshaft?" The two of them stood by a credence table near the fireplace in the great hall. The remnants of the dinner had been cleared, the children sent to bed with their nurse, the juggler thanked and dismissed with his pfennig, the other guests escorted to the door by Gunther. The hall was now sealed and even the servants sent away, leaving only Max to guard the door. Manfred filled two *maigeleins* with wine by his own hand. He proffered both, and Dietrich chose the one on the left. "Thank you, mine Herr."

Manfred grinned briefly. "Should I suspect now that you, too, are all gears and cams?"

"Please, I was conscious of the irony." They walked together from the credence table to stand near the fire. The ruddy embers hissed, and licked occasionally into flame.

Dietrich rubbed his hand across the roughly textured glass of his wine-bowl while he considered. "There was no cadence to the voice," he decided. "Or, rather, its cadence was mechanical, without rhetorical flourishes. It lacked scorn, amusement, *emphasis*, . . . hesitation. It said 'many thanks' with all the feeling of a shuttlecock flying across a loom."

"I see," said Manfred, and Dietrich raised a finger post.

"And that was another convincing point. You and I understand that by 'see' you signified something other than a direct impression on the sense of sight. As Buridan said, there is more to the meaning of an utterance than the precise words uttered. But the *Heinzelmännchen* did not understand figures. Once it learned that the 'tongue' is a part of the body, it became confused when I referred to 'the German tongue.' It did not comprehend *metonymy*."

"That's Greek to me," Manfred said.

"What I mean, my lord, is that I think . . . I think they may not know poetry."

"No poetry . . ." Manfred frowned, swirled his wine cup, and threw down a swallow. "Imagine that," he said. For a moment Dietrich thought the Herr had spoken sarcastically, but the man surprised him when he continued almost to himself, "No *King Rother*? No *Eneit*?" He lifted his cup and declaimed:

"*Roland raises Oliphant to his lips*
Draws deep breath and blows with all his force.
High are the mountains, and from peak to peak
The sound re-echoes thirty leagues away . . ."

"By God, I cannot hear those lines sung without a shiver." He turned to Dietrich. "You will swear that this *Heinzelmännchen* is only a device and not a real brownie?"

"Mine Herr, Bacon described such a 'talking head,' though he knew not how one might be fashioned. Since thirteen years the Milanese built a mechanical clock in their public square that rings the hours *with no man's hand intervening*. If a mechanical device can speak the time, why cannot a more subtle device speak of other matters?"

"That logic of yours will get you into trouble one of these days," Manfred cautioned him. "But you say it already knew some phrases and words. How was that come by?"

"They placed devices about the village to listen to our speech. They showed me one. It was no bigger than my thumb and looked like an insect, for which reason I call them 'bugs.' From what he overheard, the *Heinzelmännchen* deduced somehow a meaning—that 'How goes it?' signified a greeting, or that 'swine' signified that particular animal, and so forth. But he was limited by what the mechanical bugs saw and heard, much of which he did not properly understand. So, while he knew that swine were sometimes called 'sucklings' or 'yearlings,' he did not grasp the distinction, let alone that between the first, second, and third pen or between breeding and leader sows—by which I deduce that these folk are not swineherds."

Manfred grunted. "You still call it a *Heinzelmännchen,* then."

Dietrich shrugged. "The name is as good as any. But I coined a term in Greek to signify both the brownie and the bugs."

"Yes, you would have . . ."

"I call them *automata,* because they are *self-acting.*"

"Like the mill-wheel, then."

"Very like, save that I know not what fluid impresses an impetus on them."

Manfred's eyes searched the hall. "Might a 'bug' listen even now?"

Dietrich shrugged. "They placed them on Laurence-eve, just before your return. They are subtle, but I doubt they could have slipped into the Hof or the Burg. The sentries may not be the most alert, but they might have marked a skulking, five-shoe-tall grasshopper."

Manfred guffawed and slapped Dietrich on the shoulder. "A five-shoe grasshopper! Ha! Yes, they would have noticed that!"

IN THE parsonage, Dietrich examined his rooms carefully and finally found a bug no larger than his least finger-digit nestled in the arms of Lorenz's cross. A clever perch. The *automaton* could observe the entire room and, dark-colored as it was, remain unseen.

Dietrich left it in place. If the strangers' intent was to learn the German tongue, then the sooner that was accomplished, the sooner Dietrich could explain the need for them to depart.

"I will fetch a fresh hour-candle," he announced to the listening instrument. Then, having obtained one from the casket, concluded, "I have fetched an hour-candle." He held the candle so that it faced the bug. "This is called an 'hour-candle.' It is composed of . . ." He pinched a piece off the edge. ". . . of beeswax. Each numbered line marks one twelfth-part of the day, from sunrise to sunset. I gauge the time by how far down the candle has burned."

He spoke self-consciously at first, then more in the manner of an arts master giving a cursory. Yet, what listened was not a class of scholars, but one of Bacon's talking heads and he wondered to what extent he was understood by the device, or even whether in this instance understanding had any meaning.

· VI ·

SEPTEMBER, 1348

The Stigmata of St. Francis

THEY CALLED themselves the Krenk, or something to which the human tongue could come no closer; but whether the term was as encompassing as "human" or as peculiar as "Black Forester" Dietrich could not immediately discern. "They certainly *look* sick," said Max after one visit, and he laughed at the pun, for *Krenk* sounded much like the German word for "sick." And indeed, given their spindly form and gray complexion, the name struck Dietrich as an uncomfortable bit of divine whimsy.

Theresia had wanted to go to them with her herbs. "It is what the blessed Lord would have done," she said, which shamed Dietrich, for he himself was more concerned to see them gone than succored; and, although he admitted succor as an efficient means to that end, one must assent to the good for its own sake, and not merely as the means to another good. Yet he was reluctant to admit Theresia to the circle of those who knew of the Krenken. Beings of such strange appearance and powers would attract interest, shattering Dietrich's seclusion forever—and four was already a high number for keeping secrets. He contented Theresia by pleading the Herr's instructions, but she pressed her potions upon him. The Krenken seemed to grow well or not on their use, much as did humans.

As summer waned, Dietrich visited the encampment every few days. Sometimes he went alone, sometimes with Max or Hilde. Hilde would change bandages and clean slowly healing wounds, and Dietrich would teach the Kratzer and Gschert enough German through the good offices of the talking head so they would understand that they must leave. Their response had thus far been a guarded refusal, but whether from willfulness or incomprehension was unclear.

Max would sometimes sit with him in these sessions. Drill being to him natural, he was helpful with the repetition and dumb-play needed to communicate the meaning of many words. More often, the sergeant watched over Hilde like her guardian angel and would, when her unwonted ministry was concluded, escort her back to Oberhochwald.

The *Heinzelmännchen* acquired German quickly, for the talking head, once he learned a usage, never forgot. He owned a prodigious memory, though the lacunae in his understanding were curious. *Day,* he had intuited by listening to village talk, but *year* puzzled him entirely until it was explained. Yet how could any breed of men, however distant their homeland, fail to recognize the circuit of the sun? So, too, the word *love,* which the device confused with the Greek *eros* through some unfortunate clandestine observations into which Dietrich thought it best not to inquire.

"He is an intuitive collection of cogs and cams," Dietrich told the sergeant after one session. "Any words which are signs in themselves—such as refer to beings or to actions by beings—he apprehends immediately; while those which are signs for species or relations he finds a stumble-step. Hence, *cottage* and *castle* were clear, but *habitation* required instruction."

Max only grinned. "Perhaps he is not so well-schooled as you."

IN SEPTEMBER, the year paused, weary from the harvest, and inhaled deeply for the fall planting, wine press, and slaughter. The air grew cool and the broadleaf trees shivered in anticipation. Time enough, in this interstice between the summer and autumn labors, to finish the repairs from the "Great Fire," and to wed Seppl to Ulrike.

The nuptials took place on the village green, where the witnesses could gather 'round the couple. There, Seppl declared his intent and Ulrike, dressed in traditional bridal yellow, declared her consent, after which everyone proceeded up Church Hill. The Lateran Council had required that all weddings be public, but not that the Church participate in them. Nonetheless, despite his losses in the fire, Felix had elected a nuptial mass for his daughter's marriage. Dietrich preached a sermon on the history and development of marriage, and explained how it was a figure of Christ wed to His Church. He was well into the contrast between *muntehe,* or family alliance, and *friedehe,* the love-match favored by the Church, when he sensed the restlessness of the congregants and the growing concupiscence of the wedding couple, and drew his discourse to a hasty and ill-reasoned conclusion.

Friends and relatives paraded the couple from the church to a cottage that Volkmar had prepared for them, and watched them lie together in the bed, giving helpful last-minute advice all the while. Then the neighbors withdrew and waited outside the window. Dietrich, who had stayed behind at the church, heard the shout and the pot-banging all the way at the top of the hill. He turned to Joachim, who was helping him strip the altar.

"It's a wonder young people wed publicly at all, if that is what they must endure."

"Yes," said Joachim with a hooded look. "A woods-marriage has its advantages."

By its tone, the Minorite's remark was freighted with irony and Dietrich wondered what he had meant by it. The singular advantage of privately spoken vows lay in their easy denial afterward. Absent witnesses, who could say what was promised, or whether consent was given? A marriage promised in the throes of passion could fade with that selfsame passion. To combat this evil, the Church insisted on public weddings. Even so, many couples still exchanged vows in the woods—or even in the bed itself!

Dietrich folded the altar cloth in half, then in half again. He decided that Joachim had intended a humorous affirmation of Dietrich's own remark and said, "*Doch,*" which earned a sharp glance, quickly suppressed, from the Franciscan.

THE REBUILT cottages were blessed on the Commemoration of Pope Cornelius, still remembered as a friend to the poor and therefore an auspicious patron for such a blessing. Lueter Holzhacker led a troop of men into the Lesser Wood below Church Hill and there toppled a fir, perhaps twenty shoes tall, which they carried to the green with much ceremony. The men barked the trunk halfway to the top, leaving the uppermost branches untouched and liberating the sweet, piney scent of virgin wood. The remaining branches they decked with wreaths, garlands, and other ornaments, and a profusion of colored flags; and stood the tree in a post-hole prepared at the corner of Felix Ackermann's cottage.

Afterward, there was singing and dancing and tankards of beer and the flesh of a roast pig that Ackermann and the brothers Feldmann offered jointly as a love-gift to their neighbors. The festivities spread from the cottages down the length of the high street, spilling around the well, the oven, and into the meadow by the millpond.

The armsmen who had helped fight the fires came down from the Burg to join the celebration. They were a swaggering lot, older than their years and possessed of a hardness beside which the village youth seemed callow. More than one maiden found herself beguiled by tales of far lands and fell deeds, and more than one soldier found himself beguiled by fair maid. Fathers glowered with suspicion and mothers with disapproval. Such men seldom possessed land, and were poor matches for a peasant's daughter.

After solemnly blessing tree and cottages, Dietrich stood apart and observed the festivities. He was solitary by nature—one reason he had come to this remote village. Buridan had often chastised him for this love. *You live inside your head too much,* the master had said, *and while it is sometimes a very interesting head, it must also be a little lonely in there.* The jape had much amused the visitor from Oxford who, on encountering Dietrich mulling over his copy book in solitary places about the university, had taken to calling him *doctor seclusus.* Ockham owned the most brilliant mind Dietrich had ever encountered, but his affections often had an edge to them. A man clever with words, he had shortly after found the world composed of more than words, for he had been summoned to Avignon to answer Questions.

"They think you unfriendly," said Lorenz, jostling him loose of memories. "You stand here by the tree when everyone else is over there." He waved toward the sounds of fiddle and whistle and bagpipe, a congeries of noises with the seeming of familiar songs, yet attenuated a little by distance and the breeze, so that only snatches of tune remained sensible.

"I'm guarding the tree," Dietrich said with utter gravity.

"Are you?" Lorenz turned his head up toward the bright decorations fluttering in the treetop. The breeze whipped the flags and garlands so that the tree, too, seemed to dance. "And who might steal such a thing?"

"Grim, maybe; or Ecke."

Lorenz laughed. "What a fancy." The smith sank to his haunches and leaned back against the wall of Ackermann's cottage. He was not a large man—Gregor dwarfed him—but he was tempered like the very metal he worked: impervious to the strongest blows and as supple as the famed steel of Damascus. His hair was black, like an Italian's, and his skin had been tinted by the smoke of his forges. Dietrich sometimes called him "Vulcan" for all the obvious reasons, though his features were exceedingly fine and his voice higher pitched than one might expect of a man with such a sobriquet. His wife was a handsome woman, larger and older than he, of strong features and chaste demeanor. God had not blessed their union with fruit.

"I always loved those stories when I was young," the smith confessed. "Dietrich of Berne and his knights. Fighting Grim and the other giants; outwitting the dwarves; rescuing the Ice Queen. When I see Dietrich in my mind, he always looks like you."

"Like me!"

"Sometimes I imagine new adventures for Dietrich and his knights. I thought I would write them myself, had I my letters. There was one—I set it during the time the hero spent with King Etzl—that I thought especially fine."

"You could always recite your tales for the children. You don't need your letters for that. Did you know Etzl's real name was Attila?"

"Was it? But, no, I would never dare recite my stories. They wouldn't be true, only fancies I had made up."

"Lorenz, *all* of the Dietrich tales are fancies. Laurin's helm of invisibility, Wittich's enchanted sword, the mermaid's bracelet that Wildeber wore. Dragons and giants and dwarves. When have you ever seen such things?"

"Well, I've always supposed that in this base age we have forgotten how to make enchanted swords. And as for the dragons and giants—why, Dietrich and the other heroes killed them all."

"Killed them all!" Dietrich laughed. "Yes, that would 'save the appearances'."

"You said Etzl was real. What of the Goth kings—Theodoric and Ermanric?"

"Yes. They all lived in the Frankish Age."

"Since so long!"

"Yes. It was Etzl who killed Ermanric."

"There. You see?"

"See what?"

"If *they* were real—Etzl and Herman and Theodor—then why not Laurin the dwarf or Grim the giant? Don't laugh! I met a pack peddler from Vienna once, and he told me that when they were erecting the cathedral there, the builders found huge bones buried in the earth. So the giants were real—*and their bones were made of stone.* They named the portal the Giants' Gate because of it. They couldn't have done that if they had been only fancies."

The priest scratched his head. "Albrecht the Great described such bones. He thought with Avicenna that they had been turned to stone by some mineral process. But they may be the bones of some great animal lost in the Flood and not of giant men."

"Perhaps the bones of a dragon, then," Lorenz suggested slyly, leaning close and placing a conspiratorial hand on his arm.

Dietrich smiled. "Do you think so?"

"Your tankard is empty. I'll fetch another." Lorenz pushed to his feet, and hesitated half-turned away. "There is talk," he said after a pause.

Dietrich nodded. "There generally is. What of?"

"That you go too often into the woods with the Frau Müller."

Dietrich blinked and looked into his empty stein. He wondered why he should be surprised to learn of the gossip. "Bluntly put, my friend, but the Herr has established a lazaretto—"

"—in the Great Wood. Ja, doch. But with the Frau Müller we know also which way the rabbit runs and if she truly is caring for lepers, that *would* be a second pair of boots."

Dietrich, too, wondered that so selfish and prideful a woman had persisted in her charity. "Rash judgment is a sin, Lorenz. Besides, Max the Schweitzer goes often with us."

The smith shrugged. "*Two* men in the woods with his wife will hardly reassure the miller. I've only said what I've heard. I know . . ." He paused and turned the tankard over in his hand. It was as if his soul had retreated from the two windows in his face. The dregs of the beer dribbled out onto the dirt unseen. "I know the sort of man you are, so *I* believe you."

"You could try believing with greater certitude," Dietrich said sharply, so that Lorenz turned a startled face on him, then hurried off on his errand. The smith was a gentle man—surprisingly so, given his strength—but he was a woman for gossip.

Felix and Ilse came to give him a pair of hens for the blessing of the house. Dietrich would have refused them, yet winter would be coming and even priests must eat. The eggs would be appreciated and, later, the stew. In return, Dietrich reached into his scrip and pulled out the wooden doll and gave it to their little girl. He had polished it to remove the scorches, and had replaced the charred arms and legs with fresh sticks he had found. The hair, he had cut from his own head. But Maria dropped the doll into the dirt and cried, "That isn't Anna! That isn't Anna!" And she ran inside the rebuilt cottage, leaving Dietrich crouching in the dust.

Sighing, he replaced the doll into his scrip. It wasn't the doll, he thought. The doll was only a construction of sticks and rags. There was nothing precious about such things. He stood and picked up the wooden cage with the clucking chickens. "Come now, sister hens," he said, "I know a rooster who is anxious to meet you."

Something repaired, he thought as he returned to the parsonage, is never quite what it was before. Whatever other parts were replaced, the memories could never be.

TWO YEARS before his death, while praying fervently on Mount Alvernia, Saint Francis of Assisi received on his body an impression of the sacred wounds of Christ. Three-quarters of a century later, Pope Benedict XI, a sickly, scholarly, peace-loving man, uneasy outside the company of his Dominican order, established the feast as a token of goodwill to the rival order. So, although Hildegarde of Bingen was the saint for that day, Dietrich read the Mass *Mihi autem* to honor Francis and as a brotherly gesture toward his houseguest. This may have disappointed Theresia, for the Abbess Hildegarde, author of a well-known treatise on medicines, was a special favorite of hers; but if so, she made no protest.

The Mass had barely concluded when Joachim threw himself facedown on the freshly washed flagstones before the altar. Dietrich, putting the vessels away, thought the display unseemly. He slammed the storage cabinet and made a show of stepping around the prostrate monk as he crossed the sanctuary. "In *Galatians* today," he said, "Paul told us that it matters not whether we bear visible marks, so long as we become a new man."

Joachim's prayers cut off abruptly. After a moment, the man rose to his knees, crossed himself, and turned around. "Is that what you think?"

"In Galatia, those Jews who had not accepted Christ criticized those who had, because the Galatian pagans who had also been saved did not follow the Law of Moses. So, the Jewish Christians urged the Galatian Christians to become circumcised, hoping to use that outward sign to mollify their accusers. But the Galatians had a horror of bodily mutilation; so much turmoil resulted. Paul wrote to remind everyone that outward signs no longer mattered."

Joachim pressed his lips together and Dietrich thought he would launch some retort; but after a moment, he rose to his feet and straightened his robe. "I wasn't praying for that."

"What, then?"

"For you."

"Me!"

"Yes. You are a goodly man, I think; but you are a cold one. You would rather think about the good than do it, and you find it more congenial to debate angels and pinheads than to live the true life of poverty of the companions of the Lord—which you would know, if you thought about what Paul meant in his letter."

"Are you so holy, then?" Dietrich said with some heat.

"That men's hearts do not hold always what their lips proclaim, I am heartily aware—ja, from childhood! Many a whitened sepulcher proclaims Jesus with his tongue, and crucifies Him with hands and body! But in the New Age, the Holy Spirit will guide the New Man to perfect himself in love and spirit."

"Ja doch," said Dietrich. "'The New Age.' Was it Charles of Anjou or Pedro of Aragon who was to have started it? I've forgotten." The New Age had been prophesied by another Joachim—he of Flora. Paris had reckoned him a fraud and "a dabbler in the future," for his followers had prophesied that the New Age would begin in 1260, then in 1300, as political winds in the Two Sicilies shifted. Flora's teaching that St. Francis had been a reincarnation of Christ Himself struck Dietrich as both impious and logically flawed.

"'The man of the flesh persecutes those born of the spirit,'" Joachim quoted. "Oh, we have many enemies: the Pope, the Emperor, the Dominicans . . ."

"I should think Popes and Emperors enemies enough without taking on the Dominicans."

Joachim threw his head back. "Mock on. The visible church, so corrupted by Peter with Jewish falsifications, has always persecuted the pure church of the spirit. But *Peter* fades, and beloved *John* appears! Death stalks the land; *martyrs burn!* The world of fathers will be replaced by a world of brothers! Already, the Pope is overthrown, and Emperors rule in name alone!"

"Which still leaves the Dominicans to deal with," Dietrich said dryly.

Joachim lowered his arms. "Words hang like a veil before your understanding. You subordinate spirit to nature, *and God Himself to reason,* and so cannot see. God is not being, but *above* being. He is in all places at all times, in times and places we cannot know save by looking within ourselves. He is all things because he combines all perfections, in a way past all understanding. But when we see past the limitations of such creaturely perfections as 'life' and 'wisdom,' that which remains is God."

"Which does not seem beyond understanding, at all, and reduces God to a mere *residuum.* You preach Platonism warmed over like yesterday's porridge."

The young man's face closed. "I am a sinful man. But if I pray that God will forgive my sins, is it so terrible that I include yours, too?" He bent and rose again with a sprig of hazel in his fingers that had fallen from Theresia's herb basket. The two parted with no further words.

DIETRICH ALWAYS found his meetings with the Krenken unnerving. "It is the fixity of their features," he had told Manfred. "They lack the capacity for smiles or frowns, let alone expressions more subtle; nor are they given to much display or gesture, and that bestows on them a menacing mien. They seem like statues come to life." That had been a special terror of his from boyhood. He remembered sitting beside his mother in the cathedral church at Köln, staring at the statues in their niches, and he remembered how the flickering candlelight made them seem to move. He had thought that if he stared at them too long, they would become angry and step down from their niches and come for him.

Dietrich had concluded that it was not the *Heinzelmännchen* that spoke, but the

Kratzer who spoke through him, and he had learned the difficult trick of perceiving the words of the talking head as coming from the giant grasshopper instead—although whether boxes or grasshoppers spoke was in either case wonderful. He said as much to the Kratzer, who explained that the box remembered words as numbers.

"A number may be expressed as a word," Dietrich responded. "We have the word *eins* to signify the number one. But how can a *word* be expressed as a *number*? Ach . . . You mean a code. Merchants and imperial agents use such methods to keep their messages secret."

The Kratzer leaned forward. "You have this species of knowledge?"

"The signs we use to signify beings and relations are arbitrary. The French and the Italians use different word-signs than we do, for example; so to assign a number is not in principle different. Yet, how does the *Heinzelmännchen* . . . Ach, I see. He performs an *al-jabr* of some sort on the code." Then he had to explain what *al-jabr* was—and then who the Saracens were.

"So," the Kratzer said finally. "But these numbers use only two signs: *null* and *one.*"

"What a poor sort of number! There gives often more than one of a species."

The Kratzer rasped his forearms. "Attend! The . . . essence-that-flows . . . Fluid? Many thank. The fluid that drives the talking head flows through innumerable small mill races. *One* tells the *Heinzelmännchen* to open a sluice gate so the fluid may run down a particular race. *Null* tells him to leave the gate closed." The creature drummed rapidly on the desktop, but Dietrich was unsure what mood this represented. In a man, it might signify impatience or frustration. It was clear that the Kratzer sought to communicate certain thoughts that fit poorly within the vocabulary that his talking head had thus far provided, and so Dietrich must tease the meaning from the words much as thread is teased from wool.

The Herr Gschert had been listening to the byplay from his usual position, leaning casually against the far wall. Now he buzzed and clacked and the talking head picked up some of what he said through the "small-sound" automaton to which Dietrich had given the Greek name *mikrofoneh.* "How does this discussion use?"

The Kratzer said, "Each knowledge uses always." Dietrich did not think the utterance was meant for him and kept a blank face—although blank faces might convey weighty matters to such an expressionless folk as the Krenk. The servant who groomed the talking head turned a little and, while his great faceted eyes never looked on anything squarely, Dietrich had the uncanny feeling that the servant had glanced his way to gauge his reaction. The servant's soft upper and lower lips came together and parted in a slow, silent version of what the priest had come to consider Krenkish laughter.

I do believe that I have seen one of them smile. The thought came unbidden, and left him with a curious sense of comfort.

"The twofold number is the smallest piece of knowledge," the Kratzer instructed him.

"I disagree," said Dietrich. "It is not knowledge at all. A sentence may impart knowledge; even a word may. But not a number that represents a mere sound."

The Kratzer rubbed his forearms together in what appeared an absentminded fashion, and Dietrich thought that the act signified something like what a man would mean by scratching his head or rubbing his chin. "The fluid that drives the talking head," the Kratzer said after a moment, "differs from that which drives your mill, but we may know something of the one by a study of the other. Do you have a word that signifies this? Analogy? Many thank. Hear this analogy, then. You may break a pot into shards, and these shards into fragments, and the fragments into dust. But even the dust can be broken into the smallest possible pieces."

"Ah, you must mean the *atoms* of Demokritos."

"You have a word for this?" The Kratzer turned to Herr Gschert and, in another aside, translated by the talking head, said, "If they know such matters, there may yet give help." But the Herr replied, "Say nothing of it." On hearing this, Dietrich glanced curiously at the servant.

"The analogy," said the Kratzer, "is that the twofold number is the 'atom' of knowledge, for the least you can say about a thing is that it is—which is *one*—or it is not—which is *null.*"

Dietrich was unconvinced. That a thing existed might well be the *most* one could say of it, since there was no reason save God's grace for anything to exist at all. But he said nothing of these doubts. "Let us then use the term *bißchen* for this twofold number of yours. It means a 'little bite' or a 'very small amount,' so it may as well mean a small bite of knowledge. No one has ever seen Demokritos's atoms, either." The metaphor of a "bit" amused him. He had always thought of knowledge as something to drink—the springs of knowledge—but it could as well be something to be nibbled.

"Tell me more," said the Kratzer, "about your numbers. Do you apply them to the world?"

"If appropriate. Astronomers calculate the positions of the heavenly spheres. And William of Heytesbury, a Merton calculator, applied numbers to the study of *local* motion and showed that, commencing from zero degree, every latitude, so long as it terminates finitely, and so long as it is acquired or lost uniformly, will correspond to its mean degree of velocity." Dietrich had spent many hours reading Heytesbury's *Rules for Solving Sophismas,* which Manfred had presented him, and had found the proof from Euclid very satisfying.

The Kratzer rubbed his forearms together. "Explain what means that."

"Simply said, a moving body, acquiring or losing latitude uniformly during some assigned period of time, will traverse a distance exactly equal to what it would have traversed in an equal period of time if it were moved uniformly at its mean degree." Dietrich hesitated, then added, "So wrote Heytesbury, so nearly as I recollect his words."

Finally, the Kratzer said, "It must be this: distance is half the final speed by the time." He wrote on a slate and Dietrich saw symbols appear on the *Heinzelmännchen*'s screen. His heart thudded as the Kratzer assigned to each symbol distance, speed, and time. Here was Fibonacci's idea, letters used to state the propositions of *al-jabr* so succinctly that entire paragraphs could be said in one short line. He pulled a palimpsest from his scrip and wrote with a charcoal, using German letters and the Arab numbers. Ach, how much more clearly it could be said! His vision blurred, and he wiped his eye. *Thank you, O God, for this gift.*

"So, we see the fruits of the Holy Ghost," he said at last.

"The *Heinzelmännchen* is unsure. 'Ghost' is when you breathe out, and what has this to do with motion?"

"There was a great question for us: Does a man participate in unchanging Spirit more or less, or does Spirit itself increase or decrease in a man? We call that 'the intension and remission of forms,' which, by analogy, we may apply to other motions. Just as a succession of forms of different intensities explains an increase or decrease in the intensity of color, so the succession of new positions acquired by a motion may be considered as a succession of forms representing new degrees of that motion's intensity. The intensity of a velocity increases with speed, no less than the redness of an apple increases with ripening."

The giant grasshopper shifted in his seat and exchanged looks with the servant, saying something which the *mikrofoneh* did not this time translate. An exchange between the two escalated, growing louder, with the servant half-rising from his seat and the Kratzer smacking his forearm against the desktop, while Herr Gschert looked on with no change in his posture save the slow rhythmic scissoring of his horny side-lips.

Dietrich had grown accustomed to these wild arguments, although they unnerved him with their sudden vehemence. They were like thunder-weather, blowing up from nowhere, and passing just as quickly. The Krenken were a choleric race, like the Italians, or they were under some great strain.

When the Kratzer had reachieved his balance, he said, "This has been said by another." Dietrich knew he meant the servant. " 'You speak a word. The *Heinzelmännchen* repeats it in our tongue. But has it spoken what has been said?' "

"That is a great problem in philosophy," Dietrich admitted. "The sign is not the signified, nor may it convey the entire significance."

The Kratzer threw his head back briefly in a gesture whose meaning Dietrich had not yet plumbed. "Now we hear it," the Krenk complained. "The poor *Heinzelmännchen* is speechless. What is a 'problem'? What is a 'philosophy'? How can the ripening of a fruit or your 'holy breath' be like the speed of a falling body?"

The servant spoke again, and this time the box translated his words: "The box-that-speaks stands the word 'philosophy' not in the German tongue."

"Philosophy," Dietrich explained, "is a Greek word. The Greeks are another people, like the Germans, but more ancient and learned, save that their great days were long ago. The word means 'love of wisdom'."

"And 'wisdom' is what meaning?"

All at once Dietrich felt pity for Zeno's Achilles, running forever after the tortoise, coming always incrementally closer, yet never in fact reaching it. " 'Wisdom' is . . . perhaps, having the answers to a great many questions. Our 'philosophers' are those who seek answers to such questions. And a 'problem' is a question to which no one yet knows an answer."

"How well we know that significance."

Gschert stood away from the wall and the Kratzer turned to face the servant, by which acts Dietrich knew that it had been the servant who had last spoken, and that the servant had spoken out of turn. Whether Gschert or the Kratzer cried, "Silence!" was unclear, but the servant was unfazed. "You could ask him."

With that, the Herr Gschert sprang across the room. The leap was lightning-quick, vaulting the furniture and, before Dietrich had quite grasped what had happened, the lord was beating the servant of the talking head with his rasping forearms, raising cuts and welts with each blow. The Kratzer, too, had turned his anger on the servant and pummeled him with kicks.

Dietrich sat speechless for a moment before, without thinking, he cried, "Stop!"

and interposed himself between the combatants. The first blow to the side of his head was enough to render him insensible, so he never felt the others.

WHEN HE came again to his senses, he found himself still in the same apartment, lying as he had fallen. Of Gschert and the Kratzer, there was no sign. However, the servant sat on the floor beside him with his great long legs drawn up. Where a man might have rested his chin upon his knees, these knees actually topped his head. The servant's skin was already discoloring with the dark-green bruising of his folk. When Dietrich stirred, the servant chattered something and the box on the desk spoke.

"Why took you the blows on yourself?"

Dietrich shook his head to rid it of the ringing, but the sensation in his ears did not go away. He placed a hand on his brow. "That was not my purpose. I thought to stop them."

"But why?"

"They were beating you. I did not think that good."

" 'Think' . . ."

"When we speak sentences inside our heads that no one can hear."

"And 'good' . . . ?"

"It does me sorrow, friend grasshopper, but there is too much noise inside my head to answer so subtle a question." Dietrich struggled to his feet. The servant made no move to help him.

"Our cart is broken," the servant said.

Dietrich tried his shoulder and winced. "What?"

"Our cart is broken, and its Herr is dead. And we must stay here and die and never see our homeland again. The steward of the cart, who rules now, said that to reveal this would show our weakness, and so invite an attack."

"The Herr would not . . ."

"We hear the words you speak," the Krenk said. "We see the things you do, and all the words for these things the *Heinzelmännchen* has mastered. But the words for what is here . . ." And the creature laid a gracile, six-fingered hand across his stomach. ". . . these words we do not have. Perhaps we can never have them, for you are so very strange."

· VII ·

SEPTEMBER, 1348
The Apparition of Our Lady of Ransom

SOME IN the village, when they saw the bruises that their priest had endured at the hands of those he had sought to help, wished to drive the "lepers" from the Great Woods; but Herr Manfred von Hochwald declared that none might trespass there save by his grace. He stood a squad of armsmen on the Bear Valley road to turn back any who, from curiosity or revenge, sought the lazaretto. In the following days, Schweitzer's men turned back Oliver, the baker's son, with several other young men of the village; Theresia Gresch and her basket of herbs; and, to Dietrich's astonishment, Fra Joachim of Herbholzheim.

The motives of young Oliver and his friends were easily known. The deeds of knights were their bread and ale. Oliver grew his hair to shoulder length to ape his betters, and wore his knife tucked swordlike into his belt. The love of a good fight quickened them, and revenge for their pastor provided but a finer-sounding reason for fist and cudgel. Dietrich gave them a tongue lashing and told them that if he could forgive those who struck him, they could do likewise.

The motives that drove Theresia toward the Great Wood were at once more transparent and more opaque, for in her herb basket she had placed with the rue and the yarrow and the pot marigold, certain obnoxious mushrooms and the keen knife that she sometimes used to let blood. Dietrich questioned her on these items when Schweitzer's men had returned her to the parsonage, and proper answers could indeed be found in Abbess Hildegarde's *Physica*; yet Dietrich wondered if she had had other employments in mind. The thought troubled him, but he could not logically ask her motives when he had not yet established her purpose.

As for Joachim, the friar said only that poor and landless men needed God's word more than most. When Dietrich replied that the lepers needed succor more than sermons, Joachim laughed.

WHEN MAX and Hilde went to the lazaretto on St. Eustace Day, Dietrich pleaded that he was still too sore and repaired instead to the refectory of his parsonage, where he ate an oat porridge that Theresia had cooked in the outbuilding. Theresia sat across the table from him, absorbed in her needlepoint. He had beside the porridge a breast of hazel-hen that had been rubbed with sage and bread and a little wine and boiled. The hen was dry in spite of all, and every time he bit into it, his mouth would hurt because his jaw was swollen and a tooth on that side had come loose.

"A tincture made of clove would help the tooth," Theresia said, "were clove not so dear."

"How well to hear of absent treatments," Dietrich muttered.

"Time must be the healer," she answered. "Until then, only porridges or soups."

"Yes, 'O doctor Trotula.'"

Theresia shrugged off the sarcasm. "My herbs and bone-setting are enough for me."

"And your bloodletting," Dietrich reminded her.

She smiled. "Sometimes blood wants letting." When Dietrich looked at her sharply, she added, "It's a matter of balancing the humors."

Dietrich could not penetrate her sentence. Had she intended revenge on the Krenken? Blood for blood? *Beware the rage of the placid, for it smolders long after more lively flames have died.*

He took another bite of hazel-hen and placed a hand against his jaw. "The Krenken deal mighty blows."

"You must keep the poultice in place. It will help the bruising. They are terrible people, these Krenken of yours, to treat you so, dear father."

The words tugged at his heart. "They are lost and afraid. Such men often lash out."

Theresia attended her needlepoint. "I think brother Joachim is right. I think they need another sort of aid than that which you—and the miller's wife—have been bringing them."

"If I can forgive them, so can you."

"Have you, then, forgiven them?"

"But naturally."

Theresia laid her needlepoint in her lap. "It is not so natural to forgive. Revenge is natural. Strike a cur and it will snap. Stir up a wasps' nest and they will sting. That was why it took such a one as our blessed Lord to teach us to forgive. If you have forgiven those people, why have you not gone back, while the soldier and the miller's wife have?"

Dietrich laid the breast aside, half-eaten. Buridan had argued that there could be no action at a distance, and forgiveness was an action. Could there be forgiveness at a distance? A pretty question. How could he move the Krenken to depart if he did not go to them? But the Krenkish ferocity terrified him. "A few days more rest," he said, postponing the decision. "Come, bring the sweetcakes now by the fire, and I will read to you from *De usu partium.*"

His adopted daughter brightened. "I do so love to hear you read, especially the books of healing."

ON THE Feast of Our Lady of Ransom, Dietrich limped to the fields to assess the plowing on the tithe-lands—which he farmed to Felix, Herwyg One-eye, and others. The second planting had begun and so the lowing of oxen and the neighing of horses mixed with the jingle of harness and whippletree, the curses of the plowmen, and the whapping of mattocks and clodding beetles. Herwyg had broken the field in April and was plowing more deeply now. Dietrich spoke briefly with the man and was content with his labors.

He noticed Trude Metzger behind the plow on the neighboring manse. Her oldest son, Melchior, tugged the lead ox by a strap while her younger son, a stripling, swung a mattock not much smaller than he was. Herwyg, turning his own team about on the headland, volunteered the wisdom that the plow was man's work.

"It's dangerous for a boy so small to lead the oxen," Dietrich said to his farmer. "That was how her husband was trampled." A roll of distant thunder echoed from the Katerinaberg and Dietrich glanced up at a cloudless sky.

Herwyg spat into the dirt. "Thunder-weather," he said. "Though I've smelt no rain. But 'twas a horse what trampled Metzger, not an ox. Greedy fool worked the beast too long. Sundays, too, though I'd not speak ill of the dead. Your ox, he comes on steady, but a horse can take a mind to rear and kick. That's why I drive oxen. Hai! Jakop! Heyso! Pull!" Herwyg's wife goaded Heyso, the lead ox, and the team of six began to plod forward. The wet, heavy clay slid off the plow's mouldboard, forming a ridge on either side of the furrow. "I'd help her," Herwyg said with a toss of his head toward Trude. "But her tongue be no sweeter nor her man's ever were. And I have my own manses to plow yet, *after* I finish with yours, pastor."

It was a courteous invitation to leave; so Dietrich crossed the berm to Trude's land, where her son still struggled to turn the team. Each time the ox shifted its stance, Dietrich expected the lad to be crushed underfoot. The younger boy had sat down on the ridge and was weeping from weariness, the mattock fallen from numb and bleeding fingers. Trude, meanwhile, lashed the oxen with her whip and her boy with her tongue. "Pull him by the nose, you lazy brat!" she cried. "Left, you doodle, to the left!" When she saw Dietrich, she turned a mud-streaked face on him. "And what do you have, priest? More useless advice, like old One-eye?"

Metzger had been a surly man, given to drink and excess, though he'd been a fair plowman. Trude hadn't his cunning at the plow, but owned a portion of his surliness.

"I have a pfennig for you," Dietrich said, reaching into his scrip. "You can hire a gärtner to work the plow for you."

Trude lifted her cap and swiped a hand across her red brow, leaving another streak of dirt across it. "And why should I share my wealth with some lackland?"

Dietrich wondered how his pfennig had become her wealth. "Nickel Langerman can use the work and he has the strength for the plow."

"So why has no one else hired him?"

Dietrich thought, *because he is as ill-tempered as yourself,* but held his tongue from prudence. Trude, perhaps suspecting the imminent withdrawal of the pfennig, snatched it from Dietrich's fingers, saying, "I'll speak to him tomorrow. He lives in the hut by the mill?"

"That is the man. Klaus uses him in the mill when he has the work."

"We'll see if he is as good as your praises make him out. Melchior! Have you gotten the team straight yet? Can you do nothing right?" Trude dropped the reins and strode to the head of the team and yanked the leads from her son's hands. Leaning into them, she shortly had the team aligned and shoved the reins back at Melchior. "That's how it's done! No, wait until I have the plow in hand! God in Heaven, what did I ever do to deserve such gofs? Peter, you missed some clods. Pick up that mattock." Peter hopped to his feet before his mother could yank his head about as she had the lead ox.

Dietrich picked his way to the road and returned to the village. He thought he might visit Nickel to warn him.

"You do not seem a happy man," Gregor announced as Dietrich passed the mason's yard. Gregor had a great stone slab set up on his trestle and he and his sons were working it down.

"I've been to Trude in the field," Dietrich explained.

"Hah! Sometimes I think old Metzger threw himself under the horse to escape her."

"I think he was drunk and fell."

The mason grinned without humor. "The prime mover is the same in either case." He waited to see if Dietrich appreciated his use of philosophical language, then he laughed. His sons, not understanding what a prime mover was, understood that their father had told a jest and laughed with him.

"That reminds me," Gregor added. "Max has been looking for you. The Herr wants to speak to you, up in the Hof."

"On what matter, did he say?"

"The leper colony."

"Ah."

Gregor worked the stone, striking his chisel with hard, precise strokes. Chips flew. Then Gregor squatted to study the level, running his hand along it. "Is it dangerous, having lepers so close by?" he asked.

"The rot spreads by touch, so the ancients wrote. That is why they must live apart."

"Ach, no wonder Klaus is in such a state." Gregor straightened and wiped his hand with a rag tucked into his leather apron. "He fears Hilde's touch. Or so I've heard." The mason looked at him from under lowered brows. "So does everyone else. She's had no riding this last month, the poor woman."

"Is that a bad thing?"

"Half the village may explode from lust. Was it not Augustine who wrote that a lesser evil may be tolerated to prevent a greater?"

"Gregor, I shall make a scholar of you yet."

The mason crossed himself. "May Heaven forbid such a thing."

THE AFTERNOON sun had not yet reached the slit window, and Manfred's scriptorium lay partly in shadows undispelled by the torches. Dietrich sat before the writing table while Manfred cut in two a Roman apple and proffered half.

"I could order you to return to the lazaretto," the lord said.

Dietrich took a bite from his apple and savored the tartness. He looked at the candle prickets, at the silver ink-stand, at the leering beasts on the arms of Manfred's curule chair.

Manfred waited a moment longer then he laid the knife aside and leaned forward. "But I need your wits, not your obedience." He laughed. "They have been in my woods long enough now that I ought to take rent of them."

Dietrich tried to imagine Everard collecting rents from Herr Gschert. He told Manfred what the servant had said: that their cart was broken and they could not leave. The Herr rubbed his chin. "Perhaps that is just as well."

"I had thought you wanted them gone," Dietrich said carefully.

"So I had," Manfred answered. "But we mustn't be too hasty. There are things I must know about these strange folk. Have you heard the thunder?"

"All afternoon. An approaching storm."

Manfred shook his head. "No. That crack is made by a *pot de fer.* The English had them at Calais, so I know the sound of it. Max agrees. I believe your 'lepers' have black-powder, or they know the secret of it."

"But there is no secret," Dietrich said. "Brother Berthold discovered it in Freiburg back in Bacon's day. He had the ingredients from Bacon, though not the proportions, which he learned by trial and error."

"It would be the errors that concern me," Manfred said dryly.

"Berthold was called 'the Black' because he had been singed by his powder so often." Ockham had presented Buridan with a copy of Bacon made by the monks at Merton directly from the master's copy, and Dietrich in turn had read it avidly. "It is the niter that does the violence, as I recall, together with sulfur to make it burn and . . ." Dietrich stopped and looked at Manfred.

". . . And charcoal," Manfred finished blandly. "Charcoal of willow is best, I have heard. And we have lately lost our charcoal makers, not so?"

"You expect these Krenken to make black-powder for you. Why?"

Manfred leaned back against the stones. He twined his fingers under his chin, resting his elbows on the arms of the chair. "Because the gorge is a natural route between the Danube and the Rhine, and Falcon Rock sits like a stopper in a pipe. Trade has dried to a trickle—and with it, my own dues." He smiled. "I mean to bring down Falcon Rock."

DIETRICH AGREED that von Falkenstein, despoiler of pilgrims and holy nuns, was in want of a reining-in. Yet he wondered if Manfred realized that enough black-powder to bring down Falcon Rock was more than enough to obliterate Burg Hochwald. Dietrich contented himself with the thought that the art was a difficult one, requiring a sure touch. If the Krenken could handle the mixture safely, and Manfred learned it of them, how long before all Christendom knew? What worth, then, Burg or *schildmauer*?

In his mind, ranks of peasants bore Bacon's "fire lances" across a battlefield while da Vigevano's armored war carts hurled balls of stone from immense *pots de fer*. Bacon had described small parchment tubes that his friend, William Rubruck, had brought from Cathay, and which exploded with great noise and flash. "If a device of large size were made," the Franciscan had written in his *Opus tertius*, "no one could withstand the noise and blinding light, and if the parchment were replaced by metal, the violence of the explosion would be much greater." Bacon had been a man of great and disturbing visions. Such devices planted on the battlefield could destroy the chivalry of an entire nation.

Entering his quarters, Dietrich saw that the hour-candle was out. He placed some tinder in a flash pan and ignited it from a flint. Perhaps someday an artisan might fashion a mechanical clock small enough to fit inside a room. Then, instead of forgetting to light the candle, he could forget to lift the counterweights. Using a taper, he transferred the flame to the hour candle. Light chased shadow from the center of the room, confined it to the corners. Dietrich bent to read the hour and was gratified to find that only a little time had been lost from the sun's position. The candle must have blown out but a scant while ago.

He straightened—and across the room the globular eyes of a Krenk danced with the reflection of a hundred flames. Dietrich gasped and took a step back.

The Krenk extended its peculiarly long arm, dangling the harness worn by many of their servants. When Dietrich made no move, the Krenk shook it vigorously and tapped its own head to indicate its twin. Then it laid the harness on the table and took a step back.

Dietrich understood. He plucked the harness up and, after a study of his visitor revealed how it was to be worn, strapped it to his own head.

Krenkish heads were smaller and so the harness fit poorly. Nor were the creature's ears properly positioned, so that when Dietrich had inserted the "hearing-mussel" in his ear—as he saw the Krenk had done—the other piece, the mikrofoneh, did not hang by his mouth. The Krenk vaulted the table and seized Dietrich.

Dietrich tried to pull away, but the Krenk's grip was too strong. It made rapid passes at Dietrich's head, but they were not blows and, when the creature stepped away, Dietrich discovered that the straps now fit more comfortably.

"Does now the harness sit well—question," asked a voice in his ear.

Quite involuntarily, Dietrich turned his head. Then he realized that the earpiece must contain an even smaller *Heinzelmännchen* than the box in the Krenkish apartments. He turned to stare at his visitor. "You speak in your mikrofoneh, and I hear you through this mussel."

"*Doch,*" said the creature.

Since there could be no action at a distance, there must be a medium through which the impetus flowed. But had the voice flowed through the air, he would have heard the sound directly, rather than through this engine. Hence, an aether must exist. Reluctantly, Dietrich put the matter aside. "You are come to deliver a message," he guessed.

"Ja. The one you call the Kratzer asks why you have not returned. The Herr Gschert frets because he thinks he knows. They do not accept the reason I offer."

"You are the servant. The one they tried to beat."

There was a silence while the Krenk pondered an answer. "Perhaps not a 'servant' in your usage," it said at last.

Dietrich let that pass. "And what reason have you given them for my absence?"

"That you fear us."

"And the Kratzer fell from the stalk at that? *He* does not wear bruises."

"He 'fell from the stalk' . . ."

"It is a figure we use. To be so surprised as to fall down like ripe corn."

"Your language is strange; yet the head-picture is vivid. But, attend. The Kratzer observes your . . . your besitting? Yes. He observes that you are a natural philosopher, as is he. So he dismisses my suggestion."

"Friend grasshopper, you obviously believe you have explained something, but I am at a loss to know what."

"Those who are struck accept the grace of the beating—as any philosopher should know."

"Is it so common among you, then? I can imagine better graces."

The Krenk made the tossing gesture. "Perhaps 'grace' is the wrong word. Your terms are strange. Gschert sees that we are few where you are many. He has the sentence in his head that you would attack us—and that is why you stay away."

"If we stay away, how can we attack?"

"I tell him that our bugs have seen no warlike preparations. But he answers that all the bugs within the Burg have been carefully removed, which argues for secret preparations."

"Or that Manfred dislikes being spied upon. No, far from an attack, the Herr proposes that you become his vassals."

The Krenk hesitated. "What does 'vassal' signify—question."

"That he will grant you a *fief* and the income from it."

"You explain one unknown in terms of another. Is this a common thing with you—question. Your words circle endlessly, like those great birds in the sky." The Krenk rubbed his forearms slowly. Irritation, Dietrich wondered? Impatience? Frustration?

"A *fief* is a right to use or possess that which belongs to the Herr in return for rents of money or service. In turn, he will . . . shield you from the blows of your enemies."

The Krenk remained unmoving while the shadows in the corners deepened, and the eastern sky, visible through the window, darkened to magenta. The tip of the Katerinaberg glowed in the sunlight, unshrouded as yet by the swelling shadow of the

Feldberg. Dietrich had just begun to grow concerned when the creature moved slowly to the window and stared out at . . . What? Who could say in which direction those peculiar eyes focused?

"Why do you do this—question," it asked at length.

"It is considered a good thing among us to succor the weak, sinful to oppress them."

The creature turned its golden eyes on him. "Foolishness."

"As the world measures things, perhaps."

" 'Gifts make slaves,' is a saying among us. A lord succors to show his strength and power, and obtain the services of those he rules. The weak give gifts to the strong to gain his forbearance."

"But what is strength?"

The Krenk struck the windowsill with its forearm. "You play games with your words," the voice of the *Heinzelmännchen* whispered in Dietrich's ear, seeming eerily in that moment to be a disembodied spirit on his shoulder. "Strength is the ability to crush another." The Krenk stretched out its left arm and curled its six fingers slowly into a ball, before lifting the fist and jerking it toward the floor.

The creature raised its head to stare directly at Dietrich, who could neither move nor speak in the face of such vehemence. He need not return to the lazaretto to risk a beating by these fierce-tempered folk. The Krenken were quite capable of coming into the village, and had refrained so far only because they thought themselves too weak. Let them once suspect their own power and who knew what casual brutality they might inflict?

"There is," he began to say, but he could not finish the utterance under that basilisk glare; and so he faced Lorenz's crucifix above his prie-dieu. "There is another sort of strength," he said. "And that is the ability to live in the face of death."

The Krenk clicked its side-jaws once, emphatically. "You mock us."

Dietrich realized what the emphatic click reminded him of—the two blades of a scissors cutting something off. He remembered that, when the sign had been used, the other party had exposed its neck. Dietrich's hand rose by itself to his throat, and he put the table once more between himself and the stranger. "I intended no mockery. Tell me how I have offended."

"Even now," the Krenk responded, close by his ear though the room lay between them. "Even now—and I cannot say why—you seem insolent. I must tell myself always that you are not Krenkish and so do not know proper behavior. I have told you: Our cart is broken and we are lost, and so we must die here in this far place. So you tell us 'to live in the face of death.' "

"Then we must repair your cart, or find you another. Zimmerman is a skilled wheelwright, and Schmidt can fashion whatever metal fixtures are needed. Horses dislike your smell, and the villagers cannot spare their plough-oxen to pull your cart; but if you have silver we may buy draft animals elsewhere. If not, then once the way is known, a steady walk will . . ." Dietrich's voice trailed off as the Krenk beat his forearms arrhythmically against the wall.

"No, no, no. It cannot be walked, and your carts cannot endure the journey."

"Well, William of Rubruck walked to Cathay and back, and Marco Polo and his uncles did the same more lately, and there is on this earth no farther place than Cathay."

The Krenk faced him once more and it seemed to Dietrich that those yellow eyes glowed with a peculiar intensity. But that was a trick of the shadows and the candlelight. "No farther place on this earth," the creature said, "but there are other earths."

"Indeed there may be, but the journey there is no natural journey."

The Krenk, always wooden in expression, seemed to stiffen the more. "You . . . know of such journeys—question."

The *Heinzelmännchen* had yet to master expression. The Kratzer had told Dietrich that Krenkish languages employed rhythm rather than tone to indicate humor or query or irony. Thus, Dietrich could not be certain that he had heard hope in the machine's translation.

"The journey to Heaven . . ." Dietrich suggested, to be sure he understood.

The Krenk pointed skyward. " 'Heaven' is up there—question."

"Ja. Beyond the firmament of the fixed stars, beyond even the crystalline orb or the prime mobile, the unmoving empyrean Heaven. But, the journey is made by our inner selves."

"How strange that you would know this. How say you 'all-that-is': earth, stars, all—question."

" 'The world.' 'Kosmos'."

"Then, hear. The kosmos is indeed curved and the stars and . . . I must say, 'families of stars,' are embedded within it, as in a fluid. But in—another—direction, neither width nor breadth nor height, lies the other side of the firmament, which we liken to a membrane, or skin."

"A tent," Dietrich suggested; but he had to explain "tent," as the *Heinzelmännchen* had never seen one named.

The Krenk said, "Natural philosophy progresses differently in different arts, and perhaps your people have mastered the 'other world' while remaining . . . simple in other ways." It looked again out the window. "Could salvation be possible for us . . ."

The last comment, Dietrich suspected, had not been intended for him to hear. "It is possible for everyone," he said cautiously.

The Krenk beckoned with its long arm. "Come, and I will explain, although the talking head may not own the words." When Dietrich had come hesitantly to his side, the Krenk pointed to the darkening sky. "Out there sit other worlds."

Dietrich nodded slowly. "Aristotle held that impossible, since each world would move naturally toward the center of the other; but the Church has ruled that God could create many worlds should He wish, as my master showed in his nineteenth question on the Heavens."

The Krenk rubbed its arms slowly. "You must introduce then me to your friend, God."

"I will. But tell me. For other worlds to exist, there must be a vacuum beyond the world, and this vacuum must be infinite to accommodate the multiplicity of centers and circumferences needed to provide places for these worlds. Yet, 'nature abhors a vacuum' and would rush to fill it, as in siphons and bleeding cups."

The Krenk was slow in answering. "The *Heinzelmännchen* hesitates. There gives ja a multiplicity of centers, but what means—circumferences—question. Unless—it is what we call the—sun-ridge. Within the sun-ridge, bodies fall inward and circle the sun; beyond it, they fall outward until captured by another sun."

Dietrich laughed. "But then each body would have two natural motions, which is impossible." But he wondered. Would a body placed beyond the convex circumference of the prime mobile possess a *resistance* to its natural downward motion? However, the creature had suggested also the sun as the center of the world, which was impossible, for there would then be parallax among the fixed stars when viewed from the Earth, contrary to experience.

But a more troubling thought intruded. "You say you fell outward from one of these worlds across the 'sun-ridge' to fall upon our own?" Satan and his minions had fallen in just such a way. *These Krenken are* not *supernatural,* he reminded himself. Of this, his head was convinced, however doubtful his bowels.

Further discourse clarified certain matters and obscured others. The Krenken had not fallen from another world, but had rather traveled in some fashion behind the empyrean heavens. The spaces behind the firmament were like a sea, and the insula, while in some ways like a cart, was also like a great ship. How this was so eluded Dietrich, for it lacked both sails and oars. But he understood that it was neither cog nor galley, but only *like* a cog or a galley; and it did not sail the seas but only something *like* the seas.

"The aether," said Dietrich in wonder. When the Krenk cocked its head, Dietrich said, "Some philosophers speculate that there is a fifth element through which the stars move. Others, including my own teacher, doubt the necessity of a *quint essence* and teach that heavenly motions can be explained by the same elements we find in the sublunar regions."

"You are either very wise," said the Krenk, "or very ignorant."

"Or both," Dietrich admitted cheerfully. "But the same natural laws do apply, not so?"

The creature returned its attention to the sky. "True, our vehicle moves through an insensible world. You can neither see, smell, nor touch it from this existence. We must pass through it to return to our home in the heavens."

"So must we all," Dietrich agreed, his fear of this being fading into pity.

The Krenk shook its head and made a smacking sound over and over with its soft upper and lower lips, quite unlike the loose flapping of their laughter. After a few minutes, it said, "But we know not which star marks our home. By the manner of our travel through the inward-curling directions, we cannot know, for the appearance of the firmament differs at each place, and the selfsame star may show a different color and stand in a different place in the heavens. The fluid that drives our ship jumped in an unexpected manner and ran down the wrong mill race. Certain items burned. Ach!" He rubbed his two forearms together sharply. "I do not have the words to say it; nor you the words to hear."

The creature's words puzzled Dietrich. How could the Krenken come from a *different* world, and yet claim also to have come from a star which lay embedded in the eighth sphere of *this* world? He wondered if the *Heinzelmännchen* had translated the term "world" properly.

But his thoughts were disturbed by the sound of shoes on gravel outside the door. "My houseguest returns. It would be better if he does not see you."

The Krenk leapt to the open windowsill. "Keep this," it said, tapping his harness. "Using it, we may speak at a distance."

"Wait. How should I call you? What is your name?"

The great yellow eyes turned on him. "As you will. It will amuse me to learn your choice. The *Heinzelmännchen* tells me what means 'gschert' and 'kratzer,' but I have not permitted it to overset these terms into our speech according to their proper meanings."

Dietrich laughed. "So. You play your own game."

"It is no game." And with that, the creature was gone, bounding from the window noiselessly into the Lesser Wood below Church Hill.

•

· VIII ·

OCTOBER, 1348

Michaelmas to the Feriae Messis

MICHAELMAS CAME and with it the annual court, which the Herr held on the green under an ancient, pale-yellow linden. The tree rustled in the autumn breeze, and women pulled shawls more snugly across their shoulders. To the southeast, dark clouds had gathered over the Wiesen valley, but the air had no smell of rain and the wind sighed in the wrong direction. A dry winter, Volkmar Bauer prophesied, and talk turned to the winter seeding. Each man and woman had worn his best clothing to honor the court: hose and smock carefully darned and nearly clean, but dull against the finery of Manfred and his retinue.

Everard presided at a bench before the great tree, and the jurors sat by to ensure that no custom of the manor was violated. Richart the schultheiss brought forth the *Weistümer,* the village bylaws, written on parchment and sewn into a book, and he researched it from time to time on the rights and privileges recorded therein. This was no mean task, as rights had amassed over the years like clutter in a shed, and one man might own different rights for different strips of land.

White Jürgen, the *vogt,* presented his tally sticks and knotted strings and gave an accounting of the lord's salland for the past harvest year. The free tenants attended this recital with keen interest, comparing the Herr's increases to their own with the sort of subtle arithmetic available to those who owned no numbers beyond their fingers. Wilimer, the Herr's clerk of accounts, himself but a few years removed from haying and mowing, transcribed everything in neat miniscule onto a parchment roll of sheets glued together side-to-side. He cast his sums on an abacus and announced that the Herr owed Jürgen twenty-seven pfennig to balance the account.

Afterward, old Friedrich, the steward's clerk, took account of fines and dues. Like Wilimer, he cast his sums in Fibonacci's Arabic numbers, but he translated the results into the Roman sort for his fair copy. This introduced grave chance of error, since old Friedrich's grasp of Latin numbers was little better than his grasp of Latin grammar, where he frequently confused the ablative with the dative. "If I write the words in Latin," the man had explained one time, "I must write the numbers in Latin also."

The first fine was *buteil* for old Rudolf from Pforzheim, who had died on Sixtus Day. The Herr took possession of his "best beast," a breeding sow called Isabella—and naturally all the men debated whether this was in fact Rudolf's "best beast," rendering a variety of opinions, no two of which were compatible.

Felix Ackermann stood to pay *merchet* on his daughter, but Manfred, who had been following matters from his seat beneath the linden, announced a commutation "in view of the man's losses in the fire." This drew admiring murmurs from the assembly; which Dietrich deemed cheaply bought. The Herr could be generous in small matters.

Trude Metzger astonished everyone by paying *merchet* on herself for the lord's permission "to marry at will." This set all the women's tongues a-wagging and cast a pall of apprehension upon all the single men. The Herr, greatly amused, granted the boon.

And so it went while the sun climbed high. Heinrich Altenbach was fined four pfennigs in *chevage* for living off the manor without the lord's grace. Petronella Lürm had gleaned the Herr's fields "contrary to the prohibitions of autumn." Fulk Albrecht's son had stolen Trude's grain during the harvest. The jurors questioned the witnesses closely and, knowing the parties concerned, recommended the fines.

Oliver Becker had raised the hue-and-cry against Bertram Unterbaum on May Day past, in malice over the affections of Anna Kohlmann. Reinhardt Bent had appropriated three furrows from all the strips abutting his headland. For this offense, the man was widely hooted, for there was to the manse peasant no greater crime than stealing a furrow from a neighbor.

Manfred himself brought suit against twelve gärtners who during the July hay harvest had refused to load the hay cocks into the carts. Nickel Langermann claimed that the labor had been done in prior years "out of love for the Herr," but was not actually required by the *weistümer*. He asked that the free tenants inquire into the matter and Everard appointed an inquest from among the jurors.

At this, the court recessed for a board of bread and ale at the Herr's expense.

"Langermann fancies himself a schultheiss," said Lorenz as the crowd broke up. "He's always finding bylaws that say he doesn't have to work."

"Enough such findings," Dietrich said, "and no one will hire him, since then he won't work at all."

Max Schweitzer appeared and led him a little distance from the others. "The Herr bade me inquire about the black-powder," he murmured.

"Their alchemist recognized charcoal from the specimens," Dietrich told him, "and sulfur by its properties and appearance; but the *Heinzelmännchen* knew not what Krenkish word signified niter, so we are at an impasse. I told him it was commonly found under dung piles, but their shit differs from ours."

"Perhaps it smells sweeter," Max suggested. "And if we give him a specimen? Of niter, I mean. Alchemists can identify unknown materials, nay?"

"Ja, but the Krenken seem disinclined to make the effort."

Max cocked his head. "I wouldn't think their inclinations mattered."

"They have angst to repair their ship and return to their own country." Dietrich looked off to where Manfred stood with his retinue. The men were laughing over some matter and Kunigund, her gown wrapped in a white girdle embroidered *in orfrois* with scenes of stag hunting and hares, was torn between a ladylike dignity in Eugen's company and the desire to chase her younger sister, who had just tugged Kunigund's cap loose. Manfred thought to hold the Krenken against their will so he could learn their occult secrets. "The Herr would be wise not to press the matter," he said.

"On his own land? Why not?"

"Because the strong arm should be gently used on folk you suspect of having black-powder."

IN THE afternoon, the villagers elected beer-tasters, jurors, wardens, and other ministers for the coming harvest-year. White Jürgen declined the honor—and potential expense—of another term as *vogt,* so Volkmar Bauer was elected in his stead. Klaus was chosen again as *maier.*

Seppl Bauer shyly cast his first vote, raising his hand for Klaus along with the other householders. Or with almost all, for Trude Metzger loudly dissented and, as she was householder for her manse, cast a lone vote for Gregor. "The mason may be a dimwit," she declared, "but he is not a thief who damps the meal."

Gregor, turning to Dietrich, said, "She sweet-talks me to win my affections."

Lorenz on the other side wagged his finger. "Remember, Gregor, should you ever seek to remarry, that she has already paid *merchet* on herself, so she would be a cheap catch."

"And worth every pfennig."

"The body is but a mantle," said Theresia Gresch, breaking a silence she had held throughout the day, "which shines if true beauty lies within. So she seems plainer than she is."

"Perhaps you are one to light her lamp," Lorenz told Gregor.

Gregor scowled, now more than half-worried that his friends were plotting his remarriage. "A man would need a bonfire for that undertaking," he grumbled.

DIETRICH HAD named his nocturnal visitor Johann von Sterne—John-of-the-stars. He resumed his visits to the lazaretto, and slowly his confidence returned. The creatures would glance his way when he arrived, pause a moment, then calmly resume their activities. None threatened him.

Some worked diligently on the ship. Dietrich watched them play fire across certain seams and spray fluids and spread colored earths upon its surfaces. Air, no doubt, also figured in the repairs, for he sometimes heard the hissing of gasses deep within the nether regions of the structure.

Others occupied themselves in natural philosophy, in bizarre and patternless leaping, or in solitary walks and idleness. Some perched in trees like birds! As the autumn forest became a blaze of color, they used wonderful instruments—*fotografia*—to capture miniature "light drawings" of the leaves. Once, Dietrich recognized the alchemist by his more particular clothing, squatting in that peculiar knees-above-head posture, overlooking the stream where it tumbled over an escarpment. He hailed him, but the creature, absorbed in some contemplation, made no response and, thinking him in prayer, Dietrich quietly withdrew.

Dietrich felt a growing frustration with Krenkish laggardness. "I have seen your carpenters taken from their tasks," he told the Kratzer on one visit, "to collect beetles or flowers for your philosophers. Others, I have seen playing with a ball, or leaping up and down to no apparent purpose, indeed, sporting themselves naked. Your most urgent task is the repair of your ship, not why our trees change color."

"All those who do the work do the work," the Kratzer announced.

Dietrich thought he meant that philosophers were unskilled in shipbuilding, which was no astonishing insight. "Even so," he insisted, "there may be apprentice tasks you could perform."

At this, the Kratzer's antennae stiffened to rods, and his features, never expressive, grew more still yet. Hans, who had been occupied to the side cataloguing images of plants and paying no apparent attention to the discourse, sat upright in his seat with his hands poised over the array of types by which he instructed the *Heinzelmännchen.*

The Kratzer's eyes pinned Dietrich to his seat, and Dietrich gripped the sides of his chair in unaccountable terror.

"Such labor," the Kratzer said finally, "is for those who perform such labors."

The statement had the seeming of a proverb and, like many proverbs, suffered from a conciseness that reduced it to a tautology. He was reminded of those philosophers who, grown lately besotted with the Ancients, affected their prejudice against manual labor. Dietrich could not imagine himself shipwrecked and unwilling to assist his fellows in the necessary repairs. In such straits, even the gently born would put a hand to the task. "Labor," he pointed out, "has its own dignity. Our Lord was a carpenter and called to Himself fishermen and tent-makers and other humble folk. Pope Benedict, may he rest in peace, was the son of a miller."

"Did I hear the utterance correctly," the Kratzer said. "A carpenter may become a lord. Bwa-wa-wa. Can a stone become a bird—question. Or are all your lords base-born—question."

"I grant you," Dietrich admitted, "that a man born into his besitting will seldom rise above it, yet we do not despise the working man."

"Then we are not so different, your folk and mine," the Kratzer said. "For us, too, our besitting is written . . . I think you would say, it is written into 'the atoms of our flesh.' There is a sentence among us: 'As we are, so we are.' It would be thought-lacking to despise one for being what he was born to be."

"The 'atoms of flesh' . . . ?" Dietrich had started to ask when the *Heinzelmännchen* interrupted, "Seldom means more often than never—question, exclamation."

The Kratzer directed a series of rapid clacks at Hans, at the conclusion of which, the latter exposed his neck and addressed once more his typewriting. When the philosopher spoke again he returned to, "this curious event of the colored trees. Know you the reason for it—question."

Dietrich, uncertain what the quarrel signified and unwilling to provoke the Kratzer's anger, answered that the Herr God had arranged the color-change to warn of approaching winter, while the evergreens maintained the promise of spring to come, and thus imbued into the moods of the year sorrow and hope alike. This explanation puzzled the Kratzer, who asked whether Manfred's overlord were a master forester, at which non sequitur Dietrich despaired of explanation.

THE CHURCH celebrated the beginning of each agricultural season: to pray for a good planting or for summer rains or for a good harvest. The *feriae messis* opened the wine harvest and, in consequence, the mass *Exultáte Deo* was better attended than most. The southern slope of the Katerinaberg prickled with vineyards that produced a vintage that sold well in the Freiburg markets and provided Oberhochwald with one of its few sources of silver. But the past year had been again a cold one and there was concern that the press be bountiful.

At the Offertory, Klaus presented a bunch of ripe grapes picked from his own vines and, during the Consecration, Dietrich squeezed one of the grapes to mingle its juice with the wine in the chalice. Usually, the congregation would chatter among themselves, even lingering in the vestibule until summoned by the Preparation Bell. Today they watched in rapt concentration, engaged not by memory of the Christ's sacrifice, but by hope that the ritual would bring good luck in the harvest—as if the Mass were mere sorcery, and not a memorial of the Great Sacrifice.

Elevating the chalice high above his head, Dietrich saw nested in the vises under the clerestory the glowing yellow eyes of a Krenk.

Frozen, he stood with arms extended, until the appreciative murmur of his flock called him to himself. A superstition had been gaining favor of late that the door from Purgatory to Heaven flew open while the bread and wine were elevated, and worshippers sometimes complained if the priest made too brief an Elevation. Surely, by such a lengthy elevation, their priest had won a great many souls free, to the greater sanctification of the wine harvest.

Dietrich replaced the cup on the altar and, genuflecting, mumbled the closing words because the sense of them had suddenly fled his mind. Joachim, who knelt beside him holding the hem of the chasuble in one hand and the bell in the other, glanced also toward the rafters, but if he saw the creature, he gave no sign. When Dietrich dared once more to raise his own eyes, the unexpected visitor had withdrawn into the shadows.

AFTER MASS, Dietrich knelt before the altar with his hands clenched into a ball before him. Above, carved from a single great piece of red oak, darkened further by a hundred years of smoking beeswax, Christ hung impaled upon His cross. The wasted figure—naked but for a scrap of decency, body twisted in agony, mouth gaping open in that last pitiable accusation—*Why have you abandoned me?*—emerged from the very wood of the cross, so that victim and instrument grew one from the other. It had been a brutal and humiliating way to die. Far kinder, the faggot, noose, or headsman's ax that in modern times eased the journey.

Dimly, Dietrich heard the rumble of carts, clatter of billhooks and pruning shears, braying of donkeys, indistinct voices, curses, snap of whips, groan of wheels, as the villagers and the serfs gathered and departed for the vineyards. Quiet descended by degrees until all that was left beyond the ancient groaning of the walls was a distant, irregular kling-klang from Lorenz's smithy at the foot of the hill.

When he was certain that Joachim had not lingered, Dietrich rose to his feet. "Hans," he said softly when he had donned the Krenkish head-harness and had pressed the sigil that awoke the *Heinzelmännchen.* "Was it you I saw in the clerestory during Mass? How came you into those heights without being seen?"

A shadow moved under the roofbeams and a voice spoke in his ear. "I wear a harness that gives flight, and entered through the bell tower. The sentence was in my head to watch your ceremony."

"The Mass? Why?"

"The sentence is that you hold the key for our salvation, but the Kratzer laughs, and Gschert will not listen. Both say we must find our own way back to the heavens."

"It is a heresy many have fallen prey to," admitted Dietrich, "that Heaven can be reached without help."

The Krenk servant was silent for a moment before answering. "I had thought your ritual would complete inside my head the picture of you."

"And has it?"

Dietrich heard a sharp clack from the rafters above him and he craned his neck to spy where the Krenk had now perched himself. "No," said the voice in his ear.

"The picture of Dietrich inside my own head," Dietrich admitted, "is also incomplete."

"This is the problem. You want to help us, but I see no gain for you."

Shadows shifted in the flickering candlelight, not quite black because the flames that cast them guttered red and yellow. Two small lights gleamed in the vises. Were they the Krenk's eyes catching the dancing fires, or only metal fittings securing a beam? "Must there be always a gain for me in what I do?" Dietrich asked of the darkness, uncomfortably aware that the gain he sought was his own continued solitude and freedom from fear.

"Beings act always to their own gain: to obtain food or stimulate the senses, to win acceptance in one's place, to reduce the labors needed to possess these things."

"I cannot call you wrong, friend grasshopper. All men seek the good, and certainly food and the pleasures of the flesh and a surcease from labor are goods, or else we would not seek them. But I cannot say that you are entirely right either. What does Theresia gain with her herbs?"

"Acceptance," was the Krenk's swift reply. "Her place in the village."

"That won't make the cabbage fat. A man in want of food may drain a swamp—or steal a furrow; in want of pleasure, he may love his wife—or *fick* another's. The way to Heaven is not found in *partial* goods, but only in the *perfect* good. To help others," he said, "is a good in itself. Our Lord's cousin James wrote: 'God resists the proud and gives grace to the humble,' and, 'Religion pure and undefiled is this: to give aid to orphans and widows in their desperation.' "

"Manfred's cousin carries no weight with the Krenk. He is not—our—lord, nor is Manfred so strong as Gschert has feared. When his own folk defied him over the haycocks, he did not strike them as they deserved, but allowed—his servants—to decide the matter for him. The act of a weakling. And they came back, his own underlings, and said that the gärtners had right. Duty binds them to gather Manfred's hay, but not to place the cocks in the carts."

Dietrich nodded. "So stands it in the *weistümer*. It is the custom of the manor."

The Krenk drummed on the rafter and leaned into the ambit of the guttering candlelight so far that Dietrich thought he would topple off. "But that leaves next year the haycocks standing in the fields," Hans said, "while the serfs wait in the curia to unload. That is—thought-lacking."

A small smile crossed Dietrich's lips as he recalled the muddle that had ensued in the court following the findings of the inquest. "We gain some small amusement from paradoxes. It is a form of entertainment, like singing or dancing."

"Singing—"

"Another time I will explain that."

"It is dangerous for one who rules to show weakness," Johann insisted. "Had your Langermann made such a demand on Herr Gschert, he would be picking-food ere now."

"I do not deny that Gschert is choleric in his humor," Dietrich said dryly. Lacking true blood, the Krenken could not balance their choler properly with a sanguine humor. Instead, they possessed a yellow-green ichor; but as he was no doctor of the medical arts, Dietrich was uncertain which humor the ichor might govern. Perhaps one unknown to Galen. "But no worries," he told Hans. "The haycocks will be loaded into the carts again next mowing season, but the gärtners will do so not from *duty* but from *charitas*—or for a fee for the added labor."

"Charity."

"Ja. To seek the good of another and not your own."

"You do so—question."

"Not so often as the good Herr commanded; but yes. It gathers merit for us in Heaven."

"Does the *Heinzelmännchen* overset correctly—question. A superior being came from the Heaven, made himself your Herr, and ordered that you perform this 'charity.' "

"I would not phrase it so . . ."

"Then all fits."

Dietrich waited, but Hans said nothing more. The silence lengthened and waxed oppressive, and he had begun to suspect that his stealthy visitor had stolen away—the Krenken were not long on the formalities of greeting and farewell—when Hans spoke once more.

"I will say now a thing, though it shows us weak. We are a mixed folk. Some belong to the ship, and its captain was their Herr. The captain died in the shipwreck and Gschert now rules. Others form a school of philosophers whose task is to study new lands. It was they who hired the ship. The Kratzer is not their Herr, but the other philosophers allow him to speak for them."

"*Primus inter pares,*" Dietrich suggested. "First among equals."

"So. A useful phrase. I will tell him. In the third band are those who travel to see strange and distant sights, places where the well-known have lived or where great events have happened. . . . What call you such folk?"

"Pilgrims."

"So. The ship was to visit several places favored by pilgrims before bearing the philosophers onward to a newfound land. The ship's company and the school of philosophers say always that on such journeys into the unknown there may be no return. 'It has happened; it will happen.' "

"*Ja, doch,*" Dietrich said. "In my father's time, some Franciscan scholars sailed with the brothers Vivaldi to seek India, which Bacon's map placed but a short distance westward across the Ocean Sea. But nothing was again heard of them after they departed Cape Non."

"Then you have the same sentence in your head: *A new voyage may fare one-way.* But in the pilgrims' heads there stands always a return, and our failure to reach the correct heaven must be from someone's . . . I think your word is 'sin.' So, some pilgrims place our present failure on Gschert's sin, and even some of the ship's company say that he is nothing beside he who was captain before. One thinking himself stronger may seek to replace him. And if so, Gschert will likely raise his neck, for it is in my head that he may think the same."

"It is a grave matter," Dietrich said, "to overthrow the established order, for who is to say but that the result may not be worse. We had such an uprising twelve years ago. An army of peasants laid waste the countryside, burning manor houses, killing lords and priests and Jews."

And Dietrich recalled with sudden, unbearable immediacy, the swirling intoxication of being swept along by something greater and more powerful and more right *than oneself, the safety and arrogance of numbers. He remembered noble families immolated inside their own houses; Jew moneylenders paid in full with hemp and faggot. There had been a preacher among them, a man of some learning, and he had exhorted the crowds with the words of James:*

> Woe to you rich! Your wealth has rotted, your fine wardrobe is moth-eaten. Your gold and silver has tarnished and their corrosion is a testament against you! Here,

crying aloud, are the wages you withheld from the serfs who worked your fields! The cries of the harvesters have reached the ears of the Lord. You lived in wanton luxury on the earth; you fattened yourself for the day of slaughter!

And the Armleder army—it called itself an army, with self-proclaimed captains, and wore leather brassards for livery—sweaty, lust-mad, impatient for loot, foreboding their own death-warrants, would join in the last, so that the shout, "Day of Slaughter!" *hoarse from a thousand throats, were the last words many a wealthy lord or Jew heard in this life. Manor houses lit the night with their flames, so that a man might travel the Rhineland by their illumination as if by day. Merchant wagon trains plundered by the roadside. Itinerant peddlers, promoted by hue and cry to cosmopolitan Jew moneylenders, torn apart. Free-town burgers, fled within ancient walls, watching from the parapets while their guild-halls and warehouses burned.*

But Burg walls had withstood the undisciplined mobs, and rage faded to a realization that now only the gibbet awaited. From stone citadels had poured forth a river of steel: Herrs and knights: armsmen and guild militias and feudal levies; lances and halberds and crossbows hacking and piercing flesh and bone. Coursers swifter than the most eager of flying heels. A ragtag of farm implements, clubs, knives, billhooks thrown down by the roadside. Chivalry in mail coats riding down peasants lacking so much as breeches beneath their smocks, so that they littered the highways with the shit and piss of their terror and showed their shriveled privates as they dangled from every tree limb in the Elsass and the Breisgau.

Dietrich became aware of the silence. "Thousands perished," he told the Krenk abruptly.

The Krenk was silent still. In the quiet, the wood of the church groaned.

Dietrich said, "Hans . . . ?"

"The Kratzer was wrong. Our folk are very different." Hans leapt from roof beam to roof beam, toward the rear of the church and then up into the clerestory, where a window stood open.

"Hans, wait!" Dietrich cried. "What mean you?"

The creature paused at the open window and turned its gaze on Dietrich. "Your peasants killed their lords. That is an—unnatural—thing. What we are, we are. We have this sentence in our heads from those animals who were our ancestors."

Dietrich, dumbstruck at this offhand pronouncement, found his voice only with difficulty. "You . . . number *animals* among your ancestors?" He imagined foul couplings with beasts. Women lying with dogs. Men futtering donkeys. What might be born of such unions? Something unspeakable. Something monstrous.

"In ancient times," the Krenk replied. "There gave creatures like your honeybees in the divisions of their labor. They had no sentences inside their heads to tell them their duties. Instead the sentences were written into the atoms of their flesh, and these atoms were passed from sires and dams to their offspring, and so after an age, to us. So do each of us know our besitting in the great web. 'So it was; so it is.' "

Dietrich trembled. All beings, desiring their proper end, move toward it by nature. So a stone, being earth, moved naturally toward the earth; and a man, loving the good, moved naturally toward God. But in animals, the appetites are moved by the estimative power, which rules despotically, while in men, they are moved by the cognitive power, which rules politically. So, the sheep esteems the wolf as enemy and runs without thinking; but a man may stand his ground or flee as his reason suggests.

Yet, if the Krenken were ruled by *instinctus,* the rational appetite could not exist in them, since a higher appetite necessarily moved a lower one.

Which meant that the Krenken were beasts.

Memories of talking bears and talking wolves enticing children to their doom flickered in his memory. That the being in the rafters above him was no more than *a beast that spoke,* terrified Dietrich beyond measure, and he fled from Hans.

And Hans fled from him.

· 3 ·

NOW
Sharon

SOMETIMES SHARON felt that she and Tom did not actually have a life together, but two separate lives that shared an apartment. The whole thing ran on inertia. She never said this to Tom, and Tom was not the sort to divine her belief from subtle cues. So any mistakes in her perception, if they were mistakes, were never addressed. Instead, she set up half-conscious tests for him to fail. After her big breakthrough, she wanted to celebrate, and that was hard to do alone. So she prepared, as she had so often in the past, an intimate dinner.

Sharon was little practiced in the domestic arts. Tom had once described her as only half-domesticated. She was no gourmet cook, but then neither was Tom a demanding eater, so things usually worked out.

Yet so accustomed was she to having him underfoot that his newly recurrent absences had not yet registered as fact. She had not thought to warn him. Consequently, he was late for a dinner that he had not known would be waiting.

Subtlety was lost on Tom, but subtlety was not in it. The food had gone cold and, worse, had been warmed in the microwave. So despite the reheating, there was a chill in the room.

"Nice of you to come," Sharon said, placing the serving dishes emphatically on their trivets. She had often used that same phrase in more intimate moments, but Tom knew that this was not one of them. The complaining trivets had made that clear.

Tom was sorry. He was always sorry. Sharon suspected that contrition was a strategy he had consciously adopted, and this fed her irritation. There was something patronizing about being continually apologized to.

"Some old manorial records on loan from Harvard," he said. "Originals. We had to finish them up today and ship them back. You know how easy it is to forget the time when you're engrossed in something."

She took two salad plates from the refrigerator and put them on the table, though more gently than the serving dishes. She did, in fact, know how easy it was. " 'We'," was all she said.

"The librarian and me. I told you she's helping out with the research."

Sharon said nothing.

"Besides," he added, "it was you who talked me into trolling original manuscripts."

"I know that. I didn't think it would be every day."

"Every couple of days." He was deploying reason and fact, to no avail. Quantity was not the issue. "Say, I told you about Eifelheim, didn't I? I mean, why I couldn't find any data on it?"

"This makes the thousand and first time."

"Oh. I guess. I do repeat myself. It seems so obvious, now. Oh, well. *Lúchshye pózdno chem nikogdá.*"

"Why can't you just say 'Better late than never'?"

He looked baffled and Sharon let it pass. He really didn't know when he was doing it. She hesitated a moment after they had seated themselves. She had intended the dinner to be a celebration and was determined that it would be so. "I've cracked the geometry of Janatpour space," she said. She had imagined crying it out, proclaiming it from the rooftops. She had not imagined a surly comment, dropped into an awkward silence.

Tom may have saved his life with what he did next. He lifted his wineglass and saluted her, crying, "*Sauwohl!*" And his delight was so obviously heartfelt that Sharon remembered that she had in fact been in love with him for many years. They touched glasses and drank the toast.

"Tell me about it," Tom said. He felt aggrieved over the surprise dinner. He hated guessing wrong questions never asked. Yet he was genuinely pleased at her success and his request was not entirely meant to divert the conversation from his own tardiness.

"Well, it all suddenly clicked," Sharon began slowly, almost grudgingly, but gathered enthusiasm as she went. "The polyverse and the universe. The inside of the balloon. And light speed. That's why I'm so grateful to you, even if your help was unwitting."

Tom was two or three phrases behind. "Ah . . . The 'inside of the balloon'?"

She didn't hear him. "Do you know how it feels when two unrelated bits of information come together? When suddenly a lot of different things make sense? It's . . . It's . . ."

"Beatific?"

"Yes. Beatific. That business about light speed getting lower? Well, I checked it out and you were right."

Tom set his glass down on the table and stared at her. "I wasn't serious. I was just blowing off steam."

"I know; but sometimes steam performs work. Gheury de Bray saw a trend in 1931, and Sten von Friesen mentioned it in the *Proceedings of the Royal Society* in 1937. A few years later, a statistician named Shewhart showed that test results from 1874 through 1932 were statistically incompatible with a constant. Halliday and Resnick found that still true in 1974."

"I assumed it was measurement imprecision."

"So did I, at first. Look at the spread in the Michelson-Morley data! But precision is random, not a secular trend. The use of different methods . . ."

Tom nodded vigorously. "*A measurement is defined by the operations performed to produce it.* So different methods give different numbers. It's even worse in cliology—"

"Right." She stopped him before he could hijack the celebration. "Partly, the trend was due to physicists discovering more accurate methods. Galileo used shuttered lanterns in two towers a mile apart, and concluded that light speed was infinite. But clocks weren't precise enough back then and his baseline was *way* too short. Using stellar aberration, the mean value was 299,882 kilometers per second. But the mean value using rotating mirrors—"

"Michaelson and Morley!"

"Among others. Light speed using rotating mirrors was 299,874; using geodimeters, 299,793; using lasers, 299,792 kiss. But method changes took place sequentially; so how much was due to the method, and how much to the thing being measured?"

Tom said, "Ummm . . ." which was all he really could hope to say at that point.

"From 1923 to 1928, the five published determinations alternated between the stellar aberration method and polygonal mirrors, with averages of 299,840 and 299,800, respectively."

Tom was deep into MEGO by then. My Eyes Glaze Over. Normally, he was fascinated by matters statistic, but look up "fascination" someday. His "ummm" had turned into "unh-huh."

"But there are little hints," Sharon bubbled on. "Van Flandern—Naval Observatory—saw a deviation between the moon's orbital period and atomic clocks, and claimed atomic phenomena were slowing down. But he was called a crank, and no one took him seriously. Maybe the moon was speeding up. Even allowing for all that, there seems to be a monotonically decreasing series whose asymptote is the Einsteinian constant." She beamed in triumph, even thought she had discovered only a curiosity and not an explanation.

Tom had finished imitating a fish. "Umm. Correct me if I'm wrong, but aren't there good reasons why light speed is *supposed* to be constant? That Einstein guy? I mean, I don't know much about it, but I grew up believing in motherhood, apple pie, and the constancy of c."

"Question of scale," Sharon explained, waving an impaled cucumber at him. "Duhem wrote that a law satisfactory to one generation of physicists may become unsatisfactory to the next, as precision improves. The slope falls within the band of measurement error, so c *is* constant 'for all practical purposes.' Hell, for most *practical* purposes, we can still use Newton . . . But if we go back to the Big Clap and arm wrestle with flatness, or the horizon problem . . . You know," she said, making a sudden conversational right turn, "Dirac almost found the same thing, but from a different direction."

"Wouldn't that be a different Dirac-tion?"

Sharon really was a somber sort of creature and Tom's bent to spontaneous low humor could rub her the way cat fur rubbed amber. "Be serious, would you," she said. "Dirac found that the ratio of the electric force to the gravitational force of an electron-proton pair is roughly equal to the ratio of the age of the universe to the time it takes light to traverse an atom."

Tom laughed. "I'll take your word on that one." He filled both their wineglasses again. "Okay, but the age of the universe isn't a constant. It's increasing. . . ."

"At the rate of one second per second. Who says time travel's impossible? It's the speed and direction that's a problem." Sharon did have a sense of humor. It was more deadpan than Tom's. The Marx Brothers were more deadpan than Tom. The wine was warming her quite nicely. If Tom was a bumbler, still he meant well, and there were too many who did not to remain angry at one who did. "Have some more fish," she said. "It's brain food."

"Two helpings, then . . ."

They had not laughed together in several weeks, and the release was palpable. Problems could be obsessive, but worse, they could be solitary. It was good to connect again.

"So, there's only one point in time when Dirac's ratios could be equal," he prompted.

She nodded. "Coincidence is the usual explanation. The Anthropic Principle says that the age of the universe is what it is because that's how long it takes the universe to assemble physicists capable of estimating it. But think . . . If space and time can contort for the sole purpose of maintaining a constant ratio—velocity of light—why can't the rest of the universe be as cooperative?"

"Uh . . . ?" he prompted. Not the most incisive question, but questions weren't in it. Sharon was on a roll. Nothing like wine for lubricating the words so they tumble out faster.

"Dirac set his two ratios equal and solved for G, the gravitational constant; but his theory of slowly evaporating gravity was eventually ruled out by experiment."

"So . . . you solved his equation for c," Tom guessed.

She nodded. "And c is a function of the inverse cube root of time, which . . ."

"Which gives a decreasing speed of light," he finished. "But the asymptote is zero, not Einstein's constant, *n'est-ce pas?*"

Sharon wiggled her hand. "Haven't worked it all out yet, but the *coefficient* involves the rest masses of the electron and proton."

"Which means?"

"The coefficient isn't constant, either. Lorentz-Fitzgerald contraction. If c is decreasing, what happens to mass?"

"Beats me."

"Come on, this is grade school stuff. As velocity increases toward c, mass increases. Everyone knows that. So, switch frames. What's the difference if c decreases toward velocity?"

"Hunh, none, I suppose."

"Right, so the universe is becoming more massive."

Tom patted his stomach. "I thought it was your cooking."

Sharon gave him The Look, but he grinned until finally she had to grin, too. "Okay, I'll connect your dots." She pushed her dinner plate to one side and leaned forward with her arms on the table. "Velocity is distance over time, right? High school physics."

"They taught it just after the Lorentz-Fitzgerald stuff."

"Don't be cute."

"Can't help it."

"Well, the universe is expanding."

He almost patted his stomach again, but caught himself in time. "Big Bang. The universe started as a little ball and exploded, right? And it's been expanding ever since."

"No! That's wrong! That's newspaper science. The ur-block 'exploded!' The ur-block 'exploded!' What did it explode *into,* for crying out loud? You're thinking of stars and galaxies being flung out into space; but the ur-block *was* space. Galaxies are racing away *from each other,* not from a common center. They aren't flying farther out *into* space; space is expanding *between* them. The cosmological fluid. Get it?" A part of her—that part able to stand outside herself—could see that she had maybe drunk too much of the wine. She was babbling, and she wished she could stop, but she was goddam, freaking *happy,* and didn't want to.

Tom shook his head. "Cosmological fluid . . ." He had a sudden, Aristotelian vision of the universe as a plenum, rather than empty space.

Sharon pressed him, eager that he should understand, for she wanted to share her joy. "Look, imagine galaxies as dots painted on the outside of a balloon—"

He slapped the table in triumph. "I knew we'd get to the balloon eventually!"

"Picture yourself as a little flat bug somewhere on the balloon. *That* should be easy. Now inflate the balloon. What happens to all the dots?"

Tom looked up at the lamp that hung over the dining table and tugged at his lip. "Can I see around the curve of the balloon?"

She nodded. "Yes. But it's curved Flatland, and you can't see up, or down into the balloon."

Tom closed his eyes. "All the dots are racing away from me," he decided.

"And the dots that are farthest away?"

He opened his eyes and looked at her with a grin. "They're receding the fastest. Son of a bitch! So that's why—"

"—Astronomers use red shift velocity to estimate distance. Now plunk yourself down somewhere else on the balloon. What do you see now?"

He shrugged. "*Simil atque,* obviously."

She picked up the little peppermill from the table and set it between them. She pointed to it. "So how can the same galaxy be receding from point A . . ." She touched herself. "—*and* from point B?" She pointed to him.

Tom squinted at the surrogate galaxy. "We're living on the surface of a balloon, *hein?* Space is expanding between us, so each of us sees the other as drifting farther away." He was more right than he knew.

"The three-dimensional surface of a very weird balloon. I call it the 'perceived universe'."

"And your 'polyverse' includes the inside of the balloon."

"Right. Quantum dimensions, they're called. They're literally *inside* the perceived universe. I've been studying their orthogonality under Janatpour's hypothesis."

"And the speed of light?"

"Right." She set the saltcellar next to the peppermill. "Mark off a kilometer on the surface of the balloon. Light will take, oh, maybe a third of a microsecond to cross it. The kilometer fixed to the balloon's surface and a kilometer stick *inside* the balloon are the same. Blow up the balloon and what happens?"

"Umh. The distance *on* the balloon gets longer but the distance inside doesn't."

"And if light speed is constant *in the polyverse,* how far does the light get in a third of a microsecond?"

"As far as the original kilometer . . . Which falls short of your kilometer mark."

"Right. So a beam of light takes longer to cover the 'same' distance than it did before."

Tom pulled on his lower lip and studied the lamp again. "Cute," he said.

She leaned farther across the table. "It gets cuter."

"How?"

"I can only account for half the estimated decrease in light speed."

He looked at her and blinked. "Where'd the other half go?"

She grinned. "Distance over *time,* lover. What if seconds were getting shorter? A 'constant' beam of light would cover fewer kilometers in the 'same' number of seconds. All that stuff about 'rods' and 'clocks' . . . They're not privileged, not outside the universe. When I couple the expansion of space with the contraction of time and extrapolate backward to the Big Bang—I mean, the Big Clap—I get infinaly . . . I mean, infinitely long second—and in-fi-nite-ly fast light speed—at the decoupling; and tha's . . . Well, it's innersting, because of Milne's kinematic theory of relativity.

E-spare-men'ly . . . Ex-per-i-men-t'ly, you can't tell Milne from Einshtein. 'Til now. Here's t'me." This time, she did toast herself, draining the last of her wine. When she upended the bottle over her glass to refill it, she found that it was empty.

Tom shook his head. "I always thought the years went faster as I got older."

SHARON WOKE up with a headache and a warm, fuzzy feeling. She wanted to lie in bed. She liked the feel of Tom's arm across her. It made her feel safe. But the headache won. She slipped out from under him—not that anything short of Krakatoa would wake him—and tiptoed to the bathroom, where she shook two aspirin into her palm.

"Newton," she said to the tablets. She rattled them like dice, as she studied her reflection. "What are you smiling about?" She was a woman who put great store in her dignity, and she had behaved the night before in a decidedly undignified manner. "You know what you're like when you drink too much," she scolded her image.

Of course, you knew, her image smirked. *That's why you did it.*

"Nonsense. You've got the causal arrows backward. I wanted to celebrate my discovery. What happened afterward was spin-off."

Yeah, right. She swallowed the aspirin, washed them down. Then, because she was already up, she went to the living room and began gathering her clothes. The dishes in the dining alcove reproached her for the food hardened upon them. Now she remembered why she didn't cook more often. She hated disorder. She'd spend all day cleaning now, instead of doing physics.

"Newton . . ." Now why on Earth was Sir Isaac on her mind? He was passé, the old clockwork physics. Einstein had made him a special case, just as she would make Einstein a special case. But Newton had said that a change in velocity requires a force to explain it.

So, if time were accelerating . . .

She straightened abruptly, scattering all her clothes. "Why, what a very peculiar place this universe is!"

· IX ·

OCTOBER, 1348
The Freiburg Markets

DURING THE two weeks that followed Hans's terrifying revelation, Dietrich again avoided the Krenkish encampment; nor did Hans call him over the far-speaker, so at times, he could almost forget that the beasts were there. He tried even to dissuade Hilde from visiting them, but the woman, taking by now an unseemly pride in her ministry, refused. "Their alchemist desires I bring more divers foods, to find those more to their taste. Besides, they are mortal beings, however repulsive."

Mortal, yes; but wolves and bears were mortal, and one did not approach them lightly. He did not think Max could protect her should the Krenken turn and bite.

Yet, the Krenken spoke, and devised clever tools, so they clearly owned an intellect. Could there be a soul with intellect, but no will? These questions perplexed him, and he wrote an inquiry for Gregor to take to the Archdeacon in Freiburg.

The Herr had announced on St. Aurelia's Day that he would send a train of wagons to the Freiburg markets to sell his wine and hides and to purchase cloth and other goods. And so a frenzy of activity consumed the village. The large four-wheeled wagons were brought out, trucks and wheels inspected, harnesses repaired, axles rubbed with tallow. The villagers meanwhile studied their own stores for marketable goods, and assembled consignments of hides, tallow, honey, mead, and wine as their wit and possessions dictated. Klaus had named Gregor to drive the commune's wagon.

Dietrich found the mason in the green, seeing to the stowage of the wagons. "Be sure that barrel is tied tight," Gregor warned his son. "Good day, pastor. Have something for the markets?"

Dietrich handed him the letter he had written. "Not to sell, but give this to Archdeacon Willi."

The mason studied the packet and the red wax seal into which Dietrich had set his signet. "This looks official," he said.

"Only some questions I have."

Gregor laughed. "I thought you were the one with answers! You never go into town with us, pastor. A learned man like yourself would find much interest there."

"Perhaps too much," Dietrich answered. "Do you know what Friar Peter of Apulia once answered when asked what he thought of Joachim of Flora's teaching?"

Gregor had ducked under the wagon bed and began greasing the axles. "No, what?"

"He said, 'I care as little for Joachim as for the fifth wheel of a wagon.' "

"What? A fifth wheel? Haha! Ay, thunder-weather!" Gregor had banged his head on the cart's underside. "A fifth wheel!" he said, sliding out from under. "That's funny. Oh."

Dietrich turned to see Brother Joachim stalking off. He started after him, but Everard, who had been overseeing the estate wagons, took Dietrich by the arm. "The Herr has summoned three of his knights to serve as guards," he said, "but he wants Max to lead a troop of armsmen. Falkenstein won't plunder the train going down.

What does he need with honey—save to sweeten his disposition? But the return might prove too tempting. All that silver would jingle like the preparation bell at Mass and his greed may overcome his prudence. Max is gone to the lazaretto. Take one of the Herr's *palefridi* and go fetch him back."

Dietrich gestured toward his departing houseguest. "I must speak to . . ."

"The word the Herr used was 'now.' Discuss it with him, not me."

Dietrich did not want to visit the talking animals. Who knew to what acts their instict would drive them? He glanced at the sun. "Max is likely on his return even now."

Everard twisted his mouth. "Or else he's not. Those were the Herr's instructions. No one else has his leave to go there, God be thanked, to deal with . . . *them.*"

Dietrich hesitated. "Manfred's told you, hasn't he? About the Krenken."

Everard would not meet his eyes. "I don't know which would be worse: to see them face to face, or to imagine them." He shivered. "Yes, he's told me about them; and Max, who uses his head for more than helmet padding, swears they are mortal. For myself, I have a wagon train to organize. Don't bother me. Thierry and the others arrive on the morrow, and I'm not ready."

Dietrich crossed the valley to the stables, where Gunther already waited with a fine road-horse. "It sorrows me," Gunther said, "that I cannot offer you a jennet."

Jennets, or palfrey mules, were bred for use by women and clergy and owned a mule's more stolid disposition. Nettled, Dietrich ignored Gunther's cupped hands, and mounted from the stirrup. Taking the reins from the startled *maier domo,* he danced the horse a few paces to show it he was master, then kicked with his heels. He had no spurs—for a commoner to wear them would violate the Swabian Peace—but the horse accepted the thesis and set off at a walk.

On the road, Dietrich took his mount to a trot, enjoying the rhythm of the creature and the feel of the wind on his face. It had been a long while since he had ridden so fine a beast as this, and he lost his thoughts for a time in sheer animal pleasure. But he should not have let his pride master him. Gunther might wonder how a mere parish priest had won such horse skills.

Manfred no doubt had his reasons, but Dietrich wished he had not told Everard about the Krenken. Word would leak out in the end, but there was no point augering holes in the bucket.

AT THE place where the trees had been blown down, he spied the miller's jennet, picketed by the stump where Hilde used to leave the food. No other mount was near, but since Max would not have abandoned Hilde, he must have ridden "the shoemaker's black horse." Dietrich dismounted, slipped a hippopede onto his palfrey's hind legs, and set forth on the track that Max had blazed.

Although the day was high, he was soon enveloped in a green gloaming. Spruce and fir reached into the sky, while the more humble hazel, shorn now of their raiment, huddled naked beneath them. He had not gone far when he heard soft, womanly gasps echoing off the trees, as if the forest itself moaned. Dietrich's heart beat faster. The forest, always menacing, took on a more sinister aspect. Groaning dryads reached to embrace him with dry, naked fingers.

I'm lost, he thought, and he looked about in panic for Max's signs. He turned and a branch scratched his cheek. He gasped, ran, crashed into a white birch. He twisted away, desperate now to reach his horse. Coming to a swell of ground, he slipped and fell. He pressed his head against the ancient leafy mat and musky earth, waiting for the forest to grab him.

But the expected touch did not come, and he grew slowly aware that the moans had ceased. Raising his head, he saw below him, not the clearing where his horse awaited, but the brook where he and Max and Hilde had paused that first day. Tied to a spindly oak that twisted from the bank of the stream stood two rouncies.

Max and Hilde were there, lacing a codpiece in place, tugging a skirt back down. Max brushed leaves and dirt and fir needles from Hilde's coverslut, squeezing her breasts while he did.

Dietrich crawled backward, unseen. Max had been right. Sound did carry in the forest. Then, rising, he scrabbled back among the spruce, blundering from clearing to copse until fortune showed him the blazes, and he followed them to where he had left the palfrey.

The jennet he had seen there earlier was gone.

SINCE MAX was returning already to the village, Dietrich headed his mount also homeward, happy that he need not proceed to the lazaretto. But, coming to a bend in the trail, the beast balked. Dietrich clamped the barrel with his thighs until the horse had bolted a few paces back toward the kiln. At that, it calmed somewhat and Dietrich spoke soothingly. The palfrey rolled wild, round eyes and whickered nervously.

"Be still, sister horse," he told her. Fitting the head-harness in place, he said, "Hans. Are you on the kiln trail?"

Only the rustling of pine needles and dry branches fell upon his ears. That, and the inevitable, distant chitterings of the Krenken, which, being so natural a sound, seemed more a part of the forest than had the amorous cries of Hilde Müller in the arms of Max Schweitzer.

"Come no nearer," said the voice of the *Heinzlmännchen* in his ear.

Dietrich remained still. The sun was visible through the iron-gray lacework of trees, but stood already lower than he wished. "You bar my path," Dietrich said.

"Gschert's—artisans—want for two hundred shoe-lengths of copper wire. Know your kind the art of wire-drawing—question. It must be drawn to the fineness of a pin, with no cracks."

Dietrich rubbed his chin. "Lorenz is a blacksmith. Copper may lie beyond his art."

"So. Where finds one a coppersmith—question."

"In Freiburg," Dietrich said. "But copper is dear. Lorenz might do the task from charity, but not a Freiburg guildsman."

"I will give you a copper brick we have mined from rocks near here. The smith may keep whatever is not used for the wire."

"And this wire will further your departure?"

"Lacking it, we cannot leave. Prying the copper from the ore required only . . . heat. We have not the means to draw it. Dietrich, you do not have the sentence in your head to do this. I hear it in your words. You will not go to Free Town."

"There are . . . risks."

"So. There are then limits to this 'charity' of yours, to this rent you owe the Herr-from-the-stars. When he returns, he will thrash those who failed to do his bidding."

"No," said Dietrich. "That is not how he rules. His ways are mysterious to men." And what better proof than this encounter, he thought. He glanced once toward the clouds, as if he expected to see Jesus there, laughing. "Na. Give me the ingot and I will see to its drawing."

But Hans would not approach him, and left the ingot on the trail.

THE WAGONS set forth the next day across the plateau to the rendezvous point, where they were joined by the wagon from Niederhochwald. Thierry von Hinterwaldkopf commanded the three knights and Max's fifteen armsmen. Eugen bore the Hochwald banner.

Other wagons joined them along the way: one, from an imperial holding by Stag's Leap and another from the manor of St. Oswald's chapel. The chapter provided two more armsmen and Einhardt, the imperial knight, brought his junker and five more armsmen. Thierry, seeing his small force thus augmented, grinned. " 'S Blood, I'd almost welcome a sally from Burg Falkenstein!"

FROM ABOVE the gorge, Dietrich heard that eerie whisper in which distant valleys speak—a patois formed from the wind through the naked branches and evergreen needles below, from the rushing brook cascading off the escarpment, from a choir of grasshoppers and other insects.

The wagon track switchbacked down the face of the Katerinaberg. Inhospitable patches of gray stone and barren ground alternated with copses of desolate, windshorn beeches. The road ahead wound only a few hundred feet below them, but across insuperably steep pitches, so that Dietrich sometimes spied the vanguard coming from the other direction. Footpaths ran off where wagons could not follow. He saw ancient stairs carved into the stone hillside and wondered who had cut them.

The bottom, when they reached it, was a wild ravine, tangled with brush and toppled oaks, and flanked on both sides with great overhanging rocks and steep, wooded precipices. A rushing torrent, fed by waterfalls plunging from the heights, crashed and hissed over rocks down its center, turning to mud what little track the wagons had.

"There's Stag's Leap," said Gregor, pointing to an outcropping that jutted out over the gorge. "The story is that a hunter chased a stag through the woods near here and the beast leapt from that crag over to the Breitnau side. You see how the valley pinches up here? Still, it was a wonderful leap, they say. The hunter was in such hot pursuit that he tried to follow, though with less happy results."

BURG FALKENSTEIN, high upon one of the precipices, held the gorge tight. Bartizans dotted the schildmauer like warts on a toad, and were slit by cruciform ballistaria to give openings for hidden archers. Sentries were silhouettes in the battlement's crenels; their jibes rendered indistinct by distance. The escort feigned indifference, but they hefted their shields a little higher and kept a tighter grip on their pennoned lances.

"Those dogs won't sally against knights," Thierry said after the troop had passed with no more damage than the taunts. "Tough enough to take nuns or fat merchants, but they'd not stand fast in a real battle."

At the mouth of the gorge, the stream calmed from torrent to murmuring brook and the narrow valley broadened into green meadows. On the heights above, a square tower commanded the view of the countryside. "Falkenstein's watchtower,"

Max explained. "His *burgraf* here signals the castle when a party worth plundering passes by. Then Falkenstein sallies forth to block their advance while the men in the watchtower come out to block the retreat."

IN THE broader, softer Kirchgartner Valley, the track from Falkenstein Gorge met the Freiburg High Road. The Hochwalders circled their wagons for the night and built a fire. Thierry told off men to stand watch. "Safe enough to encamp here," Max told Dietrich. "If von Falkenstein sallies on this side, he must answer to the Graf of Urach, and that means Pforzheim and the whole Baden family."

"In olden times," Dietrich told Gregor as they ate their evening meal, "all caravans were like this. The merchants were armed with bows and swords and were sworn to each other by oaths."

"Were they?" asked Gregor. "Like an order of knights?"

"Very like. It was called a *hans* or, in the French, a *company,* because they 'shared bread.' The *schildrake* carried the banner at the head of the band—as Eugen does—and the *hansgraf* exercised authority over his brother-merchants."

"Like Everard."

"*Doch.* Save that caravans in those days were much larger and traveled from fair to fair."

"Those fairs must have been something to see. Sometimes I wish I lived in olden times. Were robber knights more common than now?"

"No, but there were Vikings from the north; Magyars from the east; and Saracens from their stronghold in the Alps."

"Saracens in the Alps?"

"At Garde-Frainet. They preyed upon merchants and pilgrims crossing between Italy and France."

"And now we must go to the Holy Land to fight them!"

Thierry overheard and grunted without humor. "If the Sultan feels like attacking me, I know how to defend myself; but if he leaves me alone, I'll not bother him. Besides, if God is everywhere, why go to Jerusalem to find him?"

Dietrich agreed. "That's why we now elevate the Host after the Consecration. So folk will know that God is everwhere."

"Of that, I would not know," Thierry continued, "but if Jerusalem was so holy, why did so many return grown wicked?" He tossed his head toward the mouth of the gorge. "You've heard the story about *him*?"

Dietrich nodded. "The devil freed his ancestor from the Saracens at the price of his soul."

Thierry wiped the juices from his plate with a crust of bread. "There is more to the tale." He put the plate aside and his junker took it for cleaning. The others at the fire clamored for the tale, so the knight wiped hands on knees, looked around the circling faces, and told them.

"The first Falkenstein was Ernst von Schwaben, a goodly knight endowed with all manly virtues—save that Heaven had denied him a son to carry his name to posterity. He took to cursing Heaven over it, which sorely afflicted his pious wife.

"A voice in his dreams told him that to make peace with Heaven, he must make pilgrimage to the Holy Land. The proud Graf was horrified at this terrible penance; but at last he smothered his own desires and departed with Barbarossa on the second great kingly pilgrimage. Before setting forth, he broke his wedding ring and, keeping half, told his wife that if he had not returned in seven years, she should consider their ties no longer binding.

"Na. The German army came to grief and Redbeard drowned; but Ernst pressed on to the Holy Land, where his sword became renowned among the infidels. In one battle, he was captured by the Sultan. With each new moon, his captor offered him release if only he would embrace the religion of Mahomet. Naturally, he refused.

"So passed the years until one day, the Sultan, impressed with his chivalry and fortitude, released him. He wandered through the desert, always toward the setting sun; until, one night as he slept, the Devil came to him."

"Hah!" said Gregor in the firelight, "I knew the fiend was in it somewhere." The serfs who had driven the estate wagons crossed themselves at the dreadful name.

"The Wicked One reminded him that the seventh year would expire on the morrow and his wife would wed his cousin. But he promised to bring him home before the morning, and that he would not lose his soul—*provided* he slept throughout the journey. So it was that he made his wicked compact.

"The Evil One changed himself into a lion which, when the knight mounted, flew off high over land and sea. Terrified, he closed his eyes and slept—until a falcon's screech roused him. He looked down horrified, where far below stood his castle. A marriage procession was entering. With a wild roar, the Evil Spirit dashed him down and fled.

"During the banquet, the *Gräfin* Ida noticed this stranger who never turned his sorrowful eyes from her face. When he had emptied his goblet, he handed it to a servant, to present to his mistress. When she glanced inside the cup, she saw . . . half of a ring."

Everyone gusted a satisfied sigh. Thierry continued.

"Thrusting her hand into her bosom, she pulled forth the other half of the ring and threw it joyfully into the goblet. Thus were the two halves united, and the wife enfolded in her husband's arms. A year later she bore him a child. And that is why the family puts a falcon on their arms."

Everard said, "One almost understands how a man might strike such a bargain."

"Always the Evil One holds out a lesser good," said Dietrich, "hoping to turn our hearts from the greater. But a man cannot lose his soul by a trick."

"Besides," said Thierry, looking with satisfaction over his audience, "Ernst could have been a saint, and Philip would still be a robber."

"That was a romantic age," Gregor suggested. "Those tales I used to hear of Redbeard and that English king . . ."

"Lionheart," said Dietrich.

"They knew how to name their kings back then! And Good King Louis. And the noble Saracen who was friend and foe of the Lionheart, what was his name?"

"Saladin."

"A most chivalrous knight," Thierry commented, "for all that he was an infidel."

"And where are they now?" said Dietrich. "Only names in songs."

Thierry drank from his goblet and handed it to his junker to fill again. "A song is enough."

Gregor turned his head up. "But it really ought to be . . ."

"What?"

The mason shrugged. "I don't know. Glorious. To save Jerusalem."

"Ja. It is." Dietrich was silent a moment, so that Gregor looked over at him. "The first who took the cross did so from piety. The Turks had destroyed the Church of the

Holy Sepulcher and barred our pilgrims from the shrines. They were not so tolerant as the Arabs, who held the Holy City before them. But I think many went also for land, and the vision grew soon tarnished. The legates could not find enough volunteers, so that Outremer lacked reinforcement. The Regensburgers assaulted those who took up the cross; and the cathedral chapter at Passau preached a 'holy war' against the papal legate, who had come recruiting."

Gregor threw his head back and laughed. "Stag's Leap."

"What?"

"Why, the knights, after chasing the Saracens out of the Alps, forgot to stop and tried to leap all the way to Outremer!"

THE HOCHWALDERS entered Freiburg by the Swabian Gate, where they paid the Graf 's toll-keeper an *obole* for each hide and four pfennigs for each barrel of wine. Walpurga's honey was taxed at four pfennigs the *sauma.* "Everything is taxed," Gregor grumbled as they passed through the portal, "except the good pastor."

The party entered a small square called Oberlinden, and so to the tavern called the Red Bear, where Everard arranged for lodgings, "although you, pastor, will probably stay with the chapter at the Dear Lady Church."

"Always tight with the pfennig," cried Gregor, who had pulled a casket of clothing from the wagon and set it beside the door to the inn.

"Thierry and Max have taken their men to the Schlossberg," the steward said, indicating the stronghold perched on the hill east of the town. "Bad enough to share a bed with the likes of this gof," wagging a thumb at the mason, "but the fewer bodies we cram into our room, the more comfortable we'll all be. Gregor, walk the priest to the minster and pay the guild for a stall in the market. Find where our wagons are to go." He tossed Gregor a small leather pouch and the mason caught it jingling in midair.

Gregor laughed and, taking Dietrich by the elbow, steered him from the inn's courtyard. "I remember when Everard was just a simple peasant like the rest of us," Gregor said. "Now he beats the kettledrum." He looked around and spotted the bell tower rising over the roofs of the modest buildings on the north side of Oberlinden. "This way."

They breasted a flood of tradesmen, soldiers, guild masters in rich coats of marten; apprentices rushing about their masters' business; miners from Ore Chest Mountain that gave the town its lead and silver wealth; country knights gawping at the buildings and the bustle; Breisgau spinsters toting baskets of thread for delivery to the weavers; a man wearing the dank smell of the river and balancing a long pole on his shoulder from which dangled a multitude of dripping fish; a "gray monk" crossing the square toward the Augustiner.

The town had been founded in the great silver rush, a hundred and fifty years before. An oath-band of merchants had taken lots fifty shoes by a hundred at an annual rent of a pfennig each, for which each settler received hereditary tenancy, use of the commons and the market, exemption from tolls, and the right to elect the maier and the schultheiss. The liberties had drawn serf and free from the countryside.

From Salt Street, they passed through a narrow alley to Shoemaker Street, pungent with leather and uncured hides. Small rivulets flowed through channels alongside the streets, a restful and cleansing sound.

"Such a great city!" Gregor cried. "Each time I come down here it seems grown bigger."

"Not so great as Köln," said Dietrich, searching the passing faces for the first widening eyes of recognition, "nor Strassburg."

Gregor shrugged. "Big enough for me. Did you know Auberede and Rosamund? No, that was before you came. They were serfs who held a manse in common near Unterbach, which they farmed to a gärtner—I have forgotten his name. He ran off to the 'wild east,' became a 'cow-knight' on one of those big cattle drives. I suppose he lives now in a 'new town' under Flemish Rights and battles the ferocious Slavs. What was I saying?"

"Auberede and Rosamund?"

"Ach, ja. Well, those two were hard workers, and cunning. At least Auberede was cunning. My father always counted his fingers after he shook her hand. Hah! While the gärtner farmed their land, they dressed some vines belonging to Heyso—that was Manfred's brother, who held the Hochwald then. They talked him into granting them custody of a storeroom near Oberbach, as well as some of the vines for a half-share in the increase. After a few years, they'd done well enough that he granted them the whole thing as a life income—manse, vineyard, storeroom, plus a wagon and some Flemish horses! Finally, weary of working for half-shares, they convinced Heyso to convert the grant to a lease. They purchased a house in Freiburg with the increase; and one day they moved here with no more farewell than that."

"Did they ever buy their freedom?"

The mason shrugged. "Heyso never went after them and after a year and a day, they were free. He farmed their strips to Volkmar, as was his right—it was salland, after all; but the women still send a man of theirs to tend the vineyard under the lease, so I think everyone is content with the arrangement."

"One serf less," said Dietrich, "is one more manse escheated to the lord. Coin is valued more than hand-service. The folk on a manor were once called a *familia.* Now, all is money and profit."

Gregor grunted. "Not enough of it, if you ask me. Here's the minster-place." The square was raucous with the clatter of hammers, creak of pulleys, snap of canvas, and the curses of workmen as they erected the booths for the market. Above them soared from the bustling square a magnificent church of red sandstone. Construction had begun soon after the town was chartered, and the nave was built in the style of that day. The choir and transept had been added later in the modern style, but with such skill as to present no clash in overall appearance. The outer walls were adorned with statues of saints beneath protective stone canopies. Under the eaves, modern gargoyles gaped and leered and, during the rains, vomited the water running off the roof. The bell tower ascended three hundred shoes above their heads. Tall windows filled with stained-glass lights pierced the walls—so many that the roof seemed to float unsupported!

"I'd think the whole thing would collapse of its own weight," Dietrich said. "The Beauvais choir vault was only a hundred and fifty-six shoes high, and it collapsed and killed the workers."

"When was that?"

"Oh, sixty years ago, I think. I heard it spoken of in Paris."

"Those were more primitive times—and the masons were French. They need all those lights because old-fashioned clerestory is too weak to illuminate the interior. But then, as you said, there is not wall enough left to hold up the roof. So they use those 'striving-pillars' to brace the wall and disperse the weight of the roof." Gregor pointed to the row of outer pilasters.

"You're the mason," Dietrich said. "I heard that the Parisians finished their great Church of Our Lady three years ago. I don't think this one is done yet. The tower wants a spire. Is that the emporium across the square? I think you must go there to have a stall assigned. Which way is the Franciscan church?"

"Straight through Minster Place to the other side of the main street. Why?"

"I have a cross Lorenz made for them, and I thought I'd take them some word of Joachim."

Gregor grinned. "Why not take them Joachim?"

THE MONKS at St. Martin's Church were assembling a large crèche in the sanctuary. Francis of Assisi had begun the custom of building a Christmas crèche, and its popularity had lately spread to the Germanies.

"We start placing figures after Martinmas," the prior explained. The Feast of St. Martin marked the popular beginning of the Christmas season, though not the liturgical one. "First, the animals. Then, on Christmas Vigil-night, the Holy Family; on Christmas day, the Shepherds; and finally on Epiphany, the Wise Men."

"Certain church fathers," Dietrich said, "ascribed the Nativity to March, which would be more reasonable than December if shepherds were watching their flocks by night."

The monks paused in their labors and looked at each other. They laughed. "It's *what* happened that matters, not *when* it happened," the prior told him.

Dietrich had no answer, only that it was the sort of historical irony that had appealed to students in Paris and he was no longer a student and this was not Paris. "The calendar is wrong in any case," he said.

"As Bacon and Grosseteste showed," the prior agreed. "Franciscans are not backward in natural philosophy. 'Only the man learned in nature truly understands the Spirit, since he uncovers the Spirit where it lies—in the heart of nature.' "

Dietrich shrugged. "I intended a jest, not a criticism. Everyone talks about the calendar, but no one does anything to fix it." In fact, since the Incarnation signified the beginning of a new era, it had been symbolically assigned to March 25, New Year's Day, and December 25 necessarily fell nine months after. Dietrich nodded at the crèche. "In any case, a pretty display."

"It is not 'a pretty display,' " the prior admonished him, "but a dread and solemn warning to the mighty: 'Behold your God: a poor and helpless child!' "

Taken somewhat aback, Dietrich allowed the prior and the abbot to escort him toward the vestibule; proceeding slowly, for the abbot, an elderly man with a wisp of whitish hair ringing his bald headskin, walked with a hobble.

"Thank you, for bringing us word of Brother Joachim," said the abbot. "We will inform the Strassburg friary." His eyes pinched in thought. "A devout boy, I recollect. I hope you have taught him the dangers of excess. The Spirituals could use a little restraint." The abbot glanced sidelong at his prior. "Tell him an accommodation may be reached. Marsilius is dead. I suppose you have heard. They're all dead now, save Ockham, and he is making his peace with Clement. He's to go to Avignon and beg forgiveness."

Dietrich stopped short. "Ockham. Do you know when?" He could not imagine Will begging pardon of anyone.

"In the spring. The chapter will meet and make a fomal plea. Clement seeks a way to take him back without making it too obvious what a fool John was to expel him." The abbot shook his head. "Michael and the others went too far when they went to the Kaiser. It is not for us to order the affairs of kings, but to care for the poor and lowly."

"That," said Dietrich, "may require you to order the affairs of kings."

The old man was silent a moment longer before saying mildly, "Have *you* learned the dangers of excess, Dietl?"

RETURNING TO the Dear Lady Church, Dietrich noticed that one of the fishwives setting up her booth had paused in her labors to watch him. He shivered against the breeze and pulled his hood up and pressed on. When he glanced back, she was tying the tent ropes. He had imagined her interest. People had long forgotten.

The Strassburg diocese governed the Elsass, the Breisgau, and most of the Schwarzwald; but an archdeacon resident in Freiburg spoke in the bishop's name. Dietrich found the man praying at the Atonement Chapel and thought it a good sign that a man so highly placed should be discovered on his knees.

When the archdeacon crossed himself and rose, he saw Dietrich and exclaimed, "Dietrich, my old! How goes it by you? I've not seen you since Paris." He was a soft-spoken man, gentle in demeanor, and with a pressing urgency to his eyes.

"I have now a parish in the Hochwald. Not so grand as yours, Willi, but it is quiet."

Archdeacon Wilhelm crossed himself. "God-love-us, yes. Too much excitement down here these past years. First, Ludwig and Friedrich fighting over the crown, then the barons—Endingen, Üsenberg, and Falkenstein—laying waste the Breisgau over God-knows-what for six years—" He gestured at the Atonement Chapel, which the barons had built in token of the peace. "—then the Armleder smashing and burning and hanging. So the madness ran from the imperials, to the Herrenfolk, to the common ruck. God be praised for these ten years of peace—God and the Swabian League. Freiburg and Basel enforce the peace on the barons now, and Zürich, Bern, Konstanz, and Strassburg have joined, as you may have heard. Come walk with me. Have you heard from Aureoli or Buridan or any of the others? Did they survive the pest?"

"I haven't heard. I'm told Ockham is to make his peace."

Willi grunted and stroked his black-and-white beard. "Until he picks his next quarrel. He must have dozed when his class discussed 'Blessed are the peacemakers.' Maybe the Franciscans don't teach that at Oxford."

In the nave, the overhead vault seemed to go on forever and Dietrich saw what Gregor had meant about illuminating the interior. By the tower entrance stood a fine statue of the Virgin flanked by two angels, carved in the old style of the previous century. The stained-glass lights were modern, save for the small round ones in the south transept, which were also in the old style. "I have a troubling theological question, your grace."

"It must be troubling if I've become 'your grace.' What is it?"

Dietrich handed him the packet and explained in elliptical terms his thoughts regarding the Krenken, whom he described only as strangers of a terrible mien, governed in large measure by instinct rather than reason. Could folk so governed have souls?

"If one is to err," Willi said, "best to err on the side of caution. Assume they have souls unless proven otherwise."

"But their lack of reason . . ."

"You give reason too much weight. Reason—and will—are always impaired to some degree. Consider how a man will pull his hand from the fire without first weighing arguments *sic et non.* Being subject to habits and conditions does not deprive a being of a soul."

"What if the being owned the seeming of a beast," Dietrich ventured, "and not that of a man."

"A beast!"

"A swine, perhaps, or a horse, or a . . . or a grasshopper."

Willi laughed. "Such a vain argument! Beasts possess the souls appropriate to them."

"And if the beast could speak and build devices and . . . ?"

Willi stopped walking and cocked his head. "Why so agitated, Dietl, over a *secundum imaginationem*? Such questions make fine school-puzzles in logic, but they have no practical significance. We were made in God's image, but God had no material body."

Dietrich sighed and Willi placed a hand on his arm. "But for the sake of old Paris days, I will give the matter thought. That is the problem with the schools, you know. They should teach the practical arts: magic, alchemy, mechanics. All that dialectic is in the air." The archdeacon waved a hand above his head, fluttering the fingertips. "Na, folk like nothing better than a good disputation. Remember the crowds at the weekly quodlibets? I'll tell you my first thoughts." The archdeacon pursed his lips and lifted a forefinger. "The soul is the form of the body, but not as the shape of a statue is *formatio et terminatio materiae,* for *form* does not exist apart from *material.* There is no *whiteness* without a white *object.* But the soul is not a form in this simple sense, and in particular, is not the shape of the material it informs. Therefore, the shape of a being does not affect the being's soul, for then something lower would move something higher, which is impossible."

"The Council of Vienne declared otherwise," Dietrich suggested. "The ninth article decreed the soul to be a form as any other form."

"Or seemed to. Poor Peter Aureoli. He tried so hard to reconcile that decree to the teachings of the Fathers, but that's what happens when you let a committee of amateurs muck around in these matters. Now, Dietl, give me an embrace and I will part to consider your problem."

The two wrapped arms for a few moments before granting each other the kiss of peace. "God be with you, Willi," Dietrich said when they parted.

"You ought to visit Freiburg more often," the archdeacon said.

OUTSIDE THE minster, Dietrich craned his neck searching the gargoyles infesting the eaves until he found the one that Gregor had mentioned: a demon clinging to the walls with spindly limbs, but with its ass stretched over the plaza. Runnels in the limbs channeled rain water through the figure's ass onto the marketplace below. Folks called it "The Shitter."

Dietrich's laughter attracted the attention of a frowsy dame selling smoked fish at a nearby booth in the minster-place. "Good day, t'ye, priest," the woman said in the accents of the Elsass. "Nothin' like the Ladychurch where you come from, I wager."

"No. Nothing like it. But here there is nothing like where I come from, either."

She gave him a peculiar look. "Contrary, are ye? I knew a man like that once, I did. I could show him a beautiful sunrise and he would quote some Paris high-and-mighty who thought it might be the Earth turning below the sun. Always had a second way to look at things." She cocked her head and studied him. "I saw y' before, and y' favor him some . . . Here, put your hand here. One thing I'd never forget is the touch of his hand on my breast."

Dietrich recoiled, and the woman laughed. "But he weren't no cold fish," she said. "No, he never recoiled from these sweet things. Nor from this more tart one, eh?" She laughed again, but slowly fell quiet. When Dietrich turned away, her voice halted him before he had taken more than a few paces. "They looked for 'im," she said. "Maybe more'n I did, for they wanted to hang 'im and I didn't want near that much. I don't suppose he was the right man for me, anyways, fine-spoken as he was. They don't look for him no more, but they might still hang 'im, if they happen on 'im."

Dietrich hurried across the square to Butter Alley, where he vanished into the nest of streets that led to the Swabian Gate. At the last, he glanced behind and saw that a boy had joined the fishwife—a dark-haired lad of perhaps twelve years, lithe and well-muscled and dressed as a fisherman. Dietrich hesitated a moment longer, but though the boy spoke to his mother, he never lifted his gaze and so Dietrich never saw his face.

OVER THE next few days, as the market bustled, Dietrich avoided Minster Place. He arranged with a coppersmith to draw the ingot. "Provided," Dietrich told him, "you draw it fine enough to pass through this eye." And he held up a device that the Krenk had given him.

The smith whistled. "The gage *is* surpassing fine, but naturally the finer the draw the less copper I use, so I certainly have the motive." He laughed a little sharply. Behind him, his apprentice sat on a swing with the drawing pliers in his hand, watching his master negotiate.

"When will it be done?"

"I must draw the wire in several reductions so it does not harden. You see, first I soften it with fire, and hammer a bit of the material through a die-hole. Then my apprentice grips it with the pliers and swings back and forth, pulling with each swing more wire through the hole. But I cannot draw it so fine as this all at once or the strand will break."

Dietrich was not interested in the finer points of coppersmithing. "So long as the breaks are not hammered together."

The coppersmith studied the ingot with covert avarice. "Two hundred shoes . . . Three days."

In three days, the market would end and Dietrich could leave this town of prying eyes. "That pleases. I will be back in that time."

HE BESPOKE also a glazier on the cost of repairing the broken church windows and secured a promise from the man to come up the mountain in the springtime. "I hear ye've got locusts up there," the glazier said. "Poor harvest. A fellow down from St. Blasien said he heard locusts all over the Katerinaberg." The man thought a little more, then added with a wink, "An' he says the monks at St. Blasien drove off a demon. Hideous lookin' creature broke into the storerooms to steal food. So the monks set a trap one night and repelled it with fire. The demon fled toward the Feldberg, but the monks burned down half their kitchen in the feat." He tossed his head, laughing. "Burned down half their kitchen. Heh. You folks live near the Feldberg. You didn't see the creature come to nest, did you?"

Dietrich shook his head. "No, we did not see that."

The glazier winked. "I think the monks were celebrating the wine harvest. I seen plenty o' demons that way, myself."

WHEN THE market ended, the wagons departed for the Hochwald with bags of coin, bolts of cloth, and a satisfied smile on Everard's face. Dietrich did not go with them, for the coppersmith's promise had proven optimistic. "It just wants a different draw," the man insisted. "The gauge is so fine that it keeps breaking." It was a plea to accept a thicker wire, but Dietrich would not hear it.

He misliked tarrying, yet without the wire the Krenken would stay forever, and he had had a vision of what that would mean. *They might still hang 'im, if they happen on 'im.* He stayed in the chapter house at the minster, dining with Willi and the others, but he never left by the south doors and he never ventured toward the River Dreisam, where the fishermen's huts lined the autumn-starved flow. He prayed for the woman and for her boy—and for her man, if she had found a new one—and he prayed that he might at least remember her name. Now and then, he wondered if he had mistaken a fishwife's ribald jape. It had all happened somewhere else. It had all fallen into a shambles under the walls of Strassburg, trampled under the hooves of the Alsatian chivalry, far from the Breisgau. It asked too much of coincidence that she be here. It demanded too much cruelty of God.

THE WIRE was at last ready on the Commemoration of Pirminius of Reichenau, and Dietrich departed with a party of miners bound for the Ore Chest, accompanying them until their roads diverged and he took the northern route to Kirchgartner Valley. There he found a caravan from Basel, led by a Jew named Samuel de Medina, in the employ of Duke Albrecht.

Dietrich thought de Medina oily and arrogant, but he had a large body of armed guards hired in Freiburg and commanded by a Hapsburg captain with a writ of safe passage signed by Albrecht. Dietrich swallowed his pride and spoke to the Jew's steward, Eleazar Abolafia who, like his master, spoke a Spanish corrupted by many words of Hebrew. "I don't forbid you walking with us," the man said with an air of vexation, "but if you cannot maintain the pace, *señor,* we leave you behind."

THE CARAVAN set forth the next morning with a jingle of bits and groaning of wagon wheels. De Medina rode upon a jennet suited to his bulk while Eleazar drove a wagon bearing a heavy oak casket. Two mounted men-at-arms rode ahead and another two behind the party. The remainder, all footmen, mixed with the other travelers, now and then glancing into the wagon bed. The party included a Christian merchant from Basel, a factor for a Viennese salt trader, and one Ansgar of Denmark, who wore a pilgrim's cloak festooned with badges representing the shrines he had visited. He was returning to Denmark from Rome.

"The pest has all but destroyed the Holy City," Ansgar told Dietrich. "We fled to the hills at the first sign and Heaven had mercy on us. Florence is devastated, Pisa . . ."

"Bordeaux, too," said Eleazar from atop the cart. "The pest appeared around the docks, and *mayor* de Bisquale set the district afire. That was . . ." He counted fingers. ". . . second day of September. But the fire burned down most of the city, including my master's warehouse—also the Chateau de l'Ambriero, where the English stay. The princess Joan was to wed our prince. She was already dead from the pest, I am told, but the fire consumed her body."

Dietrich and the pilgrims crossed themselves and even the Jew looked unhappy, for the pest slew Christian, Jew, and Saracen with equal disregard. "It has not come to the Swiss," Dietrich volunteered.

"No," said the Jew. "Basel was clean when we left. So was Zürich—though that did not stop the town from expelling my people because they thought we *might* bring it."

"But . . . ," Dietrich said, shocked, "the Holy Father has twice condemned that belief."

Eleazar only shrugged.

Dietrich dropped out of step with the wagon and found himself next to the Basler merchant, who was leading his Wallachian horse. "What the Jew won't tell you," the man murmured, "is that the Swiss have a confession. A Jew named Agimet admitted to poisoning the wells around Geneva. He and others had been sent out by the Kabbalists with secret instructions."

Dietrich wondered how much the story had been embellished in its travels from mouth to mouth. If Christendom possessed Krenkish far-talkers, the same story could be told to all, which might not ensure the truth, but would at least ensure that all heard the same lie. "Did this Agimet affirm his confession afterward?"

The merchant shrugged. "No, he denied everything, which proves he was lying; so he was tortured a second time and afterward affirmed."

Dietrich shook his head. "Such confessions are unconvincing."

The Basler remounted his gelding and from that height asked, "Are you then a Jew-lover?"

Dietrich said nothing. The danger was past, now that the bad air had been blown beyond Paris; but fear lingered in those towns that had been spared. Panic fed on rumor; and the pyre fed on panic.

So caught up in his thoughts did Dietrich become that not until he bumped into the back of the Danish pilgrim did he find the caravan halted and the supposed guards, joined by knights under the falcon banner, had encircled the caravan with drawn swords.

On the ground, with his throat neatly slashed, lay their captain. Dietrich remembered that he had come with the Jews from Basel, while the other armsmen had been hired in Freiburg to guard the casket. The dead man wore the Hapsburg eagle on his surcoat, but Dietrich had only that glance before he and the other captives were chivvied like so many sheep up the trail to the gates of Falcon Rock.

· X ·

NOVEMBER, 1348
The Commemoration of Florentius of Strassburg

PILGRIM, MERCHANT, priest, Jew were all one to the Herr von Falkenstein. His interest had lain entirely in the casket. But the possibility of individual ransoms added an extra pleasure to his coup, so he interviewed his prisoners, one by one. When it came Dietrich's turn, the guards marched him before the high seat and threw him before the Herr with no great gentleness.

Philip von Falkenstein was dark complexioned, with hair that fell in ringlets to his shoulders. He wore an ankle-length, dark green dalmatic cinched at the waist and, over that, a brocaded surcoat bearing the falcon crest. He wore his beard narrow and it seemed to Dietrich that his face had the pinched look of an empty man.

"What do you offer for freedom?" said Philip. "What is *your* most precious possession?"

"Why, my poverty, mine Herr. If you would take that from me, I will endure."

The guardsmen lining the great hall shifted their feet. The castle stone was damp and cold and smelled of niter. Falkenstein looked at him sharply and slowly a red crescent split his beard. At that signal, subdued chuckles rippled through the room. Herr Phillip said, "Who is your master and what will he do to ransom you?"

"My master is Jesus Christ, and he has already ransomed me with his blood."

This time Falkenstein did not smile. "I grant each man one jest. Two mark you as clever. Now answer straight. Who do you serve?"

The guards stiffened a little when Dietrich reached inside his scrip, but his knife had been taken from him along with the copper wire. Only the Krenkish head harness, mistaken for a sacramental of some sort, had been left him. He pressed the sigil, as he had done repeatedly since being captured. "Mine Herr von Falkenstein," he said distinctly. "I am Dietrich, pastor of Oberhochwald, a village in fief to Herr Manfred von Hochwald."

"Will he pay to have you back? Does he like clever priests who make jokes at his expense?" He turned to his clerk and whispered some instruction.

"The Duke will not take kindly to this theft," Dietrich suggested.

Philip's head snapped up. "What theft?"

"It requires no subtlety of thought to suppose that the casket contained material of some value to Albrecht. Silver, I suppose."

Philip nodded and one of the guards stepped forward and slapped Dietrich across the face. "Freiburg is rightly mine," Philip told him. "Not Urach's; not Hapsburg's. I'll have my dues."

After that, he sent Dietrich back to his cell.

BY FLORENTIUS' Day, the sky beyond the window had turned sullen, and a bitter wind pressed its way into the cell. In the distant sky Dietrich marked the lazy jot of a raptor. Dark clouds gathered in the southwest. He could taste the metallic crispness of the air. A formation of storks flew south.

Falkenstein was a greedy man and that often meant a stupid man, but Philip did not lack for cunning. The silver would be missed in Vienna, and the Hapsburg Duke, with vassals spread from the East-reich to the Swiss, was not to be trifled with. Falkenstein's hope must be that suspicion fall upon the Jew. None who knew otherwise would ever leave Falcon Rock.

Dietrich leaned through the balisteria and peered down the sheer walls of the keep to the ragged bedrock of the precipice. Not that Falkenstein need fear anyone leaving.

The distant bird had come closer and Dietrich saw now that it lacked wings. Before he had quite grasped that, the apparition swooped toward his window, and he saw that it was a Krenk wearing a peculiar body harness. Hovering, the creature packed a sort of earth to the slit window, into which he pressed a small, shining cylinder. Dietrich heard a shout from above and the clatter of hobnails on stone. He yanked the head harness from his scrip and strapped it on.

". . . away from the window. Move away from the window. Quickly."

Dietrich ran to the far corner of the cell just as thunder clapped and the air hurled him against the door. Shards of masonry pelted him; pebbles stung his cheeks. His ears rang and his arms and legs went numb. Through the dust he saw that the slit window had become a gaping portal. As he stared, a portion of the balustrade above slid loose with a grinding rasp, and a shrieking armsman plummeted, arms flapping uselessly, past the hovering demon.

"Quickly," said the voice in the head harness. "I must carry you. Do not lose your grip." The Krenk entered the cell and, with a swift motion encircled Dietrich with a girdle of some sort that snapped onto an eye on his harness. "Now we see if the weight exceeds the craftsman's boast." The Krenk sprinted toward the hole in the wall and leapt into the sky. Dietrich had one glimpse of terrified faces along the battlements, then the winds had him, and his rescuer soared through a hiss of arrows.

When Dietrich looked down, he learned the terror of the first Falkenstein riding lion-back across the inmost sea. Houses, fields, castles had become as children's blocks. Trees were shrubs; forests, mere carpets. Dietrich's head spun. He thought the ground was above him. He vomited out his stomach, and darkness had him.

HE AWOKE on the edge of the stubble field, by the Great Woods. Nearby, a yearling pig, its winter nose-ring in place, rooted under a decayed log. Dietrich sat up suddenly, causing the pig to squeal and flee. Hans sat just within the forest, with his knees above his head and his arms wrapped around his legs. Dietrich said to him, "You came for me."

"You had the copper wire."

Dietrich shook his head. "Falkenstein has it."

Hans made the tossing gesture with his arm.

"I could ask the coppersmith to draw more from what remains of the ingot, but that was his payment. He'll want another."

Hans' mandibles stuttered. Then he said, "The copper is all. It needed every effort to work that one small seam." He stood and pointed. "You can walk from here," he said through the *Heinzelmännchen.* "To fly you closer would show myself."

"You showed yourself to the guards at the Burg."

"They died. Those who did not fall when the wall collapsed, fell to my . . . *pot de fer.*"

Max's fabled weapon, revealed at last. Dietrich did not ask to see it. "What of the other captives?"

"They are nothing."

"No one is nothing. Each of us is precious in the Lord's eye."

Hans gestured toward his bulbous eyes. "But not in ours. You alone were useful to us."

"Even without the wire?"

"You had the head harness. With that, we could find you. Dietrich . . ." Hans pried a piece of bark off a fir and crumpled it between his fingers. "How much colder will it grow?"

"How cold . . . ? It will likely snow soon."

" 'Snow' is what?"

"When it warms, it becomes water."

"Ach." Hans considered that. "So, how much then this snow?"

"Perhaps to here." Dietrich marked his waist. "But it will melt again in the spring."

Hans stared statue-like for a time; then, without another word, he bounded into the forest.

DIETRICH WENT straightaway to Manfred and found the Herr in the rookery with his falconer, examining the birds. Manfred turned with a hoodwinked kestrel on his fist. "Ah, Dietrich, Everard told me you had lingered in Freiburg. I had not looked for your return so soon."

"Mine Herr, I was taken prisoner by Falkenstein."

Hochwald's eyebrows climbed. "In that case, I would not have looked for your return at all."

"I was . . . rescued." Dietrich glanced at the falconer, who stood nearby.

Manfred, following Dietrich's glance, said, "That is all, Hermann." When the servant had gone, he said, "Rescued by *them,* I take it. How?"

"One came in his flying harness and spread a paste around the slit window. There followed a thunderclap and the wall collapsed, whereat my rescuer gathered me up and flew me here."

"Ha!" Manfred made a gesture with his free hand. The kestrel shrieked and flexed her wings. "Thunder-paste, and a flying harness?"

"Nothing supernatural," Dietrich assured him. "In Franconian times, an English monk named Eilmer fastened wings to his hands and feet and leapt from the summit of a tower. He rode the breeze the distance of a furlong."

Manfred pursed his lips. "I saw no English birdmen at Calais."

"The swirl of the air, and his own fright at being so high, caused Eilmer to fall and break both his legs, so that ever after he limped. He attributed his failure to the want of tail feathers."

Manfred laughed. "Needed a feather up his arse? Hah!"

"Mine Herr, there are other prisoners in need of rescue." He explained about the Jew's caravan and the Hapsburg silver.

Manfred rubbed his chin. "The Duke lent the Freiburgers money to buy back the liberties they sold to Urach during the barons' war. I suspect the treasure was a payment on those loans. Mark me, one day the Hapsburgs will own the Breisgau."

"The other prisoners . . ."

Manfred waved a dismissive hand. "Philip will free them—once he's taken all they have."

"Not having seized the Hapsburg silver. Falkenstein's safety lies in their silence. Albrecht may assume the Jew absconded with the treasure."

"Since you have already escaped, he gains nothing by silencing the others. And a *de Medina* would not be tempted by such an amount. Albrecht knows that."

"Mine Herr, a coil of especially fine copper wire I had drawn in Freiburg for the Krenken . . . Falkenstein has taken it."

Manfred raised his gauntlet and studied the kestrel, brushing her feathers with his forefinger. "This is a lovely bird," he said. "Mark the taper of the wing, the elegance of the tail, the delightful chestnut plumage. Dietrich, what would you have me do? Attack Falcon Rock to retrieve a coil of wire?"

"If the Krenken give aid with their thunder-paste and flying harnesses and *pots de fer.*"

"I will tell Thierry and Max I have found a new captain to advise me. Why should the Krenken give a fig about Falcon Rock?"

"They need the wire to repair their ship."

Manfred grunted, frowned, and stroked the kestrel's head before restoring it to its perch in the rookery. "Then it is better lost," he said as he closed he cage. "The Krenken have many useful arts to teach us. I'd fain they not leave too soon."

WHEN DIETRICH called Hans on the mikrofoneh afterward, the Kratzer answered instead.

"He you call 'Hans' sits in Gschert's dungeon," the philosopher told him. "His sally against the Burg in the valley was not by Herr Gschert ordered."

"But he did it to retrieve the wire you need!"

"That is of no account. What matters, matters. Quicksilver falls."

Alchemists associated quicksilver with the planet Mercury, which was also quick, and Dietrich thought the Kratzer meant that the very planet had fallen from the sky. But he had no chance to ask, for the Krenkish philosopher ended the audience.

Dietrich sat at his table in the parsonage and twisted the now-silent head harness around his fingers before tossing it to the table. The Krenken had been now for three months in the woods, and wild stories were already in Freiburger ears. And the wire they needed for flight was lost.

DURING THE next two weeks, the Krenken barred Max and Hilde from their encampment. They were felling trees again, Hilde told him, and building bonfires. Dietrich wondered if some festival of theirs impended, similar to St. John's Day but requiring the exclusion of outsiders. "It isn't that," Max said. "They're planning something. I think they're afraid."

"Of what?"

"I don't know. It's a soldier's instinct."

THE FEAST of St. Catherine of Alexandria dawned close and cold, under a sky sullen with heavy clouds and a breeze not bold enough for wind. The villagers, having celebrated the *Kirchweihe* in memory of the foundation of their church, crowded from the church into the morning light, eager for the foot races and other games that marked the Kermis, only to stare dumbfounded at snowy hummocks rolling white to the horizons. During the church-vigil, a stealthy snow had thickened the land.

After a moment's awed contemplation, the children fell to with a collective shriek, and soon young and old were engaged in mock battles and fortifications. Across the valley, a troop of armsmen emerged from the castle. Dietrich thought at first that they intended to join the snow-fight, but they turned and marched at the double-quick down the Bear Valley road.

A snowball struck Dietrich on the chest. Joachim grinned and threw another, which missed. "That's how your sermons strike some people," the Minorite cried, and those in the snow-fort laughed. Only Lorenz took exception, and crushed a great block of snow over Joachim's head. Gregor, who had been organizing the opposition, took that as a signal to launch an attack, and the villagers on the farther side of the churchyard swarmed forth into a general melee.

Through the midst of this confusion, Eugen stepped his palfrey, kicking up sprays of snow, drawing silence in his wake, until he came at last before Dietrich. Only Theresia and the children remained shouting and oblivious to his appearance.

"Pastor," Eugen said, striving to keep his voice deep, "the villagers must come to the castle."

"Why?" shouted Oliver Becker. "We're no serfs, to be ordered about!" He made to throw a snowball at the junker, but Joachim, who was standing beside him, placed a hand on his arm.

Dietrich looked to Eugen. "Are we attacked?" He envisioned Philip von Falkenstein leading his men in a snowy charge to seize the escaped pastor. *We should have built the snow-forts higher . . .*

"The . . . the lepers . . . ," and here Eugen's voice did fail him. "They've left the woods. They're coming to the village!"

· 4 ·

NOW
Tom

DURING THE Middle Ages, on the Rogation Days, the peasants of a village would tour the borders of their manor and throw their children into brooks or bump their heads on certain trees so that the youngsters would learn the boundaries of their lives. Had he studied narrative history, Tom would have known that.

Consider the calls that Tom received from Judy Cao—a manuscript traced and located, or a reference newly discovered, or his approval needed on access fees levied by sundry archives and databases. There was a certain intoxication to these calls, much as a man hiking in the mountains might feel an exhilaration at the approach of a crest—not that he saw the world laid out below him, but that he saw the promise of such a horizon just beyond. To Tom, the steady trickle of information from Judy was like a cold spring in an arid place and, if a man can become drunk on water, it is in small sips of this Pierian sort.

Items had been appearing regularly in his Eifelheim file, all properly beribboned and pedigreed like dogs at a kennel show. Judy was a meticulous researcher. She had located monastic annals, uncovered manorial accounts, unearthed tantalizing odds and ends—the haphazardly preserved detritus of a vanished world. "The documents of everyday life," reliable precisely because they had not been recorded with posterity in mind.

- From a hodgepodge of "Baconalia" at Oxford: an *aide memoire* of the local knight of Hochwald recounting a discussion with "the pastor of St. Catherine" regarding the theories of Fra Roger Bacon: seven league boots, flying machines, talking mechanical heads.
- Preserved among the papers of Ludwig der Bayer in the Fürstenfeld Museum: a tantalizing reference in the writings of William of Ockham to "my friend, the *doctor seclusus* in Oberhochwald."
- Buried in the Luxembourg collection at the Charles University in Prague: a mention of "Sir Manfred von Oberhochwald" among the companions of the King of Bohemia at the battle of Crécy.
- A comment in the Annals of St. Blasien that "the Feldberg demon," having eluded attempts to capture him by fire, had "escaped in the direction of the Hochwald" after setting a larger fire that almost engulfed the monastery.
- A levy dated 1289, in the Generallandesarchiv Baden, by Markgraf Hermann VII of Baden on Ugo Heyso of Oberhochwald for six-and-a-half foot soldiers and one-and-a-half horse soldiers.
- A similar levy on Manfred in 1330 by Duke Friedrich IV Hapsburg of Austria.

- A copy of an episcopal letter in the archives of the Lady Church of Freiburg-im-Breisgau addressed to Pastor Dietrich, affirming the doctrine that "the body's appearance does not reflect the state of the soul."
- An anonymous compendium, MS.6752, in the Bibliothèque Nationale in Paris, on natural philosophy, "unusual for its wide range and systematic organization," attributed in a gloss on its 237th folio to "my quondam student, Seclusus," supposedly added by the great Arts Master, John Buridan.

If a man cannot get drunk on such sips as this, he is doomed to eternal sobriety. Why, the question of how a vassal might supply six-and-a-half soldiers to his liege is one to occupy a salon of Jesuits.

Sharon was happy for him, for this steady conduit from Judy meant that he was less in her hair, and she consequently had more time for physics and could shampoo less often. She thought this was what she had wanted and derived some welcome contentment from it. The major drawback, as she saw it, was that Tom would immediately share with her whatever sparkle of data he had been given, which she would acknowledge in a distracted and sometimes irritable manner. She was sure the information was fascinating in its own way but, like head cheese or scrapple, its enjoyment was an acquired taste.

One evening, while dining at a neighborhood Italian restaurant, Tom "shared" with her a Christmas fruitcake of facts that Judy had stumbled across in a doctoral dissertation on medieval village life. Among the records cited were a few from Oberhochwald in the 1330s. These were mostly those villagers unfortunate enough to come to the attention of the manorial courts, but some were happier cases of boons and grants. Almost as soon as he was off the cell phone and before the red clam sauce could stain his lips Tom was reciting particulars.

He had learned the names of actual people who had lived in "his" village. Being more accustomed to the broad abstractions of cliology, he had seldom encountered any of the folk behind his equations and models. He didn't know it yet, but he was being seduced by Judy Cao. He was beginning to delight in narrative history.

Thus, one Fritz Ackermann had been fined three pfennig in 1334 for "withdrawing himself from the lord's common oven"—meaning he had dared to bake his own bread at home. And in 1340, one Theresia Gresch had been granted the right to gather herbs in the common meadow and in the lord's woods.

Sharon thought the three-pfennig fine a sign of the tyranny of feudalism and said so in greater irritation than the size of the fine warranted, or indeed than Ackermann had probably expressed in paying it. Tom thought of correcting her equation of feudalism with manorialism, but said only, "Try buying your liquor across the bridge in New Jersey and you'll learn what fine the Lords of Pennsylvania levy for breaking *their* monopoly if they catch you at it."

But the lukewarm reception of his glad tidings was something of a damper and Tom felt as if he had been dumped unceremoniously into a cold stream.

The other thing about Judy's calls that sometimes irritated Sharon was their odd timing. They were as apt to come at one hour of the day as any other. Did that girl *never* sleep? And of course Tom would leap to answer the ring. It didn't matter much what he was doing. Clearing the dinner dishes? They could wait. Driving the car? That's why God invented cell phones. Sharon was the sort who regarded any great display of eagerness as unseemly. *Laid back* or *cool,* they used to say, and meant it as compliment. Tom's grin began to annoy her. A little *gravitas* would not hurt.

ONE EVENING, while Tom was deep into a travel book on the customs and legends of the Black Forest—one never knew where unexpected gold might lie unearthed—Sharon appeared in front of his recliner, wagging his cell phone at him.

"It's your new girlfriend," she said. "Again."

Tom closed the book on his finger. Sometimes he wasn't sure how to take Sharon. He would admit this now and then, after a few beers, and if Sharon were not around. They kidded each other a lot, but at times he thought her comments had an edge to them—a thin and delicate edge, because he didn't always feel the slice right off. "She's not my girlfriend," he said.

He and Sharon had been together longer than most married couples and so certain customs had grown up between them, much as moss will accumulate on a damp rock or ivy creep up the walls of hallowed halls. They had long ago agreed that possessiveness had no place in their relationship, and so regarded any show of it with a sort of horror. But that was theory. Practice was something else, for too little possessiveness may also have its hazards. Moss may be a soft and comfortable thing upon which to rest, but it is also a very same sort of thing and its flowers require a certain subtleness of thought to admire. Now and then, Tom wished that Sharon would loosen up, and Sharon that Tom would grow more steady.

Sharon, who had not meant the comment all that seriously, jiggled the phone a little in her hand as she appraised his reaction. "Turn that thing to vibrate," she told him, handing it over. "And keep it with you. That's the whole point of a *portable* phone." Without another word, she crossed to her sofa, where she curled up like the hidden dimensions of the polyverse. She found it difficult to concentrate at first on Janatpour space, which she attributed to the residuum of the interruption.

Tom acknowledged the command with an absent wave. "Did you hear that, Judy?" he asked the grainy image on the cell-phone's screen. "Sharon thinks you're my new lover."

Judy frowned and said, "Maybe I should not call you at home."

Sometimes the stuffy propriety of the younger generation was a little hard to take. "Oh, Sharon doesn't mind you calling." He dropped his voice when he said this so that he would not disturb the physicist on the sofa. "Everything's fine. What do you have for me?" In truth, he looked forward to these exchanges. Judy scratched his curiosity where it itched. *She and I click,* he had told Sharon already. *She knows historical research, which databases to tap, which archivists to contact. She knows what I'm looking for, so I don't have to explain things twice.*

And Sharon had answered, *She's a treasure, all right.*

"I think I know why the village's name was changed," Judy announced.

"*Das geht ja wie's Katzenmachen!*" Tom exclaimed—which did disturb the physicist on the sofa and earned him a glare, which he did not notice. "*Meine kleine Durchblickerin! Zeig' mir diesen Knallfekt.*"

Judy had gotten used to that sort of thing by then. She had no idea what he had said, but did have a good idea what he wanted, so a translation was not needed. She did something off the screen and the image of a manuscript replaced her face.

It is not possible to hop out of a recliner, but Tom managed it anyway. He hurried to CLIODEINOS, where he inserted his phone into the docking station, and the manuscript appeared at a more readable magnification on the monitor. The handwriting was fourteenth-century work. The Latin was awful; Cicero would have wept.

"I used the Soundex to look for variant spellings," Judy explained while he skimmed the document. "That casts a wider loop, of course, and it takes longer to sort through the . . . the . . ."

"The *Krempel.* The junk. What am I looking at?"

"It's a bull from 1377 against the Brethren of the Free Spirit. It seems that Oberhochwald's new name was not originally Eifelheim at all, but—"

"Teufelheim." Tom had skimmed ahead, and his finger now touched the screen lightly where the name appeared: *Devil-home.* He chewed on his thumb knuckle while he considered that. What sort of people had lived there, he wondered, to have earned such a name from their neighbors?

"Shun the works of Satan," he read aloud, "as we shun the unholy soil of Teufelheim. Pastor Dietrich was tried and found wanting. Be you not also found wanting, sick with heresy and sorcery. Et cetera, et cetera." Tom sat back in his chair. "The writer doesn't much care for our friend Dietrich. I wonder what he did that was so terrible—besides stiffing that coppersmith." He saved the file to his drive and Judy's face reappeared on the screen.

"The connection seemed clear to me," she said.

"Yes. Why mention Dietrich in the next sentence unless Teufelheim was Oberhochwald? Although . . ." He rubbed his ear with his finger. "In all of Swabia, I suppose there could be two Dietrichs."

"Dr. Wegner in the Language Department said that the corruption of 'Teufelheim' to 'Eifelheim' was linguistically natural."

"*Ja, wenn man Teufel spricht, kommt er.*" Tom called up the area map on a split screen and double-clicked on the village's icon so he could add the latest gloss on the name. This version of the map showed the actual geography, with landforms in shadowed relief. The village sat on a spur of the Feldberg by a steep ravine leading into the Höllental. And what better route might there be to "Devil's Home" than through "Hell Valley"? At the lower end of Hell Valley sat none other than Himmelreich—"Kingdom of Heaven." It was a topsy-turvy sort of nomenclature, with the Devil on the mountaintop and Heaven down below.

Tom saved the new information, but with a mild feeling of anticlimax, or perhaps of a slight hangover. "We still don't know why the place was abandoned, but I guess we're one step closer."

"But we do know," Judy told him. "Demons. 'Devil-home.'"

Tom was not convinced. "No," he said. "It's one more place-name in the Schwarzwald named after the Devil. Like Teufelsmühle near Staufenberg, or the Devil's Pulpit . . . There are *two* 'Devil's Pulpits,' one by Baden-Baden and the other on the Kniebis. Plus Hex Valley and Hell Valley and—"

"But did you read the descriptions of the Devils that this Dietrich supposedly conjured?"

He hadn't, but he recalled the file and this time read past the comment on the name. "Ugly sons of bitches, weren't they?" he said when he had found the passage. "Yellow, bulging eyes. Gibbering incantations. Driving men mad. 'They danced naked, but sported no manhood.'" The color control on the monitor, he noted, was fine enough to show Judy's blush. "I don't suppose demons ever won beauty contests."

"They flew, too. This must be what started those folktales about the Krenkl."

"A few sentences in a bull? No, the writer was repeating a story already in circulation. He expected his readers to understand the reference, just as he expected them to know who 'Pastor Dietrich' was. I wonder if *Krenkl* comes from *Kränklein*—South German shortens '-lein' to '-l.' "

"I thought . . ."

"What?"

"Well, the descriptions of the demons were so detailed, so vivid . . . Their appearance. Even the way the villagers behaved. Some 'saved themselves and their souls.' Others 'befriended the demons and welcomed them unto their very hearths.' "

Tom dismissed her suggestion even before she could nerve herself to make it. "All it takes is a little imagination and a bit of hysteria. The medievals were great believers in mythic beasts. They heard vague tales of the rhinoceros and imagined a unicorn out of it. The horsemen of the steppes became centaurs. They had kobolds and dwarves and . . . I saw a drawing in a psalter, in the Walters Gallery in Baltimore, that showed two weird creatures—one like a stag, the other like a big cat—walking on their hind legs and carrying a pall-draped bier between them. And there's a fresco in the crypt of the Freiburg Franziskanerkirche that shows giant grasshoppers sitting at a banquet table, probably a metaphor for the way locusts could consume entire harvests. And a carved doorpost in the Cloisters in New York portrays—"

"All right!"

The vehemence in her voice surprised him. After a moment, he said quietly, "This isn't the Middle Ages, you know. There's always a natural explanation for 'supernatural' events."

AFTERWARD, TOM remained at the PC, pulling on his lip. If bizarre visions had been the reason for the taboo, there would have been Teufelheims all up and down the Rhineland.

The medieval collapse had spawned horrors enough to depopulate a thousand Eifelheims. Cannibalism followed the famines of 1317 and 1318, when the crops drowned from incessant rains. "Children were not safe from their parents," one chronicler had written. But no villages had been shunned on that account. Peasant bands had roamed the countryside, espousing poverty and free love, sacking manors and monasteries and lynching Jews to make their point. But those who fled soon returned, even the Jews. A century of war and banditry in France destroyed the mystique of the knight, the tourney, the minstrel, and courtly love. Cynicism and despair replaced hope and anticipation. Witchcraft and heresy; flagellants and plague. The macabre cult of death, with its dancing skeletons. A new world order so closed, so paranoid, so repressive, so *stunned* by meaningless death that people forgot completely that there had ever been a different and more open world before it.

So amidst these shambles, why had Eifelheim alone remained anathema?

He pulled out the project folder and carried it to the kitchen table, where he spread the hard copies out, scrutinizing each one, as if he could wrest answers from them by sheer concentration: Manorial records of the vassals of the Margraves of Baden and the earlier Dukes of Zähringen; the knight's *memoire;* the religious treatise on the "inner world" with its awkward illuminated capital; seignorial approvals of marriages and vocations, of fines and grants; enfoeffments encompassing Oberhochwald and feudal levies upon its knight; the newspaper clipping Anton had sent him; an ecstatic prayer citing "eight secret paths to leave this earth of sorrows" and attributed at third hand to a "Saint Johan of Oberhochwald"; the episcopal letter addressed to Pastor Dietrich.

There were also the usual monkish chronicles—from Freiburg, St. Peter, St. Blasien, and elsewhere—of harvests, fairs, gossip, noble doings. One spectacular event, a lightning strike in August 1348, had set several acres of forest (and not a few superstitious minds) ablaze. The plague was then just spreading north from the coast, and the bolt had in retrospect been read as Lucifer's advent. (Had the village burned? No, the *Moriuntur* document and the business with the smith had come later.)

The bits and pieces were accumulating into a fuller picture, or at least into a sketch. The manor of Oberhochwald was one of two possessed by its knight (the other being in the gift of the Austrian Duke). The last knight to hold the fief was named Manfred, and his father had been named Ugo. The pastor at the time of the village's demise had been named Dietrich, who may have been the "*doctor seclusus*" mentioned by Ockham and who had written the *compendium* in the Bibliothèque. There was an herb-woman named Theresia (he imagined her as a gray-haired hag with a face as ragged as the Black Forest itself), a farmer named Fritz, a smith named Lorenz, and a few others whose names had wound up in that doctoral thesis. Peel back the research onion another layer, locate the originals that the doctoral candidate had used, and even more names would likely surface.

I could almost write a complete history of this village, he thought. Harvest and tax records would let him estimate economic and demographic growth. The fief records showed how it fit into the local feudal structure. The knight's *memoire* and the bishop's letter even gave him a glimpse into the village's intellectual life, such as it was.

In fact, he realized glumly, the only thing missing from the village's history was the one thing that made it worth writing—why it had so abruptly and so completely come to an end.

What if it's not there? he wondered. What if the key document had been lost? Burned to ashes in the struggles between Mercy and the Bernadines at the rag-tail end of the Thirty Years War; or during Moreau's Retreat down Hell Valley; or in the campaigns of Louis or Napoleon or a dozen other strutting would-be conquerors. Eaten by mice or mold, consumed by fire or rain or flood, crumbled in neglect.

What if it had never been written down at all?

"Tom, what's wrong? You look pale."

He glanced up. Sharon stood in the kitchen archway, a freshly brewed cup of tea in her hand. The odor of rosehips and chamomile wafted through the room.

"Nothing," he said. But he'd had the sudden, dreadful sensation that he already had a key piece of information in his hands; that he had read it several times already; and that it had meant nothing to him.

AND SO came I into the affair, although at first in only a peripheral way. I was teaching still at the Albert-Louis, and Tom sent me an e-mail asking me to find the manorial records for Oberhochwald. These were supposed to be in our university collection. I replied, Was that a personal *supposition, a* material *supposition, or a* simple *supposition? And Tom responded <LOL?> because he did not understand the joke. He supplied a list of key words and a request to search our manuscripts and incunabula for references pertaining to Oberhochwald, which I suppose was fit punishment for my attempt at* *medieval humor. Supposition theory is not much funny, especially as we don't really know what they meant by it all. They used many of the same words as we do—motion, intuition, realism, natural, occult—but their meanings lay often at odd angles to ours. Still, I promised to rummage around as best I could and, a week later, I sent him what little I had found.*

· XI ·

NOVEMBER, 1348
The Kermis

THE KRENKEN were coming into the village.

The announcement struck Dietrich like a blow to the stomach. He steadied himself with a clutch to Eugen's bridle. They meant to take the village. Given the Krenkish choler, it could be nothing else. But why, after the months of hiding? He looked up at the junker, whose face was as white as the ground. The lad *knew.* "The Herr sent hand-picked men to face them, I hope."

Eugen swallowed. "They've been told. They'll stand."

God vouchsafed Dietrich a vision of the coming events. He saw them unfold with awful clarity, as if they had already been accomplished—already *factum est.* Grim ranks of the strange creatures hurl bullets with their *pots de fer,* ignite their thunder-paste. Men are pierced, shattered. Krenken swoop from the air to strike men from above.

Max's men cry in terror. But they are men who answer fear with blows. The Krenken have their magic weapons, but a broadsword hews them as easily as a man. And once frightened men see that, they fall upon the survivors with a fury more murderous for having been born of fear; hacking and chopping to bits the creatures he had named Hans, and Gschert, and Kratzer.

Whichever way the fight might go, too many would die for the remainder to live. It would be pressed to the last. There would be no men left. Or no Krenken.

But if the Krenken were only beasts that spoke, what did it matter? One slays attacking beasts, and it would end his anxiety.

And yet . . .

Hans had flown through a rain of arrows and braved Gschert's dungeon to rescue Dietrich from Burg Falkenstein. Whatever cold Krenkish reason had driven it, it deserved more than a sword in answer. One did not put down a dog that had succored one, however fiercely it now barked.

Dietrich saw the world suddenly through Krenkish eyes—lost, far from home, neighbors to ominous strangers who could contemplate the killing of their lords, an act incomprehensible, even bestial to them. *To Hans, Dietrich was the Beast that Spoke.*

Dietrich gasped and seized Eugen's snaffle rein. "*Quickly.* Ride to Manfred. Tell him, 'they are your vassals.' He will understand. I will meet him at the millstream bridge. Now, go!"

The villagers chattered. Some had heard the lepers mentioned, and Volkmar said they would bring their illness into the village. Oliver cried that he would drive them off alone, if need be. Theresia answered that they must be welcomed and cared for. Hildegarde Müller, who alone among them realized what was coming down the Bear Valley road, stood frozen with a hand across her open mouth.

Dietrich rushed to the church, where he seized a crucifix and an aspergum and hailed the creature Hans on the head harness. "Turn back," he pleaded. "There is yet time." He draped a stole around his neck. "What is it you want?"

"Escape from this numbing cold," the Krenk answered. "The . . . hearths . . . in our ship will not burn until we have repaired the . . . the sinews of fire."

The Krenken might have spent the summer building snug cottages instead of collecting butterflies and flowers. But such chastisement was in vain. "Max brings a force to turn you back."

"They will run. Gschert has that sentence in his head. Our weapons and our form will cause them to flee, and so we will take your hearths for ourselves and not feel this cold."

Dietrich thought about the gargoyles and monsters that adorned the walls of St. Catherine's. "You may frighten these men, but they will not run. You will perish."

"Then, likewise, we will not feel the cold."

Dietrich was running already down Church Hill, a winter cloak drawn around his shoulders. "There may yet be another way. Tell Gschert to hold a white banner aloft and, when Max confronts you, hold out empty hands. I will meet you at the wooden bridge."

AND SO it was that the shivering band of two score Krenken—bundled in what hodgepodge of garments they could muster and escorted by Max's trembling, round-eyed men—approached the lord of the Hochwald. The Herr Gschert, splendid in red sash and trousers, and a yellow vest too thin for the weather, stepped forward and, at Dietrich's coaching, dropped to one knee with his shivering hands folded before him. Manfred, after the barest hesitation, enclosed those hands in his own, announcing to all who had dared draw near, "This . . . man . . . We declare Our vassal, to hold in fief the greater woods and to produce for Us charcoal and powder for the *pots de fer* and to teach the arts of his foreign land to Our men. In return, We grant him and his folk food and shelter, clothing and warmth, and the protection of Our strong, right arm." And so saying, he drew his longsword and held it before him, pommel-up, to resemble a cross. "This We swear before God and the *familia* of *Hof Hochwald.*" Then Dietrich blessed the assembly and sprinkled them with the golden-handled aspergum. Those villagers touched by the water crossed themselves, staring wide-eyed at the monsters. Some of the Krenken, noting the gesture, repeated it—to appreciative murmurs from the crowd. Dietrich blessed God for moving the Krenken to thoughtless mimicry.

He pressed the processional crucifix into the hands of Johann von Sterne. "Lead us slowly to the church," Dietrich told him, "at a pace, thus." And all set forth from the bridge and through the village to Church Hill. Dietrich followed the cross and Manfred and Gschert followed him. "May the Lord help us," Manfred whispered for Dietrich's ear.

The human heart finds comfort in ceremony. Manfred's impromptu words, Gschert's humble gesture, Dietrich's blessing, the procession and cross tempered the dread in folk's breasts, so that, for the most part, the Krenken were met by stunned silence and gaping mouths. Men clutched sword hilt or knife handle, or fell to their knees in the snow, but none dared speak against what lord and pastor had so clearly countenanced. A few shrieks pierced the still, cold air, and some clumped awkwardly through the snow in a parody of flight. Doors slammed. Bars fell home.

More would flee were flight easier, Dietrich thought, and prayed for snow. *Block the roads; choke the pathways; keep this monstrous advent contained in the Hochwald!*

When the Krenken caught sight of the "wooden cathedral," they chittered and pointed and paused to raise *fotografik* devices to capture images of the carvings. The procession bunched up short of the doors.

Someone shouted, "They fear to enter!" Then another cried, "Demons!" Manfred turned with his hand on his sword. "Get them inside, quickly," he said to Dietrich.

While Dietrich chivvied the Krenken into the church, he told Hans, "When they see a red lamp, they are to genuflect before it. Do you understand? Tell them."

The strategem worked. The villagers quieted once more when the creatures passed within and made obeisance to the True Presence. Dietrich dared relax, a little.

Hans stood beside him with the cross. "I have explained," he said over the *mikrofoneh*. "When your overlord-from-the-sky comes again, we may yet be saved. Do you know when this befalls?"

"Neither the day nor the hour."

"May he come soon," Hans said. "May he come soon."

Dietrich, surprised by the evident fervor, could only agree.

WHEN VILLAGER and Krenk alike had crowded within the church, Dietrich ascended the pulpit and related all that had transpired since St. Sixtus Day. He described the strangers' plight in most piteous terms, and had the Krenkish children stand before the congregation with their mothers behind them. Hildegarde Müller and Max Schweitzer bore witness to the injuries and deaths that had afflicted the creatures and described how they had helped place their dead in special crypts aboard their ship. "When I sprinkled them with holy water at the bridge," Dietrich concluded, "they showed no discomfort. Therefore, they cannot be demons."

The Hochwalders shifted and glanced at one another. Then Gregor asked, "Are they Turks?"

Dietrich nearly laughed. "No, Gregor. They fare from a farther land than that."

Joachim thrust his way forward. "No!" he cried for all to hear. "They *are* true demons. A glance alone convinces. Their coming is a great trial for us . . . and how we answer it may be the saving of our souls!"

Dietrich gripped the pulpit rails and Manfred, who occupied the *sedalia* usually reserved for the celebrant, growled, "I have accepted this Krenkish lord as my vassal. Do *you* gainsay me?"

But if Joachim heard, he gave no heed; rather, he addressed the *familia*. "Remember Job," he told them, "and how God tested his faith, sending demons to torment him! Remember how God Himself, robed in flesh, suffered all human afflictions—even death! Might He not then afflict demons as he afflicted Job, and even His Son? Dare we bind God with necessity and say that *this* work God cannot do? No! God has willed that these demons suffer the afflictions of the flesh." His voice dropped. "But why? But why?" This he said as if he pondered aloud, so that the assembly stilled to hear him. "He does nothing without purpose, hidden though His purpose may be from us. He became flesh to save *us* from sin. He made these demons flesh to save *them* from sin. If angels fall, then demons may rise. *And we are to be the instrument of their salvation!* See how they have suffered at God's will . . . And pity them!"

Dietrich, having sucked in his breath, let it out in astonishment. Manfred took his hand from his sword.

"Show these beings what a Christian is," Joachim continued. "Welcome them into your hearths, for they are cold. Give them bread, for they are hungry. Comfort them, for they are far from home. Thus inspired by our example, *they* will repent and be saved. Remember the Great Plea: Lord, when did we see *You* hungry? When did we see *You* naked? When? *In our neighbor!* And who is our neighbor? *Any who may cross our path!*" Here he stabbed a finger directly at the mass of impassive Krenken standing on the gospel side of the nave. "Imprisoned in flesh, they can wield no demonic powers. Christ is all-powerful. The goodness of Christ is all-powerful. It triumphs over every mean and petty and wicked thing, it triumphs over wickedness as old as Lucifer. Now we may see that *it will triumph over Hell itself!*"

The congregation gasped, and even Dietrich felt a shiver run through him. Joachim continued to preach, but Dietrich listened no longer. Instead, he noted the rapt attention of the Hochwalders; heard the clicks of Hans and a few others as they repeated the talking head's translations. Dietrich was certain of neither the logic nor the orthodoxy of the monk's words, but their effectiveness he could not deny.

When Joachim had finished—or perhaps only when he had paused—Manfred rose and announced for those who had not been at the bridge that the Krenkish leader was henceforth the Baron Grosswald and would live, together with his *ministeriales,* as a guest in the Hof and that the remaining strangers would be billeted as his council would determine.

This prospect caused much unease—until Klaus stepped forward and, hands on hips, invited the maier of the pilgrims to guest with him. The offer startled Dietrich, but he supposed that, his wife having tended their wounded, he could not appear behindhand in hospitality. After this, some opened their houses, while others muttered, "Better you than me!"

Manfred cautioned the Krenken about their choler. "I understand that your code of honor demands swift, corporal chastisement. Well and good. Other lands, other customs. But you must not handle my people so. The justice is mine alone, and to transgress it is to besmirch my honor. Should any of you transgress the laws and customs of the manor, you must answer in *my* court when it meets in the spring. Otherwise, Baron Grosswald will have the low justice among you according to your uses. Meanwhile, we want heralds to wear such head-harnesses as the Krenken may provide, so that whenever there is need to speak one with another, the nearest herald may translate."

In the silence that followed these announcements, Joachim began to sing, low at first and then more strongly, lifting his chin and throwing words to the vises and rafters, as if transported by some inner fire. Dietrich recognized the hymn, *Christus factus est pro nobis,* and at the next phrase, joined his own voice in *duplum,* at which Joachim faltered, then recovered. Dietrich took the "holding voice," or *tenor,* and Joachim the upper and their voices moved freely against each other, Joachim sometimes rendering a dozen notes to Dietrich's one. Dietrich became aware that the Krenken had stilled their chittering and stood as the statues in their niches. Not a few of them held *mikrofonai* aloft to capture the sounds.

At last their two voices fell into unison on "the refreshing fa" with which the fifth mode ended, and the church remained hushed for some moments, until Gregor's rough "Amen!" started a chorus of affirmations. Dietrich blessed the congregation, saying, "May God prosper this enterprise and strengthen our resolve. We ask this through Jesus Christ, our Lord, in the name of the Father and of the Son and of the Holy Ghost, Amen."

Then he prayed silently that the concord miraculously elicited by Joachim's unexpected sermon would not vanish in the face of second thoughts.

WHEN DIETRICH later brought Hans and the Kratzer to the parsonage, he found that Joachim had built up the fire in the main room and was adjusting the crackling logs with an iron poker. The two Krenken made exclamations untranslatable by the talking head and pushed into the room, close to the flames. Joachim stepped back, the poker in his hands and considered them.

"These are to be our particular guests," he supposed.

"The one wearing the strange furs is called the Kratzer, because when I met him he used his forearms to make a rasping sound."

"And you called their lord 'Gschert,' " Joachim said with a flat smile. "Does he know it means 'stupidly rude'? Who is the other? I've seen those garments before, in the church rafters at the *feriae messis.*"

"You saw him then—and said nothing?"

Joachim shrugged. "I had fasted. It might have been a vision."

"His name is Johann von Sterne. He is a servant who tends the talking head."

"A servant, and you call him 'von.' I never looked for humor from you, Dietrich. Why does he wear short pants and doublet while the other is wrapped in fur?"

"Their country is warmer than ours. They keep their arms and legs bare because their speech sometimes makes use of the arm-rasping. As their ship was bound for lands likewise warm, neither pilgrims nor crew brought cold-weather clothing. Only the Kratzer's folk, who had planned to explore an unknown country, did so."

Joachim rapped the poker against the stone fireplace to knock the ashes off. "He will share the fur, then," he said, hanging the poker on its hook.

"It would never occur to him," Hans Krenk answered. After a pause, he added, "Nor to me."

DIETRICH AND Joachim went to prepare beds for the strangers in the kitchen outbuilding, where the larger kitchen hearth would provide greater warmth. In the snow-path between the buildings, Joachim said, "You sang well in the church today. *Organum purum* is difficult to master."

"I learned d'Arezzo's method in Paris." That had involved memorizing the hymn *Ut queant laxis* and using the first syllables of each line for the hexachord: ut, re, mi, fa, sol, la.

"You sang like a monk," Joachim said. "I wondered if you'd ever been tonsured."

Dietrich rubbed the back of his head. "I came by the bald spot in the common course."

Joachim laughed, but touched Dietrich on the arm. "Do not be afraid. We shall succeed. We shall save these demons for Christ."

"They are not demons. You will see that in time, as I did."

"No, they are steeped in evil. The philosopher refused to share his fur with his servant. Philosophers will always have logical reasons for avoiding the good—and those reasons will always hang on their lust for material goods. A man who has little thinks little of sharing it; but the man who has much will clutch it with his dying fingers. This device . . ." Joachim fingered the cord of the head harness that Dietrich wore. "Explain how it works."

Dietrich did not know, but repeated what he had been told about insensible waves in the air, "felt" by devices which he had named "feelers," or *antennae.* But Joachim laughed. "How often you say that we ought not imagine new entities to explain a thing when those already known suffice. Yet you accept that there are insensible waves in the air. Surely, that the device is demonic is by far the simpler hypothesis."

"If this device is demonic, it did me no harm."

"Diabolical arts cannot harm a good Christian, which testifies in your favor. I had feared for you, Dietrich. Your faith is as cold as the snow, and provides no warmth. True faith is a fire that gives life—"

"If by that you mean that I don't shout and weep—"

"No. You talk—and while the words are always right, they are not always the right words. There is no joy in you, only a long-forgotten sorrow."

Dietrich, much discomfited, said, "There is the tithe barn. Fetch the straw for the bedding."

Joachim hesitated. "I had thought you went into the woods to lie with Hildegarde. I thought the leper colony a ruse. To believe that was the sin of rash judgement—and I pray your pardon."

"It was a reasonable hypothesis."

"What has reason to do with it? A man does not reason his way into a slattern's bed." He scowled and his thick brows knit together. "The woman is a whore, a temptress. If you did not go into the woods to be with her, it is certain that she went into the woods to be with you."

"Judge *her* not too rashly, either."

"I'm no philosopher, to mince words. If we are to grapple with a foe, let us at least name him. Men like you are a challenge to women like her."

"Men like me . . . ?"

"Celibates. Oh, how tasty are the grapes that dangle out of reach! How much more desired! Dietrich, you haven't granted me pardon."

"Oh, surely. I take the words of the Lord's Prayer. I will pardon you as you pardon her."

Surprise contorted the monk's features. "For what must I pardon Hilde?"

"For having such 'a woodpile stacked by the hut' that you dream of her at night."

Joachim blanched and his jaw muscles knit. Then he looked at the snow. "I do think on them, what they felt—might feel like in my hands. I am a miserable sinner."

"So are we all. Which is why we merit love, and not condemnation. Which of us is worthy to throw the first stone? But let us at least not blame another for our own weakness."

IN THE kitchen, Dietrich discovered Theresia huddled in a tight corner between the hearth and the outer wall. "Father!" she cried. "Send them away!"

"What ails you?" He reached to her, but she would not emerge from her corner.

"No, no, no!" she said. "Evil, wicked things! Father, they've come for us, they mean to take us down down down to Hell. How could you let them come? Oh, the flames! Mother! Father, make them go away!" Her eyes did not apprehend Dietrich, but looked on another vision.

This affliction he had not seen in many years.

"Theresia, these Krenken are the distressed pilgrims from the woods."

She clutched at the sleeve of his gown. "Can you not see their hideousness? Have they enchanted your eyes?"

"They are poor beings of flesh and blood, as we are."

The monk had come to the door of the kitchen outbuilding, a bundle of staw for the bedding balanced on his shoulder. He dropped it and rushed to the alcove where he went to his knee before Theresia.

"The Krenken terrify her," Dietrich told him.

Joachim held his hands out. "Come, let us go down to your own cottage. There are none there to frighten you."

"She ought not to be frightened of them," Dietrich said.

But Joachim turned on him. "In the name of Christ, Dietrich! First, give comfort; then juggle your dialectic! Help me lift her out of there."

"You are a handsome boy, brother Joachim," Theresia said. "*He* was handsome, too. He came with the demons and the fire but he wept and he carried me away and saved me from them." She had taken two more steps, supported by Joachim and Dietrich on either side, when she shrieked. Hans and the Kratzer had come to the kitchen door.

"I would observe this woman," the Kratzer said through the talking head. "Why do some of your folk respond so?"

"She is not one of your beetles or leaves, to be studied and divided by genus and species," Dietrich said. "Fright has awakened old memories in her."

Joachim took Theresia under his arm, placing himself between the herb woman and the Krenken, and hurried her through the door. "Make them go away!" Theresia begged Joachim.

Hans clicked his horny lips and said, "You shall have your wish."

He did not ask Dietrich to translate the remark for the girl, and the priest could not help but wonder if it had been an involuntary exclamation, not meant for overhearing.

THAT EVENING, Dietrich tramped into the Lesser Wood and cut down pine branches, which he wove into an Advent wreath for the coming Sunday. When afterward he looked into the kitchen, he saw Joachim's quilted, goose-down blanket laid over the shivering body of Johann von Sterne.

· XII ·

JANUARY, 1348

Before Matins, the Epiphany of the Lord

WINTER FELL like a shroud. The first snow had barely slumped under the pale sun when a second fell upon it, and path and pasture vanished alike into anonymity. The millstream and its pond froze clear to the bottom, and fish could be spied mid-wriggle in the wintry glass. Peasants in their cottages, employed in mending and repair, threw another log on the fire and rubbed their hands. The wider world had been emptied out and a pall of gray woodsmoke hung over the silence.

The Krenken huddled miserably before their hosts' firesides, seldom venturing out. The snow had halted all thought of repair to their ship. Instead, they talked about how they would someday repair it.

But after a time, even the talk ceased.

THE COMPLINES of St. Saturnius brought a wind to buffet the parsonage's shuttered windows. A low sussurus moaned through chinks in the planking. Hans had gone to the outbuilding to prepare special Krenkish foods for himself and the Kratzer. Joachim hunched over the refectory table where, under the Kratzer's critical eye, he whittled Balthazar from a bough of black oak, to add to his crèche figurines.

The door flew open, and the alchemist burst into the room and hopped immediately to the fireside, where he opened Gregor's fur coat and luxuriated in the flames. "In Germany," Dietrich said as he went to close the door, "the custom stands that we knock on the doorpost and await permission to enter." But the alchemist, whom they had named after Arnold of Villanova, made no answer. He clacked some announcement to the Kratzer, and the two fell into an animated discussion which the *Heinzelmännchen* did not translate.

Dietrich took up the stew pot that he had earlier hung to simmer over the fire and served Joachim. The Krenken were a rude and ill-mannered folk. Small wonder they quarreled so among themselves.

Hans returned from the outbuilding with two plates in his hands. At sight of the alchemist, he hesitated, then handed one to the alchemist and the other to the Kratzer. He sat himself across the table from Joachim.

"That was kindly done," Joachim said, curling another shaving from Balthazar's back.

Hans tossed his arm. "Were but one morsel left, it would be Arnold's to swallow."

Dietrich had noticed that even Gschert deferred to the alchemist, though Arnold was clearly an underling. "Why?" He spooned some soup into a wooden bowl and gave it to Hans, along with a stick of little-bread.

Instead of answering, Hans picked up the Christ-child that Joachim had previously carved. "Your brother tells me that this portrays your lord-from-the-sky; but the philosophy of the likelihood of events concludes that folk from different worlds must have different forms."

"The philosophy of the likelihood of events," Dietrich said. "That intrigues."

"Though less so," Joachim said dryly, "than Godhead made flesh. The Son of God, Hans, assumed the appearance of men at his Incarnation."

Hans listened silently to his head harness. "The *Heinzelmännchen* informs me that 'incarnation' in your ceremonial tongue likely means 'enfleshment'."

"Ja, doch."

"But . . . But this is wonderful! Never have we met a folk able to assume the form of another! Was your lord a being of . . . No, not fire, but of that essence which gives impetus to matter."

"Spirit," Dietrich guessed. "In Greek, we say *energia*, which means that principle which 'works within' or animates."

The Krenk considered that. "We have a . . . relationship . . . between spirit and material things. We say that 'spirit equals material by the speed of light by the speed of light.' "

"An interesting invocation," said Dietrich, "though occult in meaning."

But the Krenk had turned away to interrupt his fellows with untranslated exclamations. A furious debate arose among them, which ended when the alchemist donned his own head harness and addressed Dietrich. "Tell me of this lord of pure *energia* and how he enfleshed himself. Such a being, when he returns, may yet save us!"

"Amen!" said Joachim. But the Kratzer snapped his side-lips. "Enfleshment? The atoms of the flesh would not fit. Can Hochwalder impregnate Krenk? Wa-bwa-wa."

Arnold flung his arm. "A being of pure *energia* might know the art of inhabiting a foreign body." He took a seat at the table. "Tell me, will he come soon?"

"This is the season of Advent," Dietrich said, "when we await his birth at Christ Mass."

The alchemist trembled. "And when and where does he enflesh himself?"

"In Bethlehem of Judea." The remainder of the evening passed in catechetical instruction, which the alchemist noted diligently on the wonderful writing slate all Krenken carried in their scrips. Arnold asked Joachim to translate the Mass into German so that the *Heinzelmännchen* could in turn translate it into Krenkish. Dietrich, who knew how poorly the figures of one tongue might sit upon another, wondered how much of the sense would survive the journey.

VIGIL-NIGHT CAME and, with it, those villagers who otherwise seldom saw the inside of the church. With them, came Arnold Krenk. Some, upon spying this peculiar new catechumen, slipped quietly outside, including Theresia. When the Mass of the Catechumens ended, and Brother Joachim, holding high the book of Gospels, led Arnold Krenk forth for instruction, a few crept back in for the Mass of the Faithful. But Theresia was not among them.

Afterward, Dietrich threw on a coat and, gripping a torch, picked his way to the foot of the hill, where Theresia's cottage stood. He banged on the door, but she did not answer, pretending to be asleep, and so he doubled his efforts. The noise brought Lorenz from his smithy to stare at him bleary-eyed and to cast an appraising glance at the stars before returning to his slumbers.

Finally, Theresia opened the upper half of her door. "Will you allow no sleep?" she asked.

"You ran from Mass."

"While demons are present, there can be no true Mass, so I have not broken the Christ Mass law. You have, father, because you have not prayed a proper Mass."

This was too subtle for Theresia. "Who told you so?"

"Volkmar."

The entire Bauer family had also departed the church. "And is Bauer then a theologian? The *doctor rustica?* Will you come to the Sunrise Mass?" Never had he need of the question. In the past, his daughter had attended all three Christ Masses.

"Will *they* be there?"

The customs and ceremonies of the village interested the Kratzer, so also many of the stranded pilgrims. Some of them surely would attend with their *fotografia* and *mikrofonai.* "They may."

She shook her head. "Then, I must not." She started to close the door.

Dietrich put his hand up to stop it. "Wait. If 'in Christ there is no Jew or Greek, no slave or free, no man or woman,' how in Christ can I bar anyone from the table?"

"Because," she answered quite simply, "these demons are neither man nor woman, neither Jew nor Greek."

"You are a disputatious woman!"

Theresia closed the upper door. "You should rest for the Sunrise Mass," he heard her say.

Returning to the parsonage, he expressed his frustrations to Joachim and wondered if he might bar the Krenken from some Masses so Theresia and the others would attend. "The simple answer is that you cannot," the monk replied, "and like much that the Christ taught, the simple answer will suffice. Only schoolmen burden such things with quibbles." He reached across the table and seized Dietrich's wrist. "We are engaged in a wonderful task here, Dietrich. Should we bring these henchmen of Satan to the arms of Christ, the Kingdom of Heaven cannot be far off. And when the Third Age of the World comes—the Age of the Holy Spirit—our names shall be writ in gold."

But as he lay down to nap until the Sunrise Mass, Dietrich thought, *But will Theresia's name be writ among them?*

AS OFTEN happens, fear showed itself in hostility. Theresia threw snowballs at the Krenken whenever she encountered them in the open, having learned of their particular sensitivity to cold. "Of course the cold bothers them," she told Dietrich after he had chastised her. "They are accustomed to the fires of Hell." One time, her icy missiles struck a Krenkish child. After this, some of the Krenken, knowing that the mere sight of them would drive her wild, would in acts of petty revenge brave the cold merely to show themselves at her cottage window. Baron Grosswald applied the Krenkish discipline to these transgressors—not for love of Theresia Gresch, but to maintain the precarious peace—and warmth—he had eked from Herr Manfred's disposition.

Even Joachim was moved to express his disappointment. "Had you asked me who in this village would sit before the Lord," he said one afternoon while he mended a tear in his habit, "I would have named the herb woman. Lorenz told me she was mute when she arrived with you."

Dietrich, who was sweeping the floor, paused over sudden memories. "And so for two years more." He cast a glance at the crucifix on the wall, where Jesus also twisted in torment. *Why, O Lord, have you afflicted her so? Job at least was a wealthy man and so may have merited affliction, but Theresia was only a child when you took everything from her.* "Her father was a Herr in the Elsass," he said, "and the Armleder burned their manor down, killed her father and brothers, and raped her mother."

Joachim crossed himself. "God's peace upon them."

"All for the crime of being wealthy," Dietrich added pointedly. "I do not know if her father was a cruel lord or a kind one, whether he held vast sallands or only a poor knight's patch. Such distinctions meant nothing to that army. Madness had laid hold of them. They held the *type* wicked, not the person."

"How came she to escape? Tell me the mob did not . . . !" Joachim had gone white and his lips and fingers trembled.

"There was a man among them," Dietrich remembered, "who had opened his eyes and was desperate to escape their company. Yet he had been, even so, a leader, and could not slip away unremarked. So he asked for the girl as if he would bed her. The uprising had collapsed by then. They were dead men walking, and so without the law, for what greater penalty could be heaped upon them? The others thought he had only taken the child to some private place. By morn, he was many leagues distant." Dietrich rubbed his arms. "It was through this wicked man that the girl came to me, and I brought her here where the madness had never touched and she could know a little peace."

"God bless that man," Joachim said, crossing himself.

Dietrich turned on him. "God bless him?" he shouted. "He slew men and urged others to slaughter. God's blessing was far from him."

"No," the monk insisted quietly. "It was always there beside him. He had only to accept it."

For a moment, Dietrich did not speak. "It is hard to forgive such a man," he said at last, "whatever kindness moved him at the end."

"Hard for men, perhaps," Joachim retorted, "but not for God. What befell him afterward? Did the Elsass Duke take him?"

Dietrich shook his head. "No man has heard his name in twelve years."

THE INTERVAL between the Vigil-Night and the Epiphany was the longest holiday of the year. The villagers paid extra dues to stock the lord's banquet table, but were exempt from all hand-service, and so a festive spirit came over all. A spruce tree was again erected on the green and hung about with flags and ornaments, and even the meanest cottage did not lack for its dress of holly, fir, or *mistel.*

But the merrymaking did not extend to the Krenken. A too-literal translation of *advent* into the Krenkish tongue had led the stranded travelers to expect the actual arrival of the much-heralded "lord from the sky," so their disappointment was keen. While he was pleased that the strangers had looked forward to the Kingdom of Heaven, Dietrich cautioned Hans against naive literalism. "Since thirteen hundred years the Christ is ascended," Dietrich explained after the Mass for St. Sebastian, while Hans helped him clean the sacred vessels. "His disciples, too, thought he soon would return, but they were mistaken."

"Perhaps they were confused by the pressing of time," Hans suggested.

"What! Can time then be pressed like grapes?" Dietrich was both startled and amused, and smacked his lips in Krenk-like laughter while he placed his chalice in its cupboard and locked it. "If time may be 'pressed,' then it is a being on which one may act, and *being* consists of subject and aspect. A thing that is movable alters in its aspect, for it is *here,* then it is *there*; it is *this,* then it is *that.*" Dietrich wagged his hand back and forth. "Of motions, there are four: change of substance, as when a log becomes ash; change of quality, as when an apple ripens from green to red; change of quantity, as when a body grows or diminishes; and change of place, which we call 'local motion.' Obviously, for time to be 'pressed'—here *long,* there *short*—there must be a *motion* of time. But time is the *measure* of motion in changeable things and cannot measure itself."

Hans disagreed. "Spirit travels so fast as the motion of light when there is no air. At such speeds, time passes more quickly, and what is an eye-blink for the Christ-spirit is for you many years. So your thirteen hundred years may seem to him only a few days. We call that the pressing of time."

Dietrich considered the proposition for a moment. "I admit two sorts of duration: *tempus* for the sublunar realm and *aeternia* for the heavens. But eternity is not time, nor is time a portion of eternity—for there cannot be time without change, which requires a beginning and an end, and eternity has neither. Furthermore, motion is an attribute of changeable beings, while light is an attribute of fire. But one attribute cannot inform another, for then the second attribute must be an entity and we must not multiply entities without necessity. Thus, light cannot have motion."

Hans ground his forearms together. "But light *is* an entity. It is a wave, like the ripples on the millpond."

Dietrich laughed at the Krenk's witticism. "A ripple in the water is not an *entity,* but an attribute of water that results from a breeze, or a fish, or a stone thrown into it. What is the medium in which light 'ripples'?"

Hans said, "There is no medium. Our philosophers have shown that . . ."

"Can there be a ripple without water?" Dietrich laughed again.

"Very well," Hans said. "It is only *like* a ripple, but is composed of . . . very small bodies."

"Corpuscles," Dietrich supplied the word. "But if light were composed of corpuscles—a different proposition from being a 'ripple in no medium'—those bodies would impress themselves upon our sense of touch."

Hans made the tossing gesture. "One cannot argue with such reasoning." He rubbed his forearms together slowly but, as the rasps were muffled by the fur, he made no sound. "When the *Heinzelmännchen* oversets 'motion' or 'spirit,' " he said at length, "the Krenkish terms I hear may differ from the German terms you spoke. By me, the falling rock is in 'motion,' but not the burning log. When I say that by pressing a certain type on the talking head, I release spirit from the fires of the storage barrels and so animate the matter, I know what I have said, but not what you have heard. Have you finished your up-cleaning? Good. Let us to the fire in the parsonage. Here is by me too cold."

They proceeded to the vestibule, and while Dietrich shrugged into his overcoat and pulled his collar close against the chill, the Krenk spoke further. "Yet you did speak a truth. Time is truly inseparable from motion—duration depends on the degree of motion—and time does have a beginning and an end. Our philosophers have concluded that time began when this world and the other world touched." Hans clapped his two hands in illustration. "That was the beginning of everything. Someday, they will again clap, and all will begin anew."

Dietrich nodded agreement. "Our world indeed began when touched by the other world; though to speak of 'clapping hands' is but a metaphor for what is pure spirit. But, to press a thing, some actor must press upon it, since no motion exists save by a mover. How might we press upon time?"

Hans opened the church door and crouched for the bounding leaps that would take him quickly through the cold to the parsonage. "Say rather," he answered cryptically, "that time presses upon us."

THE CUSTOMS of the manor required Herr Manfred to feast the villagers in the Hof during the holy days, and so he selected according to the Weistümer certain households from the manor rolls. By Oberhochwald, the customary number was twelve, to honor the Apostles. Those who, like Volkmar and Klaus, held several manses, sat beside the lord with their wives and ate and drank off the lord's own dishes. Gärtners were invited also, though these brought their own cloth, cup, and trencher.

Gunther laid out a board of cheese, beer, swine-flesh with mustard, hazel-hen, sausage and puddings, and a stew of chicken. Manfred had told Baron Grosswald to provide the meal for his own folk from his own stores. But *charitas* went against Krenkish inclinations, and most of what Gschert laid out were German foods, eked out with but a small portion of the more particular Krenkish fare. Dietrich put the meager portions down to Grosswald's innate selfishness.

During the banquet, Peter of Rheinhausen, Manfred's minnesinger, sang from the *Heroes' Book,* choosing the passage wherein King Dietrich's band of knights attack the Rose Garden of the treacherous dwarf, Laurin, so to rescue the sister of Dietlieb, their comrade. One of Peter's apprentices played a viol, while the other tapped a small tambour. After a time, Dietrich noticed that the Krenkish guests clicked their mandibles in time to the lute. It was in such small ways that their essential humanity impressed itself upon him, and he offered contrition to God that he had ever thought them mere beasts.

Afterward, the peasants could take home what leftover food they could carry in their napkins. Langermann had brought an especially large cloth for this purpose. "The Herr's table was set with the fruits of my labor," the gärtner told him when he noticed Dietrich's eye upon him, "so I am only taking back a little of what was once mine." Nickel overstated the case, since he labored as little as possible himself, but Dietrich did not begrudge him his foresight.

The servants then cleared the tables from the center of the hall to accommodate the dancing. Dietrich marked how Krenken and Hochwalders slowly separated, like oil and water after being shaken. Some, like Volkmar Bauer, avoided the creatures and favored them with stares at once angry and fearful.

Master Peter played a dance, and the Hochwalders paired off: Volkmar and Klaus with their wives, Eugen with Kunigund, and they stepped through the measures while the other guests watched from the fireside.

Manfred turned to the noble Krenken who stood by him: Grosswald, the Kratzer, and Shepherd, who was *maier* of the pilgrims. "There is a story told of a Vigil-Night dance at Schloss *Althornberg,*" he said, gesturing broadly with a wine-filled *Krautstrunk,* whose knurled surface provided a surer grip to the drinker than did smooth glass. "In the revelry, some dancers wore hollowed-out bread loaves as clogs. Well, desecration of bread brings down naturally the Divine wrath, so thunder-weather broke out. A serving wench tried to stop the dance, but Althornberg regarded the thunder as God's applause and he ordered the dancers to continue, whereat a bolt of lightning set the castle ablaze. The serving wench alone survived—and is sometimes seen to this day on the roads around Steinbis."

Dietrich countered with the story of the Convent of Titisee. "None were admitted save beautiful heiresses, who lived high on their treasure. One dark and stormy night, there fell a knock on their door during a drunken feast, and the sisters sent their newest novice to answer. Peeping out, she saw a weary old man, white of hair, who prayed lodging for the night. Not being yet corrupted, she begged Lady Abbess to grant him hospitality, but the woman only drank a toast to his health and sent him away. That night, the rain flooded the valley and all in the convent were lost, save the young novice, who was rescued by a boat rowed by the old pilgrim. And that is the origin of the Titisee."

"Makes it so?" asked Shepherd.

"Doch," Manfred added gravely. "The story may be twice tested. First, one may peer into the depths of the lake and spy the towers of the drowned convent. The other is to dive deep into the waters. For if you dive 'deeper than ever plummet sounded,' you will hear the chimes of the convent bells. But none who have done so have returned—for the Titisee is bottomless."

Later, Hans drew Dietrich aside and said, "If none have ever returned from the bottomless lake, how does one know if the bells can be heard?" But Dietrich only laughed.

"A fable is to teach a lesson," he admonished the Krenk, "not to record a history. But mark that punishment was meted for withholding charity from a stranger, and not for some ancient pagan superstition over bread-loaves."

Little Irmgard had crept from the nursery, as children were wont to do when their elders feasted; but Chlotilde, her nurse, having discovered the escape, came after her and the child ran shrieking into the room, weaving among the tall forest of legs, until, glancing behind for her pursuer, she collided with Shepherd.

The leader of the pilgrims, who had earned her name because she spent much time gathering them and chivvying them about, gazed down upon the small thing that had nearly bowled her over, and a hush fell across the room. The dancers froze in their motions. Kunigund, seeing what her sister had done, said, "Oh" in a very small voice, for everyone knew of the strangers' choleric nature.

Irmgard looked up, and then up, and her mouth dropped open. She had seen the creatures already from a distance, but this was her first close encounter. "Why . . . ," she said in delight, "it's a giant grasshopper! Can you jump?"

Shepherd cocked her head slightly as her head-harness repeated the words; then, with a slight flex of the knees she leapt toward the rafters of the hall—to Irmgard's delighted claps. At the top of her leap, Shepherd rasped her shins together, much as a man might click his heels. Before she had touched the flagstones, a second Krenk leapt also and soon several were doing so, to an arrhythmic scritching of arms and clacking of mandibles.

So, thought Dietrich, *this is what passes for dance among their kind.* Yet the leapers made no effort to move in concert, nor did the scratching and clacking follow a *tempus.*

But Irmgard's question and Shepherd's response had broken the quiet tension in the room. The Hochwalders began to smile as they watched the Krenk leap about, for Irmgard, too, had joined in the leaping with childish glee. Even Volkmar's scowl softened.

Master Peter, hunting on his lute for a tune proper to the display, settled on a French *motetus* from *The Mirror of Narcissus.* It had no effect on the Krenkish chaos, but did entice Eugen and Kunigund to resume their intricate and patterned dance. Peter sang, *Dame, je sui cilz qui vueil endurer,* and his apprentices joined in. The tambourine player took the *triplum* and sang the lover's plea—*lie with me or I die;* while the violist took the *tenor* and sang the lover's pain.

"Does it please?" Dietrich asked Hans over the private voice-canal they sometimes used with each other. "Dance is one more bond between us."

"One more barrier. This peculiar ability of yours shows only how different we are."

"Our peculiar ability?"

"I have no word for it. To accomplish one thing by doing many different things together. Each man sings now different words to different tunes, yet they blend in ways strange but pleasing to our ears. When you and your brother sang to welcome us on your Kermis, the pilgrims could speak of nothing else for days."

"You do not know harmony or counterpoint?" But even as he spoke, Dietrich realized that they could not. They were a folk who knew only rhythm, for they did not breathe in the same manner as men did, and so could not modulate a voice. With them everything was click or scratch.

Hans indicated the Krenkish leapers. "Geese without a goosehound! When the village honored the new cottages, one man hit a skin, another blew through a tube, a third squeezed air from a bladder, a fourth scraped strings with a stick. Yet all combined into a sound to which the dancers stamped their wooden shoes and slapped their leather hose—*without being directed.*"

"No one directs your folk now," Dietrich said, indicating the leapers.

"And they do not leap in . . . 'in concert,' the *Heinzelmännchen* informs me now of the word. We do not know 'concert.' Each of us is alone inside his head, with but a single thought: 'Because we die, we laugh and leap.' "

HOW LITERALLY Hans meant the proverb did not become clear until the sun warmed the snow on the Epiphany of the Lord. Dietrich was wakened by Wanda, Lorenz's wife, who dragged him down Church Hill to a hummock of snow just off the high road behind the smithy. There, a small crowd of villagers had already gathered in silence, shivering and blowing into their hands and trading uncertain glances. Lorenz said, "The alchemist is dead."

And indeed, Arnold lay on his side in a hollow dug into the snow, folded up on himself like those ancient corpses sometimes found in timeless barrows. His nakedness startled Dietrich, as the Krenken disliked the cold even when bundled in fur. In his hand, he clutched a sheet of parchment on which were scratched Krenkish word-signs.

"Wanda saw the foot protruding from the snowbank," Lorenz said, "and we dug him out with our bare hands." He held out his palms, red and raw, as if Dietrich might doubt his word and ask for proof. Wanda wiped her dripping nose and looked away from the body. Gregor said, "He was gone when I awoke."

Seppl Bauer smirked. "One demon less to vex us."

Dietrich turned and cuffed him smartly. "Can demons die?" he cried. "Who has done this?" He looked from one to another of the small crowd. "Which of you killed this man?"

He received denials on all sides and Seppl rubbed his ear and glowered. "*Man?*" he cried under his breath. "Where is his 'crowing rooster'? He sports no manhood." And indeed, the creature proved more featureless than a eunuch.

Lorenz said, "I think he burrowed into the snow and the cold took him."

Dietrich studied how the body lay and admitted that there was none of the pungent ichor that served the visitors for blood, no evidence of bruises. He recalled that Arnold was especially melancholic even among the Krenken, and given to solitude. "Has anyone summoned Baron Grosswald from the Hof? No? You, Seppl, go now. Yes, *you.* Bring Max, too. Someone tell Klaus." Dietrich turned away to find that Fra Joachim had come down from the parsonage to gaze upon the corpse with dismay.

"He was my best catechumen," the monk said, dropping to his knees in the snow. "I thought he would be the first to come over to us."

"And what demon," said Volkmar Bauer gravely, "could live with that?"

Hans and the Kratzer had come with Joachim. The philosopher stood in frozen regard of his friend's body, but Hans stepped forward and pulled the parchment from the alchemist's grasp.

"What does it say?" Dietrich asked, but he may as well have asked the carving of St. Catherine, for Hans did not move for a long time.

Hans at last passed the parchment to the Kratzer. "It is part of your prayer," he said. " 'This is my body. Whoever eats it shall live.' "

At this evidence of piety, brother Joachim wept openly and ever after, he would name Arnold in the *Meménto étiam* of the Mass.

Both Hans and the Kratzer remained silent.

· XIII ·

JANUARY, 1348
Rock Monday

THE MONDAY after Epiphany—called Skirt Monday by the women, Plow Monday by the men—marked the end of the Christmas holy days. In most years, the men of the village contended in races to see who could plow a furlong the fastest but, with the ground snowcapped, the races were not held. But Skirt Monday went forward, and the women of Oberhochwald gleefully seized the men captive and held them for ransom. The name of the revel was a pun, for *skirt* and *revenge* sounded much the same on German tounges.

Dietrich tried, with little success, to explain the festivity to Hans and the other Krenken; but the delight of reversal escaped those bound to their estate by instinct. When Dietrich explained that on All Fools Day a gärtner would be chosen to rule as Herr for a day, they regarded him with incomprehension—and not a little horror.

Wanda Schmidt captured Klaus Müller and held him in her husband's smithy to await a ransom that proved long in coming. Some said that it was a good match, for the miller and the smith's wife were of a size and nearly of an equal strength. "Upper and nether millstone," Lorenz joked as he was led away by Ulrike Bauer. "They'd grind away the likes of me between them." The men of the village, for their part, sought capture by Hildegarde Müller. The miller's wife, however, demanded only a donation toward the relief of the destitute. Trude Metzger took away Nickel Langermann—to the amusement of all, for no one had forgotten that she had paid *merchet* on herself.

A fight broke out when Anna Kohlmann captured Bertram Unterbaum. Oliver Becker, who thought himself entitled to that fate, knocked Bertram to the ground and bloodied his nose. But instead of running to the victor, as Oliver had no doubt imagined, Anna ran to the prostrate lad and cradled his head in her lap, earning herself years in Purgatory by the names she called the baker's son. Oliver turned pale and fled from her tongue, some said with tears of his own.

Later, when Jakob and Bertha could not find their son to fire the oven, they found that both he and his meager belongings had vanished, and Jakob cursed the young man as a *bummer*.

Dietrich feared that the lad would carry tales of the Krenken to Freiburg, but Manfred refused to pursue him. "In *that* cold, through *those* drifts? No, he was a fool to run off, and likely a dead fool ere long."

At that rebuke, Dietrich knelt in church for three evenings thereafter, chastising himself that he had worried over his own safety, and not that of the distraught young man.

AT TIERCE, on the commemoration of Priscilla of the Catacombs, the Kratzer summoned Dietrich and Lorenz to meet in Manfred's hall with Hans and a third Krenk whom Dietrich did not know, and from whose girdle depended many curious tools. The Krenken spread across the banquet table parchments richly illuminated with intricate figures; though for all their fine precision, the execution was poor, lacking both the color and brilliance of French work and the wild exuberance of the Irish. Vines lay at precise angles and bore curiously geometric fruit: circles and squares and triangles, some with writing. Joachim, he thought, even with his indifferent draughting hand, could easily execute a more pleasing illumination.

"This drawing," Hans explained, "is a . . . What do you call it when something goes forth and comes back to its starting place?"

"A circuit, as when Everard makes a circuit of the Herr's estate."

"Many thank. This circuit helps move our cog through the inward-curling directions to the other world. Or so the 'servant of the essence' has said." By this, he indicated the third Krenk, who bore the name Gottfried. "His more cunning devices were ruined in the shipwreck and cannot be repaired, but this primitive one may serve in their stead. The essence runs from this point, the *mover,* out and back through a lattice of copper wires, and so animates our machines. This essence is contained in . . . storage barrels, but these barrels grow ever more depleted from lack of the generative power. This may restore them."

Dietrich stared at the illumination. "This device will speed your departure?"

Hans did not turn his head. "It may not serve," he admitted, "but it must be tried or we will be 'saved by the alchemist'." At this, the Kratzer scissored his mandibles sharply and the servant of the essence stiffened. Hans bent over the "circuit." Dietrich had noticed how the alchemist's suicide had affected his strange guests. They had become more subdued, but also snapped frequently at one another.

"Is the essence that runs through the copper," Dietrich wondered aloud, "an earth, water, air, or fire?"

Hans said nothing, so the Kratzer answered. "We call those the . . . 'four seemings of a material.' Fire, I suppose. It can burn."

"That is because fire atoms are tetrahedral, with many sharp points. It must move very fast, that being an attribute of fire."

Hans, who had been "reading the circuit," raised his head from the illuminated manuscript at that and parted his soft lips in the Krenkish smile. "Yes, very fast indeed."

"Fire seeks always its natural position, to move upward to the fourth sublunar sphere."

"Well, this sort of fire seeks a lower position," Hans said. "Or 'potency,' I think you say."

"Then it must partake also of water, which moves toward a lower sphere—though fire and water, being contrary, do not easily mix. So, your fire-water must then flow through the copper channels as water flows through mill races and moves Klaus's mill wheel from potency to act. Do these fruits on your vines signify machines? Ja? But to move a machine needs a strong current. The height of the dam is of great importance, since the greater the drop, the greater the work performed."

"The potential drop in this circuit is very great," said Gottfried, the servant of the essence, "as is the current. We have secured the remainder of the ingot left with the Freiburg smith. It will not encompass *all* repairs, but will suffice to build this device."

"What?" said Dietrich. "That was to be the man's payment!"

Hans tossed his arm. "Our need is greater. The 'bug' that traveled with you told us where his shop stood. We flew down at night and retrieved it."

"But that is theft!"

"That is survival. Are goods not distributed according to need, as you read from your book?"

"Distributed, not taken. Hans, the natural arrogance of your people has led you from the Way. You see a thing and, if you want it and you have the power, you take it."

"If we remain here, we die. Since life is the greatest good, it requires the greatest effort; so to work toward our escape cannot be called inordinate."

Dietrich started. "But life is only the greatest of *corruptible* goods, so it is not the greatest good of all, which we call God. To desire what another possesses is to love yourself *more* than you love the other, and that is contrary to *charitas.*"

But Hans only tossed his arm. "Joachim has sketched you accurately." Then he turned to the smith. "Lorenz, can you draw copper finely enough?"

"Copper wants a colder fire than iron," Lorenz said, "and then it is only a matter of piercing dies of the proper size." He grinned at the expressionless Krenk. "No worry. I will start work once Venus is ascendant."

"Venus . . ." Hans cocked his arm in a gesture indicating uncertainty.

"That planet is favorable for copper-working," the smith answered to the Krenken's evident puzzlement. "Since copper came first from Cyprus," he added helpfully.

Manfred gave his grace to the enterprise with marked reluctance, not because he expected little success but because he feared too much. "If this cog of theirs is restored," he confided to Dietrich afterward, "the Krenken will steal away, for I doubt Grosswald understands an oath of fealty. When it suits his convenience, he will discard it without a qualm."

"Being in this very different from mankind," Dietrich said.

AND SO Lorenz drew the ingot into wire, and Gottfried arranged it on a board that mimicked the pattern on the "circuit" drawing. When his magic wand touched a spool of dull gray metal, *the metal flowed* and dripped upon wire and pin alike, turning instantly solid once more and binding the one to the other. Metalworkers used such "plumbing-metal," but needed fire to make it flow, and Dietrich saw no sign of a fire. The wand, when Gottfried allowed him to touch it, was not even warm.

The work required a jeweler's touch and, when something had not been done precisely right, Gottfried would cuff his apprentices or engage in a scuffle with Hans. Even among Krenken, Gottfried was noted for his choler.

The Krenk worried over the "unclothed" nature of the wire, but his meaning remained occult, as no German word signified the clothing. When the "circuit" was ready at last, Gottfried tested it with a device he wore on his belt and—after much discussion with Hans, the Kratzer, and Baron Grosswald—pronounced himself satisfied.

THE NEXT day, an indifferent snowfall littered the still air. The party gathered in the Burg courtyard. Gottfried, bundled in furs, strapped a flying harness on, from which hung in a protective sack the device he had built. His much-abused apprentice, Wittich, would carry Lorenz to the ship in a sling. The smith had begged the boon of watching; and Baron Grosswald, at Herr Manfred's urging, had consented.

Dietrich prayed a blessing on their efforts, and Lorenz knelt upon the icy flagstones and drew the sign of the cross over his body. Before climbing the tower from which the fliers would depart, the smith embraced Dietrich and gave him the kiss of peace. "Pray for me," he said.

"Close your eyes until you are again on solid land."

"I don't fear height, but failure. I'm no copper-smith. The draw is not so fine and regular as Gottfried had asked."

Dietrich remained at the base of the tower while the others climbed the narrow, spiral stairs to the top. Just around the bend of the spiral, the two Krenken tripped on the stumbling blocks. Hans, who had stayed behind with Dietrich, commented on the mason's evident lack of skill.

"But no," Dietrich said. "The stumble-steps are so attackers climbing the tower 'trip up.' The stairs spiral right-handwise for similar reason. Invaders cannot wield their swords; while the defenders, fighting downward, have a full swing."

Hans shook his head, a gesture he had acquired from his hosts. "Your ineptness proves always cunning." He pointed skyward, though without tilting his head back. "They go."

Dietrich watched the fliers until they had become dark specks. The sentries on the walls pointed, too, but they had seen such flights now many times and the novelty of the feat had begun to fade. They had seen even Max Schweitzer fly, though with indifferent success.

"Blitzl has no little optimism," Hans said.

"Who is Blitzl?"

Hans pointed toward the fliers as they vanished into the woodland. "Gottfried. We call those who follow his craft 'Little Lightnings.' During thunder-weather great bolts of the fiery fluid cross our sky, and Gottfried works with smaller versions of the same spirit."

"The *elektronikos*!"

A Krenk's face could not show astonishment. "You know of it? But you said nothing!"

"I deduced its likelihood from philosophic principles. When your cog failed, a great wave of *elektronikos* washed across the village, creating no small havoc."

"Give thanks then that it was but a ripple," Hans told him.

IT WAS difficult to reconstruct afterward what had happened. Gottfried was in another apartment of the vessel and did not see. Perhaps Wittich had spied a loose wire and sought to adjust it. But while he handled the unclothed wire, Gottfried opened the sluice gate, allowing the *elektronikos* to pour through the channels—and through Wittich, seeking, as fluids did, the lowest ground.

"Lorenz siezed Wittich's arm to pull him away," Gottfried told Manfred's inquest afterward, "and the fluid coursed through him as well."

Like old Pforzheim, Dietrich thought. *And Holzbrenner and his apprentice.* Only stronger, as if a torrent had washed the man away. *Man's days are like grass,* he thought, *the wind blows over him and he is no more.*

"The man Lorenz did not know what would befall when he touched Wittich?" Grosswald asked. He sat by Manfred and Thierry on the judge's bench since the affair involved his folk.

Gottfried said, "He saw that Wittich was in pain."

"But *you* knew," Grosswald insisted.

The servant of the essence made the tossing motion and all could see the burns on his hands. "I moved too late."

Baron Grosswald ground his forearms slowly together. "That was not why I asked."

AFTER LORENZ'S poor burned body had been laid to rest, and Dietrich had given Wanda what comfort he could, Gregor came to the parsonage to offer his own condolences, "since the two of you were so close."

"He was a pleasant and gentle man," Dietrich said, "good to talk to and always with the air of more left unsaid. A friendship is shallow, I think, if everything between two men can be said. I'm sure there were things he wished to tell me, but there was always time for them later. Now, there is no 'later.' But Wanda's grief must be the harder."

Gregor shrugged. "She liked him well enough, but they lived as brother and sister."

"So! I hadn't known. Well, Paul commended such a life in his letters."

"Oh, she took no vow of celibacy, not so long as Klaus Müller could visit. As for Lorenz, he seemed disinclined, Wanda being *Walküre* enough to daunt any man's ardor."

"Klaus Müller and the Frau Schmidt!"

Gregor smiled knowingly. "Why not? What joy does Hilde bring to the miller's bed?"

Dietrich could not contain his astonishment. While Hildegarde Müller's wantonness was well known, he had not expected the same of Wanda, a woman by no means comely. He remembered how, on Rock Monday, Lorenz had compared his wife and Klaus to the upper and nether millstones. Had the smith known of, and perhaps tolerated, his wife's infidelity?

Fra Joachim came breathless to the door. "You are needed in the church, pastor!"

Alarmed, Dietrich stood. "What's wrong?"

"Gottfried Krenk." The young man's cheeks, red from the cold, glowed on his pale face. The dark eyes flashed. "Oh, surely, no name was more wonderfully chosen! He has embraced Jesus, and we need you to perform the baptism."

GOTTFRIED AWAITED by the baptistery, but Dietrich took him first into the sacristy and spoke to him alone. "Why do you choose baptism, friend grasshopper?" he demanded. No sacrament could be valid if its meaning was not understood. Baptism was a matter of will, not water.

"Because of Lorenz the Smith." Gottfried rubbed his forearms slowly, a gesture which Dietrich had concluded meant thoughtfulness, although the precise rhythm of the rasps might indicate irritation, confusion, or other sorts of thought. "Lorenz was an artisan, as am I," Gottfried said. "A man of low besitting, to be used as those above him would. 'In justice do the strong command; in justice do the weak submit.' "

"So the Athenians told the Melians," Dietrich said. "But I think our word 'justice' and yours do not signify the same thing. Manfred cannot use us as the Baron Grosswald uses you. He is limited by the customs and bylaws of the manor."

"How can this be," the Krenk asked, "if justice is the lord's will?"

"Because there is a Lord above all. Manfred is our lord only 'under God,' meaning that his will is subordinate to the higher justice of God. We may not obey a bad lord, nor follow an unlawful command."

Gottfried grasped Dietrich's arm, and Dietrich tried not to flinch from the horny touch. "That is the very thing! Your Herrenfolk have obligations to their vassals, ours do not. Lorenz used his own life to save Wittich, and Wittich was only a . . . One who labors at whatever is needful, but without the special skills of an artisan."

"A gärtner. But if Lorenz saw that Wittich was in pain, naturally, he tried to help."

"But it is not among us natural for the greater to help the lesser. An artisan would not help a mere gärtner; not without . . . Without your *charitas* to move him."

"To be fair," Dietrich said, "Lorenz did not know his life would be forfeit."

"He knew," Gottfried said, releasing his grip. "He knew. I had warned him against touching the wires when they were animate. I told him the fluid could strike a man like lightning. That was how he knew Wittich's peril. Yet he had no thought to stand by and watch him die."

Dietrich studied the Krenk. "Nor had you," he said after a moment.

Gottfried tossed his arm. "I am Krenk. Could I do less than one of you?"

"Let me see your hands again." Dietrich took Gottfried by the wrists and turned his hands up. The Krenkish hand was not like a man's hand. All six fingers could act as thumbs and they were long compared to the palm, which consequently appeared no bigger than a *Thaler* gold-piece. The passage of the fiery fluid had left a burn on each palm, which the Krenkish physician had treated with an unguent of some sort.

Gottfried pulled his hands away and snapped his side-lips. "You doubt my words?"

"No," said Dietrich. The black marks had seemed much like the stigmata. "Have you the love of God in your heart?" he asked abruptly.

Gottfried imitated the human nod. "If I show in my actions this next-love, then I have it inside my head, not true?"

" 'By their fruits you shall know them,' " Dietrich quoted, thinking of both Lorenz and Gottfried. "Do you reject Satan and all his works?"

"What is then this 'satan'?"

"The Great Tempter. The one who always whispers to us the love of self rather than the love of others, and so doing seeks to turn us from the good."

Gottfried listened while the *Heinzelmännchen* translated. "If when I am beaten," he suggested, "I speak inside my head—think—of beating another. If when something of mine is taken, I think to take from another to replace it. If when I take pleasure, I do not ask the other's consent. Is this what you mean?"

"Yes. Those sentences are spoken by Satan. We seek always the good, but never may we use evil means to achieve it. When others do evil to us, we must not respond with further evil."

"Those are hard words, especially for the likes of *him.*"

All voices spoken through the *Heinzelmännchen* sounded alike, but Dietrich turned, and saw in the doorway Hans. "Hard, indeed," Dietrich told the servant of the talking head. "So hard that no man can hope to follow. Our spirits are weak. We succumb to the temptation to return evil for evil, to seek our own good at the expense of others, to *use other men* as means to our own ends. That is why we need the strength—the grace—of our Lord Jesus Christ. The burden of such sinfulness is too great for us to carry alone, and so He walks by our side, as Simon the Cyrenian once walked beside Him."

"And Blitzl—Gottfried—will follow this way? A Krenk well known as a brawler?"

"I will," said Gottfried.

"Are you such a weakling, then?"

Gottfried exposed his neck. "I am."

Hans's horn lips spread wide and his soft lips fell open. "*You* say so?" But Gottfried rose and strode to the sacristy door, passing close by Hans to emerge on the altar. Dietrich looked at his friend. "He will need your prayers, Hans."

"He will need one of your miracles."

Dietrich nodded. "We all do." Then he followed Gottfried to the baptistery.

"Baptism," he told the Krenk beside the copper basin, "is the washing away of sin, just as ordinary water washes away dirt. One emerges from the water born again as a new man, and a new man needs a new name. You must choose a Christian name from among the roll of saints who have preceeded us. 'Gottfried' is itself a good name—"

"I would be called 'Lorenz'."

Dietrich hesitated at the sudden pain in his heart. "Ja. Doch."

Hans laid his hand on Dietrich's shoulder. "And I would be called 'Dietrich'."

Gregor Mauer grinned. "May I be called godfather?"

· 5 ·

NOW
Sharon

DURING THE Middle Ages, they used to burn heretics.

Now, it was never so many or so often as has been supposed. There were rules, and most of the penalties were acquittals, pilgrimages, or other impositions. If you wanted to burn, you really had to work at it; and it may say something about human nature that so many did.

Sharon did not know she was a heretic until she whiffed the smoke.

Her department head lit the first faggot. He asked her if it were true that she was investigating Variable Light Speed theories and she, with the innocence and enthusiasm of anyone filled with the holy spirit of scientific inquiry, said, "Yes, it seems to resolve a number of problems."

Now, she meant the cosmological problems: flatness, the horizon, lambda. Why the universe is so finely tuned. But the department head—his name was Jackson Welles—was dead to the spirit and was justified by the law—the law in this case being the constancy of the speed of light. Einstein said it, he believed it, and that settled it. So he had intended a completely different set of problems. "Like Noah's flood, I suppose."

The sarcasm surprised Sharon a great deal. It was as if she had been talking about auto mechanics and he had responded with a jibe about pinochle. It didn't process right away and because thought in her always induced reflection, Welles took this to mean that his arrow had sunk home, and he leaned back in his chair with his hands interlaced over his stomach. He was a lean man, hardened by treadmills, universal machines, and academic politics. He dyed his hair with great art, maintaining enough gray to suggest wisdom, but not so much as to suggest age.

They were sitting in his office, and it struck Sharon how spare the office was. Twice the girth and depth of her own, it contained only half the clutter. Textbooks, shelved and looking new, journals, photographs and certificates, all forbidding in their orderly ranks. His chalkboard held not equations or diagrams, but budgets and schedules.

It was not that Welles did not think, but that he thought about things beside physics. Budgets, grants, tenure, promotions, the administration of the department. Someone must think of such things. Science doesn't just *happen.* It's a human activity, performed by human beings, and every circus needs a ringmaster. Once, a very long time ago, a younger Welles had written three papers of exceptional merit deriving quantum mechanics from Maxwell's equations, the consequences of which were still emitting doctoral dissertations around the world; so don't think he was a *Krawattendjango*—a "tie dude," as our kids say in Germany. It is not given many men to write even one such paper. Perhaps a longing for those heady days, and an understanding that a fourth was not in him, informed his attitude.

"I'm sorry," said Sharon. "But what has VLS to do with Noah's Ark?" Even then, she thought that maybe it was some abstruse joke on the head's part. He did have a deadpan sense of humor, and Sharon was more accustomed to clowns.

"Do you really think you can prove young earth creationism?"

Perhaps it was the earnest expression on his face. The grim-set line of his mouth. Inquisitors may have had such an expression when they relaxed their charges to the mercy of the secular arm. But Sharon finally realized that he was serious.

"What," she asked, "is young earth creationism?"

The department head did not credit such innocence. He thought everyone as attuned as he to the vagaries of legislatures, school boards, and other such sources of madness. "That God created the universe only six thousand years ago? Tell me you never heard about that."

Sharon knew how Tom would have answered, and fought hard to keep his words from her lips, saying instead, "Now that you mention it, I have heard that." She really had needed the reminder. She spent most of her waking hours in Janatpour space. There were no creationists there, young or otherwise. It would have confused them and they would have gotten lost along one of those nameless dimensions of hers.

" 'Now that you mention it,' " Welles mimicked. His sarcasm was famous in the higher reaches of the school's management. Deans fled at his approach. "There is nothing so well established as the constancy of light speed."

It was the wrong thing to say, not only because there really were several other things better established, but because there is nothing guaranteed to get the back up of a no-fooling scientist than *argument from authority*. Neither Welles nor Sharon had been raised religiously and so neither of them realized that they were having a religious argument, but something atavistic rebelled in Sharon's heart. "That's the current paradigm," she said. "But a more careful inspection of the data—"

"You mean until you can *spin* the data to prove what you want!" Welles said this with no sense of irony. Kuhn may have been a poor philosopher, but he was right about the cold, dead hand of the Paradigm. "I researched it myself when I heard what you were up to, and there has been no change in the measured speed of light for several decades." He leaned back in his chair and linked his hands again under his breastbone, taking her silence as acknowledgement of the devastating impact of his rebuttal.

"Excuse me," Sharon said with only a minor tremor in her voice. "A couple of decades? That's like measuring continental drift for a few hours. Try a couple of centuries, like I did. You need a long enough baseline to—" And here her thoughts slip-slid away in an unexpected direction as her memory pulled a factoid from the hat. She examined the factoid top to botton, side to side, and around and around. Welles's eyebrows rose at the sudden silence. It was so sudden and so silent that his ears hurt. But when he opened his mouth, she raised a hand to him. "Did you know that when Birge reported the decrease in light speed in *Nature* in 1934, he'd found no change whatsoever in wavelength?"

Welles, who hadn't known the first, was equally in the dark on the second. "You mean when he reported an error in his measurement . . ."

"No, wait," she told him, "this is really interesting." She had forgotten that she was on the carpet in her department chairman's office. She had found a glittering nugget in the ore and wanted to show it to everyone, supposing they would be as delighted as she was. "Think it through, Jackson. Light speed is frequency times wavelength. So if c is dropping and wavelength is constant, frequencies must be increasing."

"So . . . ?" Welles drew the question out. He was no ignoramus. He saw suddenly where Sharon's thoughts were headed.

"So," she said, her excitement building, "atomic frequencies govern the rate at which atomic clocks tick. Of course, the speed of light has been constant since they began using atomic clocks to measure it. The instrument is calibrated to the thing it's measuring! Oh, my gosh!" She saw the chasm gaping before her; but unlike Welles, who would not step up to the lip, she leapt right into it. "Oh, my gosh! Planck's constant isn't!"

That is the way of it among heretics. They start questioning one doctrine and end up questioning everything. No wonder they used to burn them.

That grinding sound Welles heard was a paradigm shifting. But the gears were rusty. "Dr. Nagy," he said with heavy formality. "You have tenure, and there is nothing I can do about that. But if I were you, I would not be surprised if your grant were not renewed next semester."

There was the warning from the tribunal. Repent of your heterodoxy or be damned. But Sharon Nagy was on the scent of something very peculiar, and Jackson Welles knew nothing of Évariste Galois. Facing a duel at dawn, Galois had spent his last night on earth scribbling the foundations of algebraic group theory. A good night's sleep, and he might have survived the duel; but there is a certain frame of mind that prizes discovery over life itself. If death had not daunted young Évariste, what terror had loss of funding over Sharon? She was not as young as he had been, but she knew how to take a bullet.

IT WAS late when she left the university grounds. The semester had started and she had papers to grade and discussion notes to prepare. It was one of those schools that put great store in teaching and even its most prestigious scholars were required in the trenches. She held two graduate seminars and taught an upper division course in galactic structure that was well-subscribed, though her students thought her a cold fish. On a Monday she was likely to resume precisely where she had left off the previous Friday, and sometimes that meant *in media res,* while her students, bleary from weekend partying, squinted at the whiteboards and the projections from her computer, trying to remember from where the derivation had started.

It was during her preparation for the galactic structure class that she noted a further anomaly.

"Hernando," she asked the young post-doc who worked with her. "Why should cars all drive down a highway at speeds in multiples of five?"

Hernando Kelly was from Costa Rica, a "tico," as they call themselves. He was bronze, distressingly well-built, and climbed sheer rock faces for recreation. With his arm in a sling—sometimes the rock faces win—Sharon had put him to work mining databases and compiling the results. He scratched his head and tried to imagine what the question had really been about. "At multiples of five," he said, hinting for clarification.

"Right. The cars are going fifty, fifty-five, sixty, sixty-five, and so on."

"You haven't reached the speeds on the Blue Route yet." White teeth showed beneath a black moustache. "So nobody's going like sixty-two or fifty-seven or something?" At Sharon's nod, he shook his head. "Okay, I'll bite. Why?"

"I don't know," she answered happily. "I thought you knew because you were the one who told me." She held up a frequency distribution, one of several dozen he had printed off of Minitab from the "galactic empire" database. "Distribution of Galactic Redshifts," read the title above the chart. "Notice anything?"

"Well, yeah. It's comb-shaped. That means the measurement resolution is coarser than the plotting scale so you get empty bins in the histogram. I'll rescale the chart."

"Measurement resolution," she said.

"Right . . ." he said, a bit wary, for he recognized the manic tone in her voice.

"Unh-unh," she answered. "Quantized. Redshifts are quantized. Galaxies are receeding at certain speeds, and not at speeds in between."

"Why?"

"I don't know," she enthused. "That would only be an answer, and I've got something much more precious. I've got a question."

Kelly didn't see the big deal. It was like the light speed business. That had been a real bitch, because not all the literature was of equal quality. Some reports lacked the original data, some reworked previous data, some were duplicates. In some, the measurement method had been poor or the techniques for using it had not yet been perfected. Just compile all the data, the Ice Queen had told him. Oh, yeah, nothing easier.

It was all measurement error, he was convinced. Light speeds, now red shifts. He had seen "comb-shaped" histograms when he had worked summers at a metal fabricator in San Jose. The gauge had read out in increments of 0.002' and the plotting scale had increments of 0.001'. Odd numbers need not apply. He hoped the rumor wasn't true and Dr. Nagy wouldn't lose her grant because of her religious obsession. He liked working with the Ice Queen.

IT WAS a few weeks later that Sharon saw the answer, and it was a stunner.

· XIV ·

FEBRUARY, 1348
Candlemas to the Ember Days

CANDLEMAS DAY was a work holiday. At primes, the villagers gathered on the green and Joachim distributed candles to all, including the two baptized Krenken. The other Krenken stayed to themselves or watched from the edge of the green with *fotografic* devices. Dietrich blessed the candles while Joachim sang the *Nunc dimittis.* When all was ready, they formed up in procession. Klaus and Hildegarde took their accustomed places immediately behind Dietrich, reminding Dietrich irresistibly of the parable about those who would be first.

Chanting the anthem, *Adórna thálamum tuum, Sion,* Dietrich led the river of light through the early dawn, along the high street and up the hill toward St. Catherine, where he spied Theresia kneeling in the damp grass beside the church. But as the procession drew nearer, she stood and ran off. Dietrich's tongue stumbled and nearly lost its place in the anthem, but he sang the line *obtulérunt pro eo Dómino* as he passed through the church doors, as was customary.

LATER THAT day, a faint yodel from the watch tower on the Oberreid Road announced the approach of a horseman. The Krenken hid themselves at Manfred's request and did not emerge until the horseman, a messenger from the Strassburg bishop, departed on a fresh horse an hour later.

Berthold had summoned the lords of the Elsass and the Breisgau to meet at Benfeld on the eighth and discuss unrest in the Swiss. "I will be gone a week or more," Manfred told the *ministeriales* summoned to his hall. "Too many lords will attend to hope for anything shorter." Naming Ritter Thierry burgvogt in his absence, and dispatching Bertram Unterbaum to the Swiss to bring back a report, Manfred and his retinue departed the next day.

Rumors swirled in his wake. It was said that Berne had put some Jews on the pyre in November over the well-poisonings, and had written to the Imperial Cities to urge the same action on them. Strassburg and Freiburg had done nothing; but in Basel, the people rioted and, although the council banished the most notorious Jew-baiters from the city, they compelled the council to place the Jews in protective custody on an island in the Rhine.

Dietrich complained to those who had gathered at Walpurga Honig's cottage to drink her honey-wheat beer. "The Pope commands we respect the persons and property of the Jews. There was no cause for such treatment. *The pest never reached the Swiss.* It went up through France and into England."

"Perhaps," Everard suggested, "*because* Berne's swift action scared the poisoners off."

Berne actually found the poison, it was said. Everard had heard it from Gunther who had overheard the bishop's messenger. A concoction of spiders, frogs, and the skin of a basilisk had been sewn into thin leather bags that Rabbi Peyret of Chambery gave to the silk merchant Agimet to drop into wells in Venice and Italy. Had he not been captured on his return, he might have done the same in the Swiss.

Dietrich protested. "His Holiness wrote that the Jews cannot be spreading the pest *for they themselves die.*"

Everard tapped a finger aside his nose. "But not so many of them as of us, eh? Why do you suppose that is? Because they bob up and down while they pray? Because every Friday they air their bedding out? Pfaugh. Besides, the Kabbalists despise their fellow Jews as much as they do us. They're as secretive as masons and won't allow other Jews to study the hidden writings."

And "hidden writings" might be anything. Devil-spells. Recipes for poisons. Anything.

Klaus said, "We should place a guard around our own well."

"*Maier,*" said Gregor, "we have here no Jews."

"But we have *them.*" And Klaus pointed to Hans, who, though he drank no beer, squatted among them for the tallk. "Just yesterday I saw the one called Zachary standing by the well."

Gregor snorted. "Do you hear what you are saying, man? *Standing by the well?*"

Nothing was ever settled when men complained over steins of beer; and Hans said afterward, "I see now how a folk can worry themselves into agitation." Then, after further thought, he added, "Should they try to banish Krenken as they did Jews, I cannot answer for the outcome."

ON ST. AGATHA'S Day, Dietrich recited the Mass alone. There were the sick and lame to pray for. Walpurga Honig had suffered a kick from her mule. Gregor's older son, Karl, was laid up with a fever. And Franz Ambach had asked prayers for the repose of his mother, who had gone to her reward this past month. Dietrich asked also the intercession of St. Christopher for Bertram's safe return from Basel.

He gave thanks, again, that the pest had gone to England and not to the high woods. It was sinful to take joy from the suffering of others, but Oberhochwald's good fortune was annexed to it, and England's misfortune was in that annex that he took joy.

"*Meménto étiam, Dómine,*" he prayed, "*famulórum famularúmque tuárum Lorenz Schmidt, et Beatrix Ambach, et Arnold Krenk, qui nos praecésserunt cum signo fidei, et dórmiunt in somno pacis.*" He wondered if that were true about the Krenkish alchemist. He had certainly died with a "sign of faith" clutched in his hands, but self-murder was normally a bar to heaven. Yet God moved no tragedy but that some good might come of it, and, seeing how affected the visitors were by their companion's death, many of the Hochwalders who had before been wary or fearful of the Krenken, now greeted them openly and, if not warmly, with less marked hostility.

As he put the sacred vessels away, he thought to go by Theresia's cottage. Lately, he had invented reasons for pausing there. Yesterday, she had told him about Walpurga's leg and that she had set the bone. Dietrich had thanked her and waited for her to say more, but she had dipped her head and closed her window shutters.

She must by now know that she had been wrong about the Krenken. Recalling his own terror upon first sight, it was easy to forgive Theresia her more lingering dread. She would admit her error to him, she would return to the parsonage and do his chores, and in the evenings, before she returned to her cottage at the base of the hill, they would eat sweet-cakes together as they always had beforetimes and he would read to her from *De usu partium* or the *Hortus deliciarum.*

HE FOUND her arranging some herbs for drying by the glass light in her window. These herbs, she had grown in clay pots set on the sill. She bobbed to him as he entered, but continued cutting. "How goes it by you, daughter?" Dietrich said, and she answered, "Well," and Dietrich searched for something to say that did not sound like an admonition.

"No one attended Mass today." But that *was* an admonition, for Theresia had attended daily.

She did not look up. "Were *they* there?"

"Hans and Gottfried? No."

"Fine new communicants you have admitted."

Dietrich parted his lips to debate the point. After all, few ever attended the daily Mass. But he thought better of it and commented instead on the warming weather.

Theresia shrugged. "Frau Grundsau saw no shadow."

"Herwyg says it will be another cold year."

"Old One-eye *feels* the cold more each year."

"Do . . . Do your herbs prosper?"

"Well enough." She paused in her labor and looked up. "I pray for you each day, father."

"And I for you."

But Theresia only shook her head. "You *baptized* them."

"They desired it."

"It mocked the sacrament!"

Dietrich reached out and took her by the sleeve. "Who has been telling you such things?"

But Theresia pulled away from him and turned her back. "Please leave."

"But, I—"

"*Please leave!*"

Dietrich sighed and turned to the door. He hesitated a moment with his hand on the latch, but Theresia did not call him back, and there was nothing for it but to close the door behind him.

MANFRED RETURNED from Benfeld on Sexagesima, morose and taciturn and, when Dietrich came to the manor house, he found the Herr thoroughly drunk.

"War can be honorable," Manfred said without preamble, after Gunther had closed the door of the scriptorium and the two were closeted together. "A man puts on the cloth of war and his opponent also, and they meet on a field agreeable to both, and they use the tools of war, such as have been agreed upon, and then . . . God defend the right!" He saluted with a goblet, drank it dry, and filled it again from a flagon of neat wine. "God defend the right . . . Drink with me, Dieter!"

Dietrich accepted the cup, though he only sipped from it. "What befell at Benfeld?"

"The devil is loose. Berthold. Lacks all honor. Flies with the wind. A bishop!"

"If you would have better bishops, let the church choose them, and not kings and princes."

"Let the Pope choose, you mean? Pfaugh! There would be French spies in every court of Europe. Drink!"

Dietrich pulled a chair across from Manfred and sat. "How has Berthold driven you to this intemperance?"

"*This,*" Manfred filled his cup, "is not intemperance. It's what he's *not* done. He's lord o' Strassburg, but does he lead? A few lances would've settled things." He smacked the table with the flat of his hand. "Where is that Unterbaum boy?"

"You sent him to the Swiss to learn the true state of affairs."

"That was on St. Blaise's Day. He should be back by now. If that gof has run off—"

"He'd not run from Anna Kohlmann," Dietrich answered mildly. "Perhaps the road delays him. He took great pride in wearing the messenger's cloak. He'd not lightly throw it over."

"It makes nothing," said the Herr in a sudden swing of temperament. "Learned all 'n Benfeld. Y'know what happened in the Swiss?"

"I heard the Basler Jews were gathered up for banishment."

"Would they *had* been banished. Mob stormed th' compound an' set it afire, so . . . All died."

"Herr God in heaven!" Dietrich half-stood, crossing himself.

Manfred gave him a sour look. "I've no love for usurers, but . . . there was no charge, no trial, only th' mob run wild. Berthold asked Strassburg what *they* intended regarding the Jews, and th' councilors answered that they 'knew no evil of them.' An' then . . . Berthold asked th' bürgermeister, Peter Swaben, why he'd closed th' wells and put th' buckets away. By me, that was mere prudence, but there was great outcry against Strassburg's hypocrisy." Manfred emptied his cup again. "No man's safe when the mob runs loose, Jew or no. Wants only a grudge—as well you know."

At that reminder, Dietrich drained his own cup and it shook as he replenished it.

"Swaben an' his council stood fast," Manfred continued, "but the next morning, th' minster bells 'nounced a procession of the Cross-Brothers. Th' bishop detests them—all th' better folk do—but he daren't speak while th' vulgar favor them. They—*Drink, Dietrich, drink!* They marched two-by-two, the flagellants did, heads bowed, somber habits, cowls thrown up, bright red crosses front, back, cap. Up front, walked their Master, an' two lieutenants with banners of purple velvet and cloth of gold. All this in utter silence. Utter silence. Unnerved me, that silence did. Had they shouted or danced, I might've laughed. But that quiet awed everyone who saw, so th' only sound was th' hissing breath of two-hundred brothers. I thought it some enormous serpent, winding through th' streets. In th' minster-place, they chanted their litany, and I could think of but one thing."

"And what was that?"

"How *bad* th' poetry was! Hah! Th' cursed melody entangles m' thoughts. I need Peter Minnesinger to exorcise it. Wish I'd laughed, now. Might've broken the spell. Cathedral chapter all ran off, naturally. Two Dominicans tried to halt a procession out near Miessen an' were stoned for their troubles, so who dares oppose'm now? I was told Erfurt closed its gates against them, and Bishop Otto suppressed them in Magdeburg. An' th' tyrant of Milan erected three hundred welcoming gibbets outside the city walls, and the procession went elsewhere."

"The Italians are a subtle folk," Dietrich said.

"Hah! At least Umberto had a spine. The brothers stripped to the waist an' processed slowly in a circle 'til, at the Master's signal, the singing stopped and they threw themselves prostrate on the ground. Then they rose and whipped themselves with leather straps while the three in the center kept a *tempus,* so that th' smacking proceeded in unison. Meanwhile, th' crowd groaned and shivered and wept in sympathy."

"The brotherhoods were less quarrelsome in the beginning," Dietrich ventured. "A man required his wife's permission to join—"

"Which I suppose many were all too happy to give, hah!"

"—and provide four pence a day to support himself on the road. He made a full confession, vowed to neither bathe nor shave, nor change clothes nor sleep in a bed, and to maintain both silence and chastity regarding the other sex."

"A serious vow, then; though a hairy, malodorous one. And all for thirty-three days and eight hours, I was told." Manfred's brow creased. "Why thirty-three days and eight hours?"

"One day," Dietrich told him, "for each year of Christ's life on earth."

"Truly? Hah! I wish I'd known that. None of us could cipher it. But th' old leaders have all died or quit in disgust. Now, th' Masters claim to absolve from sin. They denounce mother Church, revile th' Eucharist, disrupt th' Mass, and drive priests from their churches before looting them. They enroll women now, and one hears that some vows are no longer held so dear." Manfred tilted his cup, swirled the remnants of his wine, and sighed. "I fear the curse of sobriety is overtaking me. . . . The flagellants heard of the council's obstinancy and ran wild through the Jewish quarter, drawing the townsmen after them. The Strassburgers rioted for two days, deposed Swaben and his council, and installed another more to their liking. In the end, the bishop, lords, and Imperial Cities agreed to expel their Jews. On Friday the thirteenth, the Strassburg Jews were taken up, and led the next day into their own cemetery into a house prepared for them. Along the way the crowd jeered and threw offal and ripped their clothes to find any concealed money, so that many were almost naked when they arrived."

"An outrage!"

Manfred stared into the dregs of his cup. "Afterward," he said. "Afterward, the house was fired, and I am told that nine hundred Jews perished. The mob looted the synagogue where they held their secret rituals, and found the horn of a ram. None knew its purpose, and it was supposed a means to signal the enemies of Strassburg."

"Oh, dear God," said Dietrich, "that was the *shofar.* To celebrate their holy days."

Manfred refilled his cup. "Perhaps you should've been there to educate them, but I don't think they were in a humor for learned discourse. Lover-God, I would gladly kill nine hundred Jews, if they came at me under arms and properly girded for war. But to burn them all . . . Women and children. . . . A man of honor *protects* women and children. Disorder cannot be tolerated! If a man is to be relaxed to the pyre or the headsman, let it be after a proper inquisition. *Men must be ruled!* That was Berthold's sin. He truckled to them when he should have sent his knights to *trample them under their hooves.* I tell you, Dietrich, this is what befalls when the low-born impose their will! Give us lords like Pedro of Aragon or Albrecht von Hapsburg!"

"Or Philip von Falkenstein?"

Manfred stabbed a forefinger at him. "Do not try me, Dietrich! Do not try me."

"What of the Jews who escaped?"

A shrug. "The Duke's man named Hapsburg land as sanctuary, so I suppose now they will all heigh for Vienna—or Poland. King Casimir was said to have extended a similar invitation. Oh, hold," Manfred said around a swallow of wine. He coughed and placed the goblet unsteady on the table. Dietrich snatched it before it could topple and spill its contents. "There's to be a war."

"A war? And you forgot until now to mention this?"

"I, am, drunk," Manfred said. "One drinks to forget. The Freiburg guilds have determined to break Falcon Rock. The Falcon has fouled his own nest. His ward, Wolfrianne, ran off and married a Freiburger tailor. Philip captured the man, and when she came below the walls to plead for his release, her jealous guardian returned him to her—headlong from the highest battlement. The tailor's guild demanded vengeance and the others will strike from solidarity."

"And how does that affect you?"

"You know my mind on Falkenstein . . . But the Duke's man promised aid to the Freiburgers. They bought their liberties from Urach with the Duke's silver, and their prosperity is now Albrecht's hope of repayment. Von Falkenstein robbed the Hapsburgs of one such payment." Manfred nodded to Dietrich as if to remind him. "He'll not lose another."

"He's called you out, then, for your knight-service."

"As Niederhochwald," Manfred said. "But I expect Markgraf Friedrich will join, too. Then . . . Hah! The lords of Oberhochwald and Niederhochwald will ride out together!" He drained his cup and turned the flagon bottoms-up to no avail. "Gunther!" he shouted, throwing the flagon against the door. "More wine!" Then, in a whisper to Dietrich, "He'll bring th' rot-gut, now he thinks I can't taste th' difference."

"So," Dietrich said. "Another war, then."

Manfred, slouching in his high seat, flipped a hand palm up. "The French war was a fancy. This one's duty. If the Rock can't be taken now—with the Freiburg guilds, the Duke, and the rest combined—then it cannot be done at all. But Baron Grosswald will not commit himself." He tossed his head toward the door and, by extension, toward the south tower, where the Krenkish guests were housed. "I bespoke him on my return, and he said he'd not hazard his sergeants against Falkenstein. What use their magical weapons, if I can't employ 'em?"

"The Krenken are few," Dietrich suggested. "Grosswald wishes to lose no more of his band than he already has. The last of their children died yesterday. Surely he will face an inquest when he has won his way home."

Manfred slapped the table. "So he trades his honor for safety?"

Dietrich turned on him in sudden fury. "Honor! Are the wars such a joy, then?"

Manfred shot to his feet and stood with his hands on the table before him, leaning a little forward. "A joy? No, never a joy, priest. At the wars, we must forever swallow our fears and expose ourselves to every peril. Moldy bread or biscuit, meat cooked or uncooked; today enough to eat and tomorrow nothing, little or no wine, water from a pond or butt; bad quarters, tent for shelter or the tree branches overhead; a bad bed, poor sleep with armor still on our backs, burdened with iron, the enemy an arrowshot away. 'Ware! Who goes there? To arms! To arms!' " Manfred gestured broadly with his empty *Krautstrunk*. "With the first drowsiness: an alarm. At dawn: a trumpet. 'To horse! To horse! Muster! Muster!' As sentinels, keeping watch by day and by night. As foragers or scouts, fighting without cover. Guard after guard, duty after duty. 'Here they come! Here! There are too many—No, not so many—News! News! This way—That—Come this side—Press them there—Go! Go!—Give no ground!—On!' " The Herr arrested his motions, suddenly aware that his voice had risen and that he had been pacing and and waving his arms wildly and Gunther stood dumbstruck in the doorway. Manfred spun back to the table and took up his cup, looked inside, and placed it back empty. "Such is our calling," he said more quietly as he fell back to his seat.

Silence lingered. Gunther replaced the wine flagon and carefully left. Then Manfred raised his head and speared Dietrich with his gaze. "But you'd know something of that, would you not?"

Dietrich turned away. "Enough."

"You've friends among the Krenken," he heard Manfred say. "Explain to them what *duty* means."

AT DAWN, those serfs who owed service as messengers donned cloaks with the Hochwald arms and bore the news to the lower valley and to the knight-fiefs. From Church Hill, Dietrich watched the horses dance along the snow-filled roads.

The snow that had lain thick all winter around the manor, a barrier keeping at bay the turmoil beyond the woods, was melting. Already tracks had been trampled through it. The men who carried messages would carry also rumors, and odd tales about Oberhochwald's guests would begin to circulate.

TWO WEEKS to the day, on the first Monday in Lent, horses pawed at the mud below the castle walls and snorted bright vapors in the cool March breeze. Colorful, snapping banners marked the knights who had mustered from their fiefs. Armsmen checked weapons and hitched their burdens for the trek into the valley. Wagons creaked; donkeys neighed; dogs barked. Children shouted with excitement or kissed fathers who waited afoot with solemn faces. Women, steadfast, refused to weep. The expected summons had arrived from the Markgraf, and the Herr of Oberhochwald was going to the wars.

Manfred's *palefridus* was raven-black and speckled over with white dots, as if lately bathed with soap. Its thick mane was parted on the left side of its neck, and its headgear splendidly decorated with the Hochwald colors. Hardly had Manfred mounted than it reared from joy, delighted at its master's weight in its saddle. Two of Manfred's hounds came running—behind the horse, ahead of it, behind it once more—leaping with excitement. They were trackers and they thought that this would be a hunt.

Manfred had covered his armor with a surcoat bearing his arms. His helm, slung behind his saddle for the journey, shimmered in the sunlight. His sword hilt was covered with gold. Around his neck he wore a strap with a horn shaped like a griffin's talon that measured nearly half an arm-length. Its thicker end flared into a bell and, where it tapered toward the tip, the device was decorated with pure gold and held in place with deerskin thongs. It was lustrous, like a precious stone, and when he blew on it, "it sounded better than all the echoes in the world."

His body servant was less splendidly mounted and, for saddle, he used an old feedbag. Over his right shoulder he carried the Herr's travel-bag, packed with the sundries of camp, and over his left, his lord's shield, slung in piggyback fashion. With the quiver also in his right hand and the spear tucked under the shield, he seemed more fearsomely armed than the man he served.

"It pleases," Manfred said to Dietrich, who stood beside the black horse in the trampled muck of dirt and melting snow. "The Duke had called on me for six-and-a-half men, and I dislike choosing which to send home early. They maneuver for the privilege, y'know, but never openly. Whoever receives the grace earns the enmity of his peers, and more often than not overstays his obligation rather than be thought cowardly. Now I can add the Duke's half-man to the Markgraf's half-man and so obtain a whole one." He threw his head back and laughed, and Dietrich mumbled some response. Manfred cocked an eye at him.

"You think a jest unseemly? What else might a man do marching toward possible death?"

"It is no light matter," Dietrich answered him.

Manfred slapped his gauntlets against the palm of his left hand. "Well, I'll pray my penance afterward, as a soldier must. Dietrich, much as I would tend my manor in peace, peace needs the consent of all, while one alone may raise a war. I swore an oath to protect the defenseless and punish peace-breakers, and that includes peace-breaking Herrenfolk. You priests say to forgive your enemy, and that is well, or revenge follows revenge until eternity. But between a man who will stop at nothing and one who will hesitate at anything, the advantage is generally to the former. The pagans had right, too. It is a false peace to be overforgiving. Your enemy may read forbearance as weakness and so be drawn to strike."

"And how do you determine the question?" Dietrich asked.

Manfred grinned. "Why, that I should fight my enemy—but fairly." He twisted in his saddle to see whether his corps was yet assembled. "Ho! Eugen, to the fore!" The junker, astride a white Wallachian, galloped past the cheering assembly with the Hochwald banner planted in his stirrup.

Kunigund ran to Eugen's horse and, having grabbed the check reins, cried, "Promise me you'll come back! Promise!" Eugen begged a kerchief from the girl to wear as a favor. This, he tucked in his girdle, declaring that it would keep him from harm. Kunigund beseeched her father. "Keep him safe, Father! You won't let anyone harm him!"

Manfred leaned to touch Kunigund on either cheek. "As safe as my arm and his honor permit, sweetling, but all lies in God's hands. Pray for him, Gundl, and for me."

His daughter ran to the chapel before any could see her weep. Manfred sighed after her. "She listens overmuch to the minnesingers, and holds all farewells as in the romances. If I should not return," he added, but the sentence dangled. Then, more quietly, "She is my life. I mean for Eugen to wed her, once he has won his spurs, and that he should protect Hochwald in her name; but should he . . . Should neither of us return . . . If that befalls, see that she weds well." He turned his gaze on Dietrich. "I entrust her to you."

"But, the Markgraf . . ."

"Graf Friedrich would keep her unwed, the longer to milk my land for his own pocket." His face clouded. "Had the boy lived, and Anna with him . . . Ach! There'd be none to gainsay that woman were *she* my burgvogt! *There* was a wife worthy of a man! Half of me died when I heard the midwife's wail. These past years have been empty."

"Is that why you went off to the French wars?" Dietrich asked. "To fill them?"

Manfred stiffened. "Mind your tongue, priest." He yanked on the bridle reins but, looking up, checked his turn. "Ho! What have we here?"

A clamor had gone up from the waiting knights and their attendants. Some in the encampment were pointing to the sky and cheering. Others shrieked in terror as five Krenken in flying harnesses settled like fallen leaves from the sky onto the horse-pawed field. They carried handheld *pots de fer* strapped round their middles and long, slim tubes slung over their shoulders. Dietrich recognized Hans and Gottfried—and thought it passing strange that the Krenken had once seemed so alike to him.

Wails rose from those who, having come from remote holdings, had not yet seen a Krenk. A camp-follower from Hinterwaldkopf waved in the air a reliquary she wore round her neck. Others slipped off with fearful backward glances. Franzl Longnose slapped some of the retreating camp-followers with his staff. "What, would ye run from a handful of grasshoppers?" he laughed. Some knights half-drew their swords, and Manfred called out in his battle-voice that the strangers were travelers from a distant land who had come to lend their aid with their cunning weapons. Then he added *sotto voce* to Dietrich, "My thanks for persuading Grosswald."

Dietrich, who knew how ineffective his pleas had been, said nothing.

The familiarity with which the local garrison greeted the fresh arrivals quieted many. Some muttered about "welcoming demons," but none of the country knights dared gallop off while their brothers from the Burg stood fast. When Hans and Gottfried knelt before Dietrich, drew the sign of the cross upon themselves, and prayed the priest's blessing, the murmurs faded like water sucked into the thirsty earth. Reflexively, many of those who had shouted the loudest alarms also crossed themselves, and took heart, if not ease, from this sign of piety.

"What means this?" Dietrich asked Hans amidst the commotion. "Has Grosswald then consented?"

"We shall recover the copper wire stolen by von Falkenstein," Hans said. "It may perform better than that which the blessed Lorenz drew." One of the three unfamiliar Krenken tossed his head back and made some buzz of comment; but as the creature lacked a head-harness, Dietrich did not understand him and Hans silenced the fellow with a gesture.

Manfred, having donned his own harness, approached and inquired after their corporal.

Hans stepped forward. "We have come to honor Grosswald, mine Herr. By your grace, we will fly before the column and call back reports of Falkenstein's doings through the far-speaker."

Manfred rubbed his chin. "And be out of sight of the faint-hearts among us . . . Do you have the thunder-clay?" A Krenk stroked the satchel he wore strapped across his body and Manfred nodded. "Very well. It pleases. You shall fly a vanguard."

Dietrich watched with mixed feelings the Krenken recede into the distant sky. The objections were two. The army would carry gossip on its breath, exciting a terrible curiosity; but a glimpse of Hans or his companions would give body to the whispers. *On the contrary,* Hans might recover the wire and so speed the Krenkish departure. *Ergo . . .* The question would be determined by a race between the arrival of the curious and the departure of the Krenken. In answer to the first objection, rumors were surely abroad by now, so that the gossip of this army would add but little. But to the second objection, Dietrich saw no ready answer.

On the way to Church Hill, Dietrich passed by Theresia's cottage and marked her face in the window opening. They locked gazes, and he saw again the numb, tearless ten-year-old he had carried off into the woods. He stretched an arm out and perhaps something stirred in her features, but she pulled the shutters closed before he could ascertain what that something was.

Slowly, Dietrich let his arm drop and he took a few more steps up the hill, but, suddenly overwhelmed, he sat upon a boulder and wept.

LATER THAT afternoon, Dietrich and Joachim fed the milch cow and the other animals pertaining to the benefice. The shed was warm from the heat of the beasts and rich with the odors of dung and straw. "It will please me," Dietrich said as he forked silage into the manger, "When the Krenken have gone and Theresia resumes her duties."

Joachim, who had taken the more noisome task of the chicken coop, paused and wiped the curls off his brow with the back of his hand. "Dietrich, you cannot grind a sausage into a sow."

Dietrich frowned and leaned upon his pitchfork. The cow lowed. Joachim turned and scattered feed to the chickens. There was a distant sound of banging pots in the outbuilding.

"She was always like a daughter to me," Dietrich said at last.

Joachim grunted. "Children are a father's curse. My father told me that. He meant me, of course. He'd lost a hand in the Barons' War, and it embittered him that he could no longer chop other men to pieces. He wanted me to take his place and be my uncle's heir, but I wanted God to live in me, and butchery seemed an uncertain path to the New Age." Dietrich twitched and Joachim nodded. "You taught Theresia charity, but when tried for the greatest charity of all she was found wanting. I have written it so in my journal. 'Even Pastor Dietrich's ward was tried and found wanting.' "

Dietrich shook his head. "Never say such a thing. It would hurt her. Say rather that 'Pastor Dietrich was tried and found wanting,' for I have always fallen short of the marks I have set."

The Kratzer burst into the shed, buzzing and clicking and shaking a cook's ladle. Dietrich jumped at the sudden intrusion and braced the pitchfork before him, but when he saw it was the philosopher, he pulled the head-harness from his scrip and woke it.

"Where is Hans?" the Krenk demanded. "It is past time and my meal is unprepared."

Joachim opened his mouth to answer, but Dietrich lifted a hand to still him. "We've not seen him since morning," Dietrich temporized. At this, the Krenk slammed a fist into the doorpost, said something that the *Heinzelmännchen* did not translate, and bounded from the shed.

Dietrich removed his head-harness and carefully put it to sleep. "So. He doesn't know—which means that Grosswald did not send them." He worried. Gschert had imprisoned Hans for snatching Dietrich from the dungeon of Schloss Falkenstein. What retribution might follow this new transgression?

BY TIERCE the next day, Baron Grosswald had learned of the matter and barged into the parsonage, shoving the door so hard that it banged and recoiled from the wall. Dietrich, who was praying his office at the time, jumped from the prie-dieu, dropping his book of hours so that the pages bent on themselves.

"He will show me his neck when he returns!" Grosswald cried. "Why did Manfred allow it?" Shepherd and the Kratzer pushed into the room as well, the pilgrim-leader pausing to close the door against the March chill.

"My lord baron," said Dietrich. "The Herr did not question your men's presence at the muster because he had called upon you for your duty, and presumed, when they presented themselves, that it was at your will."

Grosswald paced before the glowing fireplace in a curious springing step that, to Dietrich seemed much like skipping and yet which clearly signified great agitation. "Too many lost already," he said, though not entirely to Dietrich, for Shepherd answered.

"Three to cold, and one of them child, before you even stir to . . . *enter* village. And since—"

"The alchemist," added the Kratzer.

"Speak not his name," Grosswald warned his chief philosopher. "I will not see another life thrown away—and in so futile a gesture!"

Shepherd said to him, "If Hans gesture futile, why we husband our lives?" Grosswald swung at her, but the Krenkerin fended the blow with a deft motion of her arm, much as a knight might parry a sword cut. The two then controlled themselves, but stared at each other in the off-center, sidelong manner their peculiar eyes allowed.

"Did you expect to eat of my lord's largesse," insisted Dietrich, "with no obligation in return? Has he not granted you food and shelter through the winter?"

"You mock us," said Grosswald, shrugging off the hand that the Kratzer placed on his arm.

"I did not know that Hans *could* act contrary to your orders," Dietrich said. "Is not obedience to one's sitting written into the atoms of your flesh?"

The Kratzer, who had thus far showed his agitation by shaking in place, threw his arm to bar Grosswald. "I will answer this, Gschertl." Dietrich noted his use of the diminutive. Among grown men, it signified either endearment or condescension, and Dietrich thought the Krenken incapable of endearment.

"Our flesh-atoms," the Kratzer said, "write for us an . . . appetite . . . for obedience to our betters. But as one who hungers may fast, so may we temper our hunger for obedience. We have a proverb that reads: 'Obey an order, until you are strong enough to disobey.' And another: 'Authority is limited only by reach.' " He bowed, a human gesture, toward Shepherd, who had gone to a corner of the room by herself.

"And much depend," Shepherd said, "on man who give order." Gschert stiffened for a moment, then bounded suddenly from the parsonage, the door banging on its hinges as he departed.

Dietrich said, "I understand," as he went to close the door.

"Do you?" said Shepherd. "It wonder me. Can man fast all-time, or would hunger in end move him to desperation?"

THE NEXT day, on the feast of St. Kunigund, a riot broke out among the Krenken. They raged against one another on the high street and on the muddy green, to the amazement of villager and garrison alike. Fist and foot and forearm dealt terrible wounds and raised a clatter like swordplay with dry wooden sticks.

Frightened Hochwalders took refuge in church, cottage, or castle, so that work languished. Dietrich cried Truce to the mob on the green, but the combat swirled about him like a stream around a stone.

Pursued by four others, Shepherd bounded past him and up Church Hill. Dietrich hurried after, and found the pursuers pounding upon the carved oaken doors of the church, scarring the figures with their serrated forearms. St. Catherine had sustained a wound never delivered by her Roman tormenters. "Stop, for the love of God!" he cried and interposed himself between the mob and the precious carvings. "This building is sanctuary!"

A terrible blow laid open his headskin and he saw sudden dark and pinprick constellations. The door opened behind him and he fell backward onto the flagstones of the vestibule, striking his already aching head against the stones. Hands seized him and dragged him inside. The door slammed, muffling the clamor of the mob.

How long he lay dazed, he did not know. Then he sat upright, crying, "Shepherd!"

"Safe," said Joachim. Dietrich looked around the dim-lit church, saw Gregor lighting candles illuminating Shepherd and a number of villagers. The villagers had edged away from the Krenkerin, deeper into the building's shadows. Joachim helped Dietrich to his feet.

"That was well-said," the monk told him. " 'Stop for the love of God.' You did not debate your dialectic." The pounding on the door had ceased and Joachim went to the peephole and pushed the shutter aside. "They've gone," he said.

"What madness has seized them?" Dietrich wondered.

"They always were an ill-humored lot," Gregor said as he raised the lamplighter to touch a candle high on the wall. "As arrogant as Jews or nobles. That's twice they've beaten you."

"Forgive them, Gregor," said Dietrich. "They did not know what they were doing. I put myself between their fists and their target. Otherwise, they ignore us." It was the estimative power of instinct, he guessed. From deep within the atoms of their flesh, the Krenken did not esteem humans as friend or foe.

Shepherd squatted upon the flagstones with her knees thrust over her head and her long arms wrapped around them. Her side-lips clicked rhythmically, much as a person might hum to herself. "My lady," Dietrich said to her, "what means this riot?"

"Need you ask?" the Krenkerin said. "You and Brown-robe cause it."

Joachim had torn a strip of cloth off the hem of his robe and tied it 'round Dietrich's brow to staunch the blood. "We, the cause?" Joachim asked.

"For your native superstition, Hans turn natural order over."

"My lady," said Dietrich. "Hans acted for the common good—to recover the wire from Falkenstein. It is the nature of men, of all creation, to pursue the good."

"Is 'nature of all creation' *to do as told*—told by authority, or told by nature herself. *That* is what 'good' man does. But Hans *decide for himself* what end good, not in course of duties, not by orders from betters. Unnatural! Now, some say he act on orders—from your lord-from-sky, 'whose authority exceed even Herr Gschert.' "

Joachim cried out. "Blessed be the name of the Lord!" Dietrich hushed him with a brusque gesture. "All authority is 'under God,'" he told Shepherd, "else authority would have no limits, and justice would be only a Herr's will. But, say on."

"Now, discord among us. Words run every way, like highspringers from pouncing swiftjaw, not in orderly channels from those-who-speak to those-who-listen. As you cannot imagine . . . *celebration-inside-head* . . . of knowing one toils in one's besitting, touching upward, downward, all sides, link in Great Web, neither can you know *lacking-within-us* when Web broken. The Kratzer compare it to hunger, but hunger small thing . . ." She paused and buzzed softly. ". . . which one may bear with ease until it grow unbearable. But *this* lacking like sit on bank of flood-swollen river with . . .

with . . . your word *love-mate* . . . with love-mates unreachable on farther side."

"Heartache," said Joachim unexpectedly. "The word you want is heartache."

"Doch? Heartache, then."

Gregor the mason had come to stand with them and, when he heard what Joachim had said, remarked, "They feel heartache, do they? It's little enough they show it."

"We have heartache for Web-wholeness," said Shepherd, "and would swim angry river to restore it. We have heartache for nurseland—you say *Heimat*—and . . . and its foods."

"But there are now *heresies* among you," Dietrich guessed. "Grosswald says one thing; Hans says another. Perhaps *you,*" he suggested, "say a third thing."

Shepherd raised her masklike face. "Hans go against Gschert words, but fault to Gschert that he not speak those words. Gschertl say I too defy natural order, and mob, high and low, set upon me for that sin. But when two in discord maybe *both* wrong, Gschertl and Hans alike."

"Those who hold the middle ground," said Gregor, "are often attacked by both camps. Between two armies is a dangerous place to graze your flock."

"Discord," Dietrich said, "is a grave wrong. We must strive always for concord."

Joachim laughed. " 'I come not to bring concord,' " he quoted, " 'but discord. Because of Me husband will leave wife, children will leave parents.' So do *philosophers,* playing games with words, lose sight of their plain meanings, which can be found always inscribed in the heart."

"A bit of discord here, too," said Gregor mildly.

Dietrich said to Shepherd, "Tell your folk that any who come to the church, or who go to Manfred's court, may not be attacked, for it is the Peace of God that warriors may not attack women or children, peasants, merchants, artisans, or animals, nor any religious or public building, and by law and custom both, no one may strike another in a church or in a lord's court."

"And does this Peace serve?"

"My lady, men are by nature violent. The Peace is a sieve, and much falls through—though perhaps not as much as might otherwise."

"House-wherein-no-blows-may-fall . . ." Shepherd said in a voice which might have meant cynicism or wistfulness. "New thought. This building to grow crowded sure."

DIETRICH ASKED Thierry to put down the fighting, but the burgvogt declined. "I have here only the garrison," he explained. "Five knights, eight sentries, two gatekeepers, and a towermaster. I will not expend them to pacify those . . . those creatures."

"Why have you been left here, sir," Dietrich demanded, "if not to preserve order?"

Thierry bore impertinence less patiently than Manfred. "Von Falkenstein is no man to idle while his enemies attack, and though he cannot strike Freiburg or Vienna, he is perfectly able to ravage the Hochwald. If he sallies, I will need every man hale, alert, and under arms. Should any Krenk flee here for sactuary, he will have it, but I will not police the fighting. That is Grosswald's besitting, and I will not stand between him and his disobedient vassals."

Discontent with this ruling, Dietrich borrowed a horse from the stables, and set off toward Falcon Rock, where he hoped to obtain Manfred's intervention. The urge to press on warred with the need to pick his way carefully down the switchback along the side of the Katerinaberg and through the thickets and other obstacles in the gorge. He was still deep within the shadowed gorge when he heard a dull thump of thunder and saw a plume of dark smoke rise over the far end of the valley.

HE ARRIVED at Falcon Rock after nones, less weary in body than anxious in mind, and sought the Hochward banner in a sprawling camp of no particular order or arrangement. Noble emblems waved on all sides like the flags on a festival tree. Here, the double-eagle of the Hapsburgs; there, the golden sash of the Markgraf and the red and white bars of Urach. Elsewhere, each at its own bastion: the arms of the weavers, the silversmiths, and the other Freiburger guilds. Von Falkenstein had badly misjudged how long the guildsmen would tolerate his impositions. Now, the mechanics and shopkeepers had risen from their benches to pull the pebble from their shoe.

The camp servants were in great celebration and Dietrich saw the reason for it when he reached the head of the camp. The gates to Burg Falkenstein hung loose and the portal had collapsed, as if Sigenot had smashed it with his club. The clash of weapons and the shouts of men drifted faintly from above. The Krenkish thunderpaste had forced an entry into the schloss, but the way was narrow and, notoriously, the "gap of danger" could be held if stoutly defended. Indeed, the rubble mound below the breach had gleamed in the late afternoon sun with the armor and fittings of men and horses.

Dietrich found the Hochwald tents at last, but the Herr's pavilion was empty, his body servant nowhere in evidence. Manfred's honor would have propelled him into the gap of danger and he might even now sleep among those gleaming dead. Dietrich re-entered the tent and, finding a divan crafted in the Turkish style, set himself to wait.

AS EVENING deepened into night, the battle-sounds faded, signaling that the last of the "die-hards" had been slain or taken captive. Arms and armor fell to the victor, so many knights fought to the death, less for love of their lord than to escape penury and shame. Attackers trickled back into camp, chivvying prisoners to be ransomed, and carrying the loot with which years of highway robbery had filled Falcon Rock.

Earlier Dietrich had, from boredom, found a book in Manfred's baggage; but as it concerned falconry, it had done little to relieve that boredom, and he had found himself fretting instead over the copyist's hand or the qualities of the illuminations. When he heard the irregular tramp of hobnails outside, Dietrich put the volume aside and emerged from the tent.

Attendants had built the fire back up and Max the Schweitzer was settling his men about it. He straightened in surprise. "Pastor! What is wrong? You've been wounded!"

Dietrich touched the bandage. "There is fighting in the village. Where is Manfred?"

"At the chirurgeons' tent. Fighting! Was it that sally from the watchtower? We thought they fled toward Breitnau."

"No, the Krenken battle among themselves—and Thierry will do nothing."

Max spat into the fire. "Thierry is skilled at defense. Let Grosswald handle matters."

"Grosswald is not least among the brawlers. It is for Manfred to decide."

Max scowled. "He won't like it. Andreas, take charge of the men. Come, then, pastor. You'll never find the chirurgeon in this maze." He set off at a brisk pace and Dietrich had to match his stride to keep up.

"Is he grievous hurt?" Dietrich asked.

"He took a blow that cost him a cheek and several teeth, but I think the chirurgeon can sew it back together. The cheek, I mean."

Dietrich crossed himself and offered up a silent prayer for the Herr's well-being. The man had been a strange and cautious friend for many years, peculiar in his humors and given much to contemplation since his lady had died, visceral in his tastes, yet not without depths. He was one of the few with whom Dietrich could discuss any but the most mundane matters.

But he had misunderstood. It was Eugen, not Manfred, who sat strapped into a chair in the chirurgeon's tent. A *dentator* was removing the broken teeth one by one with a pelican, a French novelty but recently come into use. The *dentator's* muscles bulged with the effort and Eugen stifled cries with every pull. The junker's face was black from the blow it had sustained. Blood spattered his brow, chin, nose, and painted the teeth exposed by the open flap of cheek a hideous scarlet. His skull grinned through the wound. Nearby, a blood-spattered chirurgeon read from a dog-eared book while he waited.

Manfred, who stood by the chair to fortify the lad, noticed Dietrich's arrival and, by signs, indicated that conversation would wait. Dietrich paced restlessly about the tent, his mission pressing upon him.

Nearby stood a stained table on which the chirurgeon customarily worked and, beside it, a basket of dry sponges. Curious, Dietrich bent to take one up, but the chirurgeon stopped him. "No, no, *padre!* Very dangerous, those." His patois of French and Italian revealed him for a Savoyard. "They are soaked with an infusion of opium, mandragora bark, and henbane root, and the poison, he may transfer to your fingers. Then . . ." He mimed licking a finger as if to page his manuscript. "You see? Very bad?"

Dietirch backed away from the suddenly malignant sponges. "What do you use them for?"

"When the pain, he is so great I cannot-a cut without a danger, I moisten the sponge to release her fumes, and hold it under the man's nose—so—until he's sleep. But . . ." And he held a fist out, thumb and little finger extended, and wagged it. "Too much of the *fumo,* he no wake, hey? But for the most grievous wounds, maybe better he die in peace than in torment, hey?"

"May I see your book?" Dietrich indicated the volume in the chirurgeon's hands.

"He is-a called *The Four Masters.* He describe the best-a practice of the ancients, Saracens, and Christians. Masters of Salerno compile him many years ago—before the Sicilian *famigliae* kill all the Angevins. This-a book," he added proudly, "he is-a copy direct from the master's copy, but I am add to it."

"Finely done," Dietrich said, returning it. "Does Salerno then teach chirurgery?"

The Savoyard laughed. "Holy blue! Mending wounds is an art, not a *schola.* Well, at Bologna is a schola founded of Henry de Lucca. But chirugery is for clever hands—" He wiggled his fingers. "—not clever minds."

"Ja, the name 'chirurgeon' is Greek for 'hand-labor.' "

"Oho, I see you a scholar—"

"I have read Galen," Dietrich ventured, "but that was many—"

The Savoyard spat on the ground. "Galen! At Bologna, de Lucca, he cut open the cadavers and see that Galen knows shit. Galen cut up only pigs, and men are not-a pigs! I myself was apprentice when first public dissection—oh, thirty year since, I think—my master and I, we make-a the cuts while important *dottore,* he describe what he see for the students. Hah! We need no *physician* to tell us what we see with our eyes. Holy blue! You have the head wound! May I see her? Ah, she is deep but . . . Did you clean it with the *vino* as de Lucca and Henri de Mondeville command? No?" He dabbed at the cut with a rag moistened in wine. "Wine that has turned is best. Now, I dry the cut and bring-a the edges together as the Lombards do. *La Natura,* she make a viscous fluid to bind-a the edges without the needlework. I will wrap-a the wound with hemp, to draw off the heat . . ."

The *dentator* had by then finished his work and the garrulous chirurgeon took his leave to attend to Eugen's cheek. The junker, sweating and exhausted from the work on his jaw and teeth, watched the approaching knife with something approaching relief. Knives he understood. The pelican had been too much like an instrument of torture.

"HE WILL bear up," Manfred said after he and Dietrich had repaired to the Herr's tent. "The blow he took was aimed at me, so it is a scar he may wear with honor. The Markgraf himself remarked the feat and agreed on the spot that Eugen shall have his accolade. Your Hans performed a brave deed, too, which I will bring to Grosswald's attention."

"It is Grosswald's attentions that are the cause of my errand." Dietrich explained what had happened in the village. "One faction says that Hans did the proper thing, despite his master's command. 'To save us from the alchemist,' is how they expressed it."

Manfred, seated upon his camp chair, pressed his hands together under his chin. "I see." He beckoned to his servant with a hand-flip and selected a sweetmeat from the tray thus proffered. "And Grosswald's party?" He waved the servant toward Dietrich, who declined.

"They cry that Hans, by his disobedience, upset the natural order, and this they abhor above all else. I suspect other factions, also. Shepherd is wroth with Hans, but would use his faction to unseat Grosswald, whom she holds blameworthy for stranding her pilgrims."

Manfred grunted. "They are as convoluted as Italians. How stood matters when you left?"

"Once they grasped the Peace of God, many of the lowborn fled to St. Catherine or the Burg, to the frustration of their attackers, who will not risk your displeasure by violating sanctuary."

"Well," said Manfred, "I can't say I like the natural order being upset, either, but Hans did me great service this day, and for my honor I would see him rewarded, not punished."

"What service was that, mine Herr? Would it mollify Grosswald?"

"Grosswald is a man of uncertain humor." Manfred checked himself, then smiled crookedly. "How accustomed to those creatures have we grown this winter, that I should think of him as a man. Hans and his Krenkl'n swooped upon the ramparts while all attention was on the breach, slew the archers there, then assaulted the bergfried and secured the treasure-hoard!"

"Mine Herr," Dietrich said with sudden apprehension. "Mine Herr, were they seen?"

"Some in the camp saw them, I think—though only at a distance, for I cautioned them to remain hidden to the extent their honor permitted. The archers on the ramparts, naturally, saw them plain, as did the towermaster in the 'murder hole' above the gate. Him, they slew before he could pour the hot oil upon us, to the saving of many a life and horrible injury. Falkenstein's men thought their lord's demonic master had come for him at last, so their appearance sowed panic to our advantage. There will be stories, but that cannot be helped, and the demons may be thought Falkenstein's, not ours."

"There is a poetry in that," Dietrich admitted, "that the legend he used to frighten others turned like a snake to bite the man himself."

Manfred chuckled and drank wine from a goblet partly filled with resins to impart a sweet perfume to the beverage. "The Krenk who carried the thunder-paste—he was called Gerd—performed most valiantly. He flew at night to the base of the gate tower and planted there the paste. On the morrow, he fired it at the moment Hapsburg fired his *pots de fer,* so that it would seem that the shots had wrought the damage. The Duke's captain was sore amazed! Gerd used the far-speaker to accomplish this. *By Our Lady,* it seemed as if he spoke to the paste and it obeyed. Dietrich, I swear upon my sword that the line between clever art and demonic powers is a hair. Hans led his companions into the bergfried in search of the Hapsburg silver, slaying or wounding all who stood before them until the stairs ran like a river of blood—though most defenders fled on the very sight of them."

Herrenfolk were notoriously prone to hyperbole over feats of arms. The human body could bleed a ghastly amount, but a few minutes casting sums would show the impossibility of "a river" of blood, especially if "most defenders fled." "Did they find the copper?" he asked.

"Hans reasoned that the greatest resistance would lie toward the treasury, and so he attacked where resistance was greatest. But . . ." Manfred threw his head back and laughed. "For all his fine reasoning, Hans found your wire by merest chance. Falkenstein kept his lady's quarters heated—a tiled stove, no less!—and our Krenkl'n were drawn toward it. The wire was there. Her husband had given her the copper, perhaps to fashion jewelry from it. I suppose you philosophers can make something interesting of the coincidence. Perhaps that reason has its limits."

"Or that God meant for Hans to find it." Dietrich closed his eyes and offered a brief prayer of thanks that the Krenken could proceed now with their repairs.

"But, hear," said Manfred. "Lady Falkenstein had a bodyguard assigned her and, when the Krenkl'n broke into her room, he swung his sword and cut down Gerd with a single blow. And what did our little corporal do, but straddle his comrade and ward off the armsman while the others pulled the body free! First, he brandished a chair to parry a stroke, then he slung a bullet with his *pot de fer* that struck the man a glancing blow on his helm and rendered him senseless. Then, oh, valiantly done! He traced the cross over his enemy and withdrew."

"He spared him, then?" Dietrich asked in wonder, knowing the Krenkish choler.

"A wonderful gesture. And Lady Falkenstein screeching all the while for fear of the Nameless One. But she says now that her bodyguard made such a heroic fight that even a very demon was moved to recognize his valor."

"Ach. So legends grow."

Manfred cocked his head. "What better story than that both foes perform heroic deeds when they face each other? By all accounts, the man voided himself at the sight of Hans; but he stood and fought when he could have run. That man will regale his grandchildren with tales of how he traded strokes with a demon and lived—if the Duke does not hang him first. But, the Duke's silver is secured—and on its way to Vienna with the Jews—and a troop of trusted men to guard it. The other prisoners are also freed."

"God be thanked. Mine Herr, would you summon Hans and warn him of his lord's anger?"

"Too late for that, I fear. Once I had secured the treasury for the Duke, I gave Hans leave to fly his slain companion to the Krenkish crypts."

Dietrich stood in sudden alarm. "What! We must hurry back then, before it's too late."

Manfred pursed his lips. "Sit yourself, pastor. Only a fool hazards that trail in the dark. Whatever dealing Grosswald has in mind has already been dealt. However, for my honor, if Hans has not been well handled, Grosswald will pay the fine!"

Dietrich was not certain that Manfred had the power to punish Grosswald, should Grosswald not will it. The Krenken had feared the winter's cold; but their arrogance would warm with the weather, and their oaths might melt with the snows.

DIETRICH SLEPT indifferently well. He did not expect the truce among the Krenkish factions to last, for their ways required submission, not balance. Their "Web" was one not of oaths and mutual obligations, but of authority and obedience, and arrived at less by the cognitive power of their wills than by the estimative power of their appetites.

The new moon had set and, between short-lived bouts of slumber, Dietrich had watched Orion and his hounds chase Jupiter. Now the hunters, wearied of the chase, were sinking below the Breitnau heights and the Dog Star, brightest of all stars, rested yellow upon the crest of the mountain. Dietrich had read from Ptolemy in the Paris quadrivium, and Ptolemy had described the Dog Star as red. Perhaps the Greek had been mistaken, or perhaps it was only a copyist's error; but Hans had said that stars could change, and Dietrich wondered whether this were one example of the corruptibility of the heavens.

He shook his head. According to Virgil, the Dog Star portended death and disease. Dietrich watched it until it had dropped safely from sight, or until he fell asleep at last.

· XV ·

MARCH, 1349

At Sext, Ember Wednesday

DIETRICH PASSED through the spring fields on his return, and was surprised to see the tenants and serfs engaged in their customary labors. Some called out greetings; others leaned on their spades and watched him. Herwyg One-eye, working a strip close by the roadside, asked for a blessing on his plot, which Dietrich delivered perfunctorily.

"What news of the Krenken?" he asked his tenant. From the village came sounds of mallets and the smell of fresh bread in the oven.

"Naught since yestere'en, when they quieted some. Most are hiding in the church." Herwyg laughed. "I suppose that monk's preaching hurts less than being beaten."

"Then nothing was done to those Krenken who set out with the Herr?"

He shrugged. "They've not returned."

DIETRICH RODE to St. Catherine, where he found a score of Krenken in uneven rows in the nave. Some were on their feet, others in their characteristic squat. Three perched in the rafters. Joachim was in the pulpit while a thick-set Krenk wearing a head-harness translated for those who lacked one.

"Where is Hans?" Dietrich asked into the silence that greeted his entrance.

Joachim shook his head. "I've not seen him since the army left."

One of the squatting Krenken buzzed and the thickset one said through the *mikrofoneh*, "The Beatice asks whether Hans lives. It is," he added with the Krenkish smile, "a weighty matter to her."

"His band performed valiantly in the conflict," Dietrich told him. "One alone was slain and Hans avenged him in a most Christian manner. Please excuse me, I must find him."

He had turned away when Joachim called, "Dietrich!"

"What?"

"Which of them was killed?"

"The one called Gerd."

This announcement, when translated, caused a great deal of clicking and buzzing. A Krenk began sawing his arms violently and repeatedly. Others reached out in quick, tentative touches, as if tapping his shoulder for his attention. Joachim, too, descended from the pulpit, and imitated the Krenkish gesture. "Blessed are those who mourn," Dietrich heard him say, "for they shall be comforted. Sorrow is a moment, but joy is joy forever in God's presence."

Outside, Dietrich remounted and tugged the reins around. "Come, then, sister horse," he said, "I must call on your service this one last time." Kicking the horse in the ribs, he rode for the Great Woods, sending up urgent clots of mud from the sodden Bear Valley road.

HE FOUND Hans in the Krenkish vessel. The four surviving Krenken clustered in a small room lined with metal boxes on the lower level. The room's walls were scorched, and no wonder. Each box had rows of small, glass-filled windows, within which small fires burned—bright red; dull blue. Some changed colors while Dietrich watched. Other windows were dark and the box itself marred by the fires that had wrecked the ship. One box was ruined utterly, its panels bent and twisted, so that Dietrich could see that inside were many wires and small items. It was on this box that Gottfried labored with his magic wand.

He must have moved, for the Krenken turned suddenly. The Krenkish eye, Dietrich had learned, was especially sensitive to motion. When Dietrich pulled his head-harness from his scrip, Hans sprang across the room and slapped the *mikrofoneh* from his hands. Then, gripping Dietrich's wrist, led him up the stairwell to the room where they had first met. There Hans activated the "speakers."

"Gschert controls the waves-in-no-medium," the Krenk told him, "but this head talks only in this room. How did you know to find us here?"

"You were not at Falkenstein, nor seen by any in the village. Where else might you have gone?"

"Then Gschert does not yet know. The voice-canals falling under interdict forwarned us of trouble. And we had Gerd to bury and the wire to install." Hans tossed his long arm. "It is cold here, but . . . I understand now what your people mean by 'sacrifice.' You went to the battlefield?"

"Your countrymen fought over your actions, and I thought to warn you. I feared you would return to imprisonment, or worse." He hesitated. "The Herr said you forgave the man who killed Gerd."

Hans tossed his arm. "We needed the wire, not his death. This wire, drawn by a true copper-smith, may prove meet to the task. No blame to the blessed Lorenz. Copper was not his duty. Come, let us return below. Remember, only Gottfried is with us in all things. Friedrich and Mechtilde have joined only from fear of the alchemist, not from next-love."

DIETRICH WATCHED for a time as the four Krenken attached wires and touched them with sundry talismans—perhaps to bless them with some relic? Once or twice they seemed to argue, and consulted illuminated manuscripts of the "elektronik circuit." He tried to discern which of the other two was Mechtilde, obviously a Krenkerin, but though he studied them closely, he could spy no marked difference.

Growing bored, he walked about within the vessel and came to the room that the Kratzer had once named the pilot room, though there was no window to show the pilot how the vessel lay, only panels of opaque glass, several of them darkened as if by fire. One of these flickered briefly to life, accompanied by a clatter of Krenkish voices from farther below.

A padded high-seat in the center marked the captain's throne, from which he had issued orders to his lieutenants. Dietrich wondered what might have happened had that worthy survived. The captain might not have failed so badly as Gschert. Yet, being more competent than Gschert, might he not have, in typical Krenkish choler, rid himself of the risk of discovery by ridding himself of the discoverers?

God worked all things to an end. What purpose was served by the events that had so joined a reclusive scholar-priest with a bizarre creature that instructed talking heads?

Dietrich left the pilot's room and went to the outer door, where he breathed the fresh air. A distant cry echoed through the surrounding trees, and he thought at first that it was a hawk. But it was too prolonged and insistent, and it suddenly came clear: the whinny of a terrified horse.

Dietrich spun about and ran to the stairwell, nearly tripping on his robe as he hurried down the steps. "Gschert comes!" he cried, but they looked at him not at all and he realized that a human voice was to them no more than a sound, as their chittering was to him. So he grabbed Hans by the forearm.

Reflexively, the Krenk slung him aside. Hans turned and Dietrich could think of nothing better than to point toward the stairwell and shout, "Gschert!" hoping that the creature had heard the name often enough to recognize it without translation.

It must have worked, for Hans froze for a moment before unleashing a stream of chatter at his comrades. Friedrich and Mechtilde put aside their tools and sprang for the stairwell, pulling *pots de fer* from their scrips as they did. Gottfried looked up from his work with the magic wand and, first waving away the vapors with his hand, made the tossing motion toward Hans. Hans waited a moment longer, then tilted his head as far back as he could before he, too, ran up the stairwell.

Dietrich found himself alone with Gottfried, his first convert—unless one counted the alchemist's cryptic embrace of the words of Consecration. Gottfried continued to affix wires to the minute posts with his *solidare*-metal, but Dietrich thought him aware of being watched. Gottfried put the wand aside on a pad that appeared woven of metal fibers and, using a screw-twister, removed a small box from the "circuit." This, he tossed to Dietrich, who perforce must catch it, and put in its place a somewhat larger device that appeared built from odds and ends. Examining the device removed, Dietrich saw that instead of copper wires there depended from the device sundry fibers so fine as a hair and which seemed to trap light within themselves.

Gottfried clacked his mandibles and gestured to the device Dietrich now held and the more *schlampig* device he had installed in its place. He spread his hands in a very human gesture, and tossed his head several times, by which Dietrich understood that Gottfried doubted the *elektronikos* would flow through the copper wires with the same efficacy as—light?—had once flowed through the hairlike fibers.

Having thus pantomimed his doubts, Gottfried made the sign of the cross and, bending once more to the task, dismissed Dietrich with a wave of his arm.

DIETRICH FOUND Hans outside, crouched with the other two Krenken behind some metal barrels. Hans seized Dietrich's robe and pulled him too behind the barrels, where the sodden earth soaked his garments and chilled his limbs. The Krenken, he saw, were shivering, although the day was but moderately cool to Dietrich's senses. He unfastened his cloak and hung it around Hans's shoulders.

Hans cocked his head to look at Dietrich straight. Then, he handed the cloak to the Krenk squatting beside him. This one—Mechtilde, Dietrich thought—took it and wrapped it tightly around her, clenching it close about her throat. The third Krenk squatted partly upright, peering over the tops of the barrels. Where a man might scan the surroundings, he held his head so motionless as a gargoyle. The better to apprehend motion within the woods, Dietrich supposed. From time to time, the third Krenk absently fingered his neck.

The horse had stopped her whinnies, by which Dietrich thought the beast had fled—unless Gschert had slain it. He raised his head to look toward the woods and a sound like a bumblebee flew past him, followed a moment later by a sharp crack from the edge of the woods and the slap of a stone against the vessel behind him. Hans yanked Dietrich once more to the dirt and snapped his mandibles a thumb's-length from his face. The message was clear: Make no sudden moves. Dietrich glanced at Friedrich and noticed that his left antenna had bent slightly to point toward a spot in the surrounding forest. Hans crossed his antennae and, ever so slowly, eased his *pot de fer* into position to sling a bullet at his attackers.

Hans raised a great clatter with his horny side-lips, and was answered by similar buzz from the concealing forest. Dietrich pulled the head-harness from his scrip and shook it at Hans before strapping it into place.

"I told him," Hans announced when he too had donned the harness, "that his bullets would damage our only means of escape. But he worries less over our escape than over my obedience. When a man can accomplish nothing, such pride is all that is left him."

Because his private canal had been interdicted, Hans had spoken on the common canal, no longer concerned with being overheard. Gschert answered, saying, "I command, heretic. Your place is to serve."

"Truly, I was born to serve. But I serve *all* on this voyage, and not you alone. You so fear risking *one* of us, that you would lose *all* of us. If you command here, your command is that we die. You were our captain's left hand, but without the head, the hand knows not what to grasp."

In answer, another bullet was flung at them. This time, it made no slapping noise, but instead a sound like planting a foot into deep mud. Dietrich looked over his shoulder and gasped, for the Krenkish vessel glowed with a soft, internal, sourceless light, *through which Dietrich could see the trees on the other side of the ship!* Hastily, he crossed himself. Could the inanimate have ghosts? As he watched, the vessel seemed to shrink, as if it were moving away.

Hans and the others had seen as well. Friedrich and Mechtilde buzzed, and Hans said, as if to himself, "Take care, Gottfried . . . Keep it plumb . . ." Then, to Gschert: "Where is our pilot? He ought to be here to take the helm!"

"Your heresy has sundered the Web. Zachary would not come. Would you trust your life to such patchwork? Even should it drop into the Other World, will it climb forth again?"

"Then, it is at least a choice of deaths, and not the least of choices."

Fear gripped Dietrich's heart and the hairs on his head and arms began to curl. The Krenkish ship snapped suddenly into focus in its proper size and a wave of *elektronikos* passed through him and across the clearing, where corposants flickered briefly from the tips and edges of picks and poles and sundry other metal objects.

The yellow glow behind Hans's eyes seemed to dim. "Ah, Gottfried," he said.

The one called Friedrich turned on him with his *pot de fer* leveled. He clicked out some statement. Dietrich heard only the answer. "'A small leap begins a long journey.'" Friedrich hesitated, then lowered his weapon. He said something else, but Hans did not answer him.

Without warning, Gottfried appeared in the doorway of the vessel and leapt across the open area to where Hans and Dietrich crouched. He was wearing his head-harness. "I should have asked your blessing on the twisting-device, father. Perhaps it was lacking only that."

Hans placed a hand on his forearm. "The work fell short by only a little," he said.

Gottfried said, "Bwa! So said the hunter at Stag's Leap." Then he hopped atop the metal drums behind which they crouched and, spreading wide his arms, cried out, "This is my body!"

Hans pulled him to the mud a moment before a swarm of bullets flew through the space. "Those fools," Hans said. "If they damage the walls, the vessel will never sail. We must—We must—" His body made a noise like a concertine, for the Krenken possessed many small mouths about their bodies. "Ach. Will the warm-time never come?"

"Always summer comes," Dietrich said. To Gottfried, he added, "You must not despair and throw your life away because of one failure."

"His was not an act of despair," Hans told Dietrich, "but one of hope." Then, his momentary panic having left him, he concluded, "We must remove the Herr Gschert."

"That saying is easier for you than for us," Gottfried said. "You serve the Kratzer, and are not 'oath-bound' to the ship's master as are we. Yet, though it grieves me sore to bring him low, it must be done."

"How many has he brought?"

"Bwa! By the evidence, all but Zachary."

Thereafter moved a strange and a slow combat. Accustomed to joust and melee, Dietrich found the affair most peculiar, for the combatants maintained perfect stillness for long periods. His companions behind the barrels seemed statues, but statues that moved imperceptibly. Each time he looked at Hans, the servant of the talking head had moved into a different position. Such a style, he realized, must perfectly suit a nation whose eyes were responsive to motion, for perfect motionlessness would make them difficult to see. Yet it must also put them at hazard when fighting those who attack in a rush. It occurred to Dietrich that had Gschert and Manfred fought on Kermis Day, each party would have been vulnerable to the other. For to remain still in the face of a charge were fatal; while to rush against those with keen perception of movement were equally so.

Betimes, the pop of a *pot de fer* signaled a careless move, and then the Krenken showed that they were indeed capable of quick movement. Bullets whined against the barrels, or barked the limbs of trees. The fighters took up widely separate positions from which to loose their shots. The quake of a bush and snapping of twigs within the dimness of the trees signified Gschert's men doing the same. The pace unnerved Dietrich and he longed for a rush of crying rage.

With no small horror, Dietrich realized that a Krenk had appeared in the clearing itself. As still as a rock or a tree, it squatted beside a table and chairs at which the refugees had been wont to take some refreshment in warmer weather. By what imperceptible stages it had reached that position, Dietrich did not know, and when he looked again, it was gone.

Glancing then to his left, he saw a strange Krenk crouched there. Dietrich cried out in surprise and terror, and would have sprung up to his own undoing save that Hans grabbed him firmly by the shoulder. "Beatke is with us," he said, and Hans and the newcomer touched each other gently on the knees.

The woods seemed filled with locusts, for the two sides attacked with words as well, though Dietrich heard only those diatribes that passed through the *Heinzelmännchen.* Gschert's words were like honey placed before a fasting man, appeals to the heretics' inborn hunger for obedience.

"You have used your power, Gschert," Hans called out, "beyond what is just. If we are born to serve, and you to command, then your commands must be for the good of all. We do not deny our place in the Web. We deny *your* place in the Web."

Another Krenk, also one with a head-harness, though not one that Dietrich knew, said, "We who labor will be heard. You say, 'do this' and 'do that,' while you yourself do nothing. You take your ease on the backs of others."

Suddenly Dietrich became aware of more than a dozen Krenken now arrayed with Hans. None had *pots de fer,* but carried instead a variety of tools and implements. They perched in trees or behind rocks or in the gully that ran beside the clearing. "But Shepherd said that obedience was like a hunger," Dietrich said.

His plaint was carried by the common canal, and someone—which, he did not know—answered, "So it is, but a hungry man may still smite the purveyor of rotten food." Whereupon a ferocious chatter grew in magnitude from Dietrich's side of the clearing. All about him were statues which, at each glance, had altered their posture—and suddenly Dietrich was small beside his mother in the Köln Minster watching the gargoyles and the stern-faced saints slowly turn toward him. The Armleder had returned, born anew amongst the Krenken.

Between two armies is a dangerous place to graze your flock, Gregory Mauer had said.

Dietrich ran from the protection of the barrels out into the clearing that separated the two warring factions. "Stop!" he cried, expecting any moment to be stoned to death by a dozen *pots de fer.* He raised both arms. "I command you in the name of Christ Jesus to put down your weapons!"

Surprisingly, no bullets were slung in his direction. For a time, nothing stirred. Then, first one, then another Krenk rose from concealment. Hans tossed his head back and said, "You shame me, Dietrich of Oberhochwald." And he dropped his *pot de fer* to the ground. At this, the Herr Gschert emerged from the woods. "You have right," he said. "This matter is between the Hans and me alone, and it is to the neck." He stepped forward; and Hans, after a moment in which he and Beatke touched, loped across the clearing to meet him.

"What does it mean, 'to the neck'?" Dietrich asked.

"It makes true," Gschert said to Hans, "that finding ourselves on such a world we resort to the ways of our forefathers." And he stripped himself of his clothing, worn and faded sash and blouse tossed to the ground, and stood shivering in the March afternoon.

Hans had come to stand beside Dietrich. "Remember," he said, "that it is better for one man to die than a whole people, and if this will restore concord . . ." Then, to Gschert, he added, "This is my body, to be given up for many."

To the neck. Dietrich realized suddenly that Hans would not defend himself from Gschert's jaws. "No!" he said.

"Has it come to this, then?" Gschert asked.

And Hans answered, "As Arnold always knew it would. Galatians 5:15."

"Have with your thought-lacking superstition, then!"

But before Gschert could spring upon the unresisting Hans, Dietrich heard the arresting tones of a trumpet, the sound that was better than all the echoes in the world.

"IT WAS simple enough," Herr Manfred said while Max and his soldiers led the now compliant Krenken back toward Oberhochwald. "Before even I reached the village, the field hands told me that you had like a madman galloped toward the Great Wood, and that, shortly after, the Krenken followed. I pushed my men to the double-quick. We must naturally leave our horses behind the ridge, but we were clad in half-armor for the road and so the march was not difficult. I heard some of what befell over the common canal. What was the cause of it?"

Dietrich gazed out over the clearing, at the clutter of furnishings, at the lack of order. "The Krenken hunger for obedience," he said, "and Herr Gschert has served them bad porridge."

Manfred threw his head back in laughter. "If they hunger for someone to obey," the lord of Oberhochwald said, "I will serve out *that* porridge myself."

AND SO later, in the great hall, Hans and Gottfried pressed their hands together and Manfred enclosed them in his own, and they foreswore their oaths to Baron Grosswald and accepted Herr Manfred as their liege. In recognition of his valor in the battle at Falcon Rock, Manfred placed a ruby ring on Hans's right hand. Gschert was not content with this arrangement, but agreed in a Nicodemian manner that it resolved the problem of disobedience.

Shepherd accepted also when two of her pilgrims asked to be settled on the manor and to be baptized. "Those who tarry in strange lands often take up rude customs of land. We have term for it, which would overset as *'walk in steps of native-born'*. They think their cares to throw over. Later, they regret; but must be later-time in which regrets may come. You clever, priest, and have lift Hans and his heretics of one burden; but leave me with mine own." And the leader of the pilgrims studied the Herr Gschert from across the hall. "Yet, I think Hans may not be lift of all. I think your Herr Manfred not permit us to depart and that, above all things, what Hans wishes."

"Do not you all wish that?"

"Vain to will impossible."

"The word is 'hope,' my lady. When Gottfried was repairing the 'circuit,' he gave me to understand that his repair fell short of the standards of the original craftsmen. Yet he applied himself to the task with a will, and I could not help but admire him for that. Any fool can hope when success lies plainly in view. It wants genuine strength to hope when matters are hopeless."

"Thought-lacking!"

"If one presses on, God may grace the effort with success after all, and *that* end despair will never achieve. My lady, what would you, had you thrown Baron Grosswald over?"

The pilgrim-leader smiled the Krenkish smile, which always seemed to Dietrich half-mocking. "To order Hans to do as he has done."

"And yet you blame him for having done it!"

"Without orders? Yes."

Dietrich turned to face the Lady Shepherd fully. "*You* sent Gschert into the Great Woods."

"In my country," the Lady answered, "we play game of placing stones within array. Some stones remain in place and these we call . . . *Heinzelmännchen* say 'hives,' but I say 'castles' is better. From these, warrior-stones sally, and move place to place by certain rules. Game play by three opponents."

Dietrich understood. "You are playing at stones, then."

Lady Shepherd closed her side-lips with measured delicacy. "One occupy one's time as best as able. Game's intricacies help me forget. 'Because we die, we laugh and leap.' "

"Na," said Dietrich, "Hans is out of the game now. He is Manfred's vassal now."

The Krenkerin laughed. "Also, four-sided version."

· XVI ·

MARCH, 1349
Lent

WITH MARCH had come the New Year. Serfs and villagers trimmed grapevines and cut posts for fences damaged by the winter's snow. Since the truce imposed by Herr Manfred, humors had cooled, and many Krenken returned to their former guest-houses in the village. Hans, Gottfried, and a few others encamped by the shipwreck. The weather was warming, and Zimmerman and his nephews had built a shed for them heated by a stove of flagstones. This enabled them to work more hours on the repairs and, not incidently, minimize encounters with their recent foes. Gerlach Jaeger, who often ranged far hunting wolves, reported that, at eventide, he would sometimes spy them attempting their odd leaping dance "in concert."

"They ain't real good at it," the hunter replied. "They forget, and then each of 'em just does what he wants."

Dietrich often visited their camp, and he and Hans would walk the now well-marked forest paths while discussing natural philosophy. The trees had begun to green again, and a few impatient flowers spread their arms to pray for bees. Hans wore a sheepskin vest over leather-hose, his particular Krenkish clothes having long since worn out.

Dietrich explained that, although the French began the Year of the Lord already at Christmastide, the Germans took the Incarnation as the proper time. The civil year began, naturally, in January. Hans could not understand such inconstancy. "On Krenkheim," he said, "is not only the year standard, but so too the hour of the day and even to one part in two hundreds of thousands of the day."

"The Kratzer divided your hour into a gross of minutes, and each minute into a gross of eyeblinks. What task can ever be done so quickly as to need an 'eyeblink' to mark it?"

" 'Eyeblink' is your term. It 'signifies' nothing to us."

Could a man see humor in golden-faceted globes; laughter in horny lips? Above them, he heard a colored woodpecker rap against a branch. Hans clacked back at it, as if answering, then laughed.

"We find such intervals useful," he continued, "for measuring the properties of the '*elektronik* sea,' whose . . . tides . . . rise and fall countless times during an eyeblink."

"Ach so," Dietrich said, "the waves that ripple in no medium. What is by you this 'eyeblink'?"

"I must consult the *Heinzelmännchen.*" The two proceeded in silence beneath a choir of woodleafsingers and acorn-jays. Dietrich stooped by a patch of woods-masters by the trail. He plucked one of the pale pink flowers and held it close to his eyeglasses. The underground parts made a good red dye and Theresia could use the remainder in her remedies, save that she would not walk the Great Woods so long as the Krenken were there. Reason enough for Dietrich to dig a few up for her and place them in his scrip.

"An eyeblink," Hans announced at last, "is two thousand and seven hunded and four myriads of the ripples of unseeable light from . . . a particular substance which you do not know."

Dietrich stared at the Krenk for a moment before the absurdity overwhelmed him, and he burst into laughter.

AS THEY returned to the camp, Hans asked after the Kratzer. Dietrich told him of his many quodlibets with the philosopher over points of natural philosophy, but Hans interrupted. "Why has he not come to our camp?"

Dietrich studied his companion. "Perhaps he will. He complains of weakness."

Hans suddenly stilled and Dietrich, thinking he had seen something in the forest, stopped also and listened. "What is it?"

"I fear we hold the Lenten fast too seriously."

Dietrich said, "Lent is a demanding season. We await the Lord's resurrection. But the Kratzer is not baptized; so why does he also fast?"

"From fellowship. We find comfort in that." More, Hans would not say, but passed the remainder of the walk in silence.

AT THE camp, Ilse Krenkerin approached Dietrich. "Is it true, pastor, that those who swear fealty to your lord-from-the-skies will live again?"

"Doch," Dietrich assured her. "Their spirits live forever in the communion of saints, to be reuinited with their bodies on the Last Day."

"And your lord-from-the-sky is a being of *energia,* and so can find the *energia* of my Gerd and replace it in his body?"

"Ach. Gerd. Were you then his wife?"

"Not yet, though we spoke of finding a '*no equivalent*' on our return. He was of the crew and I was but a pilgrim taking passage, but he seemed so . . . so commanding . . . in his ship's livery, and goodly in form. It was for my sake—that I need not drink the alchemist's broth—that he counterspoke the Herr Gschert and joined the heretics. If your sky-lord will reunite us in a new life, I would swear my fealty also to him."

Dietrich said nothing of Gerd's unbaptized state. He was unsure of the correct reasoning. The law of love held that no man could be condemned for lacking beliefs he had never had opportunity to learn; but it was true also that only through Jesus could a man enter Heaven. Perhaps Gerd would be admitted to that limb of Heaven reserved for the virtuous pagans, a place of perfect natural happiness. But if so, and Ilse accepted the Christ, they would not be reunited. It was not an easy question, but he promised to arrange instruction for her and for two others in the camp who also asked.

He was pleased at their interest, and curious also what "the alchemist's broth" might be.

TO RAISE a junker to knighthood was a costly matter, since honor required celebrations worthy of the occasion: festivities, banquets, gifts, a competition of minnesingers, and *bohorts,* the "playing at lances." So lords often raised several junkers at once to share the costs. When Manfred announced that he would raise Eugen, Thierry agreed to raise his Imein, as well.

The Zimmermans constructed a stand of benches in the meadow from which folk could watch the contests, and the sounds of hammer and saw drowned the grumbling at the extra work. A serf named Carolus was so wroth at the additional work that he ran off. His property escheated to Manfred, who bestowed the manse in halves to Hans and Gottfried.

"The land is servile," Dietrich warned the new tenants, "so you'll owe hand-service for it to Manfred, but you yourselves are free tenants." He suggested they engage Volkmar Bauer to assume the plowing and reaping in return for half-shares in the harvest. Volkmar complained naturally that he was hard-pressed to work his own manses and those he owed the Herr; but he was a forethoughtful man and his kin might someday need additional furlongs. So arrangements were made by which divers obligations of the strips were rented to others, and the terms were witnessed by the schultheiss and written into the weistümer. While the transaction did not win Volkmar's love for the Krenken, it did still the vogt's more overt hostilities.

On the day before the knighting, which was the Third Sunday in Lent, the junkers fasted from dawn to dusk. Then, breaking fast at sunset, they put on robes of the purest white English wool and spent a vigil-night on their knees in the chapel. Eugen's wound was healing, as the Savoyard had promised, though the scar was prominent and his smile would always have a sinister curl to it. Imein, who had fought creditably but without a wound, regarded the scar with something approaching envy.

"I much regret the meanness of the festivities," Manfred confessed to Dietrich that evening as he inspected the viewing stands. "Eugen deserves more, but we must yet conceal our Krenkish vassals. Einhardt will be much vexed that I did not invite him to play at lances with us."

Einhardt was the imperial knight by Stag's Leap. "I suspect the old man has heard rumors by now," Dietrich suggested, "but is too courteous to indulge his curiosity."

"That pleases. My daughter dislikes bathing him because he smells so. He seldom uses soap, though he was taught since childhood proper bathing. 'French vanities!' he says. I suspect he triumphed on the battlefield because his opponents ran from his stink." Manfred threw his head back and laughed.

"Mine Herr," said Dietrich, "I pray you not tilt your head . . . Among the Krenk it is a mark of submission—and an invitation to the superior to bite the neck in twain."

Manfred's eyebrows shot up. "Is't so! I'd thought them laughing."

"Each man sees what his own experience has taught him. You did not punish Grosswald for disturbing the peace. To us, forebearance is a virtue; but to them it signifies weakness."

"Hah." Manfred walked a few more steps with his hands clasped behind the small of his back. Then he turned and inclined his head. "Hans's gesture at Falcon Rock, when he spared his enemy . . . Did that signify also weakness?"

"Mine Herr, I know not; but his ways are not ours."

"They must learn *our* ways, if they are to stay on my manor."

"If they stay. Their desperation to regain their own country is what drove Hans to his disobedience."

Manfred considered him thoughtfully. "But why such desperation? A man might long for his homeland, for family or lovers or . . . or wife, but longing eventually dies. Most longing."

ON THE morrow, the junkers emerged from the chapel and were bathed to symbolize their cleanliness, after which they were dressed in linen undergarments, tunics brocaded with gold thread, silk stockings, and embellished shoes. Crimson cloaks were hung about their shoulders, so that the assembly gasped with delight when they re-entered the chapel. The Krenken painted many pictures with their *fotografia.*

The chaplain celebrated the Mass, while Dietrich and brother Joachim sang *Media vita in morte sumus* in choir. The choice was meet; for while the words reminded the young men that death lurked always in their chosen life, the tonalities of the fourth mode lessened the choleric yellow bile, which a warrior must ever restrain.

After the Mass came the *schwertleite.* Eugen and Imein placed their swords upon the altar and promised their services to God. In his homily, Father Rudolf cautioned them to imitate the knights of olden days. "In these degenerate times, knights turn against the anointed of the Lord and lay waste the patrimony of the Cross, despoil the 'paupers of Christ,' oppress the wretched, and satisfy their own desires with the pain of others. They dishonor their calling and replace their duty to fight with lust for booty and innocent virgins. You must demonstrate instead your honor, loyalty, justice, generosity, and especially your balance—avoiding all excesses. Honor priests, protect the poor, and punish criminals, as in days of old."

Dietrich wondered whether the knights of olden times had been as pure and upstanding as they were now remembered. Perhaps Roland and Ruodlieb and Arthur had been men no better or worse than Manfred—or von Falkenstein. And yet, was it not a good thing to seek the ideal, regardless how poorly it may have been practiced, to imitate the *ideal* Roland and not the fallible man he may have been?

Father Rudolf blessed the two swords. Then Manfred dressed Eugen in a double-stitched shirt of linked mail, shoes of iron ringlets, a *topfhelm* with windows, and a shield bearing Eugen's new device: a white rose crossed by a thistle. Once Imein was similarly accoutered by Thierry and both were kneeling before the altar, Manfred took up each man's sword in turn and laid the accolade upon his shoulder. Formerly, this had been done with a hand-slap across the face, but this new French custom had lately become popular in the Germanies.

Afterward, a *banquet* was laid in the great hall. An ox roasted upon a spit outside the manor house, and serfs hurried in and out with great platters bearing haunches and sausages. Laid out were pepper cabbage, candied songbirds baked into pies, eggs pickled in red beets, baked ham in black vinegar sauce, grated sweet beets and carrots combined with raisins. The iced cream and sorbets were also drizzled with the black vinegar sauce. Feasting was accompanied by juggling, mimes, and song. Peter Minnesinger performed a passage from Hartman von Aue's *Erec* describing the rage of his fellow knights against a count who had beaten his young wife. Dietrich wondered if Manfred had ordered the passage as a gentle reminder to his daughter's betrothed.

The bohorts took place in the afternoon. The contenders and their ladies progressed about the field while the spectators admired their colorful surcoats and livery. Eugen was especially remarked, for he was well-liked. The villagers hooted Imein lustily when the two newly raised knights took their positions at opposite ends of the field.

Dietrich watched with Max and Hans from the stands, distant enough that the horses did not smell the Krenk. "We played a game much like this at Paris," Dietrich remarked.

"What!" said Max. "You? At lances?"

"No, it was the game of obligations. One student was assigned to be the interlocutor and another to be the respondent. The interlocutor's task in the debate was to trap the respondent into maintaining a contradiction. The respondent's task was to avoid the traps. It helped us develop nimble wits."

Max grunted. "Hah, hardly as fine a display as this!" He swept his arm around the curial grounds.

"Ach, but the Church disapproves of such displays," Dietrich said.

Hans clacked his mandibles. "Small wonder! To risk life for sport!"

"It's not that," Dietrich told him. "It's the display of vanity and pride that is objectionable."

"You will thank God for all the vanity and pride," said Max, "when you must trust your lives and property to the skills they practice here."

"It is to their skills that our lives and properties are usually forfeit," Dietrich said. "I think folk may one day be thankful more for the skills that natural philosophers practice."

Kunigund, who was queen of love and beauty for the contest, tossed her kerchief, and the two knights spurred their mounts with a shout, leveling their lances as they closed. Imein cleverly deflected Eugen's point with a feat of his shield, and caught the other full on with his own. Eugen flew over his horse's rump and lay stunned on the field until the attendants carried him off. Kunigund rose to go to him, but Manfred restrained her with a hand on her shoulder.

"Bwa! We Krenken might enjoy this game," said Hans, "if the blows were not pulled."

"Times change," Max said. "In the old days, the crowd would shout, 'Be cheerful!' and applaud any well-turned feat. Imein did good work with his shield in that passage. Very prettily done. But now, you hear them yell. 'Stab and attack!' " Max suited gesture to his words. " 'Poke out his eyes!' 'Chop off his foot!' "

Hans waved his arm across the stands. "They cried no such thing."

Max leaned forward to watch Thierry and Ranaulf enter the lists. "No, but elsewhere. Here, chivalry is not yet forgotten."

THAT EVENING, Dietrich ventured into the Lesser Woods behind Church Hill, gathering certain roots and cuttings, the moon and he being both in the proper frame for such a task. A few herbs also had answered to the spring warmth, although the butterheads would not bloom for several months. Some plants he left whole. Others, he sliced and boiled to make a paste. Still others, he ground to powder with a pestle and tied into muslin bags for infusions. He would make of these medicines a gift to Theresia. The unexpected offering would delight her and she would invite him inside to talk and they could restore the life they had had together.

Dietrich prepared the salves and unguents in the kitchen outbuilding, while Joachim prepared also dinner, and the Kratzer warmed himself by the fire. The Kratzer questioned Dietrich closely about the attributes of each specimen, and Dietrich told him that this was a purgative and that was a simple against fevers. The Krenkish philosopher picked up a root that Dietrich had not yet washed. "Our alchemist," he said, "considered both too much and too little the future. He never proofed these substances, only those you offered us as food. Perhaps in one of these would have lurked our salvation."

"Your salvation," Dietrich told him, "lies in the Bread and in the Wine."

"Ja," said the Kratzer, still studying the root. "But bread *of what grain?* Wine brewed *of which fruit?* Ach, had Arnold persevered, he might have found the answer in this unpromising wood."

"One doubts so," said Dietrich. "That is mandrake, and a poison."

"As we will all learn," Joachim said from the kettle, "if you let it into my stew."

"A poison," said the Kratzer.

Dietrich spoke. "Doch. I have lately learned that it induces sleep and a relief from pain."

"Yet, that which poisons *you* may sustain *us,*" the Kratzer said. "Arnold should have continued his proofings. Our physician has not his skill at alchemy."

"What was it Arnold sought?"

The Kratzer rubbed his forearms slowly. "Something to sustain us until our salvation."

"The Word of God, then," said Joachim from the fireplace.

"Our daily bread," said the Kratzer.

Dietrich thought the concordance too neat. The words he heard the Kratzer speak were only those that the *Heinzelmännchen* had matched to Krenkish clicks and hums. "What means 'salvation' to you?" he asked the creature.

"That we should be taken from this world to the next, and so to our home beyond the stars, when your lord-from-the-sky at last on Easter comes."

"Faith is vain," said Joachim, "without charity. You must follow the Way that is Jesus—shelter the homeless, clothe the naked, comfort the afflicted, feed the hungry—"

"Ach!" cried the Kratzer. "Could I but feed the hungry! Yet, there is food which nourishes and that which merely fills." He rubbed his forearms slowly together, a sound like a grinding millstone and hopped to the doorway, the upper half of which was open to the late afternoon, and stared out toward the Lesser Wood. "I have never—" he said after a silence. "Your word is 'wed,' though among us it wants three to accomplish. I have never wed, but there are colleagues and nest-brothers that I would see once more, and now I never shall."

"Three!" said Joachim.

The Kratzer hesitated a moment and his mandibles parted, as if on the edge of speech; then he said. "In our language, the terms would mean the 'sower,' the 'eggmaker,' and the . . . The *Heinzelmännchen* does not overset the word. Call it the 'wet nurse,' though it nurses *before* the birth. Bwa-wa-wa! We are truly 'der,' 'die,' and 'das'! To watch one's niggling crawl into the nurse's pouch is said to be a profoundly moving experience . . . Ach, I have grown too soon old, and such matters are for the young. Mwa-waa. Never more will I see my nest-brothers."

"You must not lose hope," said Joachim.

The Kratzer turned his great yellow eyes on the monk. "Hope! One of your 'inner words.' I know what you signify by 'swine' or 'palfrey' or 'schloss,' but what is 'hope'?"

"When all else is lost," Joachim told him, "it is the one thing you may keep."

AT THERESIA'S cottage, Dietrich's knock was answered first by silence, then by a furtive movement by the shutters, then by the upper door opening. Awkwardly, Dietrich pulled from his scrip the bag of medicines he had prepared and extended them to the woman who had been the only daughter in his life. "Here," he said. "I made these for you. One is a sleep-inducement made of mandrake for which some instruction is required."

Theresia did not take the bag. "What temptation is this? I am no witch, to deal in poisons."

" 'The dose makes the poison.' You know that. I taught you."

"Who gave you this poison? The demons?"

"No, it was the Savoyard physician who treated Eugen." Only a chirurgeon, but Dietrich did not mention that. He shook the bag. "Take it, please."

"Which is the poison? I won't touch it."

Dietrich took the sponge he had infused with the Savoyard's mixture.

"I wish you hadn't made it. You never dealt in poison before *they* came."

"It was the Savoyard, I told you."

"He was only their instrument. Oh, father, I pray every day that you break free of their spell. I have asked for help for you."

Dietrich felt cold. "Who have you asked?"

Theresia took the remainder of the bag from him. "I remember when I saw you first," she said. "I could never remember, but now I do. I was very small, and you seemed enormous. Your face was all blackened from smoke and people were screaming. There was a red beard . . . Not yours, but . . ." She shook her head. "You snatched me over your shoulder and said, 'Come with me.' " She began to close the upper door, but Dietrich held it back.

"I thought we could talk."

"About what?" And she closed the door firmly.

Dietrich stood silently before the cottage. "About . . . anything," he whispered. He had longed so for her smile. She had always delighted in his gifts of medicines. *Oh, father!* the child cried in his memories. *I do love you so!*

"And I love you," he said aloud. But if the door heard, it did not answer, and Dietrich had barely dried his tears before he reached the parsonage at the top of the hill.

SHORTLY BEFORE vespers on Holy Thursday, a herald arrived from Strassburg bearing a parcel sealed with ribbons and with the episcopal arms impressed into bright red wax. The herald found Dietrich in the church preparing for the morrow's Mass of the Pre-sanctified, the only day of the year when no Consecration was prayed. Warned by the farspeaker, Hans and the other Christian Krenken, who were helping drape the crosses and statues in black, had leapt into the rafters and hidden themselves in the shadows above.

Dietrich inspected the seals and saw no sign of tampering. He hefted it, as if its weight would reveal its matter. That someone as august as Berthold II knew his name frightened him beyond measure. "Know you what this touches upon?" he asked the herald.

But the man denied knowledge and departed, though with many a wary glance at his surroundings. Joachim, who was also helping in the church, said, "I think rumors have reached the bishop's ears. That man was sent to deliver a message, but he was also told to keep his eyes open."

The Krenken dropped to the flagstones and resumed their work with the shrouds. Gottfried, last to drop, said, "Shall we give him something to see?" Then he departed, laughing.

Dietrich slit the seal on the packet and unfolded it. "What is it?" Joachim asked.

It was an indictment from the episcopal court that he had baptized demons. If there were any surprise in the contents, it was that they had been so long in coming.

It came suddenly upon Dietrich that it was on this night, at about this time of day, that the Son of Man had been betrayed by one of his own. Would they come for him tonight, as well? No, he had a month's grace to respond.

He read the document a second time, but the words had not changed.

"A MONTH'S grace," said Manfred when Dietrich came to his scriptorium with the news.

"By law," Dietrich answered. "And I must provide a list of my enemies, so the investigating magistrate may decide whether the charges have been laid in malice. There must be at least *two* witnesses before a judge will act. The bill does not name them, which is unusual."

Manfred, sitting in his curule chair at his desk, curled his fingers under his chin. "So. How long is your enemy list?"

"Mine Herr, I did not believe I had any."

Manfred nodded toward the indictment. "You have at least two. By Catherine's wheel, you are naïve for a priest. I can name a dozen here in the village."

Dietrich thought irresistibly of those who had objected to Hans's baptism, who feared the Krenken beyond reason. The punishments for false witness were severe. Years ago, a man in Köln who had accused his son of heresy out of spite over the lad's disobedience had been placed in the stocks, where he had died. Dietrich went to the slit window and sucked in the evening air. Firelight glowed in cottage windows in the valley below. The forest was a rustling black under a twinkling sky.

How could he name *her*, and deliver her to such a fate?

· 6 ·

NOW
Tom

TOM AND Judy met at the Pigeon Hole to discuss her latest findings over a couple of cheesesteak hoagies. Searching for Pastor Dietrich, Judy's worm had turned up a ton of *klimbim.* "Do you know how many medieval Germans have been named Dietrich?" She rolled her eyes up to Heaven, but secretly she knew how much work one eureka took. The journey of a thousand miles really does begin with a single step; it just doesn't end there. "Wrong century; wrong kingdom. Saxony, Württemberg, Franconia . . . A 'Dietrich' in Cologne, even a 'Dietrich' in Paris. Those, I could eliminate. The tough ones had no particular year or place associated with them. Those I had to read one by one. And *this* one?" She waved the printout in the air. "The idiots didn't put 'Oberhochwald' in their index. Otherwise, it would have popped out long ago." She bit her hoagie savagely. "Jerks," she muttered.

This was a book excerpt. During the 1970s, an enterprising group of liberals had published a book called *Tolerance Through the Ages,* whose contents were intended to show enlightened attitudes in many times and places. Along with Martin Luther King's *I have a dream . . .* speech and Roger Williams's *The Bloody Tenet* was a letter from Pastor Dietrich to his bishop.

To the Rt. Rev. Wilhelm Jarlsberg, Archdeacon of Freiburg in the Breisgau

I beseech your good offices to present with my humble prayers this apologia to his grace, Berthold II, Bishop of Strassburg.

I have remained meekly silent while my detractors, hoping to turn your heart against me, have laid a charge against me with the tribunal of the Holy Office. Reason and truth will prevail, I thought. Yet, this latest incident regarding the flagellants in Strassburg causes me to wonder whether reason be yet highly regarded in Christendom.

My accusers have told you that we in Oberhochwald have welcomed demons into our homes. By your most gracious leave, I respond in this manner.

Question. *Whether Pastor Dietrich of Oberhochwald has treated with demons and sorcerors and foully abused the blest sacrament of baptism under vehement suspicion of heresy.*

Objection 1. *It would seem that I have treated with demons because my guests have employed various occult devices and practice arts unknown to Christian men.*

Objection 2. *It would seem that I have treated with demons because my guests are said to fly by supernatural means. And such flight is said to be like that of the witches who meet on the mountain called the Kandel.*

Objection 3. *It would seem that I have treated with demons because my guests are peculiar in their appearance.*

On the contrary, it is written that Christ died to save all men. Baptism cannot therefore be withheld from willing converts, but only by force or by impairment of the will is the grace of the sacrament corrupted. Further, Canon Episcopi *clearly states that witchcraft, albeit a civil crime, is no heresy. Thus the request of my accusers is improper in both theology and law.*

Reply to Objection 1. *Worldly things are either natural or unnatural. But a thing is termed* unnatural *because it lies outside nature's usual course, not because it invokes the supernatural. So, a stone thrown upward is said to exhibit unnatural motion, for it would never exhibit such motion by its own nature. Now, artificial things include not only constraints of nature of this kind, but also mechanical contrivances such as clocks or eyeglasses. So an herb woman employing some hidden quality of a plant is said to practice magic, because the true essence has not yet been uncovered, and only the efficacy is known. But "hidden" does not mean forever unknown, for these essences, being real, are discoverable, and it would be vain for nature to have a property potentially knowable that cannot be actually known, and as it becomes more generally known to scholars, it ceases to be occulted. For example, we read now God's Word through the medium of wonderful eyeglasses. Though these be but mechanical contrivances, many of the simple folk do mistrust them. My guests employ devices like those described by Roger Bacon, which, while their essences remain occult, are generally regarded as things of this world.*

Reply to Objection 2. Canon Episcopi *declares that witches do not fly to their Sabbats, save in dreams induced by belladonna and other noxious herbs, and that to believe otherwise is sinful. Therefore, my accusers err when they claim that my guests fly by supernatural means. Flying, should it be possible, will be accomplished either through God's Will or through the skills of clever artisans.*

Reply to Objection 3. *Demons cannot abide the touch of Holy Water. Yet, the water of baptism caused them no discomfort, in particular he who took the Christian name Johannes. Therefore, he is no demon.*

Thus do I refute my accusers. "Whatsoever ye do to the least of My children, ye do unto Me." I have aided wanderers lost and hungry, some grievously hurt, when they appeared here this summer past. Granted, Fra Joachim finds them ugly and names them demons, despite their evident mortal ills, but mortal they are. They fare from a far land, and folk there have naturally a different form; but if Pope Clement can by his marvelously rational bull open his palace at Avignon to the Jews, then surely a poor parish priest may shelter helpless wayfarers, no matter the color of their skin or the shape of their eyes.

Christ with us this Year of Grace 1349. Given by my own hand at Oberhochwald in the Margravate of Baden, on the Commemoration of Gregory Nazianzen.

Dietrich

"Quite a remarkable man," said Tom, folding the printout.

"Yes," said Judy quietly. "I should have liked to have known him. My parents were also 'helpless wayfarers.' They lived in a boat on the water for three years before their 'Pastor Dietrich' found them a home."

"Oh. I'm sorry."

She shrugged. "It was a long time ago, and I was born here. The American story."

He tapped the pages with his fingernail. "This brother Joachim, on the other hand, sounds like a bigot, denouncing Dietrich to the Inquisition like that and calling the people 'demons.'"

"Dietrich mightn't have known who his accusers were."

"Anonymous denunciation? Sounds like the Inquisition."

"Well . . ."

Tom cocked his head. "What?"

"In the beginning, a lot of accusers wound up dead—killed by the heretics—so they were promised anonymity, and severe penalties were imposed for false accusations."

He blinked. "The Inquisition had *rules*?"

"Oh, yes. More stringent than the royal courts, in fact. For example, they prepared a summary of the case where they changed all the names to Latin pseudonyms and presented it to a group of men chosen for their reputation in the community—the *boni viri,* the good men—who could then review it without prejudice. We know of cases where the accused deliberately committed blasphemy to get transferred out of the royal court to the inquisitorial court."

"They used torture, though, didn't they?"

"For questioning, never for punishment. But *everybody* used torture back then. The tribunals allowed it only long after the imperial courts had introduced it. The inquisitors' own manual called it 'deceptive and ineffectual,' and allowed it only as the last resort, or when guilt was already clear from other evidence. Back then, a confession was *required.* They couldn't convict on other testimony. Torture was allowed only once, and could not cause loss of limb or endanger life, and anything said must be sustained by oath given afterward."

Tom wouldn't buy it. "But a persistent prosecutor could find loopholes in that."

"Or a corrupt one. Certainly. It was more like a modern grand jury than a trial."

"Are you sure? I always thought . . ."

"It was my dissertation in narrative history."

"Oh. That's why you learned Latin, then?" In truth, Tom was often surprised by the granular details of history. Working as he did with the big picture, the particulars could vanish into faceless stereotypes.

He studied the printout again. How much more information was hidden the same way, deep in a Black Forest of words seven centuries thick? "I'd guess they were Chinese. Dietrich's guests, I mean. The comments about skin color and eye shape. Oriental, at any rate."

"There was such travel in the fourteenth century," Judy admitted. "Marco Polo and his father and uncle. And William Rubrick, who was a friend of Roger Bacon."

"What about travelers in the other direction? Did anyone from China head west?"

Judy wasn't sure, but the Pigeon Hole was a Hot Spot, so she pulled out her wireless and poked an inquiry. After a few minutes she nodded. "We know about two Chinese Nestorians who came west. Hunh! At the same time the Polos were going east. They may have passed each other on the way. Hey, one of them was named Marco, too. That's weird. Marco and Sauma. When they reached Iraq, Marco was elected *Catholicos,* the Nestorian Pope, and he sent Sauma on embassies to the Roman Pope and the English and French Kings.

"So Dietrich may have sheltered a similar party," Tom said, tugging his lower lip, "one that met with disaster. Attacked by robber barons, maybe. Some were wounded, he says."

"Perhaps," Judy agreed, "but . . ."

"But what?"

"Chinese aren't *that* different. And they can't *fly*. So why call them flying demons?"

"If their arrival coincided with an outbreak of ergot hallucinations, the two events may have been connected in the popular mind."

Judy pursed her lips. "If so, Dietrich seems to have converted at least one hallucination to Catholicism. Johann. Do you suppose it's the same person as Johannes Von Sterne, the one whose baptism was referred to the bishop's court?"

"I think so. And this was Dietrich's response. Remember, the *moriuntur* document?"

"Yes. I think it must have been part of a journal kept by Pastor Dietrich."

"*Bestimmt.* In a small village like Oberhochwald, the priest was probably the only literate man. Here. These came from Anton this morning in an e-mail." Tom handed her printouts of some pdf files I had sent him. "He dug around over in Freiburg for me."

Judy read through them avidly. Sure, she was only a research assistant, but that doesn't mean she didn't care—about the research, among other things. When she finished, she set them down on the table and frowned a little. Then she paged back and re-read some passages.

"Did you catch that part about their names?" Tom asked. " '*He is called Johann because his true name is too difficult for our tongue.*' He would never have heard a non-Indo-European language before."

Judy nodded absently. "He must have studied Hebrew if he was the *doctor seclusus* that Ockham mentions. And he would likely have heard Arabic at some time. But—"

"Did you read the part where Johann and some of his companions helped care for the villagers during the Plague?" Tom retrieved the pages from Judy, who continued to look at the space they had occupied between her hands. Tom licked his thumb and flipped through the sheets. "Here it is. '*Hans and three of his countrymen daily visit the sick and bury the dead. How sad that those who hid from their sight will not emerge to witness true Christian charity.*' " He took a sip of his soda. " '*And so Johann and I prayed for strength together, and gave comfort to those pilgrims who have grown despondent.*' "

Judy made up her mind about something. It was only an intuition and she was afraid to give it voice, because she didn't really know what that voice would say. She took the pages from him, leafed through them, and pointed with her finger. "What do you make of this . . . ?" The abruptness in her voice earned her a curious look before Tom read the indicated passage.

"I'm not sure what you mean," he said when he had finished. "Dietrich found Hans alone one night looking at the stars. They talked a while and Hans asked how he would ever find his way home again. A homesick traveler, *n'est-ce pas?*"

"No, Tom. He wrote that Hans *pointed to the stars* and asked how he would find his way home again."

"So? People in those days used the stars as guides in traveling."

She looked away; pushed her cheesesteak aside. "I don't know," she said. "It's just a feeling. Something we've read. It means something different . . . Not what we think it means."

He didn't answer her. He took a last bite from his hoagie and put it down unfinished. Despite the cornucopia of material they had unearthed, they were still no closer to finding the reason for Oberhochwald's abandonment. He chewed on that for a while instead.

Shun them as we shun the unholy soil of Teufelheim. In its last year of existence, Oberhochwald was an ordinary village. Yet, a mere generation later it was being called the Devil's Home.

He didn't realize it, but he was dabbling in the occult—the essence of the matter was still hidden—and he would need a bit of magic to uncover it.

· XVII ·

APRIL/MAY, 1349
Until Rogation Sunday

BY SPRING, it seemed as if the Krenken had always been there. They had settled into the rivalries, rhythms, friendships, and jealousies that marked village and manor, and had begun to participate in ceremonies and revelries. Perhaps, being deprived of the company of their own folk, their *instinctus* drove them to seek such comfort. When Franzl Long-nose was wounded by outlaw knights encamped in a cave below the Feldberg, two Krenken used their flying harnesses to scout for the outlaws, though to no avail.

"Men of von Falkenstein's," Max told Dietrich later, "who took to the woods when the Rock fell. I had thought them fled toward Breitnau."

Shepherd's long awaited coup fell on Low Sunday. Many Krenken, through too-literal a translation, had expected the "Herr-from-the-sky" to arrive on Easter and rescue them, and were afterward much disheartened. Shepherd (who had not so misconstrued) had carefully positioned her people, awaiting just this disappointment. She had insinuated herself into Herr Manfred's company, always between Gschert's lips and Manfred's ear. She intended that Manfred should grow accustomed to hearing her advice in addition to—and eventually, instead of—Gschert's. Manfred, no stranger to intrigues among his vassals, was keenly aware of her maneuvers. "She thinks to depose him," he told Dietrich one evening as he and Dietrich and Max strolled the castle walls. "As if my oath to protect him would mean nothing."

Dietrich said, "She told me that the Krenken play a game of position and maneuver among themselves. I think she is bored, and this is a way of relieving her tedium. A curious folk."

"A *patient* folk," Max answered. "God might've created them for ambush work or sentry-go; but for intrigue, the dullest Italian could rob them blind."

Shepherd seemed affronted when Manfred rejected her assumption of power and instead set guards over Baron Grosswald. Dietrich was unsure how great an obstacle they would have proven had Shepherd pressed her coup to the limit, but the Krenken seemed disinclined to anger their host. Most of the pilgrims and one of the Kratzer's philosophers declared their fealty to Shepherd, who settled in the end for secession.

Gschert accustomed himself to the role of "Herr of the Krenken," and he "beat the kettledrum," as folk said, even though the secession, first of Hans and his companions and then of Shepherd and her pilgrims, greatly reduced his besitting. Most of the ship's crew remained loyal to him, and perhaps he had convinced himself that this was indeed the rightful and customary bound to his authority. He was seen betimes standing rock-hard on the castle parapet, gazing out across the world with those great yellow eyes and thinking no one knew what. Dietrich never did pierce the consciousness of that cruel and haughty lord.

MAY BLOSSOMED from April's bounty, and wildflowers speckled the meadows and high woods. The rich odor of rising sap and the fragrance of honey-clover anointed the air. Diligent bees flitted among the blossoms, griping bears newly roused. But in the age-old honey-struggle between bear and bee, it was men who held the balance, for they hunted the one and farmed the other.

On Walpurgisnacht, bonfires lit the hilltops to frighten witches from their covens. As custom required, Manfred spent the day playing with the villagers' illegitimate children; while those selfsame peasants danced around festooned poles and leapt through fires and ensured a plentiful supply of such children for future years.

Dietrich and Hans sat on the church green, overlooking the celebration. "It is said that the ancient red-haired race who once held these lands lit such fires to mark the middle of the springtime."

"The folk you call pagans," Hans said.

"One sort of pagan. The Romans had outgrown such frivolities, one reason why their empire fell. It was much too serious to last."

"Then the Christians took these customs from the pagans."

Dietrich shook his head. "No, the pagans *became* the Christians and merely kept their own ways when they did. So, like the Romans, we give gifts during Christmastide and, like the Germans, we decorate trees on festive occasions."

"And like the red-haired race, you light bonfires and dance around poles." Hans parted his lips. "Underseeking your customs was the Kratzer's great work, and I have the sentence in my head that this example will please him. Perhaps . . ." He stiffened for just a moment. "Perhaps I will visit him."

Below, among the celebrants, the philosopher plied his *fotografik* device.

ON ROGATION Sunday, Hans and the other enfoeffed Krenken joined the villagers in the annual progress of the manor. Dietrich led them forth after Mass, garbed in a flowing embroidered green cape and bearing holy water in a brass bucket on which was engraved the image of a spring bursting from a rock. Behind him, in order of precedence, marched Klaus and Hilde, then Volkmar and his kin, and the other *ministeriales* for that year, and behind them the mass of villagers, two hundred strong, chatting and laughing, with children darting among them as random and as humming as the bees in the meadows. Hans and Gottfried walked beside Dietrich, the latter bearing the aspergum and the former, the pail.

But Dietrich remembered when the child Theresia skipped with that same aspergum clenched in her fist; and Lorenz the smith had carried the pail and held the cape. Had Gottfried taken up Lorenz's old duty as he had taken Lorenz's name? Now Theresia lingered fearful in the procession's rear.

Manfred escorted them astride a white palfrey whose mane had been braided and perfumed and inset with fresh violets. With him were Eugen and Kunigund and—on a small white pony—little Irmgard, done up in a lace girdle to mark her chastity and with unbound hair flowing to her waist. Kunigund, being now wed, enclosed her hair with a wimple. Everard strode with his wife Yrmegard and his son Witold a few paces behind the Herr's party. "He's no more noble for traipsing in his lord's muck,"

Klaus whispered to his wife, loudly enough that Yrmegard scowled and gripped her husband's arm.

Dietrich had earlier explained to Hans that this was a ceremony only for the *familia;* which was why Joachim, like the soldiers in the Burg, had remained behind. Nevertheless, the Kratzer and a few Krenkish pilgrims followed with their *fotografik* devices.

The ground was yet sodden from the previous week's rains, and soon were hose and shoes spattered and Manfred's horse mud-stained to her hocks. Whenever they came to a boundary marker, Richart Schultheiss would point it out and parents would toss their children in *this* stream or bump their head against *that* tree, to general laughter and repeated demands to "do it again!"

"A curious custom," Hans said as they progressed. "Yet it touches. One cannot love a world. It is too large. But a fleck of ground so far as his eye can see, one may hold precious above all."

After stopping for a midday meal, and a visit by the curious to the Krenkish vessel, the villagers emerged on the far side of the Great Woods, where the ground dropped sharply toward the Bear Valley road. Manfred had reined in on a spur of rock to essay the descent when he suddenly held a palm up. "Quiet!" The chatter of the peasants gave way to louder cries of "Silence, there!" and "The Herr wants silence!"

Finally, there was the sound only of soft breezes and rustling branches from the woods behind them. Everard began to make some remark, but the Herr hushed him with a gesture.

Faintly, they heard it: the tocsin of a distant bell.

It was a single note, tolling slowly, borne half-heard like a leaf on the blustery winds. "Angelus already?" someone asked. "No, the sun is yet too high." "Too deep for St. Catherine's peal. Is it St. Peter's?" "St. Wilhelm, I think." "No, St. Wilhelm tolls three bells."

Then the wind shifted and the faint ringing died. Manfred listened further, but the sound did not repeat itself. "Whose bell was that?" he asked Dietrich.

"Mine Herr, I did not recognize it. St. Blasien owns a bass bell called the Paternoster, but this was higher-pitched. I think it was more distant than those we usually hear, and some freak of wind brought it to our ears."

Manfred scowled toward the Swiss, the direction from which the ringing had seemed to come. "Basel, perhaps?"

Hans cried, "Smoke! And five riders."

Everard leapt atop a protruding boulder and shaded his eyes. "The monster has right. Altenbach's steading burns! A dust cloud moves off toward the northeast. That five riders are under it," he added as he dropped off the stone, "I will take the word of the bug-eye."

Manfred ordered his serfs across the valley to help put out the fire. Hans called the other baptized Krenken to his side. After a deal of pointing and clacking, he and Beatke leapt toward Altenbach's steading, while Gottfried and another hopped into the woods, toward the wrecked ship. The fifth stood irresolute.

"How can they leap so far?" Klaus wondered, for this was the first time he had seen the Krenken in open country. "Do they wear seven-league boots?"

"No," Dietrich explained, "beings made of earth move naturally toward the center of the earth. But these beings are drawn less strongly because they come from a different earth. Hans told me that on Krenkhome his weight, or 'gravitas,' was greater than here."

Klaus grunted, unconvinced, and started after the others. Dietrich seized Theresia by the wrist. "Come, the Altenbachs may need your salves."

But she pulled away from him. "Not while *they* are there!"

Dietrich held his hand out. "Will you lend *me* then your tote?" When Theresia did not move, he whispered, "And so we see it. First you recoil from these strangers from beyond the firmament; then you recoil from helping your own folk. Did I teach you this from childhood?"

Theresia thrust her bag into his hands. "Here. Take it." And then she burst into tears. "Watch over Gregor," she said. "That big fool risks his soul."

As Dietrich hurried after, Gottfried and Winifred Krenk passed overhead in flying harnesses, with metal buckets of some sort dangling from them. Glancing back, he noted the small knot of villagers who had stayed behind. Theresia. Volkmar Bauer and his kin. The Ackermanns. And one of the Krenken. Well, one did not need two hundred men to fight a single fire! Yet, loping by his side were Nickel Langermann and Fulk Albrecht's son—and even Klaus Müller! Nickel grinned. "Altenbach will owe me favors for this," he said. "It never hurts to have a rich peasant owe you." Fulk said, "Hold your flap and hurry, or the fire is out before we get there."

WHEN, BREATHLESS, Dietrich had reached the steading, Manfred met him at the gate. "He needs your sacrament, pastor," he said, in a voice sharp as flint.

Dietrich entered the smoldering cottage, where the Krenken were putting the flames out with foam they pumped from their curious buckets. On the packed earth floor, Altenbach sat with his hands folded over his midriff, as if after a satisfying meal. Behind him, a woman wept. When he saw Dietrich, Altenbach grimaced. "Thank God ye've come in time," he said. "I'd fain not have her journey alone. Shrive me of my sins, but be damn quick about it."

Dietrich saw blood oozing between the fingers. "That's a sword-cut!" he said. *And a fatal one* . . . This he did not voice, though he suspected Heinrich knew.

"I thought it would hurt more," the peasant said. "But I feel cold, as if I had winter in my belly. Father, I have lain with Hildegarde Müller, and once I struck Gerlach Jaeger in anger . . ." Dietrich leaned close so that others could not hear the confession. For the most part, the man's trespasses had been stirred only by short-lived passions. There was no true wickedness in him, only the stubborn pride that had driven him to live apart. Dietrich drew the sign of the cross, using his own spittle, and offered him the words of God's forgiveness.

"Thank you, father," Heinrich whispered. "It would grieve me to have her alone in Heaven. She *will* be with God, won't she, father? Her sin does not condemn her."

"*Her* sin . . . ?" Dietrich raised his head and searched the room for Altenbach's wife, and saw that the woman weeping in the corner was Hilde Müller. Beside her, Gerda Altenbach lay with her throat slit and her clothing ripped from her, although a blanket now covered her decency. "No," he told the dying man. "She committed no sin, but was sinned against, as St. Thomas taught."

Altenbach relaxed. "Poor Oliver," he said.

"Your sons are Jakop and Jaspar, no?"

"Brave lads," he whispered. "Defend their mother . . ." Then he gave up his ghost. When his hands fell away, his guts spilled from him.

"All dead," said Manfred from the doorway and Dietrich turned to him. "The two boys are in the yard." The Herr's glance flickered toward Gerda, rested on Heinrich. "There was a gärtner who worked for him. Calls himself Nymandus. He hid in the woodpile and witnessed all. Tried to flee from me, so he must be off someone's manor. 'Nymandus,' indeed! It's little I care for sending him back. He saw five men in mail, but much disheveled, so I take them to be those outlaws from Falcon Rock that Long-nose ran into. They defiled Altenbach's wife, killed him and his sons, made off with his chickens and yearlings. I think the food was their object. Nymandus said the leader had red hair, which sounds like Falkenstein's Burgvogt from the watchtower." The Herr heaved a deep breath and stepped outside into the yard. Dietrich followed him.

"I'll send Max out," Manfred said, "but there are too many dells and meadows in those hills, and a small band might lurk unseen for a long time . . . Dietrich . . ." He hesitated. "The baker's son was with them."

"So. That was what Heinrich meant."

"Nymandus heard his master call the boy by name. He's hanged himself for certain now, the fool. It lacks now only his capture and a stout rope."

"Evil companions led him astray . . ."

"They've led him to the gallows. Altenbach's older boy—Jakop, was it?—raked him with a sickle and laid open his cheek." He paused, perhaps reflecting on the similar wound, more honorably obtained by Eugen. "And it was Oliver who cut him down."

Dietrich had noticed the two boys lying where they had fallen in the barnyard, a bloody sickle clasped in the elder brother's hand. Had Oliver imagined himself a knight doing battle? He had owned a lively imagination, capable of imposing its fruits on the world about him. Now he was a murderer of children. Dietrich whispered a prayer—for Jakop and Jaspar, for Heinrich and Gerda, and for Oliver.

"Ja," said Manfred, noting the gesture. "I don't know if poor Altenbach saw them fall. I hope he died thinking his sons would carry on his blood."

In the silence that followed, the sound of the distant bell came once more. Dietrich and Manfred looked at one another, but neither said what he thought the omen presaged.

· XVIII ·

JUNE, 1349

At Tierce, The Commemoration of Ephraem of Syria

JUNE CAME and, in the timeless wheel of the seasons, the winter fields were harvested and the resting field plowed for the September planting. Fully half the plowdays were allotted to the Herr's salland, so that while the *weistümer* called for rest from labors at eventide, the free tenants kept hand to plow on their own manses to make up the lost time. One of Trude Metzger's oxen had died of a murrain the week before, and so she harnessed a cow to her team, though with marked lack of enthusiasm on the cow's part.

Dietrich and Hans watched the villagers at work from a slab of granite at the edge of the Great Woods. In the rock's crevices, Dietrich marked the large, blue flowers of adder-heads, and resolved to tell Theresia of their location. Nearby, the spring that ran near the Krenkish camp tumbled into the valley. "What foods grow you in your country?" Dietrich asked. "They must differ from those we grow here."

Hans became as one with the granite slab on which he squatted. This absolute stillness into which the Krenken sometimes fell no longer frightened Dietrich, but he did not yet understand what the habit signified.

Then Hans's antennae twitched and he said, "The terms do not overset well, but we grow plants much like your grapes and beans and turnips and cabbage. Your 'wheat' is something strange to us; and likewise our foods include some strange to you. Greatleaf! Twelvestem! Ach! How my throat longs for their smack!"

"May you taste them soon. Is your vessel yet ready to depart?"

A parting of the soft-lips. "You tire of my company?"

"Never that, but there will be . . . difficulties should you remain much longer."

"Yes. I have heard you consort with demons." Hans's lips gaped and he made threatening gestures. "Perhaps I will fly to this Strassburg and frighten the bishop into surrender."

"Pray, do not."

"Rest easy. Soon, your 'demons' shall trouble you no more." He hunched forward, as if poised to leap, and stretched forth his arm. "I see movement on the Bear Valley road."

Dietrich shaded his eyes against the distance. "Dust," he said at last. "Use your farspeaker and alarm Baron Grosswald. I fear he must hide his people once again."

AT FIRST the travelers were shadows against the westering sun, and Dietrich, waiting in the road astride his rouncy, heard the weary clop of the hooves and the whining complaints of the axle well before he could discern their features. But as they closed, he saw that the man astride the jennet wore a fringed *talith* and curled his long, graying hair into elaborate ringlets. It needed no yellow star on his cloak to identify him. A second man, meanly dressed and both sharper of feature and darker in complexion, and wearing his hair in two thick, black braids, slouched upon the wagon bench with a servant's resignation. The awning overhanging the wagon shielded two women garbed in veils.

The Jew noted Dietrich's garb and said, with the briefest dip of his head, "Peace to my lord."

Dietrich knew that Jews who were strict observers of their Law were forbidden to greet or to return the greeting of a Christian, and so by "my lord" the man had meant in his heart his own rabbi and not Dietrich. It was a deft stratagem by which he could observe both the innumerable laws of his tribe and the conventions of courteous discourse.

"I am Malachai ben Schlomo," the old man said. "I seek the lands of Duke Albrecht." His voice reeked of Spain.

"The Duke disposes a fief nearby called Niederhochwald," he told them. "This is the road to Oberhochwald, held by the same Herr. I will take you to him, if it pleases."

The old man brushed with his fingers, a gesture that meant to lead on, and Dietrich turned his horse toward the village. "Have you come from . . . Strassburg?" Dietrich asked.

"No. Regensburg."

Dietrich turned to him in surprise. "If you seek Hapsburg lands, you have come the wrong way."

"I took what roads I could," the old man said to Dietrich.

Dietrich brought the Jew to Manfred's hof, where he told his story. The blood libel had sparked riots in Bavaria, it seemed, and Malachai had been forced to flee, his home burned, his possessions plundered.

"That was infamous!" Dietrich exclaimed.

Malachai dipped his head. "I had suspected so; but my thanks for the confirmation."

Dietrich ignored the sarcasm and Manfred, much affected by the man's woes, bestowed sundry gifts on him and conducted him personally to the manor house in Niederhochwald, where Malachai would await a party of the Duke's men to escort him safely across Bavaria to Vienna.

THE ONE place in Oberhochwald where the Jews would not betake themselves was inside the church of St. Catherine, so many of the Krenken had hidden themselves there. Dietrich, entering to prepare for the Mass, spied the gleaming eyes of Krenken perched among the rafters. He repaired to the sacristy and Hans and Gottfried followed. "Where are the others?" he asked them.

"At the camp," Hans told him. "Though it is warm now, they have grown soft these past months, and find the woods less congenial than the village. We, in turn, find their company less congenial, and so have come here. The Kratzer asks when they can emerge."

"The Jews depart tonight for the Lower Woods. Your folk may return to their labors tomorrow."

"That pleases," said Hans. " 'Work is the mother of forgetting.' "

"A difficult mother," Gottfried said, "with so little food to sustain one."

This puzzled Dietrich, the Lenten fast being long past. But Hans held a hand out to silence his companion. He hopped to the window, from which he viewed the village. "Tell me about these Jews and—their special foods."

Gottfried had turned to the vestments and appeared to study them, but in that head-half-cocked way that showed he was also listening closely.

"I know little of Jewish foods," Dietrich said, "save that some, like pork, they shun."

"Much like us," Gottfried said, but Hans again silenced him.

"Are there other foods, which *they* eat, but you do not?"

By the stillness of the Krenken, Dietrich knew that the question was important. Gottfried's comment, with its implication of judaizing tendencies, troubled him. "I know of none," he said carefully. "But they are a very different folk."

"So different as Gottfried from me?" At Hans's question, Gottfried turned from his inspection of the Mass vestments and flapped his soft lips.

Dietrich said, "I see no difference between you."

"Yet his folk came once to our land and . . . But that is the foregone-time, and all has changed. You may have noticed that Shepherd speaks differently. In her *Heimat*, what we call Grand-Krenkish is little used, so the *Heinzelmännchen* must twice translate. By us, you and Malachai seem much the same, save for the hair and the garb—and the food. Yet we overheard that your folk attack them and drive them from their homes and even kill them. It cannot be this usury I hear of. As thought-lacking as it is to kill a man because you owe him money, it is doubly so to kill a man because you owe someone else money."

"Rumors of the well-poisonings have outrun the pest, and men do mad things from fear."

"Men do foolish things." Hans ran his finger down the edging that held the glass light in the window. "Does killing their neighbor stem the 'small-lives' that make disease? Is my life longer if I have shortened another's?"

Dietrich said, "Pope Clement has written that Christian piety must accept and sustain Jews; so these massacres are the work of sinful and disobedient men. He contends that Jewish and Christian learning make one whole, which he calls 'Judaeo-Christian.' Christendom issued from Israel as a child from a mother, so we must not anathematize them as we do heretics."

"But you do not like them," Hans said. "You have shown it so."

Dietrich nodded. "Because they rejected the Christ. For so long as the Savior was to come, the Jews were chosen by God to be a light to the nations, and God placed many laws on them as a sign of their holiness. But once the Savior was come, their mission ended, and the light was given to *all* the nations, as Isaiah prophesied. The laws that set them apart were void; for if all peoples are called to God, there can be no distinctions among them. Many Jews did believe, but others clung to the old Law. They incited the Romans to kill our blessed Lord. They killed James, Stephen, Barnabas, and many others. They sowed dissension in our communities, disrupted our services. Their general Bar Kochba massacred the Jewish Christians and drove many into exile. Later, they betrayed Christians to Roman persecutors. In Alexandria they lured Christians from their homes by crying that the church was on fire and then attacked them when they emerged; and, in far-off Arabia, where they ruled as kings, they massacred thousands of Christians at Najran. So you see the enmity is of long standing."

"And is this Benshlomo so old that he performed those fell deeds?"

"No, they befell long ago."

Hans tossed his arm. "Can a man be guilty of a deed done by others? What I see is that there stands a limit to this *charitas* that you and Joachim preach, and enmity may be returned for enmity." He struck the window frame repeatedly with his forearm. *"But if vengeance is the law, why did I leave the Kratzer?"* This outburst was greeted with silence by both Gottfried and Dietrich. Hans turned from the window. "Tell me I have not made a fool's choice."

Gottfried handed Dietrich an alb of white linen. Donning it, Dietrich recalled that it represented the garment with which Herod had draped the Lord to revile him as a fool.

"No," he told Hans. "Of course not. But the Jews have been enemies for generations."

Hans turned from the window to face him in the human manner. "Someone once said, 'Love your enemies.' "

Gottfried turned once more to the table, and said, "Father, you have worn white vestments of late. Should I lay those out?"

"Yes. Yes." Dietrich turned from Hans, his thoughts in turmoil. "St. Ephraem is a doctor of the church, and so: white, which is the sum of all colors and signifies joy and purity of soul."

"As if such ritual mattered," said Brother Joachim from the doorway. He stepped into the room. "You have acquired two sacristans, I see. Do they know their tasks well? Do they know with which fingers to touch and hold the holy armor so that you may gird yourself to battle the devil and lead the people victorious to the eternal Fatherland?"

"The sarcasm is heavy-handed, brother," Dietrich told him. "A lighter touch is needed for the best effect. Men crave ceremonies. It is our nature."

"It was to *change* our nature that Jesus came among us. Di Flora's *Everlasting Gospel* eliminates all need for signs and riddles. 'When that which is perfect is come, forms and traditions and laws will have fulfilled their purpose and will be done away with.' No, we must travel deep within ourselves."

Dietrich turned to the two Krenken. "All that over whether linen be white or green! By the holy saints, Joachim, such *minutiae* obsess you more than they do me."

"About such things, we know nothing," Hans said. "But he has right over the inward-curling directions. To find our Heavenly home, we must travel in directions not of height or length or breadth, and through a time not of duration."

"We could always walk," said Gottfried, flapping his soft lips, but Hans clicked his horny lips and his companion cut his laughter short. "We have been cut off from home," he said, "and from our companions. Let us not be cut off from each other."

THE NEXT day, Dietrich came upon a man in close study of the church walls. Seizing him by the surcoat, he discovered it was the Jew servant. "What make you here?" he demanded. "Why were you sent?"

But the Jew cried out, "No tell master I come. No tell, please!"

The distress was so palpable that Dietrich judged it genuine. "Why?"

"Because . . . Is unlawful for us to walk near house of . . . of *tilfah.*"

"Truly? So, does it not defile *you*?"

The servant cringed. "Honored one, I base-born rascal, not so pure and holy as master. What can defile me?"

And was that irony that Dietrich heard in that voice? He nearly smiled. "Explain yourself."

"I hear of them, carvings, from hof servants and think I come see. We forbid to make images, but I am loving beauty."

"By His wounds, I believe you speak the truth." Dietrich straightened and released his grip on the man's sleeve. "How are you called?"

The man doffed his cap. "Tarkhan Hazer ben Bek."

"A large name for such a small man." Tarkhan wore a long, tasseled scapular beneath his rough coat, and his thick braids were unlike the delicate curls his master affected. "You are not Spanish."

"My people from east, from borderlands of Letts. Perhaps you know Kiev?"

Dietrich shook his head. "Is it far, this Kiev of yours?"

Tarkhan grinned sadly. "So far as edge of world. Once was mighty city of my people, when we hold Golden Empire. Now, who am I whose fathers once were kings?"

Dietrich found himself amused. "I would invite you to my table, and learn of this Golden Empire; but I fear you would pollute yourself."

Tarkhan crossed his hands over his breast. "Mighty ones, like master, so pure even small things are polluting them. Now he think golden-eye demon watching him and he draw seal of Solomon around rooms. But me, what matter? Beside, good manners never pollute."

The mention of golden-eyed demons held Dietrich momentarily speechless. Had the Krenken gone to the Lower Woods to peek at this exotic stranger? "I . . . I think I may have some porridge, and a little ale. I cannot place your accent."

"Is because my accent has no place. In Kiev, are Jews and Rus, Poles and Letts, Turks and Tatars. Is wonder I understand myself!" He followed Dietrich into the parsonage.

Joachim had just placed two bowls of porridge on the table. He stared, and Tarkhan favored him with a cautious smile. "You preacher I hear of."

"I am no friend to Jews," Joachim replied.

Tarkhan spread his hands in mock astonishment. Joachim said no more, but fetched a third bowl and some bread from the kitchen. These he placed on the table, just out of Tarkhan's reach. "No wonder," the Jew murmured to Dietrich as he gathered his food, "you sometimes burn them."

"Beware of too much cleverness," Dietrich whispered in return.

Each prayed grace after his own fashion. Tarkhan said over the clack of wooden spoons on wooden bowls, "Hof servants say you man of learning, much travel, and study nature."

"I was a scholar at Paris. Buridan was my master. But of this Kiev, I know nothing."

"Kiev, merchant city. Many come and go, and this wonders me when I boy. I taking service with ben Schlomo because he travel, so I seeing many place." He spread his hands. "So, I know he forbids 'Maimonism'? He say council of rabbis declaring forty years ago *scientia* not proper to Jews. Talmud only should be study. I should know this? I ask, where in Talmud this written, and he tell me only pure may study Talmud—which I am not. Oy!" He raised his eyes to Heaven in silent entreaty—or rebuke.

Joachim grunted. "Your master is right about the vanity of worldly knowledge, but wrong about which book should be studied."

The Jew took another spoon of porridge. "Everywhere I go, I hear this thing. In Muslim lands, too, but there, only Koran fit for study."

"The Muslims were wonderful scholars once," Dietrich said. "And I have heard of your Maimonides—as great a scholar as our Thomas and the Saracen Averröes."

"Master is calling Maimonists worse heretics than Samaritans. 'Destroy, burn and root them out,' he say. Is popular idea, I am thinking, for all folk. Muslims, too." Tarkhan shrugged. "Oy! Everyone else persecute Jews. Why not other Jews? Maimon himself was flee Cordoba because Ispanish rabbis persecute him. Until master say this," he added, "I never hear of him. So I was follow teacher I never hear?"

Dietrich chuckled. "For a Jew, you are a man of wit."

Tarkhan's grin vanished. "Yes. 'For a Jew.' But I find it so in all land. Some men wise, some fools; some wicked, some good. Some all of that, sometimes. I say Christian can be save in his religion, as Jew can in his, or Muslim in his." He paused. "Master is never telling you this, but we escape Regensburg because guilds take arms and fight Jew-killers. There gave in that city, two hundred and seven and thirty righteous gentiles."

"May God bless those men," said Dietrich.

"Omayn."

"Now," Dietrich said, as he carried the bowls to the sideboard, "let us sit by the hearth, and hear of this Golden Empire."

The Jew planted himself upon a stool while Dietrich stirred the logs to encourage the flames. Outside, wind rushed and the afternoon windows darkened with the clouds.

"This tale from old time," Tarkhan said, "so how much true? But is good tale, so no matter. In old times, in north of Persia, live 'Mountain Jews,' Simeon tribe, put there by Asshurrim. But many laws forgot until King Joseph find Talmud again. They know Elijah and Amos, Micah and Nahum, but now come flatland Jews from Babylon tell of new prophets: Isaiah, Jeremiah, Ezekial. Then pagan Turks come over to One God. Together we create Golden Empire. Our merchants go I'Stamboul, Baghdad, even Cathay."

"Merchants," said Joachim, who had affected not to listen. "You had much gold, then."

"Among Turks each direction is having color. South white, west gold, and Khazars then west-most of all Turks. Itli Khan name seven judges. Two judging our people by Talmud; two judging Christians; two judging Muslims by *shari'a.* Seventh judge pagans, who were worship sky. Many years our khan fight Arab, Bulgar, Greek, Rus. I see in old book, Jewish knight in chainmail riding steppe pony."

Dietrich stared in astonishment. "I have never heard of this empire!"

Tarkhan struck his breast. "Like all grown proud, Lord bring us low. Rus take Kiev and Itli. All this happen long ago, and most are forgotting, save some, like me, who love for old tales. Land rule now by Mongols and Poles; and I, whose fathers once kings, must serve Ispanish moneylender."

"You don't like Malachai," Dietrich guessed.

"His mother find that hard. Ispanish Jews proud, with strange customs. Eat rice cakes for Passover!"

WHEN DIETRICH later showed Tarkhan to the door, he said, "It has grown dark. Can you find Niederhochwald?"

The Jew shrugged. "Mule can find. I ride with him."

"I would . . ." Dietrich dipped his head, looked away for a moment at the stars. "I would thank you. Though I never wished your people any harm, never before have I seen a Jew as a man. Always it was 'a Jew is a Jew!' "

Tarkhan scowled. "True. But by us, Greek and Roman *notzrim* are same."

Dietrich recalled how the Krenken had seemed at first alike. "It is the strangeness," he said. "Just as the trees of a distant forest blend into an indistinguishable whole, so do the singularities of strangers fade when their appearance or customs are distant from our own."

"You may have right," said Tarkhan ben Bek. "Master, he travel many years, see only pollution. Though master is think he seeing you before, when he much younger."

THE TROUBLING thought that he had been recognized stayed with Dietrich, and he gave thanks that Malachai was safely segregated in the Lower Woods and would not see Dietrich again before he departed for Vienna.

AT MIDDAY on the Feast of St. Barnabas, a lone rider, astride a jennet mule and clad in the brown robes of a Minorite, worked his way up the track from St. Wilhelm and entered the manor house.

"I'll not go back," Joachim sneered when Dietrich mentioned the stranger. "Not while Strassburg's prior is a truckling Conventual who has forgotten every humility that Francis taught." Later, as they went to clean the church, he pointed across the notch that separated the two hills. "He's coming here. If he *is* a Conventual, I'll not kiss his hairy—"

The stranger monk studied the crest of Church Hill, pausing when he caught sight of the two watchers. There seemed no face within the cowl, only a black emptiness, and the notion sprang irresistibly to Dietrich's mind that this was Death, now these dozen years overdue, treading a weary mountain trail in search of him. Then a flash of white showed within the shadow and Dietrich realized that it was only the angle of the sun that had made that hood seem so empty. Immediately another apprehension replaced it: namely, that the rider was an *exploratore* sent by the Strassburg bishop to question him.

His unease grew as the inexorable mule plodded to the hilltop. There, the rider threw back his cowl, revealing a thin face, long in the chin and crowned by a laurel of tangled white hair. There was something of the fox in it, and of the deer surprised by a hunter, and the lips seemed those of a man who had lately mistaken for new wine a jar of old vinegar. Though time had aged him, had drawn him out more gaunt than ever, had spotted his northland-pale skin, five-and-twenty years sloughed off in an eyeblink and Dietrich gasped in surprise and delight.

"Will!" he said. "Is it truly you?"

And William of Ockham, the *venerabilis inceptor* bowed his head in mock humility.

RESIGNED BY now to the periodic intrusions of strangers, the Krenken had absented themselves from the public space; but perhaps having grown bored, they played this time a precarious game of hide-and-seek, keeping themselves just out of sight rather than flying off to the Great Wood. As Dietrich escorted his visitor about the village, he marked, from the corner of his eye, the sudden leap of a Krenk from one concealment to another.

The church walls held Will Ockham's tongue mute, a feat no Pope had yet accomplished. He stood before them some time before he began to circuit the building, exclaiming with delight over the *blemyae,* complimenting the peredixion tree and the dragon. "Delightfully pagan!" he declared. Some Dietrich must explain: the Little-Ash-Men of the Siegmann Woods, or the Gnurr of the Murg Valley, which seemed to emerge from the woodwork itself. Dietrich named the four giants supporting the roof. "Grim and Hilde and Sigenot and Ecke—the giants slain by Dietrich of Berne."

Ockham cocked his head. "Dietrich, was it?"

"A popular hero in our tales. Mark you Alberich the Dwarf in Ecke's pedestal. He showed King Dieter to the lair where Ecke and Grim lived. Giants don't like dwarves."

Ockham thought about that for a moment. "I shouldn't think they'd even notice them." He regarded the dwarf further. "At first, I thought him grimacing in his effort to hold the giantess up; but now I see that he is laughing because he is about to toss her over. Clever." He studied the kobolds under the eaves. "Now *those* are surpassingly ugly gargoyles!"

Dietrich followed his gaze. Five Krenken perched nude under the roofline, frozen in that preternatural stillness into which they sometimes fell, and pretended to uphold the roof. "Come," Dietrich said quickly, turning Ockham about. "Joachim will have prepared our meal by now." As he chivvied his guest along, he glanced backward over his shoulder and saw one of the Krenken open and close his soft lips in the Krenkish smile.

DIETRICH AND Ockham passed the evening over a supper of pumpernickel and cheese and wholesome amounts of ale. News of the great, wide world drifted through the High Woods on the lips of travelers; and Ockham had been at the center of that world.

"I was told," Dietrich said, "you are to make your peace with Clement."

Will shrugged. "Ludwig is dead, and Karl wants no quarrel with Avignon. Now that all the others are dead—Michael, Marsiglio, and the rest—why pretend that we were the true Chapter? I sent the Seal of the Order back, the one that Michael took with us when we fled. The Chapter met on Pentecost and told Clement of my gesture, and Clement sent to Munich offering better terms than Jacques de Cahors ever did. So we will kiss and pretend that all is well."

"You meant Pope John."

"The Kaiser never called him anything but 'Jacques de Cahors.' He was a religious man."

"Ludwig, religious!"

"Certainly. He created his own pope and carted him all over Italy. You can't get more religious than that. But when you have said 'hunting' and 'feasting' and 'bohorts,' you have limned the man in all his essentials. Oh, and securing his family's good fortune. A simple man, easily guided by his more subtle advisors—he would never have gone into Italy but for Marsiglio's wheedling—but his stubbornness could rebut the subtlest of reasoning. Karl, on the other hand, is much taken with the arts, and intends a university for Prague to rival Montpellier or Oxford, if not Paris itself. A place free of the rigid orthodoxies of established scholars."

He meant free of Thomists and Averröeists. "A place where they may pursue nominalism?" Dietrich teased.

Ockham snorted. "*I* am no nominalist. The problem with teaching the Modern Way is that lesser scholars, excited by the novelty, seldom bother to master my insights. There are lips on which I heartily wish my name had never rested. I tell you, Dietl, a man becomes a heretic less for what he writes than for what others believe he has written. But I will outlive all my enemies. The false pope Jacques is dead, and that old fool Durandus. One hopes the odious Lutterell will soon follow. Mark me. I shall dance on their graves."

" 'Doctor Modern' was hardly an 'old fool' . . ." Dietrich ventured.

"He sat on the tribunal that condemned my theses!"

"Durandus himself once faced the tribunal," Dietrich reminded him. "Peer-review is the fate of all philosophers worth reading. And he did exert his influence favorably on two of your propositions."

"Out of fifty-one on trial! Such a mewling favor is more insult than the honest hostility of the odious Lutterell. Durandus was a falcon that had choosen not to fly. He would have been less a fool had he been less brilliant. One does not criticize a stone for falling. But a falcon? Come, who else did we know at Paris?"

"Peter Aureoli . . . No, hold. He was raised archbishop, and died the year before you came."

"Is an archbishopric often so fatal?" Ockham said with amusement.

"You and 'Doctor Eloquent' would have found much in common. He shaved with your razor. And Willi is archdeacon now in Freiburg. I posed him a question this past market."

"Willi Jarlsburg? The one with the pouty lips? Yes, I remember him. A second-rate mind. An archdiaconate suits him, for there he will never be called upon to utter an original thought."

"You are too harsh. He always treated me kindly."

Ockham regarded him for a moment. "His sort would. But a kindly man may yet own a second-rank intellect. The assessment is no insult. The second rank is far more than what most scholars achieve."

Dietrich recalled Ockham's agility in taking shelter behind his precise words. "The Herr brought me a tract by a young scholar now at Paris, Nicholas Oresme, who has a new argument for the diurnal motion of the earth."

Ockham chuckled. "So, you still debate the philosophy of nature?"

"One does not debate nature; one experiences nature."

"Oh, surely. But John Mirecourt—you will not have heard of him. They call him 'White Monk.' A Capuchin, as you might suppose. His propositions were condemned at Paris last year—no, it was in forty-seven—by which accolade we know him for a thinker of the first rank. He has shown that experience—*evidentia naturalis*—is an inferior sort of evidence."

"Echoing Parmenides. But Albrecht said that in investigations of nature, experience is the only safe guide."

"No. Experience is a poor guide, for tomorrow one may have a contrary experience. Only those propositions whose contrary reduces to a contradiction—*evidentia potissima*—can be held with certainty." Ockham spread his hands to invite rebuttal.

Dietrich said, "A contradiction in terms is not the only sort of contradiction. I know that grass is green from experience. The contrary can be falsified by *experientia operans.*"

Ockham cupped his ear. "Your lips move, but I hear Buridan's voice. Who can say but that, in some far-off place, one may not find yellow grass?"

Dietrich was brought short by his recollection that, in the Krenkish homeland, the grass was indeed yellow. He scowled, but said nothing.

Ockham pushed himself to his feet. "Come, let us proof your proposition with an experience. The world turns, you said."

"I did not say that it *did* turn; only that, *loquendo naturale,* it *might.* The motion of the heavens would be the same in either case."

"Then why seek a second explanation? Of what use would it be, even were it true?"

"Astronomy would be simplified. So, applying your own principle of the least hypothesis—"

Ockham laughed. "Ah. Argument by flattery! A more potent argument by far. But I never intended entities in nature. God cannot be bound by simplicity and may choose to make some things simple and others complex. My razor applies only to the workings of the mind." He was already striding toward the door and Dietrich scurried to catch up.

Outside, Ockham studied the indigo sky. "Which way is east? Very well. Let us apply experience. Now, if I move my hand rapidly, thus, I feel the air pushing against it. So, if we are moving toward the east, I should feel an east wind on my face, and I—" He closed his eyes, and spread his arms. "—feel no wind."

Joachim, climbing Church Hill, stopped in the path and gaped at the scholar, who seemed to have adopted the attitude of the Crucified.

Ockham turned toward the Lesser Wood. "Now, if I face north . . ." He shrugged. "I feel no change in the wind whichever direction I face." He paused expectantly.

"One must arrange the experience," Dietrich insisted, "so that all matters affecting the conclusion are accounted for, which Bacon called *experientia perfectum.*"

Ockham spread his hands. "Ah, so the common senses are insufficient for this special sort of experience." Grinning as if he had triumphed in a quodlibet, he returned to the parsonage, Dietrich again in his wake. Joachim, following, latched the door and went to the pot for a stein of ale. He sat at the table beside Dietrich and tore a piece of bread off the loaf and listened with a smirk.

Dietrich pressed the argument. "Buridan considered the objections to a turning earth in his twenty-second Question on the heavens, and found a response for each, save one. If the entire world moves, including earth, water, air, and fire, we would no more feel a resisting wind than a boat drifting with the current feels the motion of the river. The one compelling objection was that an arrow loosed straight up does not fall west of the archer, which it would if the earth were turning underneath it, for an arrow moves so swiftly that it cuts *through* the air and thus would not be carried along by it."

"And this Oresme has resolved the objection?"

"Doch. Consider the arrow at rest. It does not move. Therefore, it begins already with the motion of the earth and, when loosed, possesses two motions: a rectilinear motion up and down, and a circular motion toward the east. Master Buridan wrote that a body impressed with motion, will continue in its motion until the impetus is dissipated by the body's gravity or other resisting forces."

Ockham shook his head. "First the earth moves, then the people move with it to explain why they do not constantly stumble; then the air must move with it to answer a second objection; then the arrow, to answer another; and so further. Dietl, the *simplest* explanation for why the stars and the sun appear to circle the earth is that they *do* circle the earth. And the reason why we feel no motion in the earth is that the earth does not move. Ah, 'Brother Angelus,' why waste your powers on such trivia!"

Dietrich stiffened. "Do not call me that!"

Ockham turned to Joachim and said, "He would be at his readings before the morning bells and stayed at it by candlelight after the evening bells, so the other scholars called him—"

"That is a long time since!"

The Englishman tilted his head back. "May I still call you *doctor seclusus*?" He grunted and sought another bout of ale. Dietrich retreated into silence. He had thought to share a fascinating idea, and Will had somehow created a *disputatio*. He should have remembered that, from Paris. Joachim glanced from one to the other. Ockham returned to the table. "This is the last of the ale," he said.

"There gives more in the kitchen," Dietrich answered.

They discussed the "calculators" at Merton and the death of Abbot Richard of Wallingford, who had invented a new "triangular" geometry and an instrument, the rectangulus, much favored by navigators. "And to speak of navigators," Dietrich added, "the Spanish have discovered new islands in the Ocean Sea." He had the tale from Tarkhan, who had it in turn from his master's agents. "They lie off the coast of Africa, and boast great flocks of canaries. So it may be that a 'new way' across Ocean may be found, leading to the 'oversea lands' on Bacon's map."

"One may more easily explain Bacon's Land by a cartographer's imagination and the lure of blank spaces." Ockham smiled and added, "Much as your rustic woodcarvers here have filled in the walls of your church with giant grasshoppers and the like."

Joachim had a slice of pumpernickel in his mouth and nearly choked until Dietrich had helped him to swallow some ale to help it down. Ockham rose, saying, "I'll fetch more ale from the kitchen." But Joachim gasped, "No, there waits also a giant grasshopper."

Unsure of the jest, Ockham barked puzzled laughter.

· XIX ·

JUNE, 1349

At Nones, The Commemoration of Bernard of Menthon

MANFRED STYLED his banquet "a symposium," and promised a quodlibet between Dietrich and Ockham as the post-prandial entertainment. But as some entertainments were not to everyone's taste, this did not supplant Peter's singing or the dwarf's acrobatics or the juggler's display of plates and knives. The dwarf's trained dog drew but a pursed lip from Will Ockham; but Kunigund and Eugen laughed hugely, especially when the dog tugged the dwarf's hose down to reveal his bare ass. Einhardt, like Manfred, paid more particular attention to the singing. "Einhardt has held me ill," Manfred had confided earlier to Dietrich, "for missing the bohorts, so this is my peace to him." Dietrich, having verified the knight's famous stink, gave thanks that his corpulent wife, Lady Rosamund, sat between them.

The sideboard was laden with game birds and aged venison, and continually refreshed by a never-ceasing bustle of servants bearing platters, retrieving empty trenchers, and spreading on the floor fresh rushes mixed with flowers to surrender their scents when stepped upon. Behind each seat a page awaited the diner's every need. Tarkhan ben Bek, brushed and combed into respectability, did service for his master, for Malachai's rites did not permit him to eat of Manfred's bounty, but only of his own provisions, prepared under his supervision. Normally, two of Manfred's hounds would prowl the room, scavenging scraps that fell from the table; but, from respect for the Jew's sensibilities, the animals had been barred from the feast. Their piteous howling could be heard faintly from the kennels outside.

Eugen sat at Manfred's right and Kunigund, his left. Beside them were Dietrich and Will, with Malachai the Jew to Will's right. Malachai's wife and daughter remained in seclusion, disappointing Eugen, who had anticipated the exotic sight of veiled women. Lady Rosamund was hardly compensation.

To Einhardt's left, at the table's foot sat Thierry von Hinterwaldkopf. The knight had already delivered his required service-days, but Manfred hoped to induce him to serve additional days from love to help hunt the outlaws.

In the corner beside the fireplace, Peter Minnesinger sat with his two assistants. "If it please mine Herr," he said, twisting his strings until they sang true, "I would sing from Parzival."

"Not that horrid French tale!" Einhardt complained.

"No, lord knight." Peter draped his hair and settled the lute upon his lap. "I would sing Wolfam von Eschenbach's version, which all men know is the noblest rendition of the story."

Manfred waved a hand. "Something less weighty," he said. "Something touching love. Play *Falcon Song.*" A devotee of the New Art, Peter oft complained of Manfred's fondness for the old-fashioned minnesong, in which all was figure and symbol, and would have preferred a more modern lyric, in which real people moved through real landscapes. *Falcon Song* was, however, artfully constructed, and no line could be changed without spoiling its symmetry. Its author, anonymous as poets of olden days often were, was known only as "He of Kürenburg."

> "I raised me a falcon for more than a year
> When I had him tamed as I'd have him be
> And I'd dressed his feathers with rich golden bands,
> Aloft high he soared and flew to other lands.
>
> Since then have I seen him gracefully flying:
> Sporting upon his foot silken tyings
> And his coat of feathers glittered golden.
> May God bring together who would lovers remain."

Listening, Dietrich marveled at how God could appear in sudden and unexpected places, for *Falcon Song* had given him God's answer to the problem of Ilse and Gerd. It mattered not that Ilse had been baptized and Gerd had not, for God would bring lovers together.

And more than lovers. Had Dietrich not raised Theresia as he'd have her be? Had she not "flown to other lands"? Had he not seen her since, "gracefully flying"? Surely, God would bring them together once again. A tear wound its way down his cheek and Kunigund, ever attentive to those about her, noticed, and placed her hand on his.

AFTERWARD, AMID the clatter of silverware and krautstrunks, table-talk settled on matters of the world. The House of Bardi had followed the House of Peruzzi into insolvency, Ockham told them, and Malachai added that silver had become scare. "It is all going East, to the Sultan to pay for silk and spices."

Dietrich said, "In his tractate on money, that mine Herr gave me, young Oresme wrote that money can be understood just as the rainbow or magnetism. He states that, 'If the prince sets a ratio on the coins that differs from the values of silver to gold in the market, the underrated coin will vanish from circulation, and the overrated alone remains current.' "

"A philosophy of money?" said Ockham.

"Silver *does* buy more gold in the East," Malachai said, tugging his beard.

"So it 'flies to others lands!' " laughed Kunigund.

"May God not keep silver asunder from those who love it," added Thierry with a sly glance at the Jew.

"Bah!" said Einhardt. "Then the prince merely fixes the prices of silver and gold in the market to match the values he sets on the coin."

"Perhaps not," Dietrich replied. "Jean Olivi argued that a thing's price derives from the assessments of those who seek to buy it—regardless what merchants demand or princes decree or however much labor went into its making."

Ockham laughed. "It's Buridan's wicked influence. Oresme is his pupil, as was Brother Angelus, here." He nodded to Dietrich. "And another from Saxony, called

'Little Albert,' is already much talked of. Ah, Dietl, you should have stayed at Paris. They would speak of you in the same way."

"I leave fame for others," Dietrich answered curtly.

WHEN TALK turned later to politics, Ockham recounted the infamous progress of the Wittelsbach court through Italy twenty years before, when they had burned the Pope in effigy. "After all," he said, "what say has a Frenchman in the election of the Roman Kaiser?"

"Sauwohl!" said Einhardt, saluting with his cup.

"I had thought to use this as the topic for the disputation," said Manfred, gesturing with a haunch of venison for the wine to be poured. "Tell us your arguments, Brother Ockham, if they are not merely that you ate at Ludwig's table?"

Ockham rested his chin on his palm and curled one finger by his ear. "Mine Herr," he said after a moment. "Marsiglio wrote that *no one* could gainsay the prince in his own land. Of course, he meant that 'Jacques de Cahors' could not gainsay Ludwig—which pleased Ludwig greatly. And what he really meant was that he was a Ghibelline, and blamed the Pope for every ill in Italy."

" 'Ghibelline,'" said Einhardt. "Why cannot the Italians pronounce 'Vibligen'?"

Manfred studied the back of his hand. "And you did not agree . . . ?"

Ockham spoke cautiously. "I argued that, *in extremis,* and *if the prince is become a tyrant,* then it is legitimate for another prince—even a pope—to invade his country and overthrow him."

Einhardt expelled his breath and Thierry stiffened. Even Manfred grew still.

"As the Breisgau lords," Dietrich interjected quickly, "overthrew von Falkenstein."

Einhardt grunted. "Outlaws, *doch.*" The sudden tension eased.

Manfred cast Dietrich an amused glance. He tossed the bone of his venison to the floor and turned again to Ockham. "And how are we to know when the prince is become a tyrant?"

Ockham's page refilled the Englishman's krautstrunk and Ockham took a swallow before answering. "You have heard the maxim, 'What has pleased the prince has the force of law.' But I glossed that, 'What pleases the prince *reasonably and justly for the sake of the common good* has the force of law.' "

Manfred studied his guest carefully and rubbed his cheek. "The prince," he said, "has always in mind the common good."

Ockham nodded. "Naturally, a prince who rules with God's law in his heart will do so; but men are sinners, and princes are men. So, men have certain natural rights directly from God, which the prince may not alienate. The first such: a man has a right to his own life."

Eugen gestured with his knife. "But he may be murdered by an enemy, or fall to the pest or other injury. What right to life has a man drowning in a river?"

Ockham raised his forefinger. "That a man possesses a natural right to his own life means only that his defense of that life is *legitimate,* not that his defense will be *successful.*" He spread his hands. "As for other natural rights, I number the right to freedom against tyranny, and the right to property. That last he may forego, *when in so doing he pursues his own happiness.*" Ockham cut into a sausage set before him by a page. "As the Spirituals do in imitation of the poverty of the Lord and His Apostles."

Thierry laughed. "Good. That leaves more for the rest of us."

Ockham waved a dismissal. "But with Ludwig dead, every man must look to himself, so I am for Avignon to make my peace with Clement. This really is a most excellent sausage."

Einhardt slapped the table. "You are thin for a monk, but I see you have a monk's appetite." Then, turning to Eugen he said, "Tell me how you won that scar," and, flushing, the young Ritter recounted his deeds at Burg Falkenstein. At the tale's conclusion, the imperial knight raised a cup to him. "Old strokes, worn with honor!" he cried.

He and Manfred then refought the battle of Mühldorf, where Einhardt had ridden for Ludwig Wittelsbach and Manfred for Friedrich Hapsburg, each of whom had sought the imperial crown.

"Ludwig cut a fine figure," Einhardt wheezed, "You must've remarked it, Ockham. You knew him. Very striking body, tall and slender. How he loved to dance and hunt stags!"

"For which reason," Manfred countered, "the imperial dignity sat lightly upon him."

"No *gravitas*?" Einhardt swallowed a mouthful of wine. "Well, your Hapsburgs are grave. I'll give you that. Old Albrecht couldn't pass the table salt without pondering the political implications. Hah! Before your time, I think. I was only a junker, myself. 'Hard as diamond,' that's what folks said about him."

"Yes," said Manfred. "Look at what he did in Italy."

Einhardt blinked. "Albrecht did nothing in Italy."

Manfred laughed and slapped the table. "Just so. He once said, 'Italy's a lion's den. Many tracks go in; none come out.' " The table broke out in laughter.

The older knight shook his head. "Never understood why Ludwig went in there. Nothing south of the Alps but Italians. Can't turn your back on 'em."

"It was at Marsiglio's urging," Ockham said. "He hoped the emperor would settle the civil wars there."

Manfred plucked a fig from the bowl and caught it in his mouth. "Why shed German blood to settle Italy's quarrels?"

Einhardt said, "Now, the Luxemburgers are the sort the minnesingers warble over. Karl keeps his purse open for 'em, so I suppose they'll sing about him, too. That's why I followed *Ludwig*. Between your dour Hapsburgers and the flighty Luxemburgers, the Wittelsbachs are plain-spoken, beer-drinking German folk, as simple as this sausage."

"Yes," said Manfred, "as simple as that sausage."

Einhardt smiled. "Well, they'd have to be fools to want the crown at all." He frowned over a dish of *blancmange* the servant set before him. "This, I must say, is more like a Luxemburger."

Thierry said, "Speaking of all that, what's become of old 'Pocket Mouth'?"

Malachai the Jew answered. "We heard in Regensburg that *Gräfin* Margaret remains loyal to her new husband and the Tyrolean revolt is over."

"No blame to her," said Thierry. "Her first husband was both stupid and impotent. A wife might endure one or the other, but not both."

"Hah!" said Manfred, raising a cup. "Well said!"

"Marriage is a sacrament," Dietrich objected. "I know you defended Ludwig on this, Will, but not even an emperor may annul a marriage."

Einhardt leaned past his lady and shook a fork at Dietrich. "No, a marriage is an *alliance*. The Great Houses," he said, tapping his temple, "they are planning *decades* ahead—decades!—shoving their children like chess pieces into the marriage beds of the Empire. But that is where Ludwig was so clever—for a sausage-head. 'Pocket-Mouth' detested Hans-Heinrich, but she would not discard a marriage-alliance with Luxemburg without obtaining another of equal value. So, Ludwig gives her a divorce—*and then marries her to his own son!*" He smacked the table with his palm so that the cups danced. "So, pfft! Luxemburg loses the Tyrol to Wittelsbach."

"For so clever a move," Thierry said, "it proved a bit too obvious."

"So," said Einhardt, "Ludwig makes a second chess-move. He holds Bavaria, and his son holds now the Tyrol *and* the Brandenburg Mark, which neatly surrounds Bohemia—in case Luxemburg makes the trouble, *ja?* So when the other Houses complain of the nepotism, he takes Carinthia from the Tyrol, which changes nothing but makes everyone happy."

"And you'll notice," added Manfred, "that Hapsburg gained Carinthia—*without* the need to kiss the Ugly Duchess."

More laughter. Einhardt shrugged. "What matter? Luxemburg rules Europe now. You'll not see a Hapsburg again on the imperial throne."

Manfred smiled at his own *blancmange.* "Perhaps not."

"Three votes sit in Luxemburg's pocket."

"With four needed," Thierry said. "Have they resolved the dispute in Mainz?"

Einhardt shook his head. "The Pope's new lapdog—who is it?" He snapped his fingers.

"Gerlach of Nassau," Ockham told him.

"The very man. He's tells everyone he's the new archbishop, but Heinrich won't surrender his See. You see how clever all this is? Gerlach is nobody. Who fears House Nassau holding Mainz?"

"*If* he can oust Count Heinrich," said Thierry.

"So." Einhardt counted off on his fingers. "Karl holds the Bohemian vote himself, and his brother Baldwin is archbishop of Trier. That's two. And when House Luxemburg says, 'frog,' Archbishop Waldrich asks how high he should jump. Except *he* thinks he is King of Frogs. Ha-hah! So Köln's vote makes three. As for the Wittelsbachs . . . Well, little Ludwig holds Brandenburg, as I've said; and his brother Rudolf is Count Palatine, which makes two votes. With Mainz uncertain, both families play court to the other Rudolf, the Duke of Saxe-Wittenburg. Hah! House *Welfen* holds the balance!"

Manfred said mildly, "The balance will change before the electoral college need vote again. Yet . . . No one thought Ludwig would drop dead, either."

"The Kaiser's party was hunting in the woods around Fürstenfeld," Ockham remembered. "I was at the lodge with the others when they brought him in. A peasant found him lying in the field beside his horse, as if he had no more than fallen asleep."

"A man in the summer of his life, too," Einhardt said. "Apoplexy, I heard."

"Too many sausages," Manfred suggested.

"He did not die hungry," Ockham admitted.

"Nor will I," said Einhardt. "This is excellent food, Manfred. Too bad not all of us can enjoy it." He glanced at Malachai. "Now, what's this I hear about your guesting demons?"

The question, coming unexpectedly as it did, brought momentary silence to the table.

"I have founded a lazaret in the Great Wood," Manfred said casually. "The lepers there are hideous in appearance, but are mortal as you or I." Thierry grinned at nothing; Eugen looked into his cup. Lady Kunigund watched her father. Ockham listened with keen interest. Malachai tugged repeatedly at his beard and his eyes missed nothing.

"Hah. Some o' your men've been spreadin' tales, then," Einhardt replied. "Said you brought 'em down to Falcon Rock that time." The old man turned to his wife and said, "Y'see, my dear? Nothin' to those stories."

Lady Rosamund was a fleshy, indignant woman. "Then, what of that *thing* I saw?" She turned to the Hochwalders. "Since two weeks, I hear a strange clicking from my rose garden, but when I look, I see . . . I don't know what. Hideous yellow eyes, enormous arms and legs . . . Like a giant grasshopper. It leapt from the garden into the sky and *flew,* flew away in this direction. Then I see my roses chewed on and spat on the ground!"

"A giant grasshopper . . ." said Malachai slowly.

Einhardt patted her arm. "Some beast had gotten into the garden, dear. That was all." But he studied Manfred with a cool eye.

ON THE morrow, Dietrich escorted Ockham as far as the pass on the Oberreid road. Ockham led his mule, which he had named "Least Hypothesis," and he paused and rubbed its nose. He had thrown back his cowl, so that in the dawn his wild hair seemed a laurel of flame against the rising sun. He said, "You've let your tonsure grow out, Dietl."

"I am a simple priest of the diocese now," he said, "a mendicant no longer."

Ockham studied him. "You may have foresworn your vow of poverty, but I cannot say you have gained wealth by doing so."

"Life here has its gifts."

"Had you learned to flatter the Kaiser, you would need not live in the back woods."

"Had you learned to live in the back woods, you would need not flatter the Kaiser."

Ockham smiled faintly and looked off to the east, toward Munich, Prague, Vienna, the capitals of the Great Houses. "A touch," he said; and, a moment later, "There was an excitement to it, a feeling that we were accomplishing things in the world. 'If you defend me with your sword,' I told Ludwig, 'I'll defend you with my pen.' "

"I wonder if he would have, had it come to the test."

Ockham shrugged. "Ludwig had the better of the bargain. But when he has been long forgotten, men will remember me."

"Is it so bad a thing," wondered Dietrich, "to be forgotten?"

Ockham turned away and tightened the cinch on the mule's saddle. "So tell me about demons and grasshoppers."

Dietrich had seen him study the church roof and knew he had marked the absence of the "gargoyles." And Einhardt's lady had described them.

Dietrich sighed. "There are islands farther even than the Canary Islands. The very stars of Heaven are distant islands, and on them live . . ."

"Grasshoppers," suggested Ockham, "rather than canaries."

Dietrich shook his head. "Beings much as you and I, but bearing an outward form resembling grasshoppers."

Ockham laughed. "I would accuse you of multiplying entities, saving only . . ." He glanced again toward the church eaves. "How do you know that these grasshoppers live upon a star?"

"They told me so."

"Can you be certain that they spoke the truth? A grasshopper may say what it wishes and be no more truthful than a man."

Dietrich reached into his scrip. "Would you speak with one?"

Ockham studied the head-harness that Dietrich brought forth. He touched it gingerly with his finger. "No," he said, withdrawing his hand. "Best I know as little as possible."

"Ah." Dietrich looked away. "Manfred told you of the indictment."

"He asked if I would speak for you before the prosecuting magistrate."

Dietrich grunted.

"Yes, as if the word of a heretic would carry weight with *them.* Should any ask concerning matters diabolical during my sojourn here, I can truthfully answer that I saw nothing."

"Thank you, old friend." The two embraced and Dietrich helped Will mount.

Ockham seated himself. "I fear you have wasted your life in this crappy little dorp."

"I had my reasons."

And reasons, too, for staying. Dietrich had come to Oberhochwald seeking only refuge, but it was now his corner of the world, and he knew each tree, rock, and stream as if he had had his head banged against them in his youth. He could not live again in Paris. It had seemed better then only because he had been younger, and had not yet known contentment.

AFTER THE "Old Inceptor" had ridden away, Dietrich returned to the village, where he encountered his farmer, Herwyg One-eye, on his way to the fields. "He be gone, pastor," the old man cackled. "And not too soon."

"So?" Dietrich asked, wondering what possible grudge Herwyg might hold against Ockham.

"Left Niederhochwald this morning, cart, harem, and all. Set out for Freiburg at first light."

"The Jew?" Dietrich felt suddenly cold in the June sun. "But he was faring to Vienna."

Herwyg rubbed his chin. "Can't say; don't care. He's a wretched creature. Kurt the swineherd, what is married to my cousin, heard the old Jew say he'd put an end to the Angelus. What infamy! Without the bells, how would folk know when to halt work?"

"The Angelus," said Dietrich.

Herwyg leaned closer and lowered his voice, though there were none to hear him. "And the wight must've caught glimpse o' your special guests, too. Kurt heard'm exclaim about unclean beasts and flying demons. Kurt, he come up here right off, 'cause he wants t'be the first with news." Herwyg hawked and spat into the dirt, but whether that signified the Jews, his cousin's taste in husbands, or merely a phlegmy throat, Dietrich did not wait to hear. He sought the empty church, where, amidst the images of suffering saints and outlandish creatures, he fell to his knees and begged again the absolution that he had begged for more a dozen years.

· XX ·

JUNE, 1349

From the Commemoration of St. Herve

THE HERR found him there, prostrate on the flagstones, and turned and sat on the sanctuary step beside him. "I've sent Max and his men to fetch the Jew," he said. "There are but few roads he could take, encumbered as he is with his cart. Max's men are ahorse. He'll bring him back."

Dietrich rose to his knees. "And then what?"

Manfred leaned back on his elbows. "And then we'll see. I'm improvising."

"You can't hold him forever."

"Can't I? No, I suppose the Duke will wonder. A factor for the Seneor family cannot simply disappear. But our worries run together, Dietrich," he added. "Friedrich would have questions for me, as well. I took you in."

I could run, Dietrich thought. Yet, where would he run this time? What lord would take him in? The New Towns in the wild east were hungry for settlers, and asked few questions about a man's past. Dietrich returned to his prayers, but his thoughts were now disturbed with self-love. So he employed recitations, hoping that the thought might follow the words. After a while, he heard Manfred rise and go.

THE SUN was lowering when the commotion drew Dietrich forth at last to gaze upon the party returning up the cleft between Church Hill and the castle. It was Max and his party, with a single prisoner bound and hoodwinked on a guided horse. Folk were streaming from their cottages or running in from the spring fields to learn what had befallen.

Joachim came up behind Dietrich. "Is that the Jew?" he asked. "Why is he bound up like that? What does Manfred plan to do with him?"

He plans to kill him, Dietrich thought. He cannot hold the man, for the Duke was sending an escort to bring him to Vienna; nor can he give the man his liberty, for the Markgraf would punish him for sheltering Dietrich these past twelve years. Dietrich remembered what Max had once said about serving two masters. But an accident . . . Death would be more convenient for everyone.

Except Malachai, of course.

"Where are you going?" Joachim asked him.

"To save Manfred."

HE FOUND the Herr on his high seat at the far end of the castle hall, beneath the Hochwald banner. As he entered, Dietrich heard the door to the bergfried slam closed and saw Manfred heave a troubled sigh.

"Mine Herr!" Dietrich cried. "You must free the Jew!"

Manfred, sitting with his chin upon his fist, looked up in surprise. "Free him!" He sat back against the chair. "You know what would follow?"

Dietrich clenched his fists by his side. "Ja. Doch. I know. But sin demands repentance, not further sin. A Jew is made in the image of God, no less than, than a Krenkl, and a remnant of them will one day be saved. God will accept Malachai for his faithfulness to the old dispensation, *for His promise is from generation to generation.* God made His people a covenant, and God does not foreswear Himself. Malachai sought our protection, and I swear what I swore at Rheinhausen that day when you found me: to no one who comes to me shall I allow harm. I swear it even should that vow place me between him and you."

Manfred's face went cold. "You touch on my honor. Do you love the flames so much that you would weep over the torchbearer?"

"He has good cause."

Manfred grunted. "And you accept the penance that would follow?"

Old Rudolf Baden had been Markgraf during the uprising, but Friedrich might have inherited his father's grudges along with his lands. The church courts would take Dietrich from the secular courts if he appealed; but that might only exchange noose for faggots. Yet, Carino had murdered his inquisitor, Peter of Verona, and ended his days in great saintliness in the priory of Forli—where the prior was Peter's own brother. "I ask no indulgences," he said.

Manfred lifted his gaze toward the corner of the chamber. "You heard what he said?"

"I heard."

Dietrich spun about, and there to his left stood Malachai the Jew, only somewhat battered, and by his side, a disheveled Tarkhan ben Bek. Malachai approached Dietrich and looked him closely in the eyes. Dietrich flinched, but then accepted the scrutiny with meekness.

Finally, Malachai stepped away. "I was mistaken," he said to Manfred. "This is not the same man." Then he turned abruptly on his heel and strode for the door. "I will await the escort in Niederhochwald—and trust to my spells until then."

Tarkhan followed him out, but stopped where Dietrich stood. "You lucky man," he whispered. "You *very* lucky man, master never wrong."

DIETRICH FOUND Max in the common room of the castle's bergfried, where Theresia was sewing his cuts up. He looked up when Dietrich entered and gave him a grin.

"Your Jews were fortunate," Max said. "Had we not pursued, they were dead men, and the women worse. The outlaws fell upon them two leagues past the Lesser Wood, where the Oberreid road passes through that narrow defile in the Dark Woods. A good place for ambush. I had marked it myself. Is that wine, woman? Wine's for drinking, not for wounds!" He grabbed the cup from her and gulped a swallow.

"Pfaugh!" He spat it on the ground. "That's vinegar wine!"

"Your pardon, soldier," Theresia said, "but I understand the practice is recommended by the Pope's physicians and the Italian doctors."

"Italians use poison," Max said. "But as well the outlaws chose the defile," he continued, "for they had no sign we were on the Jews' heels until we had fallen upon their rear. Their lookout had abandoned his post to join in the looting. God was with us and—" Max looked about the guardroom and lowered his voice. "And that servant of his had a sword in his bundle, a great curved blade like the Turks use. That gave us another edge in the fight, so I'll not argue the legalities of it.

"I had marked my man: an ill-looking buggerer, more scar than skin. I could see he was no stranger to daggerwork, for he came at me with his weapon in the underfist position, so I fell into the stance called 'the unbalanced scales'." He waved his arms, trying to demonstrate from a seated position, much inconveniencing Theresia. "But, damn me, if he didn't overfist his dagger and reverse his stroke. A clever ruse.

"Now a dagger is well and good to force a point between the links in a coat of mail, but it's no good at all for slashing. My quillon took him off his guard, and instead of the forearm block he expected, I gave him a stroke across the belly. He had fast hands, though. I give him that. A daggerman wants quickness more so than strength."

Theresia clucked while she bandaged his arm. "Ach, the poor man."

Max scowled. "That 'poor man' and his fellows murdered twelve people since they fled Falcon Rock, including Altenbach and his entire family."

"He was a wicked man, I am sure," she answered, "but he has now no chance of repentance."

"He has now no chance of another murder. You are too tender, woman."

Too tender, Dietrich thought, yet in some ways no more tender than flint; and in other ways less like flint than glass.

DIETRICH STAYED with Max after Theresia had left. "Manfred said that you took none captive, save Oliver."

Max was silent for a space, then he said, "It is a bad gambit to block a man's dagger with your shoulder. I must remember that the next time." He flexed his shoulder and winced. "I pray it does not stiffen on me. Would you tell God that at Mass? I will pay seven pence. Pastor . . ." He sighed. "Pastor, Oliver was ours to deal with. The others were carrion, but Oliver was one of us, and we must hang him with our own hands."

And so it was.

Manfred summoned the jurors to the courtyard, where Nymandus the gärtner swore to Oliver's presence among the outlaws and to his murder of the Altenbach boy. The young man made no response, but whispered, "I rode a horse and carried a sword. I struck blows for the poor and in honor of the queen of love and beauty."

No, Dietrich thought, *you struck blows* upon *the poor—because your queen of love and beauty chose another.* He wondered what the other outlaws had made of him. Had they, too, imagined themselves free men defying oppressive lords?

None spoke in Oliver's behalf, not even his father, who loudly disowned his son and cried that this was the fate of all those who aspired above themselves. But afterward, he returned to his bakery and sat for hours staring at the cold, cold oven.

Only Anna Kohlmann wept for him. "It is all for cause of me," she said. "He would only win my heart with daring feats."

And instead of winning a heart, he had lost a neck. "Mine Herr," Dietrich said when Manfred had asked for any to speak, "if you hang him, he will have no chance for repentance."

"You see to the next life," the Herr answered. "I must see to this one."

The Krenken who had crowded into the court clattered their agreement along with the other Hochwalders when the jurors returned their verdict and Manfred pronounced sentence of death. Gschert von Grosswald and Thierry von Hinterwaldkopf, who flanked Manfred on the bench, concurred in the judgment, Gschert with a simple scissoring of his horny lips.

So the next morning at dawn, they led the prisoner forth, bound and gagged, bleeding from a dozen wounds, face blackened by countless blows. His eyes darted like two mice above the rag jammed into his mouth, seeking escape, seeking succor, finding nothing but dull contempt from those around him. His own father spat upon him as he was led down the high street toward the linden tree for judgement.

LATER, WHEN Dietrich went by Theresia's cottage to see to her welfare, he encountered Gregor outside her door, nursing one hand with the other. "My little finger, I think," the mason said. "It wants a splint. I jammed it between two stones."

Dietrich rapped on the doorpost and Theresia pulled open the upper door and, seeing Gregor, brightened into the first smile Dietrich had witnessed since the advent of the Krenken. Then she caught sight of Dietrich. "Greet God, father," she said before turning to address Gregor. "And how goes it by you, mason?"

Gregor raised his bloody hand in mute appeal, and Theresia gasped and rushed him in. Dietrich followed, leaving the upper door open for the air. He watched Theresia cleanse the wound and bind it to a splint with a hemp bandage, although it seemed to Dietrich that the mason was not one to quail at such small hurts. Only after she had cared for Gregor did Theresia address Dietrich. "And are you then also wounded, father?"

Yes, he thought. "I came only to see how matters go with you," Dietrich said.

"It goes well," she said, turning up her eyes to his face.

Dietrich waited for her to say more, but she did not; and so he took her by the shoulders and kissed her on the brow, as he had so often in her childhood. Unaccountably, she began to weep. "I wish they had never come!"

Dietrich said, "Gottfried-Lorenz has assured me that they will soon go home."

"To one home or another," Gregor said. "Two more died this past week. I think they die of homesickness."

"No one dies of homesickness," Dietrich said. "The cold killed some—the alchemist, the children, a few others—but summer is come."

"It's what Arnold once told me," the mason insisted. "He said, *'We will die because we are not at home.'* And again, he said, *'Here, we eat our fill, but are not nourished.'*"

"That is senseless," said Dietrich.

The mason scowled, and glanced at Theresia, and then at the open doorway, through which the sounds of birds thrilled the morning air. "It puzzles me," the big man admitted. "Your friend, the Kratzer, said once that he wished for half the hope that Arnold had. Yet, Arnold murdered himself, and the Kratzer did not."

"Their talking head may not understand such words as 'hope' or 'despair.'"

"What difference," said Theresia, "whether they die or depart?"

Diertrich turned and took her hand in his, and she did not pull away. "All men die," he told her. "What matters in God's eye is how we have treated one another in life. 'Love the Lord with your whole heart and your whole soul, and love your neighbor as yourself.' This command binds us to one another and saves us from the snares of vengeance and brutality."

"There is no shortage among Christians of vengeance and brutality," Gregor observed.

"Men are men. 'By their fruits you shall know them,' not by what name they call themselves. Sudden grace may come upon even the most wicked of men. Ja, even the most wicked of men . . . I have—I have seen this myself."

Theresia reached out and touched his cheek to brush away a tear. Gregor spoke: "You mean Gottfried-Lorenz. Grosswald called him choleric, and now he is the humblest of Krenken."

"Ja," said Dietrich, glancing toward him. "Ja. I meant like Gottfried-Lorenz."

"But I think Grosswald intended no praise by calling him humble."

Theresia was weeping also and Dietrich returned her favor. "No, he would not," he answered. "By him are forbearance and forgiveness weakness and folly. A man with power uses it; one without, obeys. But I believe all men thirst for justice and mercy, whatever is written in the 'atoms of their flesh.' We have saved six of his folk—perhaps seven, for of the alchemist I am uncertain."

"Justice *and* mercy," said Gregor. "Both at once? Now, there stands a riddle."

"Father," said Theresia suddenly, "can one love and hate the same man?"

A bee had found its way into the cottage and hunted diligently among the herbs that Theresia grew in small clay pots on her windowsills. "I think," Dietrich said at last, "that it may be not the same man, but rather two: the man he is now and the man he once was. If a sinner truly repents, he dies to sin and a new man is born. That is what it means to forgive, for it defies reason to blame one man for the deeds of another."

He feared to press the matter further and left the cottage shortly after with Gregor. Outside, the mason rubbed his injured finger absently. "She is a sweet woman, if a simple one. And she may not be entirely wrong about the demons. It may be as Joachim says—the supreme test. But who is tested? Do we lead them to humility, or do they lead us to vengeance? Knowing men, I fear the second."

AT BREAKFAST the next morning, the Kratzer opened a flask that he kept in his scrip. The contents proved a murky broth, which the Krenk stirred into his porridge. He screwed the cork back into place, but sat frozen with the flask in hand for some time before returning it to his scrip. The Kratzer pulled a spoonful of porridge to his lips, hesitated, then returned spoon and contents to the bowl and pushed it away. Dietrich and Joachim exchanged puzzled glances, and the Minorite rose from his seat and went to the pot to check the porridge.

"Does it fill, but not nourish?" Dietrich asked in jest, remembering what Gregor had said the day before.

The Kratzer responded with that stillness in which his folk seemed to turn to stone. Always unnerving to Dietrich, the gesture became suddenly clear. Certain animals responded to danger by likewise remaining still. "What is wrong?" Dietrich asked.

The Kratzer stirred his porridge. "I ought not speak of it." Dietrich waited and Joachim watched with a puzzled frown. He ladled porridge into his own bowl but, although he had to reach past the Kratzer to do so, the Krenk did not move.

"I have heard some among you," the Kratzer said at last, "speak of a famine that befell many years ago."

"More than thirty years past," Dietrich said. "I had been lately received into orders and Joachim was not even born. It rained mightily for two years and the crops drowned in the fields from Paris to the Polish marches. There had been small hungers before, but in those years there was no grain anywhere in Europe."

The Kratzer rubbed his forearms together forcefully. "I was told that people ate grass," he said, "to fill their bellies—but the grass did not sustain them."

Dietrich stopped eating and stared at the Krenk.

"What?" Joachim asked, sitting down.

Dietrich sensed the sidelong glance of the creature, who remained otherwise entranced by some inner vision. "How much longer," he asked the Kratzer, "will your particular stores last?"

"We have eked them out since the beginning, but drop-by-drop even the mightiest sea must one day empty. Some hold out great 'hope,' but their way is hard, perhaps too hard for some of us. It has pleased me," he added, "that your 'early time' came before the end. I should have missed seeing your flowers bloom, and your trees come back to life."

Dietrich looked on his guest with horror and pity. "Hans and Gottfried may yet repair—"

The Kratzer kratzled his forearms. "That cow comes not off the ice."

PRAYING A horse from Everard, Dietrich sped to the Krenkish encampment, where he found Hans, Gottfried, and four others in the lower apartment of the strange vessel, clustered around a "circuit" illustration, and making a great chitter of discussion. "Is it true," Dietrich demanded bursting in, "that your folk will soon starve?"

The Krenken paused in their work and Hans and Gottfried, who wore head-harnesses, turned about to face the door.

"Someone has told you," Hans said.

" 'Jaws have hinges,' " Gottfried commented.

"But is it *true*?" insisted Dietrich.

"It has truth," Hans said. "There are certain . . . materials—acids is your alchemic word—which are essential for life. Perhaps four score of these acids befall in nature—and we Krenken need one-and-twenty of them to live. Our bodies produce naturally nine, so we must from our food and drink obtain the others. That food which you have shared with us holds eleven of those twelve. One is lacking, and our alchemist found it nowhere in all the foodstuffs he proofed. Without that particular acid, there is one . . . I must call it a 'firstling,' as it is the first building block of the body, though I suppose it should wear one of your Greekish terms."

"Proteios," Dietrich croaked. *"Proteioi."*

"So. It puzzles me why you use different 'tongues' to speak of different matters. This Greekish for natural philosophy; the Latinish for matters touching your lord-from-the-sky."

Dietrich seized the Krenk by his forearm. The rough spines that ran its length pricked his hand, drawing blood. "That makes nothing!" he cried. "What of this *protein*?"

"Without this acid, the *protein* cannot be formed, and lacking it, our bodies slowly corrupt."

"Then we must find it!"

"How, my friend? How? Arnold spent sleepless nights searching for it. If it eluded his keen eye, how may we discover it? Our physician is skilled, but not in the arts of the laboratory."

"So, you chewed upon the roses near Stag's Leap? You robbed the monastery at St. Blasien?"

A toss of the arm. "As if one could know by tasting! Yes, some of our folk try this or that. But the best source of the *protein* lies at our journey's end. The missing acid lies within our own particular food, which we eke out to supplement that which your people have provided." Hans turned away. "Our ship will sail before the hunger grows acute."

"What is in the broth that the Kratzer will not eat?"

Hans did not turn around, but his voice whispered in Dietrich's ear as if he stood by his side. "There is one other meat that has this *protein,* and the supply of it is not yet exhausted."

Dietrich did not understand for a long moment. Then Gottfried said, "This is my body, to be given up for us. Your words have given us hope," and the full horror of the stranger's situation fell upon him, nearly crushing him with its weight.

"You must not!"

Hans turned once more to face Dietrich. "Would you have *all* die, when *some* might live?"

"But—"

"You have taught that it is good to offer one's body for the salvation of others. We have a sentence. 'The strong devour the weak.' It is a sign, a *metaphor,* but in times of great hunger in our past, it has befallen in fact. But you have saved us. It is the *offer* and not the eating that saves, and the strong too may offer themselves to save the weak among us."

DIETRICH RETURNED to Oberhochwald numbed. Could he have mistaken the Krenken? It was not beyond reason. The *Heinzelmännchen* did not understand the significances of words and associated the signs only from usage. *Evidentia naturalis,* he thought.

Yet clearly the Kratzer was distressed by the thought. So much so that he would not even taste the broth. Dietrich shuddered anew at the memory. Of whom had that broth been distilled? Arnold? The children? *Had any of them been hurried to their deaths to prepare the broth?* That thought was most horrid of all. Would the Krenkish *instinctus* move them willingly to the stewpot?

Arnold had given his own life. "This is my body," he had promised the other Krenken in his death-note. A terrible parody, Dietrich now realized. Having failed in his search for the elusive acid, he had despaired and quit the struggle. And yet he had retained, like the legendary casket of Pandora, one last tenuous hope—that Hans and Gottfried might repair the ship and sail the Krenken back to their heavenly home. Anything that extended the needed foodstuffs would add that many days to the effort. Unwilling himself to follow the path he saw necessary, the alchemist had taken the only path he could, for the sake of others.

And so he had died a Christian after all.

THE RIDER wore the livery of the Strassburg Bishop and Dietrich watched his approach from a crag overlooking the Oberreid road. Hans, who had warned him of it, perched beside him, clinging somehow to the very rock so that, although he leaned far beyond the precipice, he did not fall as a man might. A different center of gravity, he had explained once to Dietrich, showing him a trick with straws, a pfennig, and a cup. "Does he bring your arrest?" the Krenkl asked. "We would fight to keep you from their hands."

"'Put away your sword,'" Dietrich quoted self-consciously. "Your attack would hardly allay what fears they nurse." Hans laughed then clacked into his farspeaker a warning to the others.

He watched the herald turn his mount up the track toward St. Catherine.

Looking about, Dietrich realized that Hans had departed without a sound, a Krenkish ability eerily akin to ghostly vanishing. *I must keep the herald from the parsonage,* he realized, for the weakening Kratzer lay within. He gathered his skirts and hurried to the head of the path just as the herald reached its top, bringing the man to an abrupt halt. "Peace be with you, herald," Dietrich said. "What mission brings you here?"

The man searched from side to side, glancing even above his head, and clutched his cloak more tightly about him, though the day was warm. "I carry a message from His Excellency, Berthold II, by grace of God bishop of Strassburg."

"Indeed, I spy his badge on your cloak." If they had come for him, why had they sent only this one man? Yet, if the message were an order to return to Strassburg with the messenger, he would do so meekly. In the distant fields, some of the peasants had paused at the furrow to stare toward the church. At the hill's base, the arrhythmic clang-clang of Wanda Schmidt's hammer had ceased while she watched events transpire above her.

The herald pulled forth a parchment, folded and tied with a ribbon and sealed with wax. This he tossed to the ground at Dietrich's feet. "Read this at Mass," the man said, and then, with marked hesitation, "I have more parishes to visit, and should like a pot of ale before I leave."

That he had no intention of dismounting had become clear. His rouncy was haggard and nearly blown. How many parishes had he already visited, how many more yet to go? Dietrich saw now other packets in the herald's pouch. "You may pray a horse from the Herr's stables," he said with a gesture across the valley.

The messenger said nothing, but regarded Dietrich with wariness. The parsonage door banged open and a bird took sudden flight from the eave, and the herald started with a terrible fear distorting his face.

But it was only Joachim bearing the requested ale. He must have been listening from the window. The bishop's man regarded the Minorite with suspicion. "No surprise finding one of *them* in this place," he sneered.

"I could dip a sponge in the pot and offer you the ale on a hyssop reed," said Joachim, who had not the reach to hand the mounted man his cup.

The herald bent and snatched the cup from the Franciscan's hands, quaffed his fill, and tossed it to the dirt. Joachim knelt to retrieve it. "I have offended my lord," he said, "by offering him not a golden cup studded with emeralds and rubies."

He was ignored. The herald gestured to the message in the dust. "The pest is come to Strassburg."

Dietrich crossed himself and Joachim forgot to rise. "God help us all," Dietrich whispered.

· XXI ·

JUNE, 1349
The Nativity of St. John the Baptist

THE MASS, *Recordáre, Dómine,* was said at nones, and St. Catherine's filled with the dreadful curious. Burg and dorp alike were there, and the Krenken as well, even those unbaptized, for all knew that some portentious word had reached the pastor. Manfred and his family, forewarned, stood in front to provide an example. Dietrich celebrated jointly with the chaplain, Father Rudolf, a vain and haughty man much consumed with the prestige of his benefice. Yet Rudolf's pale countenance, like the ruin of a Roman temple, demanded pity and Dietrich gave him the Savior's words, *Be not afraid, for I am with you always.*

The bishop's letter, when read aloud, had not the heart-draining sound of the herald's flat pronouncement. A few citizens had fallen ill with the unmistakable signs, but not in the vast numbers felled in Paris or, the year before, in Italy. Yet, all parishes were warned to prepare themselves. Special prayers were begged for Strassburg—and for Basel and Berne, for the pest was now known to have been in Berne in February, and in Basel by May.

At this news, Anna Kohlmann threw herself weeping to the flagstones and would not be comforted. "Bertram!" she cried. "Ach, Bertram!" Manfred, who had sent the boy to Berne, maintained a stoic countenance.

Into this commotion crawled from the rear of the nave Ilse Krenkerin. Like the Kratzer, she was much weakened by her refusal to drink the elixir, and moved only by use of oddly shaped crutches; but these she abandoned and went to Anna on hands and knees, where she proceeded to poke at the girl. Some cried out at the attack. But Joachim breasted the crowd and stood over the two girls, crying that this was only the Krenkish caress.

"I know the sentences inside your head," Ilse told Anna, and the *Heinzelmännchen* spread the words to a score of head-harnesses, and whispers spread it further. "I died when Gerd fell. But he fell in his duties to the common good, and I will see him when my energy enters the lands of the Herr-from-the-sky." Joachim repeated these simple words of faith for the assembled congregation. This brought mutters of agreement and much nodding of heads, but little comfort to Anna Kohlmann.

After services, Dietrich and Father Rudolf unvested in the sacristy. "The bishop wrote only that it *might* come here," the chaplain said. "Only that it *might*. Not that it *would.*" He seemed to take much comfort in grammar. "And Strassburg is distant. The Elsass borders on the French-reich. Not so distant as Avignon or Paris, but . . ."

Dietrich said only that such reports were often exaggerated.

FOR SEVERAL days thereafter, folk remained shuttered in their cottages or told one another that the pest would not come so high into the mountains. Bad air is heavy, Gregor announced with confidence, and seeks always a lower level. But Theresia said that God had fashioned His instrument and only repentance could stay His hand. Manfred was more thoughtful. "Those bells we heard on Rogation Day," he said to Dietrich. "They were in Basel, I think, and carried to us by a freak of wind. God was warning us."

Hans suggested marking the times and locations of the outbreaks on a land-chart, by which Dietrich supposed he meant a *portolan*. But, as none such existed in the village and most other such charts were symbolic in intent, the suggestion came to nought. The Krenken knew not the geography to compile what Hans called a "true chart." Still, all men knew that to travel from Berne to Basel to Strassburg was to pass by Freiburg and thus the roads into the High Woods. A turn to the east, and . . . It had been, withal, a narrow escape.

ILSE KRENKERIN died a few days after the Pestilence Mass, and Dietrich sang the Dead Mass for her in St. Catherine's. Hans, Gottfried, and the other baptized Krenken carried the bier into the church and set it down before the altar. Shepherd attended in silence, for Ilse had been of her party of pilgrims. She paid no mean attention to the ceremony, though whether from reverence or mere curiosity, Dietrich could not say.

Only a few villagers came, as they were for the most part yet huddled in their cottages. Norbert Kohlmann came and Konrad Unterbaum and their families; so also, surprisingly, Klaus and Hilde. Hilde wept at the sight of Ilse's body and her husband was helpless to comfort her.

Afterward, the Krenken bore their companion away to be stored in the cold-boxes until her flesh was needed. "I bandaged her wounds," Hilde said as the Hochwalders watched the Krenken progress the Bear Valley road toward their ship. Dietrich looked at her.

"She was hurt in the shipwreck," she said, "and I bandaged her wounds."

Klaus placed an arm around her shoulder, saying, "My wife is tenderhearted," but she shrugged the arm off.

"Tenderhearted! It was a terrible penance, imposed upon me! Ilse *stank*, and a snap of her jaws could take my wrist off. Why should I weep for her? She is one burden less for my penance." She wiped her face with a kerchief, turned, and nearly collided with Shepherd as she fled.

"Explain, Dietrich," Shepherd said. "All recitation over corpse! All water shaken; all smoke swung and swirled! What you accomplish? What good for Ilse? What good? What good? What I tell her birth-givers?"

She reared her head and clacked her side-lips so fast as to make a buzzing that grew sensibly into a musical note, and a remote part of Dietrich's mind was delighted to learn that a tone was a high frequency of clicks. She leapt away, not toward the fine cottage of Klaus and Hilde, where she had been staying, but out across the resting fields toward the Great Wood. Konrad Unterbaum said, "I never thought *them* like us before today. But I know her heart; that I do."

JOACHIM SAT on a small stool by the Kratzer's cot and spooned a little porridge into the creature's mouth. Outside, weathercocks turned and dark clouds tumbled over one another as they raced across the sky. A distant cloud over the lowlands flashed. Dietrich stood by the open window and smelled rain in the air.

"Your weather pleases," said a voice in the head-harness, and it seemed so hale that

Dietrich needed a moment to mark it as the Kratzer's. It ought to gasp and sound weak, as befit his estate, but the *Heinzelmännchen*'s art did not extend so far. "The change in the air caresses my skin. You do not have this sense. No, you do not feel the pressing of the air. But, ach! That tongue of yours! So supple an organ! We taste nothing so intensely as you. How fortunate that is! How fortunate. With a school of philosophers will I return to this place to study. Not since the bird-folk of Cliff-home World have I known any so fascinating as you."

The Kratzer raved when he spoke of returning, since it was growing ever more evident that he would not be leaving—save in the manner that all men left this world. Dietrich felt a great wash of pity and he stood by the cot to carress the strange creature in his own strange way.

EACH DAY, Dietrich and Joachim prepared a meal for the weakening Kratzer, trying divers materials in the hope that one might contain the substance that his body craved. They made stews of unlikely fruits, and teas of doubtful herbs. Nothing could do more harm than doing nothing more. The philosopher had put aside untasted the flask containing the alchemist's vile brew, and each day his horny skin grew more mottled. "He bleeds within," explained the Krenkish physician, when Dietrich had called upon her skills. "If he will not drink the broth, there is naught I can do. And even should he drink," she added, "it but prolongs the dying. All our hope is in Hans, and Hans has gone mad."

"I will pray for his soul," Dietrich said, and the physician tossed her arm for souls, for life, for death, for hope.

"You may believe that the *energia* can live without the body to support it," the Krenkerin replied, "but ask no such foolishness from me."

"You have the plow before the ox, doctor. It is the spirit that supports the body." But the doctor was a materialist and would not hear it. Good in small things, as such folk often were, she esteemed the Krenkish body as but a machine, like a waterwheel, and gave no thought to the rushing waters that moved it.

WHEN, AFTER a week had gone by with no further word, the dread of the pest began to fade and people laughed at those who had shown so much fear before. By the Nativity of John, festivities drew them forth from their cottages. The tenants sent their tithe of meat to the parsonage and lit bonfires on the hills, even on the Katerinaberg, so that the vigil night was pocked with ruddy glows. Boys ran about the village drawing fiery arcs with their torches to chase away dragons. At the last, a great hoop of wood and brush was lit on the church green and rolled downhill, and a great sigh lifted from a hundred lips, for it toppled to its side halfway down. The children delighted in the flames and diversions, but their elders clucked over the bad luck thus signified. The fiery wheel more often reached the bottom without falling, the old women told the old men, who nodded without contradiction, although memory might run otherwise.

Hans parted his lips. "Underseeking your customs was the Kratzer's great work, and I have the sentence in my head that this example might please him."

"He is dying."

"And so, deserving a comfort."

Dietrich fell silent. When a few moments had gone by, he said, "You loved your master."

"Bwa-wa! How could I not? It is written in the atoms of my flesh. Nevertheless, one more bite of knowing to feed his mind would please him." He stiffened abruptly into immobility. "Gottfried-Lorenz calls. There is trouble."

GOTTFRIED WORE a floral crown and had shed his leather hose to leap among the revelers. Few remarked the custom any longer, as he had no shameful organs to display. At least, none that women would recognize as such. Somehow, in the whirling, he had swiped Sepp Bauer across the crown with his serrated arm, and the young man lay now prostrate amid the flickering torches. Some in the crowd made ugly growls in their throats. Others gathered by the moment, asking questions.

"The monster attacked my son!" Volkmar declared. He swept his arm around his neighbors. "We all saw." A few nodded and muttered. Others shook their heads. A few cried that it was chance. Ulrike, swollen with child, shrieked to see her husband lying so. "You beast!" she cried at Gottfried. "You beast!"

Dietrich saw anger, confusion, fright, recognized the signs. He noticed from the corner of his eye, a handful of other Krenken gathering in the outer darkness, and one, who held the rank of sergeant among them and was known therefore as Hopping Max, had unfastened the flap on the scrip that held his *pot de fer.* "Gregor," Dietrich called to the mason. "Fetch Max from the castle. Tell him we have a matter for the Herr's justice."

"The Markgraf 's, you mean!" Volkmar shouted. "Murder is for the high justice."

"No. See! Your son breathes. It wants only the scalp sewn back in place and a little rest."

"Not by you," Volkmar replied. "Your tenderheartedness to these demons is a scandal."

What might have happened then remained unknown, for Max arrived with a half-dozen armsmen and imposed the Herr's peace upon them; and Manfred, when he arrived much put out at the late hour, ruled the matter accidental and declared that a full trial of the facts would await the annual court at Michaelmas.

The crowd sullenly dispersed, some giving Volkmar a slap on the shoulder, others giving him a look of disgust. Gregor said to Dietrich, "Volkmar's not a bad man, but his tongue can slither out of his food-hole before he knows it. And he says things with such certitude that he cannot after deny them without seeming foolish."

"Gregor, at times I think you are the cleverest man in Oberhochwald."

The mason crossed himself. "God forbid, that is no great feat."

WHEN THE revelers had dispersed and Dietrich was alone with Hans and Gottfried, Hans said, "The Herr is a clever man. In three months, sits the court, and long before, all questions are moot."

Gottfried touched Dietrich on the shoulder, startling him. "Father, I have sinned," the Krenkl said. "It was no accident. Sepp taunted me, and I struck without thinking."

Dietrich regarded his convert. "Guilt may be altered by circumstances," he allowed. "If your *instinctus* overcame you—"

"Striking him was not my sin."

"What, then?"

"Afterward . . . , I was happy."

"Ah. That *is* serious. How did he provoke you?"

"He called himself happy that we would soon be gone."

Dietrich cocked his head. "Because you starve? He hoped for your death?"

"No, he meant our ship. I did not think. He might have meant a 'fare well.' He could not have known of our failure."

Dietrich stopped and grabbed Gottfried by the arm, which caused the Krenk to freeze and check an instinctive blow. "Failure?" Dietrich demanded. "What means this?"

"The wire will not serve," he said. "There is a measure . . . You know how a rope will snap if too much weight pulls on it? Our *electronik* mill snaps also, though in a different way. With each proofing, it grows less strong. We cast the sums and . . ."

Gottfried fell silent and Hans touched him several times about the torso. "But the doctrine of chances, brother," he told Gottfried, "gives no certainty. There gives yet a chance of success."

"There gives yet a chance that Volkmar Bauer will caress me," Gottfried answered. He faced Dietrich directly, after the human fashion. "The weakening is such that our ship can drop into the abyss between the worlds, but will likely lack the power to climb back out on the farther shore. A hard fate."

"Or an easy one, brother," said Hans. "Who has ever come back to tell us which?"

Gottfried batted Hans's arm away and sprang down the hill. Dietrich watched him go. Then he turned on Hans.

"You always knew you would fail."

Hans's eyes were unreadable. "A *schlampig* device like that? Wire drawn with pliers by a boy on a swing? No clothing for the wire to contain its fluids? We made the work as sound as we could, but it is more rags and patches than that coat of Manfred's jester. I thought failure likely from the start."

"Then . . . why the pretense?"

"Because you were right. When the alchemist failed, my folk might have seen nothing before them but lingering death. We gave them something else these past five moons. Hope may be a greater treasure than truth."

RETURNING TO the parsonage, Dietrich found the Kratzer lying upon his pallet, his soft lips opening and closing, though too slowly to signify laughter. He recalled that Hans had made once the same sign beneath an anonymous sky. *He is weeping,* Dietrich thought, and found it oddly affecting that, for Krenk as for man, the outward appearance of tears was so like that of laughter.

The Kratzer was a materialist. Was that why he wept? All men naturally feared death. Yet a materialist, holding naught beyond the threshold, might dread the passage more. He leaned over the Krenkl's pallet, but saw only his own myriad reflections in those strange, golden eyes. There were no tears, could be no tears and, lacking them, how could the melancholic humor be bled?

The Krenken were impaired in all expressions; their humors heightened by containment, like the black-powder in one of Bacon's paper tubes. They wept more deeply, angered more brightly, celebrated more wildly, idled more slowly. But they knew no poems, and sang no songs.

And yet, as a man might be happy who knew of naught else—happy before waterwheels and eyeglasses and mechanical clocks, when life was harder than in these more modern times—so too could the Krenken live content until finding themselves in the Hochwald.

Dietrich crossed to the outbuilding to obtain some grain with which to make a porridge. Upon the windowsill, above the grain sack, sat the Kratzer's flask. It was fashioned of a white, semi-opaque material that the Kratzer had named "rock-oil," and the sun, passing through the clarified oilskin that served as a light in that window, cast the contents in shadow. Dietrich took the flask in hand.

He was not mistaken. The level had diminished.

Returning to the parsonage, Dietrich gazed down at the philosopher. *I know now why you weep, my friend.* The spirit was willing, but the flesh was weak, and the Kratzer's dread had pulled the stopper that his revulsion had meant to keep sealed. "Do you know what he drank?" Dietrich asked the monk, who knelt in prayer.

Joachim's murmurs stopped, and he nodded, once. "With this very spoon, I fed him. I poured into him his friends and companions. God moves mysteriously." Then he sat back on his heels. "The body is but a husk; only the spirit is real. We respect our body as the image of God, but *their* bodies are not God's image, and so might be used in ways not permitted to us."

Dietrich did not contest the casuistry. He watched the Minorite scoop up the fine, dark-green granules that the Kratzer's body expelled and pour them into a waste-bucket. "But if the body is consumed," he asked, "what remains for the ressurection of the dead?"

Joachim wiped the creature clean. "What remains when worms consume it? Do not limit God. With Him, are all things possible."

SHORTLY AFTER the Nativity of John, a peddler arrived from the direction of Bear Valley, leading a pack mule full of goods. He prayed the Herr's leave to set up a stall on the village green for a few days. A swarthy man with wide, thick moustaches, and with bangles on his wrists and two hoops of gold in his ears, he fired his tin-pot up and promised miracles of repair. He displayed also ornaments he had procured in the East. He gave the name of Imre and claimed Hungarian blood. He did a brisk business on sundry trifles, and mending pots and pans.

At Angelus the following day, Dietrich approached him as he packed his goods away for the night. "You have something, I fix?" the man asked.

"You are far from home," Dietrich suggested.

That elicited a cheerful shrug. "Man stay home, man no peddler," the other replied. "Only Soprón shopkeeper. Sell to neighbors, what profit? What I make, they make. Here, when you see these things like I bring?" He dipped into a coffer and emerged with a white pallium done up in fishes and crosses and edged in bright colors of red and blue. "When see the scarf so fine?"

Dietrich pretended to study the material. "You'd fetch a better price for it in Vienna or Munich than in a little hill dorp."

The man licked his lips and glanced to the side. He tugged on his moustache. "City guilds no like the peddlers; but here, how often see one?"

"More often than you may think, friend Imre. Freiburg is no great trek." He did not mention that tales of demons had kept such traffic at bay of late. That Imre might spy an incautious Krenk was a chance to which Dietrich had resigned himself. "Now, if you would return to me Volkmar's brooch, I will give you a word of advice. Substitutions of base metal are too bald for so small a village, where each man knows his few gauds with greater intimacy than do your city folk." Imre grinned and dug into his scrip, retrieving the ornament. Dietrich checked the clasp on the back and saw that it had been repaired with considerable skill. "A man of your craft need not resort to such petty theft." He handed over the tin piece that the peddler had substituted. "If you are once marked a thief, who will trade with you?"

Imre dropped the false brooch into his scrip with a careless shrug. "Men of skill must also eat. Think vogt want me sell for him brooch in Freiburg. Fool wife, keep money."

"You would be advised to leave," Dietrich told him. "Volkmar will talk to the others."

Again, the man shrugged. "Peddler come, peddler go. Otherwise, no peddler."

"But do not go to Strassburg or to Basel. The pest has appeared there."

"Oho . . ." The Magyar looked east, toward Bear Valley. "So. Then I no go those places."

THE PEDDLER returned to Oberhochwald three days later, although Dietrich did not learn of it until after noon. Manfred himself, riding at exercise with Eugen and one of the castle knights, came upon him on the track from Niederhochwald. Imre declared that he had private words for the Herr, and Manfred led him a little to the side. Eugen sat his horse close by and, on hearing the Herr gasp and thinking him treacherously struck, rendered the peddler senseless with the flat of his sword. This proved an injustice, as Manfred related to a council hastily called afterward in the great hall.

"The pest is come into the Breisgau," he announced without preamble.

· XXII ·

JUNE, 1349
Until Nones, The Seven Holy Brothers

THE PEST *is stalking us,* Dietrich thought. It had crept incrementally closer, from Berne to Basel to Strassburg, turning now to Freiburg. Would it come next into the mountains? It had crossed the Alps, so climbing the Katerinaberg would be no great feat.

"This Imre had reached the glade at Church-Garden," Manfred continued, "where he encountered a party of Freiburgers riding at the canter toward the gorge. There were a dozen, all told: a merchant by his surcoat, his lady, maids and servants in livery, and a few others. They would have trampled our peddler down, had he not pulled his mules aside in haste. A bag fell from their pack horse as they passed, and the merchant ordered a servant to reharness the load, even as he and the others pressed on. The servant worked in terrible haste, spilling clothing and other goods and gathering them up again in clumsy fingers. Imre helped him re-secure it."

"More likely he yanked it loose as it passed," said Klaus, and the others tittered nervously.

Manfred did not smile. "That was when the servant told him of the pest, and that hundreds were each day dying in Freiburg."

"Did he verify the servant's tale, mine Herr?" Everard insisted. "Perhaps the man exaggerated. Servants are notorious liars."

Manfred spared him a curious glance. "Imre reasoned that if a man as educated as a guild-merchant deemed it wise to flee east, he would be a great fool himself to continue west. The servant with the pack horse quickly outdistanced Imre's mules, yet Imre came upon his load shortly after, scattered along the trail up the gorge. He supposed that the roughness of the trail had caused the pack to come loose again and, lacking his master's voice in his ear, the servant had this time abandoned all and fled. Imre thought the clothing too fine to lie deserted so he gathered them into his own pack."

Klaus said, "I misdoubt he helped tie the man's bundle with that very end in view." He spoke too quickly and too sharply and rubbed one hand with the other as he looked at each councilor in turn.

"A little farther on," Manfred continued grimly, "he came upon the body of the merchant's lady, lying as she had fallen from her horse. Her face was deep blue and distended in agony, and she had vomited black bile over herself. Beside which, her neck was broken in the fall."

Klaus had no quip his time. Everard had gone pale. Young Eugen caught his lip between his teeth. Baron Grosswald did not move. Dietrich crossed himself and prayed God's mercy for the unknown woman. "And her husband stopped not to aid her?" he asked.

"Nor the servant. Imre says that in pity he placed over her form a blanket from the abandoned bundle, daring naught else. But," and Manfred slumped a little in his high seat, "I have not said all. The peddler confessed that he had come west in flight. The pest was in Vienna already in May and in Munich this month, but he kept silence for fear we would expel him."

At that, there were many exclamations. Everard cursed the peddler. Klaus exclaimed that Munich was, after all, many leagues distant, and the malady might travel north into Saxony, rather than west into Swabia. Eugen worried that the pest was surrounding them, east and west. Dietrich wondered about the Jews, who had set off in that direction with the Duke's escort.

Baron Grosswald, silent until now, spoke up. "Illness stems from countless creatures, too small for thought and borne in divers ways—by touch, on the breath, in the shit or piss, in the spit, or even on the breeze. It matters not which way the roads wind."

"Such foolishness!" Eugen cried.

"Not so," said Dietrich, who had heard already this thesis from Hans, as well as from the Krenkish physician. "Marcus Varro once proposed that very thing in *De re rustica. . . .* "

"Which is very interesting, pastor," said Klaus in a high, tight voice, "but this pest is not like other afflictions, and so may not spread like those of the monsters." To Gschert: "Can you swear that what you say of *your* small-lives is true of *us*? I've heard your folk remark more than once on our differences."

Gschert tossed his arm. " 'What may be, may be; but what is, must be.' I have other concerns than this *mal odour* of yours. You may live or you may die, however you may deny it, as the luck of the small-lives have it. As for us, we may only die." The affectless tones of the talking head endowed his pronouncement with a fatal chill. Dietrich wanted to tell the monster that his reasoning had failed, had asserted the consequent. What *must be* is; but what *is* need not be, but can through the grace of God be changed.

But Manfred struck the table with the pommel of his dagger. Dietrich marked how white the knuckles were that held it. "Could your physician not mix for us a medicine?" the Herr asked. "If the pest is natural, then the treatment must be natural, and we have no theriac in the village."

But Gschert shook his head in the human fashion. "No. Our bodies—and yours, I must suppose—have naturally many small lives within, with whom we live in balance. An 'anti-life' compound must take careful aim so that only the invader is slain. Your bodies are too strange to us; and we would not know friend from foe among your small-lives, even did our physician know the art. Subtle skills are called for in fashioning a compound to hunt and destroy an invading small-life. To create a new one from whole cloth, and for creatures whose bodies she does not know, is beyond her."

Silence fell, and Manfred sat still for a time while the others watched. Then he pressed both palms to the table and pushed himself to his feet, and all eyes but Gschert's turned to him.

"This is what we shall do," Manfred announced. "Everyone knows it is death to have contact with the sick. So. We must cut ourselves off and have nothing to do with the outside. No one may use the road through the village. Any who come hither from Freiburg or elsewhere must pass around, through the fields. Anyone trying to enter the village will be turned away—by force of arms, if need be."

Dietrich took a slow breath and studied his hands. Then he looked up to Manfred. "We are commanded to show charity to the sick." A low sigh ran around the table. Some cast eyes down with shame; others glared at him.

Manfred rapped the table with his knuckles. "This is not uncharity," he declared, "since we can do nothing to help them. *Nothing!* All we can do is allow the pest among us."

That drew loud exclamations of assent from all save Dietrich and Eugen.

"There are rumors," Manfred added, "that we harbor demons. Very well. Let it be known. Let the Krenken fly about at will. Let them be seen in St. Blasien and St. Peter; in Freiburg and Oberreid. If folk are too frightened to come here, we may yet keep this . . . this Death at bay."

THAT EVENING, Dietrich organized a penitential procession for the morn to pray the intercession of the Holy Virgin and St. Catherine of Alexandria. The procession would be barefoot and in rags and the penitents would wear blessed ashes on their brows. Zimmerman would take the great cross down from above the altar and Klaus would carry it on his back. "A bit late for that, priest!" Everard complained when he was told of it. "You were sent to tell us God's will! Why'd you not warn us of His anger years ago?"

"It is the end of the world," Joachim said quietly, and perhaps even with satisfaction. "The end of the Middle Age. But the New Age arrives! Peter departs; John comes! Who will be worthy to live through these times?" Yet, the monk's eschatology perhaps meant no more than Everard's complaints, or Klaus's jokes, or Manfred's severity.

After making the arrangements, Dietrich knelt in prayer in his room. *Be mindful, O Lord, of thy covenant,* he prayed, *and say to the destroying angel: Now hold thy hand, and let not the land be made desolate, and destroy not every living soul.* When he raised his eyes, he saw Lorenz's strange iron crucifix and bethought himself of the smith. A strange and gentle man in whom God had blended both strength and mildness; a man who had died trying to save a monstrous stranger from an unseeable peril. What had God intended by that? And what had God intended by moving a violent and wrathful Krenk to take Lorenz's name—and as much of his mildness as the Krenkish nature could assume?

Rising from the prie-dieu, he saw Hans squatting knees-above-head behind him. Donning the Head-harness, he admonished his guest. "You must make some sound when you enter, friend grasshopper, or you shall kill me from surprise."

A faint parting of the soft lips indicated a wan smile. "Among us, noise is evidence of clumsiness. In the atoms of our flesh, it is written that we make no sound, and the most silent are the most admired, and esteemed the most attractive. When our forefathers were animals, lacking thought and speech, we were prey to terrible flying things. And so, when we were pagans, we worshipped swooping, fearsome gods. Death was a release from fear—and our only prize."

" 'Do not be afraid.' Our Lord said that more often than he said anything else."

Hans clacked his side-lips. "Do you have the sentence in your head that tomorrow's procession will halt this pest of yours, that it will bar the small-lives from the High Woods?"

"If it is as you say, no. No more than prayer can stay a charging horse. But that is not why we pray. God is no such cheap juggler as to play for a pfennig."

"Why, then?"

"Because it will focus our minds on last things. All men die, as all Krenken die. But how we approach that death matters, for we will receive another life according to our merits."

"When your folk submit, you kneel before your Herr. Among us, we squat as you see."

Dietrich accepted this, and after a moment he asked, "For what purpose have you prayed?"

"For thanks. If I must die, at least I have lived. If my companions have perished, at least I have known them. If the world is cruel, at least I have tasted kindness. I had to cross to the far side of the sky to taste it but, as you say, the world is full of miracles."

"There is no hope, then, for your folk?"

" 'One thing alone removes all chance of death; and that thing is death.' But hear me, Dietrich, and I will tell you a sentence that my folk have learned. *The body may be strengthened by an exercise of the spirit.* Do you understand me? One man may welcome death, and so find it. Another man may will himself to live, and in that will may lie the difference in their fates. So, if these prayers and processions muster your *energia,* you may better resist the entry of the small-lives into your bodies. As for me, I have an answer to my own prayer."

"And what is that?"

But Hans refused to say. He hopped to the bedside of the dying Kratzer and affixed to the wall before his eyes a brightly colored reproduction of the meadow-scene that Dietrich had first noted on the strange "view-slate" on the Kratzer's desk. Hans then squatted by the bedside for a time in silence. Then he said, "For every Krenk, the sentence is that he would see his birth-nest once more. What you call his 'heimat.' However he fares through the world-inside-the-world, whatever wonders he finds in distant places, there gives always that place for him."

Hans unfolded to his feet. "Our ship will sail," he said. "In another week, perhaps two. No more." Then without another word he left the parsonage.

DURING THE week that followed the procession, a curious humor came over the folk of Oberhochwald. There gave much merriment and spontaneous laughter, and they told one another that Munich and Freiburg were far off and what happened there did not affect the High Woods. Folk left their harrows to sport in the field. Volkmar Bauer gave Nickel Langermann a meat pie and his wife cared for little Peter, who had fallen ill with the murrain. Jakob Becker walked through the village and left a loaf of bread at each cottage and two at each hut and afterward visited the grave in which his son had been laid.

Gregor and his sons brought Theresia Gresch to Mass on the Fifth Sunday in Pentecost. This Mass was better attended than most, and afterward Gregor said that if people were frightened more often, the village would be a friendlier place, and he laughed as if at a great and terrible joke.

Dietrich gave thanks for the newfound concord but when, after that week, nothing had happened, the village slowly returned to normal. The free tenants once more spurned the gärtners and serfs; the horseplay in the fields ceased. Dietrich wondered if the penitential procession had, as Hans had suggested, strengthened their spirits to resist the bad air; but Joachim only laughed.

"How heartfelt is a penance that fades so soon?" He shook his head. "No, true contrition is longer, broader, deeper than that, for this sin was so long with us."

"But the pest is not a punishment," Dietrich insisted.

Joachim turned his eyes away. "*Do not say that,*" he whispered fiercely in the soft confines of the wooden church—and the statues seemed to whisper back in creaks and moans. "If it is not punishment, it is nothing; and it is too terrible a thing to be nothing."

THAT NIGHT, quietly, the Kratzer died.

Joachim wept, for the philosopher had never accepted Christ and had died outside the arms of the Church. Hans said only, "Now, he knows."

Dietrich, to comfort the servant of the talking head, said that God could save whom He would, and there was a limb of Heaven reserved for the virtuous pagans, a place of natural happiness.

"Do I experience that which you call 'grief '?" the Krenk wondered. "We do not *weep* as you do; so perhaps we do not *feel* as you do. But there is a sentence in my head that I will see the Kratzer no more, that never more will he give me instruction, never more strike me for my faults. Since a long time, I have not paid *homage* to him—I use your term—and since that time, I have looked on him differently. Not as a servant looks on a master, but as one servant looks on another, for are we not both servants of a greater Lord? The sentence in my head is that this pleased him in some way, for even now I cannot bear that I have disappointed him."

He turned to the window, where he stared down Church Hill to the village and beyond that to the Great Woods. "He would not drink, and I did. The strength he refused was mine to repair the ship. Which of us was right?"

"I do not know, my friend," said Dietrich.

"Gschert drank, *and did nothing.*"

Dietrich did not answer him. The Krenk's lips worked slowly.

After a time, the physician came with two other Krenken and they carried off the mortal remains of the Kratzer to their vessel, there to prepare him for the nourishment of others.

FRIDAY, ON the commemoration of the Seven Holy Brothers, the Krenken departed the High Woods. Manfred bade them a ceremonial farewell in his manor hall, inviting their leaders and those who had hosted them. To Shepherd he gave a necklace of pearls, while to Baron Grosswald he gave a coronet of silver to signify his rank. Perhaps for the only time, Dietrich thought the Krenken leader affected. He set the laurel upon his head with great care and, though Shepherd split her lips in the Krenkish smile, the knights and armsmen present gave forth a loud "Hoch!" that startled the Krenken.

Manfred summoned Dietrich, Hilde, and Max. "I had not the heart to forbid it," he said. "Their ship's rudder has been fully repaired, and they have no cause anymore to linger." He paused. "If they stay, all will follow poor Kratzer to the tomb. As you three were the first to welcome them, I am sending you with them to bless their craft. I hope for their speedy return now that they know which winds carry them here. The Baron Grosswald has promised to return with skilled physicians and apothecaries, who may aid us against the pest."

"Mine Herr," said Dietrich, "their rudder—" He could not continue and said only, "I, too, wish them fair winds and calm seas."

They rode the Herr's rouncies past golden fields to the clearing where the vessel lay. Dietrich suggested they picket the horses at the charcoal kiln and walk the rest of the way, lest the nearness of so many Krenken panic them. Dietrich noted that Max wore now a scrip on his belt in which nestled a handheld *pot de fer*. "You have finally secured one, I see."

Max grinned and slipped the machine from his scrip. "Hopping Max gave it me before they decamped for their ship."

"What will you do when there are no more bullets for it?"

Max shrugged. "Is there a flaw in my weave? They've taught us how to make safely the black-powder, and that is enough. To make bullets for this device wants arts mechanical which we do not have. The bullets we use for our slings are too irregular in size and shape. But it is a cunningly wrought piece, and I will keep it for its beauty and as a think-piece for the strange events of this past year."

"Last night, Joachim begged Shepherd and others to stay."

Max cocked his head. "He hates them so? If they stay, they die."

"He believes that our great work was to win these creatures to Christ, and this labor alone has kept the pest from our homes. If the Krenken depart unbaptized, he says, the pest will come."

Max laughed. "He calls them demons still? I've helped cart too many of their bodies to believe that anymore."

Hilde joined them at the base of the ridge. She handed Dietrich the bundle that contained his vestments. Max carried the bucket and the aspergum. "It will please me when they are gone," she said, "and matters put back in order."

Dietrich took his companions by the hand. "Have your own guests said aught about this voyage to you? Shepherd? Augustus? Any of them?"

"Why?" said Max. "What is wrong?"

Dietrich released them. "I do not know whether this is a terrible sin or a wonderful act of hope. Come." With that, he led the way up the ridge and down the other side, where the Krenken stood about in divers attitudes, preparing to embark. They were fewer than before, and many were in the extremes of their particular illness, their skin having mottled. Most of these stood or squatted alone, but a few were supported by their fellows or carried in pallets. They stood in silence.

Baron Grosswald had erected a table and cunning machines to repeat in Krenkish Dietrich's words. "You must make swift," he said over the private canal, "or our resolve may falter." Dietrich nodded to show that he had heard, and donned the purple vestments used in the Mass for Pilgrims and Travelers. He would not celebrate the Mass, of course, but the prayers were of special merit to the occasion.

He crossed himself. "*In nómine Patris, et Filii, et Spiritus Sancti . . .*" A few of the Krenken repeated the gesture. The wind whipped through the trees, bending the branches and causing them to bow.

"*Rédime me, Dómine,*" he prayed for his guests. "Redeem me, O Herr, and have mercy on me: for my foot has stood on the straight path. Judge us, O Herr, for we have traveled in innocence. If we should walk in the shadow of death, we will fear no evil, for Thou art with us.

"Direct our steps according to Thy word; and let no iniquity have dominion over us. God has given his angels charge over us, to keep us in all Thy ways. In their hands, they will bear us up, lest we dash our foot against a stone.

"Perfect Thou, O Herr, our goings and our comings, that our footsteps be not moved from the straight path. Incline Thy ear and hear my words. Show forth Thy wonderful mercies." Then, raising his arms, he cried, "Send Thy grace before these pilgrims to guide their steps, and let it follow after them and accompany them in their paths, so that by the protection of Thy mercy, we may rejoice in both their progress and in their safety."

Dietrich progressed around the vessel, blessing it with holy water which Max carried in the bucket for him, and finished by drawing the sign of the cross over the assembled Krenken, saying, "Go with God." After this, the pilgrims, still silent, filed on board their ship. Some of them bowed or genuflected to Dietrich as they passed, though he did not think they meant more than courtesy. "Good-bye, my Krenkl'n," he said again and again. "May God go with you." One replied over the private voice-canal, "I will carry your message of charitas home with me." Dietrich gave her a particular blessing even while his eyes searched among the passing figures.

"What seek you?" Max asked him.

"A face." Yet, in an odd fashion, while he had learned to mark individuals, seeing the Krenken now standing in ranks, their particulars faded once more into the sameness he had perceived on his earliest encounters. It was as if, on the cusp of their departure, they had grown once more indistinct.

Perhaps Hans and the others, bound by duty to their posts, were already inside.

Some Krenken hesitated at the ramp and a few made to turn back. These, Grosswald's henchmen encouraged with blows and shoves. One of the henchmen was Friedrich, who had stood with Hans when Hans and Gottfried had defied Grosswald. He froze on noticing Dietrich's regard, then pushed his way through the jostling pilgrims into the ship.

Shepherd and Grosswald were last to board. The captain of the ship paused and seemed about to speak, but then he merely smiled in the Krenkish manner. "Perhaps the magic works."

Shepherd was the last. She stood halfway up the ramp and looked about the clearing. "Strange world; strange folk," she said. "Lovely, but deadly. There worse shores on which to beach, but none so cruel." She turned to go, but Dietrich held out the three head-harnesses.

"We won't need these anymore," he said, though Shepherd would not understand now that he had taken it off.

But Shepherd only touched the *mikrofoneh* with a fingertip and pressed them back on Dietrich, along with her own. At the head of the ramp, she chittered a last, untranslated statement, then she was inside and the door closed upon her and the ramp clanked into its recess.

DIETRICH INTENDED to watch the vessel out of sight, for he was consumed by a curiosity as to how it proposed to do so. Hans had insisted that it moved on a cushion of magnetism in a direction "inside of all direction." Dietrich had read Pierre Maricourt's *Epistola de Magnete* in Paris, and he remembered that magnets had two poles and that like poles repelled each other, so what Hans had told him was allowed by natural philosophy. But what had Hans meant when he said that these "inner directions" receded without regard to where one stood? Maricourt—Bacon's "Master

Peter"—had written also that an investigator "diligent in the use of his own hands . . . will in a short time correct an error which he would never do in eternity by his knowledge of natural philosophy and mathematics alone." And so, Dietrich determined to watch the Krenkish ship recede and, if he and Max and Hilde watched from different points, test the proposition that it would recede in all directions at once.

Yet, after he had explained his *experientia,* and Max and Hilde went toward their assigned positions, several Krenken bounded down upon them and, seizing them in their long serrated arms, carried them away behind the far side of the ridge.

THE KRENKEN pinned them to the loam and held them motionless. Max shouted and tried in vain to reach his *pot de fer.* Hilde screamed. Dietrich's heart beat against his ribs like a captive bird. The Krenk who held him to the ground ground his side-lips together, but Dietrich could make nothing of it without the head-harness. Hilde subsided into heaving sobs.

"Hans?" said Dietrich, for the Krenk who held him to the earth wore leather hose and a loose blouse of homespun that fit ill on his frame. The Krenk had opened its mandibles, perhaps to answer, perhaps to bite Dietrich's neck in two, when a sudden wind swayed the upper reaches of the spruces and birch. Limbs creaked, birds took wing. Deer bolted through the underbrush. An odd tension gripped Dietrich and he sucked in his breath and waited. It was like the morn when the Krenken arrived, only not so strong.

Terror and unease flowed through him like the millstream over the wheel. The wind rose to a howl and lightning snapped like bolts from a crossbow, striking trees all about and causing branches to burst. The thunderclaps echoed off the Katerinaberg, piled one upon the other, died slowly away.

The brief storm ended. The trees bowed for a moment, then steadied. The Krenken who had pinned Dietrich and his companions to the earth straightened and stood very still while their antennae waved about. Dietrich, too, sniffed the air and detected a faint odor at once metallic and pungent. The Krenkish heads moved fractionally and Dietrich understood that they were looking at one another. Hans clicked something and Gottfried stepped forward from where he had been waiting in the trees with several large coffers and sundry equipments and climbed to the top of the slope.

From there, he chittered something short and intense and those holding Max and Hilde and four others waiting in the woods bounded toward the top of the ridge, where, after several loud rounds of clacks, they poked one another with stiffened fingertips.

Dietrich and Max climbed to their feet. A moment longer, and Hilde joined them. They followed the eight Krenken to the ridgetop.

The clearing below lay empty.

All that remained of the great vessel were the stumps of many trees, the broken remnants of others, and a scattering of debris overlooked or ignored in the departure. One by one, the Krenken bounded down the slope, where they stood in utter silence.

One bent and retrieved some object from the ground, which he held indifferently, but which Dietrich, watching from the ridge, knew he studied with great intensity, for he twisted it first one way, then another, which is what the Krenken often did to sharpen the vision of their strange eyes.

"That device," said Hilde, and Max and Dietrich both turned to her. "I saw it often in the hands of their children. It is some plaything."

Below, the Krenken squatted and hugged their knees high above their heads.

· 7 ·

NOW
Sharon

SHE HEARD him call distantly, a tiny, insect-voice, squeak-squeaking her name. But her universe was too lovely to leave. No, not the *uni*-verse, the *poly*-verse. *Twelve* dimensions, not eleven. A triplet of triplets. The rotation groups and the meta-algebra made sense now. The speed of light anomaly fit, too. She squeezed the polyverse, and her pulse quickened. Smart lad, that Einstein. He got it just right. A twist. Kaluza and Klein were no dummies, either. And bend, and . . . *There!* If she warped it in *that* way . . .

There is an altered state that overcomes one in such moments, as if the mind had slipped into another world. Everything else becomes distant, and time itself seems suspended. Motion ceases. The sun stands still. In such moments, famous mathematicians make cryptic marginal notes.

Sharon's eyes refocused and she saw Tom's face staring into hers. "I had it!" she said. "It was beautiful. I almost had it! Where's my notebook!"

It appeared magically in her hands, open to a blank page. She snatched the pen from Tom's fingers and scribbled fiercely. Partway through she invented a new notation. *Please,* she thought, *let me remember what it means.* She marked an equation with a star and wrote: *[*] is true!!* She sighed, and shut the book. "Wait'll I tell Hernando," she said.

"Who's Hernando?"

She scowled at Tom. "I don't know whether to be angry because you interrupted my train of thought, or glad because you had my notebook handy. How did you know?"

"Because you don't normally pour your tea on your scrambled eggs."

Only then did she remember she was eating breakfast. She looked down and groaned. "I must be losing my mind."

"No argument here. I knew it was notebook-serious as soon as your eyes glazed over." He took her plate to the sink and rinsed it off into the disposal. "You can have one of my soft-boiled eggs," he told her over his shoulder.

She shuddered. "I don't know how you can eat those things." She snagged a piece of bacon from his plate.

He sat back down. "I saw that. Do you want some tea? No, *I'll* pour."

Soon she was sipping on "the Earl." Tom set the pot down. "So what was the big revelation? I've never seen you zone out quite that thoroughly."

"You don't understand GUT physics."

And Sharon didn't understand cliology; but Tom knew something Sharon did not, although he didn't know he knew it. And that was that when your words come out of your mouth and back into your ear, your brain gives them a second rinse, and cleans them up a little better. All Tom knew was that when he tried to explain things to Sharon, his own thinking clarified. "You go ahead," he said. "I'll sit here, smile benignly, and nod in all the right places."

"I don't know where to start."

"Start at the beginning."

"Well . . ." She took a sip of tea as she thought it over. "All right. At the Big Bang—"

Tom laughed. "Whoa! When I said to start at the beginning, I didn't mean the Beginning."

She tried again. "Look. Why did the apple fall on Newton?"

"Because he was sitting too close under the apple tree?"

She pushed back from the table. "Forget it."

"Okay, okay. Gravity, all right?"

She paused and studied him. "Are you interested in my work, or not?"

"Did I have your notebook ready for you?"

So he had. How did the cliche put it? Actions speak louder than words. And a good thing, too, because his words could be so irritating. She reached across the table and patted his hand. "You're right, Tom. But I'm still trying to figure this out, so I'd rather not be distracted by witty remarks." She had almost said "half-witty remarks."

Tom shrugged and sat back in his chair. He had heard "half-witty," anyway. "All right. Apples fall because of the force of gravity. Wasn't that already discovered?"

"And why do currents flow?"

"Electromagnetism. Do I get a prize?" Surliness had crept into his voice.

"Why does time run faster?"

He opened his mouth to reply, closed it, and grew thoughtful. "Some sort of force," he said slowly, almost to himself.

Gotcha! she thought. No smart-ass comeback for that one. "Exactly. Accelerations require forces. Uncle Isaac said so. Look at it this way. We don't 'move forward' through time; we 'fall downward,' pulled by a sort of temporal gravity. I call it chronity." *Pulled by what?* she wondered. Something at the end of time? *How Aristotelian! Jackson would have a cow. Or something at the beginning. God. Hah! No, better make that the Big Bang. No sense pushing the chair's hot buttons.* "Or maybe we're pushed," she continued. "I haven't decided on plus or minus signs yet."

"So," Tom mused. "*Tempus fugit,* after all." Sure, he had promised no witty remarks. He hadn't broken that promise.

She sighed. It was hard to remain cross with Tom. He was so damned cheerful when his own work was going well. "I know my equations are true," she mused aloud. "I need to know if they are fact."

MORE PEOPLE should make that distinction. It's one thing to have a bird in an equation; quite another to have a bird in your hand. A *fact* is an accomplishment, *factum est.* In German, "deed-matter." Tom, who had been reading more Latin and Middle German lately than English, knew immediately what she meant.

But it was easier to hypothesize occulted forces lurking behind the walls of the world than it was to find them. After all, she couldn't just tear down those walls, could she?

Could she?

Never underestimate a determined woman. Universes are flimsy things in their hands.

"CERN CAN rent me some time in about four months," she told Tom a week later as she bustled in the door feeling pleased with herself. "Meaning they will give me chickens if I supply the eggs."

Tom nodded, figuring this was one of those right places. He was at his desk, reading a copy of the manorial accounts of Oberhochwald that I had sent him from Freiburg. It was missing many pages, and it stopped several years short of the crucial time; but who knew where gold might lie buried?

"It would just be preliminary, of course," Sharon went on. "CERN can't go back in time far enough."

He might have nodded at that one, too; but it really demanded more. "Say what?"

"The really big accelerators recreate conditions as they were in the first seconds after the Big Bang. We can stick our noses a little way into the balloon and see a world in which the seconds were longer and the kilometers shorter."

"And this is helpful because . . . ?"

"Chronity. I need to detect it, verify it. And I can't as long as I'm stuck in the present with all the forces frozen out. You see, a fifth force upsets the paradigm. Forces were classified on two axes: strong versus weak and long range versus short range. The schema was so neat that everyone figured there could only be four forces."

"Heh, sounds like the four Aristotelian elements Judy told me about. The two axes were hot versus cold and wet versus dry. Hot and dry gave you fire—"

There were only two people in the apartment. How did Judy manage to squeeze in? "This isn't the Middle Ages," she snapped. "We're not prisoners of superstition!"

Tom said, "Uh?" wondering where that remark had come from. Sharon set her briefcase on her desk and opened it, stared at its contents. After a while, Tom said, "So, like, which force is, umm, strong and long range?"

Sharon took her notebook out and turned it absently. "Electromagetism," she said. "And the *weak* long-range force is gravity."

"Maybe I'm putting on weight, but gravity doesn't feel so weak to me."

"Yeah, but you need a whole planetful to feel it, don't you?"

Tom laughed. "Got me with that one."

"And the short-range forces are the strong and weak nuclear forces."

"Wait," said Tom, "let me guess which one is the strong one."

Sharon dropped her notebook to the desk. She said nothing, but said it loudly.

"Okay. So, how does chronity fit in?" Tom asked her.

"By redefining the ranges. Long range and short range only apply to the familiar three spatial dimensions. Other forces might propagate along the hidden dimensions. You see, forces are space warps. Einstein showed that gravity was a warp caused by the existence of matter. I mean, the earth orbits the sun, right?"

Tom had been so immersed in medieval research that the question seemed weirdly counterfactual. The earth was in the center and the sun circled in the fourth heaven. The lack of sensible parallax of the fixed stars had disproven heliocentrism centuries before. But he knew by now to avoid smart-ass answers. If he knew that more often, he'd have less stress in his life. "Okay . . ."

"So, *how does the earth know the sun is there?* No action at a distance, right? Answer: the earth doesn't know jack about the sun. It just follows the path of least resistance and rolls around the lip of the funnel. So if gravity is a warp in space-time, what is electromagnetism?"

Tom was no fool. He knew when he was being spoon-fed an answer. He stared at his desk lamp, trying to imagine that it was really some sort of space warp.

"But to make it work, Kaluza and Klein had to tack some extra dimensions onto the universe. Then we discovered the nuclear forces and tried to create warp models for them. When the smoke finally cleared, we had eleven dimensions on our hands."

Tom's mouth dropped open. "*Merde!* You mean physicists kept adding imaginary dimensions just to make their space-warp metaphor consistent? Sounds like Ptolemaic astronomers adding new deferants and epicycles."

"Those dimensions are no more imaginary than Newton's 'force fields.' And it wasn't arbitrary. Certain symmetry relations . . ."

Tom held his hands up, palms out. "Okay, okay. I surrender."

He hadn't, and she knew it. "Don't patronize me! This is physics. This is *real.* And it's a hell of a lot more important than why some backwoods German village was abandoned when obviously everyone in it died!"

This really was a very wrong thing to say; and more than factually wrong. What happens to human beings may actually be more important than what happens to physical theories. But it was wrong on a personal level. Sharon had created a warp in her own personal space, and the force it represented repelled.

Tom stood. "I have to walk over to the library. I've got a meeting with Judy."

"More Eifelheim?" she asked without turning. But it was not so simple a question as two words. English really is a tonal language—if you have an ear for the tones.

"*Tempus fugit,*" he said after a moment, answering the question she hadn't quite asked. "*Quae fuerant vitia mores sunt.*"

Sharon did not respond. Tom pulled his hard-copy files and stuffed them into the pouch he used for his portable. Judy seemed a pretty girl, given the current preference for wholesomeness. Did Tom find that attractive? Why had he probed so insistently over Hernando? "I do like you, you know."

Tom slung his pouch over his shoulder. "I wish you'd tell me now and then."

"It's an established fact, like gravity. It doesn't need continual reminders."

He looked at her seriously. "Yes, it does. When you're near a cliff."

She looked to the side, perhaps expecting a precipice. Tom waited and when, after a while, she had said nothing more, he started for the door. He looked back before he closed it and saw that Sharon had not moved.

SHE HAD to tell someone; so she told Hernando.

"If I had to guess," the nucleonic engineer said when she had called him, "you have a warp model for your time-force."

"*If* I add a twelth dimension. But that messes up the accepted models for the other four."

"Until now," he guessed.

"Right. It came to me in a flash. You see, the subatomic 'zoo' was organized by the quark theory by 1990. Turned out, all those subatomic particles were aliases for three families of three particles. Well, I've organized my twelve dimensions in the same way: as three sets of three: Space, Time, and something I haven't named yet."

"That only makes nine," he pointed out. He did not point out that he probably knew the subatomic zoo better than she did.

"Plus three 'meta-dimensions' that link the three triplets on a higher level." She doodled while she talked. A triangle with a smaller triangle at each corner. It was only an icon, really.

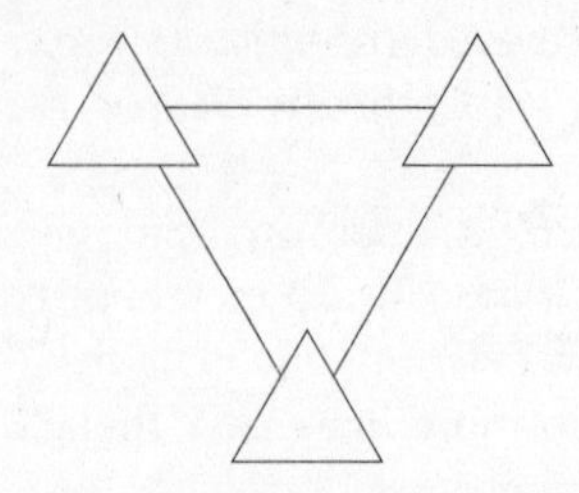

"I call it the polyverse. Our universe is the subset that we can sense. A warp in the polyverse can intersect the universe in various ways, depending on its orientation. Like the blind men and the elephant, we think we're seeing different forces, but they're just different 'cross sections' of a single warp."

"Hmm. We can't *see* these 'hidden dimensions,' can we?"

"No. The extra dimensions form the inside of a balloon. The original monoblock was slightly asymmetrical. When it expanded in the Big Bang, some of its dimensions were rolled up. They're still there: inside the quarks; inside you, me, everything."

"Maybe," said Hernando, "but the simplest explanation for not seeing them is that they're not there."

SHARON TRIED to patch things up with Tom over dinner. She waited until he came home from the library—was he planning to read every book in that place?—and announced that she was treating him to goulash and palatschinken at Belváros Café. Tom, who had already eaten cheesesteak hoagies with Judy at the Pigeon Hole, knew that there were times when a few extra calories was a bargain price, and agreed with as much cheer as he could muster. "Jo!" he said, getting into the mood. "*Paprikás csirkét kérek galuskával és uborkával. És palacsinta!*"

She even let him chatter on about long-dead people in ghost towns, the gist of which was that there had been a hospice called St. Laurence somewhere in the Black Forest in the late fourteenth century dedicated to Plague victims and operated by a small order of friars named after "St. Johan of Oberhochwald." What that had to do with anything, Sharon did not know. He started to show her the emblem of the Order, but her patent disinterest stopped him. Instead, he asked about her own work.

That was her cue. "What's wrong with the sequence nineteen, fourteen, two?"

"Umm . . . The gap between fourteen and two is too great?"

"Right. In the Beginning, there was just a single Superforce, because the extra dimensions hadn't rolled up yet. As the energy levels dropped, the polyverse warped and the individual forces, ah, 'froze' out of the soup. Gravity became separate at Planck scale energy, 10^{19} proton masses; the strong nuclear force at unification scale, or 10^{14} proton masses; and the weak force at Weinberg-Salam scale, ninety proton masses, which is about 10^{2}."

For once in his life, Tom was able to leap ahead of her. "And you think your chronity 'froze out' somewhere in between."

She grinned. "My guess is about 10^{8} proton masses. I call that Nagy-scale energy because I'm just so freaking modest. CERN can't reach that; but maybe the new L4 accelerator will. Even back in the 1980s, they could reach Weinberg-Salam scale. They fused the weak force with electromagnetism and created the electroweak force."

"Wait, I remember. That's the breakthrough that gave us the antinuclear shield, right?"

"Eventually. The weak force governs atomic decay. Once we could hitch it to electromagnetism, the fission suppression field was only a matter of time. Holy shit!"

Tom blinked. Perhaps it was from the flash of insight. "What?"

"We know how to manipulate electromagnetism. If we can fuse chronity with the electroweak force . . . that should be able to manipulate the time force."

"Time travel?"

"No, no. But time is three dimensional. Nagy-scale energy gets us *inside the balloon*, and we could . . . well, go anywhere. Light speed is still the upper limit; but if we go far enough in the right direction, the kilometers become very short and the seconds become very long, and we can pick any freaking light speed we want!" Well, taking a shortcut through the inside of the balloon would be a neat trick topologically, like a donut jumping through its own hole; but, who knew? With the proper energies, focused in the proper directions . . .

He blinked again. "Instantaneous interstellar travel?"

She shook her head. "As near as makes no difference. Tom, we wouldn't need spaceships, at all. *We could drive our cars to the stars.* With protective suits, probably, we could walk! A single stride would cover interstellar distances."

"Seven league boots! Sounds like you've discovered hyperspace."

"No. *Hypo*-space. Topology is conserved. The eight hidden dimensions are *inside* the universe, remember? To travel to other worlds, we have to travel inside." She laughed, but this time he was oddly quiet. "Tom?"

He shook himself. "Nothing. I just had the oddest feeling of déjà vu, is all. As if I'd heard all this before."

· XXIII ·

JULY, 1349

The Feast of St. Margaret of Antioch

JOACHIM WAS tolling the Angelus bell when Dietrich left Nickel Langermann's hut, where he had lanced malignant pustules on Trude Metzger's arms and on the back of little Peter's hand. The pustules worried him. The "wool-sorters' disease" was often fatal. Lost in such thoughts, he blundered into a press of chattering villagers returning from their fields. "Come to visit your daughter, old man?" he heard people call. "Ach, Klaus! Klaus! Here comes your father-in-law!" "That is a hard path for a frail old man; are you well?"

And there stood Odo Schweinfurt, from Niederhochwald, blinking dully in the setting sun. The old man searched up and down the high street, saw the mill, and set off in that direction. "No, the miller's cottage is over there!" someone called out, and Odo turned uncertainly.

The commotion drew Hilde from her cottage. "My father is here?" Hilde asked. Then with delight more feign than fair, she cried, "Daddy!" But he stank of the pigs he tended and she came no closer than her nose allowed. Klaus stood behind her, still in his white-powdered apron from the mill, and regarded the old gärtner narrowly. He had not his wife's disdain for the man's calling, but his nose was no less gentle for that. "What do you want, Odo?" he asked, for he misdoubted any came to his door without some want.

"Dead," said the old man.

"Bread? Does Karl not feed you? Such an ungrateful son!" He laughed, for Hilde's brother was well-known as a pinch-pfennig.

"No," said Hilde, wiping her hands on her coverslut. "He said 'dead.' Who is dead, Daddy?"

"All. Karl. Alicia. Gretl. Everyone." He stared around at the press of villagers, as if searching, searching.

Hilde's hand flew to her mouth. "His whole family?"

Odo sank to his wasted haunches in the dirt of the high street. "I've not slept for three days, nor eaten since yestermorn."

Dietrich stepped forward. "What happened?" he demanded. *Dear God,* he prayed, *let it be the murrain.*

"The blue sickness," Odo said, and those who stood close by groaned. "Everyone in the Lower Wood is dead. Father Konrad. Emma Bauer. Young Bachmann. All of them. Ach, God is cruel to kill my son and my grandchildren before my eyes—and spare me after." He turned his face to the sky and shook both fists. "I curse God! I curse the God that did this!" Dietrich heard the word run through the crowd like a flight of arrows whisking through the air. *The pest! The pest!* Folk began to edge away.

Even Klaus stepped back. But Hilde Müller, with a countenance white as the clouds, took her villein father by the hand and led him toward her home. "He will be the death of us," Klaus warned her.

"It is my penance," she said, with a toss of her head.

"It's a hard path up from the lower valley," Herwyg One-eye told anyone who would listen. "Bad air cannot climb it." But none answered him and each fled in silence to his own place.

IN THE morning, Heloïse Krenkerin flew over the Lower Wood and reported a pair of women living under a lean-to on the far end of the fields there. They had a small campfire and ran into the woods on catching sight of Heloïse. A third must have been hiding there, as well, for someone loosed a bolt when she swooped down for a closer look. At best, no more than a handful lived; unless others had fled to St. Peter or Bear Valley.

The Herr heard this report in his high seat and fingered an old scar on the back of his right hand. Dietrich studied the councilors, who sat along the black oak table in the manor hall. Eugen, pale and wide-eyed on his right; Thierry, who had ridden from Hinterwaldkopf on another matter and who sat now grim-visaged by his liege's left; Everard, cheeks flushed and eyes dully glazed; Klaus, anxious and unable to hold himself still; Richart, his law books useless in this matter, casting his attention here and there as others spoke. Dietrich and Father Rudolf represented the ghostly arm, and Hans spoke for the eight Krenken.

"Wiped out?" Manfred said at last. "Half my living gone, *and we heard nought until now?*"

Everard spoke low, though not so low as to go unheard. "When a man's family dies, your living seem less weighty." A rebuke from one so obsequious as Everard drew startled glances. The steward gave off a sharp, pungeant odor that Dietrich could not name. *Drunk*, Dietrich decided from the reddened cheeks, the slurred voice, the glazed look.

"Heloïse saw a body on the trail." Max continued his report. "Perhaps they sent a man to notify you but he died on the way."

"As well he did not succeed," said Thierry, whose fists were stones on the table.

"Praying mine Herr's grace," Klaus said, "but my wife's father says it was no more than three days from the first death to his flight."

Manfred frowned. "I have not forgotten, *maier*, that you broke my curfew."

"My *wife* bid him welcome . . ." He straightened. "Would you turn away your own father?"

Manfred leaned forward over the table, and spoke in measured tones, "In. An. Eyeblink."

"But . . . He was amongst us before anyone knew he had come."

"Beside which," the schultheiss said, glad for something covered by law and custom, "those of each village have the right to visit the other."

Manfred gave his lawman an astonished look. "There stands a time for rights," he said, "and a time for what is needful. I gave orders that *no one* might enter this village."

Richart was scandalized; Klaus genuinely puzzled. "But . . . But, this was only Odo!"

Manfred rubbed his face. "*No one,* maier. He may have brought with him the pest."

"Mine Herr," said Hans, "I am no scholar of these things, but the speed of the pest argues that the small-lives quickly devour their . . . We would say 'host,' though the guest is unwelcomed. These small-lives act so quickly that, did Odo carry them, he must show already the signs; and he does not."

Manfred grunted and his bearing was yet skeptical.

Everard giggled and spoke to Klaus. "You are a fool, miller, and your wife rides you. And anyone else she can mount."

Klaus darkened and rose from his seat, but Eugen raised a hand. "Not at mine Herr's table!"

Manfred, for his part, snapped, "Steward, remove yourself!" When the man did not move, he cried, "Now!" and Thierry rose with a hand on his sword-hilt.

But Father Rudolf spoke in a querulous voice, "No, no, this will not do. This will not do. We mustn't fight one another. *We* are not the enemy." And he took Everard by the elbow and helped him to his feet. Everard squinted at the assembly as if only now seeing them. Rudolf guided him toward the door and he staggered out, blundering first into the doorpost. Max closed the door behind him. "He stinks," the sergeant said.

"He is afraid," Dietrich answered, "and drunk because he is afraid."

Manfred's eye was hard. "I will brook no excuses! Max?"

"There were fresh graves in the churchyard down there," the sergeant continued, "but also bodies lying about—in the green, in the fields, one man dead even at the plough."

"Unburied, you say?" Dietrich cried. Had it come upon them *that* suddenly?

A finger jutted from Manfred's fist. "No, pastor! You will not go down there."

"To bury the dead is one of the commands that the Lord fastened upon us." A great ball of ice had formed within Dietrich as he thought about what awaited there.

"If you go down the mountain," Manfred told him, "I can not permit your return. The living here need your care."

Dietrich formed an objection, but Hans interrupted. "It will by us go easier."

"Then you, too, must be barred from returning," Manfred said to the Krenk.

Hans worked his lips in a brief Krenkish smile. "Mine Herr, my companions and I are forever barred from 'returning.' What is one lesser exile within a geater? But, the small lives that devour your folk would likely not attack mine. The . . . How do you say it when kinds change?"

"*Evolutium,*" suggested Dietrich. "An unfolding of potential into actual. An 'out-rolling' toward an end."

"No, that is not the right term . . . But what it means, mine Herr, is that *your* small-lives know not *our* bodies, and would lack the . . . the key to enter our flesh."

Manfred pursed his lips. "Very well, then. Hans, you may bury the dead at Nieder-hochwald. Take only Krenken with you. When you return, wait at your former lazaretto in the woods for signs of the pest. If no signs appear in . . . in . . ." He cast about for some interval that might provide protection. "In three days' time, you may return to the village. Meanwhile, *no one* may enter this manor."

"And what of my wife's father?" Klaus insisted.

"He must go. It sounds harsh, miller, but it must be. We must look to ourselves."

EVERARD LAY facedown in the path near the curial gate. Klaus laughed, "The sot had puked his guts out."

The sun was high but the breeze off the Katerinaberg carried with it enough chill to mitigate the heat. The roses had come into their time and their sharp tendrils had entwined themselves around the trellises of the Herr's garden. But the earth here by the gate had been scuffed bare by countless obedient feet, and the yellows of the butterheads emerged more miraculously from the barren ground.

Amidst the color, Everad twitched.

"He'll be sore when he sobers up," Max observed, "thrashing on the ground like that."

"He may choke on his vomit," said Dietrich. "Come, let us carry him to his wife." Dietrich strode ahead and knelt by the steward.

"He seems comfortable where he is," said Max. Klaus laughed.

The vomit beside the path was black and loathsome, and Everard himself exuded a repellant odor. His breath wheezed like a bagpipe; and his cheeks, when Dietrich touched them, were hot. The steward twitched at the gentle touch and cried out.

Dietrich stood abruptly, taking two steps back.

He collided with the miller, who had come forward crying, "Awake, drunkard!" The steward and the maier had been rivals and partners for many years and bore each other that mix of friendly contempt that such associations often engendered.

"What is it?" the sergeant called to Dietrich.

"The pest," Dietrich told him.

Max closed his eyes. "Herr God in Heaven!"

Dietrich said, "We should carry him to his cottage." But he made no move. Klaus, hugging himself, turned away. Max returned to the manor house, saying, "The Herr must know."

Hans Krenk shouldered them aside. "Heloïse and I will carry him." The pagan Krenkerin, who had been resting nearby from her flight, joined him.

On the hill opposite, Joachim tolled the midday bell, announcing lunch to the workers in the fields. Klaus listened a moment, then said, "I thought it would be a bleaker scene."

Dietrich turned to him. "What would be?"

"This day. I thought it would be marked by terrible signs—lowering clouds, ominous winds, a crack of thunder. Twilight. Yet, it is so ordinary a morning that I grow frightened."

"Only now frightened?"

"Ja. Portents would mean a Divine Mover, however mysterious His moves; and the wrath of an angry God may be turned away by prayer and penance. But it simply happened. Everard grew sick and fell down. There were no signs; so it may be a natural thing, as you have always said. And against nature, we have no recourse."

In the steward's cottage, they scattered ledgers and rolls from the table and placed Everard there, as if serving a suckling pig. His wife, Yrmegard, wailed and clutched at her hands. Everard had begun to kick and twitch, and his face was now sensibly hotter. Dietrich pulled the man's shirt away, and they saw the boils on his chest.

"The murrain," said Klaus in relief.

But Dietrich shook his head. The resemblance was keen, but these were not the pustules of the "wool sorter's illness."

"Place cold rags on his forehead," he told Yrmegard. "And touch not the boils. When he thirsts, allow no more than sips. Hans, Heloïse, let us move him to his bed."

Everard howled when they picked him up and the Krenken nearly dropped their burden. "Heloïse will stay with him," Hans announced. "Yrmegard, come no closer.

Small-lives may travel in the spit, others from touch or the breath. We do not know which may be the case here."

"Shall I give my husband to the care of demons?" Yrmegard demanded. She wrung her hands in her coverslut, but made no movement toward the bed. Young Witold, her son, clung to her skirts and stared wide-eyed at his twitching father.

Outside the cottage, Klaus turned to Dietrich. "Everard never came near my father-in-law."

Hans tossed his arm. "The small-lives may be carried by the wind, like the seeds of some plants. Or they may ride on other animals. Each kind travels in preferred ways."

"Then none of us is safe," wailed Klaus.

Hooves clattered in the courtyard, and Thierry and Imein galloped past, leaping their horses across the low stone wall and jumping the moat that encircled the grounds. Klaus, Hans, and Dietrich watched them pass through the village and thence the fields, where lunching peasants marveled at the sight and, not yet knowing the cause, cried out in admiration for the horsemanship.

But by the evening Angelus, everyone had heard the news. Those returning from the fields slipped away to their cottages without a word. That night, someone threw a rock through the fine tinted glass light that Klaus had placed so proudly in the window of his house. In the morning, no one stirred from his dwelling. They peeked through wooden shutters at the deserted street, as if the poisoned breath of the pest waited to pounce on whoever might show himself.

AFTER DIETRICH prayed Mass the next morning to a congregation of Joachim and the Krenken, he walked to the crest of the hill to gaze upon the village emerging from the shadow of night. Below, the smithy was dark and cold. A rhythmic creak sounded in the morning air—Klaus's mill wheel, disengaged and slowly turning. A cock noticed sunrise and the sheep in the murrain-infested flock bleated piteously at their brethren who had fallen during the night. A faint mist lay over the fields, white and delicate as spun flax.

Joachim joined him. "It is like a village of the dead."

Dietrich made the sign of the cross. "May God avert your words."

There was another silence before Joachim spoke again. "Do any need succor?"

Dietrich tossed his arm. "What succor can we give?"

He turned away, but Joachim seized him. "Comfort, brother! The body's ills are the least of ills, for they end only in death, which is but a little thing. But if the spirit dies, then all is lost."

Still, Dietrich could not proceed. He had discovered that he was afraid of the pest. *Media vita in morte summus.* In the midst of life we are in death, but *this* death terrified him. He had seen men with their guts hanging in strings from a sword thrust into the belly, screaming and hugging themselves and soiling their clothes. Yet, no man went to battle without accepting that chance. But this sickness took no sense of risk or hope, and struck where and whom it willed. Heloïse had spied a man in Niederhochwald dead at his plough; and what man goes into his strips accepting that such a death might await him there?

Hans laid a hand on his shoulder, and he started at the touch. "*We* will go," the Krenk said.

"A demon treading the high street calling out for the sick? *There* is comfort for those folk."

"So, we are demons, after all?"

"Men afraid may see demons in the familiar, and direct their fear of the insensible to a fear of the sensible."

"Thought-lacking!"

"So it is; but it is what folk do."

Dietrich took a step down the path, hesitated, then continued unsteady to the bottom. Coming first to Theresia's cottage, his call was answered by a shrill voice he barely recognized.

"Go away! Your demons brought this on us!"

The charge was illogical. The pest had wasted regions that had never seen a Krenk; but Theresia had never been swayed by keen reason. He continued to the smithy, where he found Wanda Schmidt already speaking with Joachim.

"You did not have to come," Dietrich told the monk as the two proceeded on either side of the high street, but Joachim only shrugged.

And so they went, house by house until, at the far end of the village, they reached the gärtners' huts. Entering the Metzger cottage, Dietrich assured himself that Trude suffered no more than the murrain. The black streaks on her arm showed that the poison was spreading in her. *Trude will die,* he thought, keeping the belief from his face and lips as he prayed a blessing on them.

He returned to the cusp where Church Hill and Castle Hill met, where he awaited Joachim, who crossed the meadow from the miller's cottage. Sheep baa'ed at the Minorite as he passed among them. "Are they well?" Dietrich asked, indicating the cottages that lined the other side of the meadow, and Joachim nodded.

Dietrich let out a gust he hadn't known he held. "None other, then."

Joachim kicked a dead rat from the path and looked up Castle Hill. "There is yet the curia—and there is where the pest first showed itself."

"I will ask among Manfred and his folk." Impulsively, he embraced the monk. "You had no need to expose yourself. Care of this flock is mine."

Joachim studied the sheep dying in the meadow, as if wondering which flock Dietrich had meant. "The vogt is derelict in his business," he said. "Dead sheep ought to be burned, or the murrain will destroy the flock. My father's sheep were once afflicted so, and two of the shepherds died with them. It was my fault, of course."

"Volkmar has now other worries than the village sheep."

Joachim grinned suddenly. "But I do not. 'Feed my sheep,' the Master said, but not all food is bread. Dietrich, that was a hard journey down that high street, but a journey is made lighter with a companion."

In the end, Everard alone was ill, and he seemed to be resting now peacefully. Dietrich dared hope that it might go no further. Hans clicked his mandibles at this, but said nothing.

GOTTFRIED AND Winifred Krenk took two of the flying harnesses and flew to the lower valley to bury the unfortunate folk of that place. There were so many corpses that they used the thunder-paste to dig the graves. Dietrich wondered if that were a proper way to dig a grave, but then reflected that a grave dug all at once might be proper for a village that had died all at once. He spoke the words over them using the far-speaker that Heloïse had taken with her.

Afterward, Hans replenished the fire barrels of the talking head by unfolding a triptych made of glass. This glass converted sunlight into the *elektronik* essence.

Philosophically, one sort of fire might be converted into another sort of fire, but the practical alchemy eluded him.

"Why has the pest come here?" Dietrich asked suddenly.

Hans watched the sigil on the body of the *Heinzelmännchen* that signified how full the fire barrels were. "Because it has come everywhere else. Why not here? But, Dietrich, my friend, you speak of it like a beast that goes and comes with a purpose. There is no purpose."

"That holds no comfort."

"Must there be comfort?"

"Life without purpose is not worth living."

"Is it? Listen, my friend. Life is ever worth living. My . . . You would say, my 'grandsire.' My 'grandsire' spent many—months—huddled in a broken nest—a town—wrecked by . . . by an aerial assault. His nest-brothers were gone down in flames. His nurse had died in his arms from a violent expression worse than that of black-powder. He did not know where he would find his next meal. But his life was worth living, because in such straits, finding that next meal gives purpose; the next dawn marks your success. Never was he more alive than in those months when he lived so close by death. It was my own hatching-brood—which wanted for nothing—that found life oppressive."

WHEN TUESDAY dawned with no further instances of the pest, the villagers crept from their cottages and spoke together in hushed voices. Word had come from the manor that Everard was resting and his fever seemed a little milder. "Perhaps the village will escape with no worse," Gregor Mauer said, when Dietrich passed through the village that morning.

"May God grant it so," Dietrich answered. They stood in the mason's workyard, amidst stone dust and chips. Gregor's two sons idled nearby in leather aprons and wearing thick gloves. Little Gregor, a hulking youth near ten stone in weight, held a plumb in his hand and was swinging it absently.

"Pastor . . ." Gregor seemed oddly hesitant. He studied the dust in his courtyard, pushing it with the sole of his boot. A glower sent his sons off. Little Gregor poked his younger brother with his elbow and grinned at his father over his shoulder.

"No respect," said Gregor. "I should have sent them away for their 'prenticing." He sighed. "Pastor, I would wed Theresia. She is your ward, to give in marriage."

Dietrich had not looked for this day. In his heart, Theresia remained a tearstained waif, blackened with the soot of her burning home. "Does she understand your wish?"

"She consents." When Dietrich made no answer, he added, "She is a sweet woman."

"She is. But her heart is deeply troubled."

"I have tried to explain about the Krenken."

"There is more than that. I think she impresses her inner demons upon the outer ones."

"I . . . don't understand."

"Something Hans told me about the soul. The Krenken have made a philosophy of it. I call it *psyche logos.* They have divided the soul into parts: the self—that which says, *ego,* the conscience—which sits above *ego* and rules it, the original sin below it, and, naturally, the vegetative and animal souls of which Aristotle wrote. They say . . ." He grew suddenly irritated with himself. "But that is of no matter. What I mean is . . ." He smiled briefly. "There stand matters in her past of which you know nothing."

"It is less her past than her future that concerns me."

Dietrich nodded.

"Then we have your blessing?"

"I must think on it. There is no man I'd rather give her to than you, Gregor. But it is a decision for the rest of her life, and not one to be made on a moment's fancy."

"The rest of her life," Gregor said slowly, "may be no long time."

Dietrich crossed himself. "Do not tempt God. None else have fallen ill."

"Not yet," Gregor agreed, "but the end of the world is coming, and in Heaven there is neither marriage nor giving in marriage."

"I told you I would think on it." Dietrich turned to go, but Gregor's shout turned him round.

"We don't need your permission," the mason said, "but we wanted your blessing."

Dietrich nodded, hunched his shoulders, and left the stoneyard.

AFTER VESPERS, Dietrich ate a simple meal of bread and cheese washed down with ale. He had cut extra pieces for Joachim, but the young monk had not reappeared. Hans squatted by the open window, listening to the insect song called up by evenfall. From time to time, the Krenkl bit into a piece of bread that had been dipped into the life-giving elixir. Even so, some bruises had already marked his skin. The stars, reflected in his huge eyes, seemed to twinkle inside his head. "There stands a sentence in my head," he said, "that one of those must be Home-star. If God is good, He'd not abandon me with no glimpse of it. I only wish I knew which. Perhaps . . ." He extended a long forearm, a long finger, ". . . that one. It is so bright. There must be some reason it is so bright." He buzzed with his side-lips. "But no. It is bright because it is close. The philosophy of chances tells me that Home-star is unknowably distant, in an unknowable direction, and not one of those lights even shines in Krenkheim's skies. Even that tenuous bond is denied me."

"The sky is deep, then?" Dietrich said.

"Immeasurably deep."

Dietrich came to the window and gazed into the black dome overhead. "I always thought it a sphere hung with lamps. But some are near and some are far, you say, and that is why they seem brighter or dimmer? What holds them up? The air?"

"Nothing. There is no air in the void between the stars. There gives no 'up' or 'down'. If you were to ascend into Heaven, you would go up and up until the earth loses its grip and you float forever—or until you came within the grip of another world."

Dietrich nodded. "Your theology is correct. In what medium do stars then swim? Buridan never believed in the quintessence. He said that Heavenly bodies would continue always in what motion the Creator gave them, for there would be no resistance. But if the sky be not a dome that holds the air in, it must be filled with something else."

"Must it? There was a famous . . . *experientia*," Hans told him. "A Krenkish philosopher reasoned that, were the Heavens filled with this fifth element, there would be a 'wind' as our world moved through it. He measured the swiftness of light first one way, then the other, but he found no difference."

"Then young Oresme is wrong? The earth does *not* move?"

Hans turned and flapped his lips. "Or there is no quintessence."

"Or the quintessence moves with us, as the air does. There are more than two possibilities."

"No, my friend. Space is filled with nothing."

Dietrich laughed for the first time since finding Everard. "How can that be, since 'nothing' is no thing, but the lack of a thing. If the sky were filled with no thing, something would move to fill it. The very word shows it. *Vacuare* is 'to empty out.' But *natura non vacuit.* Nature does not empty. It needs effort to make something empty."

"Na . . ." Hans replied with hesitation. "Does the *Heinzelmännchen* overset properly? Our philosophers say that the nothing does contain what we call the 'nothing-spirit.' But I misdoubt your folk would know of this. How would you say it with your philosophical tongue?"

"The noun of *vacuare* is *vacuum,* which expresses an abstract action as a factual thing: 'that which is in the state of having been emptied.' So: *Energia vacuum.* But we read that 'the spirit of God moved over the Void,' so it may be that you have found the very breath of God in this 'vacucum-energia' of yours. But, attend." Dietrich raised a finger. "Your vessel moves across insensible directions that lie within all of nature."

"Ja. As the inside of a sphere is 'insensible' to those who apprehend only its surface."

"Then, your Krenkheim star is not so far away at all. It is within you at all times."

Hans froze for a moment, then briefly parted his soft lips. "You are a wise man, Pastor Dietrich, or a very confused one."

"Or perhaps both," Dietrich admitted. He leaned from the window. "I see no sign of Joachim, and it grows now too dark to go about with no torch."

"He is in the church," Hans said. "I saw him go in at nones."

"So! And not yet out? It is past vespers."

Alarmed, Dietrich hurried across the church green, stumbling a bit over the half-seen, starlit terrain, coming up with a rush against the carved support post at the northwest corner of the church. Ecke the Giantess lowered upon him; Alberich the Dwarf leered menacingly from the pedestal. The wind swayed and gave them voices. Dietrich staggered up the stairs, paused and laid a gentle hand on St. Catherine's sinuous form, upon her sorrowful cheek. A night owl passed by with a sound that was almost silence. Fearful of what he might find within, he threw the doors open.

The starlight, attenuated by its passage through the stained glass, left the interior dim. Dietrich heard a dull, slow slapping sound from near the altar.

He ran to the sanctuary, where he tripped upon a prostrate form. There was a familiar stink to the air. "Joachim!" he cried. "Are you well?" He remembered Everard lying in his vomit and his reeks. But this smell was the sharp, sanguine odor of blood.

He groped the body and found it nude above the waist, found the smooth young flesh streaked with bloody furrows. "Joachim, what have you done!" But he knew the answer, found the flail with his searching hands and pried it from the Minorite's grip.

It was the knotted rope that the monk wore as cincture, sodden now with blood. "Ach, you fool! You fool!"

The body stirred in his embrace. "If I drink the cup to the full," a voice whispered, "it may pass from others." The head turned and Dietrich saw eyes bright in the fragile starlight. "If I suffer the pains of ten, then nine may be spared. There," he laughed, "that's an algebra, isn't it?"

A cold, blue light suffused the interior of the church as Hans entered with a Krenkish lamp. "He has hurt himself," the creature said when he had approached.

"Ja," said Dietrich. "To take our suffering on himself." Had he been whipping himself for the entire four hours since Hans had seen him enter the church? Dietrich seized the monk more tightly, kissed him on his cheek.

"He thought by whips to stay the small-lives?" said Hans. "That is not logical!"

Dietrich gathered the body in his arms and stood. "To the Devil with logic! All of us stand powerless. At least he tried to do *something*!"

ON WEDNESDAY, Manfred summoned Dietrich to the chapel to commemorate Kaiser St. Heinrich: a just ruler from a day when the Germanies had possessed both rulers and justice. "The good Father Rudolf," Manfred explained the summons, "took my gray last night and fled."

Dietrich had never liked the chaplain, but this news startled and disturbed him. The Herr's chapel was well appointed with gold vessels and silk vestments, and its chaplaincy was a comfortable benefice that made few demands and stood its holder higher than a mere village priest. Rudolf was a good man and gave God honor, but there was that small portion of his heart in which he treasured Mammon.

In the chapel's rear stood Eugen and Kunigund and her sister Irmgard, Chlotilde the nurse, Gunther, Peter Minnesinger, Wolfram and their families, Max, and a few others of the Herr's household, waiting quietly closed in on themselves for the Mass to begin. Dietrich lowered his voice to a whisper. "He abandoned his benefice?" Serfs would at times flee their manor. Less often, a lord would abandon his fief. But it was not seemly for any man to desert his sitting in life. "Where will he go?"

Manfred nodded. "Who can say? Nor do I grudge him the horse. Flight gives a chance, and I'd not deny a man his chances."

Afterward, Dietrich stood at the gate to the curial grounds and gazed sightlessly over the village, thinking about Fr. Rudolf. Then he spun on his heel and walked to the cottage of Everard Steward.

"How fares your man today?" he asked when Yrmegard had opened the upper door.

Yrmegard looked over her shoulder. "Better, I think. . . . He . . ." Abruptly, she threw the lower door open. "See for yourself."

Dietrich crossed the threshold. He took a short breath, hesitant to draw too much of the bad air into his lungs. "Peace be with all here. Where is Heloïse?"

"Who is that? The demon? I thought all demons had Jew names. I chased it out. I'd not have it squatting here ready to seize my husband's soul should it leave his body."

"Yrmegard, the Krenken have been with us since Kermis-day . . ."

"They were only waiting their chance."

Everard's cottage was divided into a main room and a sleeping room. The steward held several strips of land and the extra wealth showed in the opulence of his dwelling. The man himself lay in the sleeping room. His brow was dry and hot to the touch. The swellings on his chest had been joined by others in his groin and under his arms. One, by the left arm, had grown to the size and coloring of an apple. Dietrich took a cloth to the bucket, soaked it, folded it, and laid it across the man's brow. Everard hissed and his hands became claws.

Dietrich heard Yrmegard shush the crying boy. Everard opened one eye. "Quiet, boy," he said. The words were slurred because his tongue was swollen and refused to stay inside his mouth. It was a slimy, gray, wet snail seeking escape from its shell. "A good boy like a porridge and the bird sings," Everard said, with one earnest eye pinned on Dietrich.

"He is mad," said Yrmegard, edging closer to the bed. Witold ran weeping from the cottage.

"He is conscious," said Dietrich, "and he is speaking. That is miracle enough. Why ask for reasoned discourse?"

He tried to feed Everard some water, but it dribbled down his chin due to the unruly tongue. He coughed and groaned, but this seemed a better thing than the vomiting and shrieks of the previous day. *It is passing,* he thought in relief.

FROM CASTLE HILL, Dietrich took the back trail to the meadow bordering the millstream. There he found Gregor and Theresia sitting on the bank, throwing pebbles into the pond. He halted before they had seen him, and he heard, above the waters rushing onto the mill wheel, the bells of Theresia's laughter. Then someone put the camshaft into its gear and the great paddle wheel began to groan and turn.

There had been a time when the sound of it had delighted Dietrich. It was the sound of labor lifted from the shoulders of men. But there was something in it this day of complaint. Klaus came forth from the mill to watch the wheel turn and judge the current and the drop. Satisfied, he turned and, spying Dietrich, called a greeting. Gregor and Theresia turned also and Dietrich, being thus discovered, approached them.

"You have my blessing," he told Gregor before the mason could speak. He placed his left hand in turn on the brow of each, sketching the cross with his right as he did so. The touch served double duty: he detected no sign of fever in either, but he did not speak of that. "She is a good woman," he told Gregor, "and pious when her terrors permit, and her skills in the healing arts are truly a gift from God. On her terrors, do not press her, for she wants comfort and not inquisition." He turned to Theresia, who had began to weep. "Listen to Gregor, daughter mine. He is a wiser man than he believes."

"I don't understand," Theresia said, and Dietrich knelt before her.

"He is wise enough to love you. If you understand nothing beside that, it would suffice an Aristotle."

Gregor walked with him a space toward the mill. "You changed your mind."

"I never opposed it. Gregor, you had right. Each day may be our last and, whether our time be long or short, the smallest happiness added to it is worth its while."

At the mill, Klaus dusted his hands with a rag while the mason and the herb woman walked off together. "So?" he asked. "Does Gregor get what he wants?"

Dietrich said, "He gets what he asked for. Pray God they are the same."

Klaus shook his head. "You are too clever sometimes. Does she know what he wants to do with her? I mean, down there. She is a simple woman."

"You are grinding wheat today?"

Klaus shrugged. "The pest may kill us all, but there is no reason to starve while we wait."

THAT WAS the third day's grace.

· XXIV ·

JULY, 1349

At Primes, The Commemoration of St. Hilarinus

THURSDAY DAWNED and the wind blew hot and from the west, hissing through the black spruce and stirring the half-grown wheat. The heavens faded into a blue so pale as to be alabaster. In the distance, toward the Breisgau, small, dark plumes rose, suggesting fires in the lowlands. The air twisted from the heat, conjuring half-seen, invisible creatures to stalk the land.

Dietrich sat by Joachim's cot and the young man turned his back so that Dietrich could anoint the welts. Dietrich dipped his fingers in the bowl he had prepared and smeared the ointment gently on the wounds. The Minorite shuddered at the touch. "You might have died," Dietrich chided him.

"All men die," Joachim answered. "What concern is it of yours?"

Dietrich set the bowl aside. "I have grown accustomed to having you about."

As he rose, Joachim twisted to face him. "How goes it with the village?"

"It has been three days, with no further afflictions. Folk are telling one another that the pest has moved on. Many have returned to work."

"Then my sacrifice has not been in vain." Joachim closed his eyes and laid his head back. In moments, he was again asleep.

Dietrich shook his head. How could he say that the boy was wrong?

WHEN DIETRICH left the parsonage to ready the church for Mass, he saw One-eyed Herwyg, Gregor and his sons, and others were on their way to the field, hoes or mowing scythes across their shoulders. Jakob's oven was lit, and Klaus's mill turning. Only the forge stood yet cold and silent.

Dietrich remembered how Lorenz would stand by the anvil, sweaty in his apron, and wave to him from below. Perhaps Wanda had found a man's task at last too much. Or perhaps she lacked for charcoal.

He made his way downhill, past the sheepfold, where stood a bare handful, all uncertain and with a sickly mien. The decimation of the village beasts had passed barely remarked for the greater dread of the pest. Cattle and sheep had fallen to the murrain. Rats, too, lay about, though that was a blessing. Herwyg's dog barked, sat, and scratched furiously at his fleas.

Dietrich stepped inside the open-walled smithy, picked up a hammer that lay upon the anvil, and cradled it in his two hands, finding it curiously heavy. Lorenz had swung it one-handed high over his head, yet Dietrich could barely lift it. A barrel of ox shoes and another of horseshoes stood nearby. In the quenching barrel, a green film had grown on the suface of the water.

A raven's cry drew his attention. He watched it circle, drop into the smithy's back garden, then rise again. And circle.

Dropping the hammer, Dietrich rushed out the rear exit, and there he found Wanda Schmidt sprawled upon her back amidst the beans and cabbage, arms waving as if reaching toward the sky. Her tongue, black and swollen, protruded from dry cracked lips. The raven swooped again, and Dietrich chased it off with a stick.

"Water," the prostrate woman gasped. Dietrich returned to the smithy, found a cup by the quenching barrel, and filled it. But when he extended the cup to the stricken woman, her thrashing arms batted it away. Her face was red with fever, so he found a rag, soaked it in water, and laid it across the woman's brow.

Wanda shrieked, arching her back and flailing her arms until she had knocked the cloth aside. Retrieving it, Dietrich found the rag already dry. He crumpled the rag in his hands, and sank to his haunches. *Why, O Lord?* he pleaded. *Why?*

Yet that was an impious thought. *This pest comes not from God,* he reminded himself, *but from some mal odor borne on the wind.* Everard had breathed it; now Wanda had, too. She had had no late contact with the steward, so the Krenkish theory of small-lives jumping from man to man seemed now proven false. Yet there must be *reason* to it. God had "ordered all things by measure, weight, and number," and so by measuring and weighing and numbering, mere men could learn the "eternal ordinances by which He set the courses of the stars and the tides of the sea."

Wanda cried out, and Dietrich edged away. The mere glance of a stricken one could infect. Blue flames shot forth from the eyes. The only safety lay in flight. He scrabbled to his feet, and backed through the smithy to the high street, where he stood breathing rapidly.

Without, all seemed in order. He heard the rasping saw from Boettcher's cooperage, the sheering cry of a hawk circling high over the autumn fields. He saw Ambach's pig rooting through the garbage along the high road, the flash off the water dripping from the mill's paddle wheel. He felt the wind's hot breath on his cheek.

Wanda was too large a woman to move alone. He must run for help, he told himself. He ran first to the stoneyard, but Gregor had taken his sons out to mow hay. Then, recalling that Klaus and Wanda had lain together, he ran to the eastern end of the village.

ODO SWUNG the upper door open, but gazed at Dietrich without recognition. "The curse is complete," the old man said, a riddle he forebore explaining. Dietrich reached past him and, unlatching the lower door, pushed his way inside. "Klaus!" he shouted. Old Schweinfurt stood by the open door, gazing upon the empty street. A groan issued from above, and Dietrich scrambled up the ladder to the sleeping loft.

There, he found the miller upon a three-legged stool drawn close to the bed. The bed boasted a headboard and, at its foot, an oaken chest with iron hinges and carved with the image of a waterwheel. Upon the bed lay a mattress stuffed with ticking and, upon the mattress, lay Hilde.

Her golden hair was twisted and matted with sweat, and her frame racked by coughs. She stared with near-Krenkish eyes. "Summon pastor Dietrich," she cried. "Dietrich!"

"Here," Dietrich said, and Klaus jerked to that soft statement where he had not reacted to the earlier knocks and shouts. Without turning, he said, "She complained of headaches when she awoke and I thought little of it and went to start the wheel. Then . . ."

"Dietrich!" cried Hilde.

Dietrich knelt beside the bed. "Here I am."

"No! No! Bring the pastor to me!"

Dietrich touched her gently on the shoulder, but the woman jerked away.

"She has lost her wits," Klaus said, in a voice preternaturally calm.

"Have the boils appeared?"

The maier shook his head. "I know not."

"If I may lift her gown up to inspect . . . ?"

The miller stared at Dietrich for a moment, then began to laugh. They were great rolling laughs that shook his frame and died abruptly. "Pastor," he said gravely, "you are the only man in this dorp who has prayed my grace before looking." He moved aside.

Dietrich lifted the nightgown and was relieved to find no swellings in her groin, though reddish spots near her secret place showed where they intended their appearance. When he tried to look at her chest and under her arms, the gown caught and she flailed about. "Max!" she said. "Send for Max! He will protect me!"

"Will you give her the last rites?" Klaus asked.

"Not yet. Klaus . . ." he hesitated, but then said nothing about Wanda. The miller would not leave his wife like this. When he rose, Hilde clutched at his robe. "Fetch Dietrich," she begged him.

"Ja doch," Dietrich answered unfastening her grip. "I go now to fetch him."

Outside, he paused for breath. God was a clever sort. Dietrich had fled the pest in one house, only to find it in another.

HANS AND Gottfried helped him move Wanda to her bed. When Dietrich returned to the parsonage, Joachim took one look at his face. "The pest!" he said. At Dietrich's nod, he threw his head back and cried, "O God, I have failed You!"

Dietrich laid a hand on his shoulder. "You have failed no one."

He shrugged off the touch. "The Krenken are gone back to Hell unshriven!"

When Dietrich turned away, Joachim snatched his sleeve. "You cannot let them die alone."

"I know. I go to Manfred to pray his grace for a hospice."

HE FOUND the Herr in the great hall, sitting between a roaring fire in the hearth and a second built in a large cauldron placed on the other side of the room. The entire household had huddled there, even Imre the peddler. Servants came and went, bearing wood to feed the fires. They left slowly and returned quickly.

Manfred, who sat at the council table scratching with a pen on a sheet of parchment, spoke without looking up. "The fires worked for your pope. De Chauliac recommended it when I bespoke him in Avignon. The element of fire destroys the bad air . . ." He waved the pen in dismissal. ". . . somehow. I leave science to those trained in it." His eyes darted to the corners of the room, as if he might spy the pest lurking there. Then he bent once more to the parchment.

Fire might be effective, Dietrich thought, since it loosened the stiffened mass of bad air and caused it to rise. Bells, too, might break up the mass by shaking the air. But if the pest was carried by innumerable *mikrobiota,* Dietrich did not see where the flames would help—unless, like moths, the small-lives were drawn to the fire for self-immolation. Of these thoughts he said nothing. "Mine Herr, Wanda Schmidt and Hilde Müller have been struck by the pest."

"I know. Heloïse Krenkerin warned us by the farspeaker. What do you want of me?"

"I pray your grace to establish a hospital. Soon, I fear, too many will lie ill to—"

Manfred tapped the pen against the table, blunting its point. "You stand too much on ceremony. A hospital. Ja, doch. So be it." He waved a hand. "For what good it may do."

"If we cannot save their lives," Dietrich said, "we can at least make their dying gentler."

"A great comfort that must be. Max!" He dusted the parchment and folded it in quarters. In a gobbet of wax poured off a candle, he impressed his signet. He studied the ring afterward, twisting it a little on his finger. Then he looked to little Irmgard who stood close by with her nurse, snuffling through her tears, and he smiled briefly at her. He handed Max the letter and another that he had already finished. "Take these to the Oberreid road and give them to the first respectable-looking travelers you see. One is for the Baden Markgraf, the other for the Hapsburg Duke. Freiburg and Vienna have already their own problems, but they ought to know what has befallen here. Gunther, go with, and saddle a mount for him."

Max looked unhappy, but he bowed his head and, pulling his gloves from his belt, strode toward the door. Gunther followed, looking, if possible, even less happy.

Manfred shook his head. "I fear death is in this house. Everard fell after he exited this very room. How fares he?"

"Quieter. May I move him to the hospital?"

"Do what you think needful. Do not ask my permission again. I am taking everyone to the *schloss*. I barred folk from entering the village and none heeded me. Now Odo has brought this on us. The *schildmauer* at least I can bar against intruders. Each man must look now to his own house and to his own kin."

Dietrich swallowed. "Mine Herr, all men are brothers."

Manfred made a long, sad face. "Then you have much work ahead."

DIETRICH CALLED on Ulf and Heloïse to carry Everard to the makeshift hospital in the smithy. Neither Krenkl had yet accepted Christ. They had stayed, Hans had suggested, because their fear of death in the "gap between the worlds" exceeded their fear of death by starvation. But when he asked Ulf about this, the Krenk only laughed. "I fear nothing," he bragged over the private canal. "Krenk die. Men die. One must die well."

"With *charitas* in the heart."

An arm toss. "There is no 'charitas,' only courage and honor. One dies without fear, in defiance of the Swooper. Not that one believes, naturally, in the Swooper, but it is a saying of ours."

"Then why did you stay behind when your vessel left, if not from dread of this 'gap'?"

Ulf indicated the Krenkerin striding ahead of them. "Because the Heloïse stayed. I promised our spouse—Understand you our man-woman-nurse? Good. The nurse stays always at the nest. I swore a . . . a blood-oath to it that I would by our Heloïse stay. Some truth-seekers claim that the gap lacks time, and so prolongs death forever.

The Heloïse feared that above all. By me, is all death the same, and I snap my jaws at it. I stayed because of my oath."

THE STENCH, when they entered Everard's cottage, was a palpable thing. The steward lay naked upon his bed, save for a dry, filthy rag placed over his brow. Dark blue-black lines ran up his limbs from the groin and armpits. Of Yrmegard or Witold, there was no sign. Dietrich bent over Everard, thinking him dead, but the man's eyes flew open and he half-rose in the bed. "Mother of God!" he cried.

"I must lance the boils before we move him," Dietrich said to Ulf, gently pressing the steward supine. The black rivers of poison running out the arms and legs suggested that he was already too late. "Where are your wife and child?" he asked Everard. "Who cares for you?"

"Mother of God!" The steward clawed at himself, raking his skin with his nails, and shrieking. Then, abrubtly, he lay back quietly, panting and gasping, as if he had repelled an assault from the ramparts and was resting now for the next attack.

Dietrich had washed the knife already in sour wine, and Ulf suggested heating it in the fire as well. The hearth smoldered in sullen red embers. No firewood stood ready. *She has fled*, Dietrich thought. *Yrmegard has abandoned her husband.* He wondered if Everard knew.

The boils were as large as apples, the skin stretched tight and shining around them. He chose the one under the right arm and touched it with the point of his scalpel.

Everard howled and thrashed, striking Dietrich with his fist and knocking the scalpel from his hand. Dietrich knelt, seeing double from the blow, then groped among the rushes for the fallen blade. When he rose, Everard lay on his side, hugging his arms tight against himself and with his knees drawn up. Dietrich walked to the stool beside the bed and sat for a moment, rubbing his temple and thinking. Then he called Hans by the farspeaker.

"There is a basket in my shed, marked with the cross of the Hospitallers," he told his friend. "Bring to the steward's cottage one of the sponges you will find in it—but handle it with care. It has been steeped in mandrake and other poisons."

Hans arrived soon, and stood with the other Krenken to watch. Dietrich moistened the sponge in the water barrel behind the cottage and returned, holding it at arm's length. Then, as the Savoyard had instructed, he held it firmly against Everard's nose and mouth while the steward clawed at his hands. Long enough for sleep, the Savoyard had said, but not so long as for death. Everard went suddenly limp, and Dietrich tossed the sponge into the fire. Too long? No, the man's chest rose and fell. Dietrich crossed himself. "Blessed Jesus, guide my hand."

The blade's touch did not awaken the steward, but he groaned and struggled a little. Hans and Ulf held his limbs steady. The boil was tough and Dietrich pressed harder with the point.

Suddenly, it split, and a vile, suppurating black filth oozed forth, bearing with it the most abominable stench. Dietrich clenched his teeth and applied himself to the remaining boils.

When he was done, Heloïse handed him a rag that she had meanwhile boiled and soaked in vinegar. With this, Dietrich mopped up the slime and cleaned the man's body as best he could. "I would not touch the pus," Ulf advised, and Dietrich, who had had no such intention, ran outside and bent double, vomiting out that morning's breakfast and gulping in great gasps of mountain air. Hans, following, touched him briefly several times. "It was bad?"

Dietrich gasped. "Very bad."

"My . . ." Hans touched his antennae briefly. "I must wash them." Then he said, "The steward will not live."

Dietrich blew his breath out. "We must ever hope, but . . . I think you are right. His wife has taken their boy and run off. He has none to care for him."

"Then we will do it."

They placed Everard on an ambulance that Zimmerman had fashioned, and Ulf and Heloïse took up the handles before and after. Dietrich walked alongside and held the litter steady as they negotiated the hill. He remembered how St. Ephraem the Syrian had fashioned three hundred ambulances during a famine in Mesopotamia. *We will need more,* he told himself.

Hans stayed to burn all the rags and clothing, and kill whatever small-lives they harbored. Ulf called to him. "Save a portion of the pus for my inspection."

"Why did you ask that?" Dietrich said as they proceeded down the hill.

"I labored with the instruments in our craft's lazaret," Ulf told him. "We have a device, which Gschert left with us, that enables us to see the small-lives."

Dietrich nodded, though he did not understand. Then he asked, suddenly, "Why do you help us with the sick, if you have no faith in *charitas*?"

The pagan Krenk tossed his arm. "The Hans is now the Krenkish Herr, so I follow him. Besides it employs my days."

Which was, withal, a Krenkish sort of answer.

WANDA SCHMIDT died the next day, on the Commemoration of St. Maternus of Milan. She kicked and writhed and bit her own tongue in twain. Black blood welled up from within her and spilled forth from her mouth. She heard not the words of comfort that Gottfried Krenk spoke to her; perhaps she did not even feel the gentle pokes which stood among his kind for caresses.

Afterward, Gottfried accosted Dietrich. "The Herr-from-the-sky would not save the woman of the blessed Lorenz. Wherefore did we pray His aid?"

Dietrich shook his head. "All men die when God calls them back to Himself."

And Gottfried answered, "Could he not have called her more softly?"

KLAUS AND Odo brought Hilde to the hospital on an ambulance that they carried between them. When they had lain her on a pallet in the smithy, near the fire that Dietrich had built in the furnace, Klaus bid Odo return to the house, and the old man nodded distractedly, and said, "Tell Hilde to hurry back and cook my dinner."

Klaus watched him go. "He sits on the stool before the fireplace, and stares into dry ashes. When I enter the room, he turns his eyes toward me for only a moment before he is drawn back to the fascination of cinders. I think he is already dead—in here." He beat his breast. "All else is mere ceremony." He knelt to stroke Hilde's hair. "The beasts are dying, too," he said. "Along the roadside I saw dead rats, several cats, and Herwyg's old hound. One-eye will miss that dog."

Dear God, Dietrich prayed, *will you scour the earth of all living things?* "What is this?" he asked, fingering the sleeve of Klaus's jerkin. "It looks like blood. Has she vomited blood?"

Klaus dropped his eyes to the stains and stared at them as if he had never seen them before. "No," he said. He touched one of the spots with his fingertip, but it came away with no color, so the blood there was already dried. "No. I . . . I followed . . ."

But whatever the miller had been about to say was lost to his hesitation, for Hilde rose from her sickbed and stood suddenly upright. At first, Dietrich thought it a miracle; but the woman began to turn and spin and sing la-la-la, flailing her arms. Klaus clutched at her, but her arm struck him a mighty blow to the cheek that nearly felled him.

Dietrich went to the pallet's other side and tried to grab one arm while Klaus grabbed the other. He took hold of her wrist and used his own weight to bear her down. Klaus did the same. Hilde continued to twist side to side, singing wordlessly. Then, abruptly, she ceased and lay still. Klaus's head snapped up. "Has she . . . ?"

"No. No, she breathes."

"What does it mean? The dancing."

Dietrich shook his head. "I know not . . ." Her pustules were grown large, but there were yet no streaks of poison on her arms. "May I see her legs?" Wordlessly, Klaus lifted Hilde's skirt, and Dietrich studied her groin and thighs and was relieved to see no streaks there, either. "Gottfried," he called, "bring the old wine."

Klaus dipped his head. "Ja, ja, I need also a drink. Will she rest now?"

"It's not to drink. I must wash my lance."

Klaus laughed suddenly, then reverted to morose silence.

Gottfried brought a pot of vinegar and Dietrich washed the blade in it. Then he held it in the smithy fire until the handle became hot. He would not chance the soporific sponge this time. Those he must save for ones like Everard, where the chance of life and the risk of death were more closely balanced.

"Hold the bowl," Dietrich said to Gottfried, handing him a clay basin. "When I lance the pustule," he added to Klaus, "the pus must drain into the bowl. Ulf said that we must not let our flesh contact it, but the Krenkl do not believe it affects them."

"There is but one way to discover that," said Gottfried.

"He is a wise demon, then." Klaus studied the Krenkl. "She took care of *them*; now *they* take care of her. I understand the one act no better than the other." He stared at the knife.

"Fear not," Dietrich said. "De Chauliac told Manfred that this course was often effective, if not delayed too long."

"Cut then! I could not bear it should she—"

Dietrich had honed the lance to razor-keenness. He brought it through the pustule with a clean stroke. Hilde gasped and arched her back, though she did not scream as Everard had. Dietrich had firm hold of her arm and the putrescence spilled into Gottfried's bowl. He looked to see if it contained blood and was relieved to see that it did not.

Though less vile than Everard's eruptions, the pus stank badly enough. Klaus gulped and retained his stomach by sheer will, though he did recoil.

Soon, the grim effort was over. Dietrich poured more of the vinegar over the wounds. He was uncertain why this might be efficacious, but medical doctors had taught so since the great age of Aquinas. Vinegar burned, so perhaps the element of fire burned out the small-lives.

AFTERWARD, DIETRICH walked with Klaus to Walpurga Honig's cottage, where they sat on the bench before it. Klaus rapped his knuckles on the window shutter and, a moment later, the ale-wife opened it and shoved a pot of ale into his hands. She glanced at Dietrich, reappeared with a second pot, then slammed and bolted the shutter. The sudden noise startled little Atiulf Kohlmann, sitting in the dirt across the street, and he cried out for his mommy.

"Everyone is afraid," Klaus said, with a gesture of the pot. He took a sip, closed his eyes, and began to weep, the pot dropping from nerveless fingers and spilling his ale in the dirt. "I don't understand," he said after a time. "Has she wanted for anything? Her mere word was its purchase. Brocades, girdles, wimples. Silken small-clothes one time in the Freiburg—Italian work, and did that not cost me? 'French paint' for her face. I put food on her table, a roof over her head—and not a hut like her father's. No, a *wooden* building with a *stone* fireplace and a chimney to heat the bed-loft. I gave her two fine children and, while God saw fit to call the boy back too young, I saw our 'Phye fairly wed to a Freiburg merchant. Only God knows how Freiburg fares this day." He studied his hands and wrung one with the other. He looked east, toward the lowlands.

"Yet she seeks other men," he said. "Everyone knows it, but I must pretend otherwise—and take my little revenges when I weigh out the meal. I jested when I lifted her skirt for you. But I think now you really were the last man in Oberhochwald to see that sight; though I did not think so at one time. I thought you went into the woods to be with her, pastor. Priest though you are, you're a man. So I followed one day. That was when I saw the monsters for the first time. Yet *they* were not so terrible a sight as my Hilde, splayed upon a bed of forest leaves while that crude sergeant entered her."

Dietrich remembered one of the miller's horses tethered in the clearing and thinking then that it was Hilde's. "Klaus—" he said, but the miller continued with no indication of having heard.

"I'm an agile man in the marriage bed. Not so agile as in my spring, but I've had no complaint from others. Oh, yes, I've swyved other women. What choice had I? *Your* choice? No, I burn like your Paul. I don't know why she turns from me. Do other men speak sweeter words? Are their lips more agreeable?"

And now the miller raised his eyes to look at Dietrich squarely. "You could tell her. You could make it a commandment. But . . . I don't want her submission. I want her love, and I can't have that, and I don't know why.

"I saw her first in her father's swineyard, feeding the pigs. Her feet were bare in the muck, but I saw the princess in the mire. I was apprenticed to old Heinrich—Altenbach's father, that was—who held the Herr's mill before me, so my prospects were good. My Beatrix had died in that terrible winter of 1315, and all our children with her, so my seed would die with me, unless I wed again. I proposed a marriage to her father and paid *merchet* and the Herr consented. No woman here ever had so fine a wedding-feast, save only the Herr's own Kunigund! I learned that night that she was no virgin, but what woman is by that age? It did not bother me then. Perhaps it should have."

Dietrich laid a hand on Klaus's shoulder. "What will you do now?"

"He was not gentle with her, that pig sergeant. For him, just another *'loch.'*"

"Wanda Schmidt has died."

Klaus nodded slowly. "That sorrows me. We were good friends. We shared the same lack, but filled it with each other. I know it was a sin, but . . ."

"A small sin," Dietrich assured him. "There was no evil, I think, in either of you."

Klaus laughed. His thickset body shook like an earthquake in a barrel, and tears started in the corners of his eyes. "How often," he said when the laughter had settled into melancholy, "in your dry, scholastic sermons, have I heard you say that an 'evil' is the lack of a 'good'? So, tell me, priest," and the eyes he turned on Dietrich overflowed with emptiness, "what man had ever lacked as much as I have?"

They sat in silence. Dietrich handed the miller the pot of ale he held and the miller drank from it. "My sins," he said. "My sins."

"Everard is dead also," Dietrich told him, and Klaus nodded. "And Franzl Longnose from the castle. They put his body outside the walls this morning." He looked toward the towers behind the battlements. "How fares Manfred?"

"I don't know."

Klaus set both pots on the sill for Wanda to take back. "I wonder if we ever will."

"And the Unterbaums are gone," Dietrich said. "Konrad, his wife, their two surviving children . . ."

"Toward Bear Valley, I hope," said Klaus. "Only a fool would hie for the Breisgau with the pest in Freiburg. Where is Atiulf 's mother?"

They stood and crossed to the boy crying in the dirt. "What is it, my small?" Dietrich asked, kneeling beside the lad.

"Mami!" Atiulf howled. "Want mami!" He ran out of breath and sucked in for a great bellow that ended in a paroxysm of phegmy coughing.

"Where is she?" Dietrich asked.

"Don't know! Mami, *I don't feel good!*"

"Where is your father?"

"Don't know! Vati, make it stop!" Then the couging racked his body once again.

"And your sister, Anna?"

"Anna's sleeping. Don't wake her! Mami said."

Dietrich looked at Klaus, and Klaus looked at him. Then they both looked at the cottage door. The maier set his jaw. "I suppose we must . . ."

Klaus opened the door and stepped inside, and Dietrich, with the boy in hand, followed.

There was no sign of Norbert and Adelheid, but Anna lay on a pallet of straw, with a countenance of peace and contentment.

"Dead," Klaus announced. "Yet not a sign on her. Not like poor Everard."

"Atiulf," said Dietrich sternly, "was your sister ill when you went to bed last night?" The boy, still whimpering, shook his head. Dietrich looked to Klaus, who said, "Sometimes the murrain strikes people so, when it enters the mouth instead of the skin. Perhaps the pest acts the same way. Or she has died from grief over that boy."

"Bertam Unterbaum."

"I would have thought better of Norbert," Klaus said, "than that he left his boy to die."

Reason would have told him to fly, Dietrich thought. If the boy was doomed, what purpose was served by staying—and falling himself victim? And so all reasonable people had fled—from ancient Alexandria, from Constantine's Plague-wracked army, from the Paris Hospital.

Klaus picked the boy up in his arms. "I will take him to the hospital. If he lives, he will be my son." Norbert had acted contrary to his temperament, but Klaus's offer was astonishing. Dietrich offered a blessing and they parted company. Dietrich continued toward the Bear Valley end of the village for no other reason than that he had started out in that direction.

A cottage door flew open and Ilse Ackermann ran from it with Maria in her arms. "My little Maria! My little Maria!" she shrieked over and over. The girl was a blackened figure soiled with vomit, with lips and tongue dark blue, and blood flowing freely from her mouth. She exuded the pest's peculiar odor. Before Ilse could say more, the girl spasmed and died.

The woman cried out one more time and dropped her daughter to the ground, where she lay like the blackened doll that the selfsame girl had rescued from the fire. The pest seemed to have invaded every thumb's-length of her body, rotting it from within. Dietrich backed off in horror. This sight was more dreadful than Hilde with her delirium, or even Wanda with her blackened, lolling tongue. This was Death in all his awful majesty.

Ilse threw hands to her face, and ran off toward the autumn field where Felix labored, leaving her daughter in the dirt behind her.

DEATH HAD buffeted Dietrich from all sides and too quickly. Everard, Franzl, Wanda, Anna, Maria. Peaceful or agonizing; long or short; rotting with stench or simply falling asleep. There was no order to it, no lawfulness. Dietrich quickened his pace. The pest, after three days' rest, had redoubled its efforts.

Vile fruit dangled from the linden tree in the green: a human figure twisted in the hot July breeze. It was Odo, Dietrich saw as he edged closer, and he thought first of suicide. But the rope was tied to the trunk and there was nothing under his feet from which he might have jumped. Then he understood. Returning to his son-in-law's house, Odo had been waylaid and killed for the sin of bringing the pest.

Dietrich could endure no more. He ran. His sandals clapped against the wooden planks of the millstream bridge and found the Bear Valley road. The track was baked hard in the sun, except where it ran between the swell of the land. Here, the rivulet had turned it to mud, which splattered Dietrich's legs as he splashed through it. At the bend, he came upon one of the Herr's rouncies, a gray one, fully saddled and caparisoned, nibbling from some succulent bush by the pathside.

A sign! he thought. God had sent a sign. Seizing the reins, he scrambled up the bank and settled himself into the saddle. Then, without a look behind, he directed the unwilling horse eastward.

· 8 ·

NOW
Sharon

THE SUBCONSCIOUS is a wonderful thing. It never sleeps, no matter what the rest of the mind does. And it never stops thinking. No matter what the rest of the mind does. Sharon was in the middle of her galactic structure class—seven upper-class physics majors—when, in turning about after making a point, her eyes fell on the poster-sized chart of the distribution of redshifts.

Of course.

She fell silent, and the student who had just answered her question shifted uneasily in his seat, wondering where his answer had gone wrong. He tapped his stylus staccato on the tabletop and looked for support to his classmates. "What I meant . . ." he temporized, hoping for a hint.

Sharon turned around. "No, you were quite right, Girish. But I just realized . . . Class dismissed."

Now the singular difference between the graduate species and his undergraduate cousin is that the graduate student may be discontent with such an unexpected boon. For the most part, they are there because they *want* to be, and not because society says they ought to be. And so they filed out of the seminar room buzzing to one another while Sharon fled to her office, where she scribbled furiously.

When Hernando entered half an hour later, tossed his cap on the bookshelf, and dropped his backpack beside his desk, she was so deep into it that she never noticed him. He stared at her for a while before he settled himself to sort out his notes for his nucleonics lecture.

"It's because time is quantized," Sharon said, drawing Hernando out of his own contemplation.

"What? Time is quantized? Yeah, I suppose. Why not?"

"No, it's the redshifts. Why the galaxies are receding at discrete velocities. The universe sputters."

Hernando spun his chair to face her. "Right."

"Okay, vacuum energy. Einstein's lambda, the one he called his biggest blunder."

"The cosmic fudge factor he threw in so he could get the result he wanted."

"Right. So, Einstein was a genius. Even when he made a mistake it was brilliant. Lambda is pushing the galaxies apart faster and faster. But the amount of energy in the vacuum depends on the speed of light—and vice versa."

"That's what your theory seems to suggest."

She ignored his doubts. "If light speed drops, it reduces the amount of energy the vacuum can hold. So where does the excess energy go?"

Hernando pursed his lips and looked thoughtful. "Outside the universe?"

"No, *inside* the universe. Into ordinary radiation and matter. Into dust clouds and microwaves, stars and planets and galaxies, into whales and birds and college professors."

The post-doc whistled. "The Big Bang itself . . ."

"*And* with no wacky inflaton field needed as an epicycle. Quantized time is the only thing that explains the redshift gaps."

"Measurement resolution?" Hernando suggested. "Limited samples? Unrepresentative samples?"

"That's what they told Tifft when he discovered it. And . . . they were right about a lot of it; but they were also champions of orthodoxy clinging to the existing dogma. Look, *light* is quantized, *space* is quantized, what makes *time* so special? It's just another dimension of the continuum."

"Oh, that's a convincing argument. Besides, if you're right, it's not exactly a *continu*-um."

"And that's why there are gaps in the redshifts. What looks like a continuous motion picture is really just a series of frames. The universe has 'cracks' in it."

The muscular young man laughed. "And what's in those cracks?"

"Oh, wouldn't we love to know! Whole other universes, I think. Parallel worlds."

Hernando cocked his head and looked thoughtful. "Objective evidence?" he said after a time.

"That's where you come in."

"Me?" He looked alarmed, as if Sharon was about to send him into one of those parallel worlds.

"You need to build me a chronon detector."

"Sure, my afternoon is free after my two o'clock lecture. I suppose a chronon is . . ."

"A 'quantum' of time."

He thought about it. "Cool beans. But how do you detect something like that?"

"You and me, Hernando, we're going to figure that out. Think of it. Someday, you may walk on another planet, or on a parallel world."

The post-doc snorted. "I got something to do that weekend."

Sharon leaned back in her chair, certain now that she had his skeptical mind hooked. Every enthusiast needs a skeptic, or she would run out of control.

· XXV ·

JULY, 1349
Ferial Days

THE GRAY was disinclined to flight, and her stubborn walk was a compromise between Dietrich's desire to gallop and her own desire not to move at all. When they reached the stretch by the meadow gate where the bushes gave way to open land, and the mare saw untied, wind-scattered sheaves of half-mown hay, she turned off the road and tried to nuzzle the rope from the gatepost. "If you are that hungry, sister horse," Dietrich conceded, "you'll not last the journey." Leaning down, he undid the latch and the horse quickstepped into the meadow like a child shown his birthday cake.

While Dietrich waited impatiently for the gray to feed, curiosity turned his mind to the saddlebags, and he wondered to whom beside God he owed this boon. Searching, he found a linen maniple, dyed bright green and embroidered in thread-of-gold with crosses and the chi-rho. Below that were stuffed other priestly vestments of surpassing beauty. He settled himself in the saddle. What more sign could he ask that the horse had been sent for him to find?

When the mare had eaten her fill, Dietrich turned her toward the shade of the Great Wood. There was a stream there, he remembered, where the horse could drink, and the canopy would be relief against the awful heat.

He had not entered the wood since the Krenkish vessel's departure, and the expression of summer foliage had altered its aspect considerably. The woods-masters and wild roses suffused the air with their fragrances. Bees hummed. New growth had obscured many of the blazes that Max had cut. Yet, the horse seemed purposeful. Dietrich supposed that she smelled the water and gave her free rein.

Unseen creatures bolted from their path, disturbing the shrubs and the hazel. A blue-winged tail-mouse watched his progress for a space before flying off. Petrarch, it was said, found peace in nature and had once climbed Mount Ventoux near Avignon for no reason but the prospect from its summit. Perhaps the savagery of his writings, his distortions and libels, owed something to his love of savage places.

Dietrich came upon the clearing where the stream pooled before completing its rush down the mountainside. The horse dipped her head and began to drink and Dietrich, reflecting that he too would grow thirsty on the road, dismounted and, hobbling the mare with a hippopede, walked upstream a few paces to drink.

A stone fell into the pool, and Dietrich leapt back. Above him, upon a projecting ledge where the water tumbled into the pool, squatted Heloïse Krenkerin. Dietrich awoke his head-harness. "Greet God," he told the other through the private canal.

The Krenkerin reached to the side and slung another stone into the pool. "Greet God," she said. "I thought your kind avoided these forests."

"They are fearful places," Dietrich agreed. "What brings you here?"

"My folk find . . . quiet-inside-the-head in places like this. It has . . . what is your word . . . *Maze.* Balance."

"Arnold used to sit there so," Dietrich said. "I spied him once."

"Did you . . . He, too, was of the Great Isle." She threw another stone into the pond, refreshing ripples that had begun to subside. Dietrich waited, but she said no more until he turned to go.

"When you stand still," Heloïse said, "you seem to vanish. I know that is the way our eyes are fashioned, and the Ulf tried to explain how yours were different; but he is only . . . one-who-labors-with-machines-for-physicians, and not a physician himself." She tossed another stone. "But that makes naught." The stone struck directly in the center of the fading ripples, and Dietrich thought that each of her tosses had struck precisely the same spot. Was it the motion of the water that drew her aim? Humans gauged distance more exactly than Krenken; but Krenken gauged motion more exactly. Thus God assigned to each folk gifts suitable to their being.

"How fares Ulf?" the Krenkerin asked. "Shows he the spots?" And she extended her arm so that Dietrich could see the dark-green mottling that presaged the strange starvation of his guests.

"Not that I have seen."

She ran a finger around a large blemish. "Tell me, is it better to die quickly or slowly?"

Dietrich looked down while he scuffed the dirt with his foot. "All beings seek naturally to live, so death is an evil, never to be sought for its own sake. But all beings seek also to avoid pain and terror. As to die quickly lessens these, a quick death is therefore, if not a 'good,' at least a lesser defect of the good. But a quick death gives also no chance for repentance and expiation to those one has wronged. So, a slower death may also be thought a lesser evil."

"It is true, what is said of you." A fifth stone followed the others. "The Ulf stayed because Hans asked for his particular skills, and he obeyed as if Hans had been a . . . one-set-above."

"Is that what he told you?"

"I could not leave him. Yet, each day I smell my death step closer. That is not right. The Death ought to swoop like your hawk; not stalk like your wolf. 'So it was; so it is.' "

"Death is but a doorway to another life," Dietrich assured her.

"Is it."

"And our Herr, Jesus Christ, is the gate."

"And how pass I through this gate-that-is-a-man?"

"Your hand is already on the latch. The way is love, and you have shown that already by your acts."

So also had her husband. It wondered Dietrich, as he returned to his horse, that both had stayed because each believed the other would. Thus does one turn from care because it is a duty to duty because one cares. He stepped into the stirrup and seated himself. "Come to me when you return to the village," he said, "and we will talk." With that he tugged the reins and headed the gray toward the trail.

The horse had indeed been a sign, and a miracle as well. The sign had been to lead him here, so that God might gently admonish him through the mandibles of a stranger. The cup would pass from Heloïse no more than it had passed from the Son of Man in the Garden, so what presumption it was to think that it could pass from him! "Lord," he prayed, "When did I see You sick or in distress and fail to comfort You?"

He leaned forward and stroked the horse's head and she gave him a whicker of pleasure. "You are a miraculous horse," he told her, for God had permitted her to come into the presence of a Krenkl without panic.

Along the way back, he said a prayer for the repose of the soul of Father Rudolf. God had presented Dietrich the means of flight, and with it a warning of the rewards awaiting flight.

THE HORROR built much like a rainstorm: first a few, then a period of quiet when folk believed the menace past, then a few more, until at last a torrent. Folk cowered in their homes. In the fields, crops rotted and hay wilted unscythed. A few joined Dietrich and the Krenken at the hospital. Joachim, when he had recovered from his stripes; but also Gregor Mauer, Klaus Müller, Gerda Boettcher, Lueter Holzhacker. Theresia Gresch labored over her herbs, preparing those that eased pain or induced sleep, though she would not enter the smithy.

Gottfried had dedicated the hospital to St. Laurence, though Dietrich suspected that he meant the late smith, not Sixtus's deacon. Having been told by Dietrich of the Knights of the Hospital, the creature took to wearing a surcoat with the cross of the Order blazoned on the upper left.

Folk sickened slowly—and suddenly; from coughing fits—and boils. Herwyg One-Eye seemed to blacken before Dietrich's horrified gaze, as if a shadow had passed across his soul. Marcus Boettcher lingered, like Everard, in agony and convulsions. Volkmar Bauer's entire family perished: his wife, Seppl, even Ulrike and her newborn babe. Only the vogt himself lived, and he precariously.

Days fell together: Margaret of Antioch, Mary Magdalen, Appolinaris, James the Greater, Berthold of Gasten . . . Losing track of the feasts, Dietrich celebrated unnamed ferial days.

Burials brought people out. Marcus Boettcher. Konrad Feldmann and both his girls. Rudi Pforzheimer. Gerda Boettcher. Trude and Peter Metzger. At each death, Dietrich rang the church bell. Once for a child, twice for a woman, thrice to signify a man. Who would hear, he wondered? He imagined the peals drifting ever fainter over a landscape devoid of life.

The churchyard filled, and they dug graves in fresh ground that Dietrich consecrated irregularly. Again and again, Dietrich told himself, *Not all die.* Paris lived, and Avignon. Even in Niederhochwald, a handful had survived. Hilde seemed to grow better, and Little Gregor, and even Volkmar Bauer.

Reinhardt Bent would steal no more furrows from his neighbors, nor Petronella Lürm glean the Herr's fields. Fulk's woman, Constanz, died in the sudden fashion. Melchior Metzger led a delirious Nickel Langermann to the hospital. "It isn't fair," the young man said, as if blaming Dietrich. "He had the murrain and he grew well. Why strike him this second time?"

"There is no 'why,'" Hans answered from the bedside of Franz Ambach. "There is only 'how,' and that no one knows."

ULF HAD been working with a device that magnified very small things, by which Dietrich had named it *mikroskopion.* Through this, Ulf had studied the blood of both the stricken and the hale. One day, when Dietrich had come to the parsonage to wake Joachim for his turn in the hospice, Ulf showed them on the image-slate numberless black flecks of varied shapes and sizes, like dust motes caught in a beam of sunlight. Ulf indicated one particular curl. "This one never appears in hale blood; but always in those stricken."

"What is it?" Joachim asked, only half-awake.

"The enemy."

But it was one thing to know the face of the enemy, and quite another to slay him. Arnold Krenk might have succeeded, or so Ulf said. "Yet, we have not his skills. We can but proof a man's blood and say if the enemy is present within him."

"Then," said Joachim, "all who do not yet bear this mark of Satan must flee."

Dietrich rubbed the stubble on his chin. "And the ill can be restrained from flight, lest they spread the small-lives farther abroad." He glanced at Joachim, but said nothing of logic. "Ja, doch. It is little enough, but it is something."

MAX WAS the natural leader of such a flight. He knew the forests better than any but Gerlach the hunter, and was more accustomed to leading men than was Gerlach.

Dietrich went to the Herr's stables and saddled a sleek, black courser. He had tightened the cinch and was proposing that the beast accept the bit when Manfred's voice said, "I could have you flogged for your presumption."

Dietrich turned to find the Herr behind him, bearing a great hunting bird on his left forearm. Manfred nodded toward the horse. "Only a knight may ride a courser." But when Dietrich began to remove the bridle, he shook his head. "Na, who will care? I came forth only because I remembered my birds, and thought to free them before they starved. I was in the rookery when I heard you fumbling around. I plan to unbar the kennel and the stable, too, so it is well you came now. I suppose you mean to flee as Rudolf did."

The ease of the supposition angered Dietrich, not least because it struck too truly; but he said only, "I go to find Max."

Manfred raised his gauntlet and stroked the falcon, which craned its head, sidestepped a bit on the thick, leather glove, and screeched. "You know what the gauntlet means, don't you, precious one? You yearn to spread your wings and fly, don't you? Max has flown, too, I suppose, or he would have returned ere now." Dietrich made no answer, and Manfred continued. "But it is bred into his character to return to me. Not Max; this beauty. Max, too, now that I think on it. He'll circle and circle, searching for the welcoming arm below and will not see it. Is it right to release him to such sorrow?"

"Mine Herr, surely he will accustom himself to his new circumstances."

"So he will," Manfred answered sadly. "He will forget me and the hunts we carried out together. That is why the falcon symbolizes love. You cannot keep a falcon. You must release him, and then he will return of his own will, or . . ."

"Or 'fly to other lands.'"

"You know the term? Did you study falconry? You are a man of parts, Dietl. A Paris scholar. Yet, you know horsemanship and perhaps hunting with birds. I think you were gently born. Yet you never speak of your youth."

"Mine Herr knows the circumstances in which he found me."

Manfred grimaced. "Most delicately put. Indeed, I do. And had I not seen you stay the mob at Rheinhausen, I would have left you there to be slaughtered with the rest of them. Yet it has, on the whole, been well. I have copied many of our conversations in memoranda. I never told you that. I am no scholar, though I think myself a practical man, and I have always delighted in your ideas. Do you know how you make a falcon return to you?"

"Mine Herr . . ."

"Dietrich, after all these years, you and I may 'duzen,' and dispense with formalities."

"Very well . . . Manfred. One cannot make a falcon return, though one may easily bar it from returning. A falconer must master his emotions, must make no sudden moves that could frighten the bird off."

"Would that more lovers knew that art, Dietrich." He laughed and then, in sudden silence, his face grew long. "Eugen has the fever."

"May God save him."

Manfred's lips twitched. "His death is the end of my Gundl. She'll not live without him."

"May God deny her wish."

"Do you think God hears you anymore? I think He has gone away from the world. I think He has grown disgusted with men and will have no more to do with us." Manfred stepped outside the mews and, with a sweep of his arm, launched the falcon. "God has flown to other lands, I think." He watched for a moment, admiring the bird's beauty, before he ducked back inside the mews. "I hate to break troth with him in such a manner." He meant the bird.

"Manfred, death is but a falcon launched to 'fly to other lands.'"

The Herr smiled without humor. "*Apropos,* but perhaps too easy. When you return with the black, give him hay, but do not stable him. I must see to the other beasts." He turned, hestitated, then spread his arms. "You and I may never meet again."

Dietrich took the embrace. "We may, should God grant us both our hearts' desires."

"And not our deserts! Ha. So we part on a jest. What else can a man do amidst such sorrow?"

DIETRICH DID not at first notice Max, save that the heavy buzz of flies under the summer heat led him to the spot. He hunched his shoulders and slid from the horse's back, tying the beast with special care to a nearby oak. Procuring a kerchief, he plucked blossoms from patches of wildflowers and crushed them within the cloth to release their perfume before tying the kerchief to his face. He broke off a branch from a hazel bush and, using it as a broom, swept it across the sergeant's body, dispersing its aerial diners. Then, with as much dispassion as he could muster, he looked upon the carcass of his friend.

The physicians of Bologna and Padua had made anatomies on bodies dried in the sun, or consumed in the earth, or submerged in running water, but Dietrich did not think they had ever done so on a body in this state. His stomach leapt through his mouth, and so visited a final indignity on the man. When he had recovered, and had refreshed his "flower-pocket," Dietrich confirmed what he had glimpsed.

Max had been stabbed in the back. His jerkin was rent there, at the kidneys, and a great gout of blood had issued forth. He had fallen forward, in the act of drawing his quillon, for he lay upon his right arm with the handle of the long dagger in his death-hardened grip and the blade half out of its sheath.

Dietrich staggered to a nearby stone, a block that had tumbled countless years before from the escarpment overhead. There, he sobbed—for Max, for Lorenz, for Herwyg One-eye and all the others.

DIETRICH RETURNED to the hospital after vespers. For a time, he watched Hans and Joachim and the others walk among the sufferers, applying cool cloths to fevered brows, spooning food into indifferent mouths, washing the bandages used to cover the sores in tubs of hot, soapy water and laying them out to dry, a practice Hugh de Lucca and others had commended.

At last, Dietrich stepped inside where Gregor watched over his ailing son. "Everyone says he has my face," Gregor said, "and maybe that's true when he's awake and tries to be like me; but when he's asleep, he remembers that he is *her* firstborn, and her shade looks out at me from inside his heart." He was silent for a moment. "I must look after Seybke. The two of them fought. Always scuffling like two bear cubs." Gregor craned his neck. "Gregerl's not a pious boy. He mocks the church, despite my scolds."

"The choice is God's, not ours, and God acts not from petty spite, but from boundless love."

Gregor looked around the smithy. "Boundless love," he repeated. "Is that what this is?"

"It is no comfort," Hans interjected, "but we Krenken know this. There is no other manner in which the world could be fashioned that would bear life. There are . . . numbers. The strength of the bonds that hold the atoms together; the . . . the strength of the *elektronik* essence; the attraction of matter . . . Ach!" He tossed his arm. "The sentences in my head wander; and it was not my calling. We have shown that these numbers can be no other. The smallest change in any, and the world would not stand. All that happens in this world, follows from these numbers: sky and stars, sun and moon, rain and snow, plants and animals and small-lives."

"God has ordered all things," Dietrich quoted from the Book of Wisdom, "by weight and measure and number."

"Doch. And from those numbers come also ills and afflictions and death and the pest. Yet had the Herr-in-the-sky ordered the world in any other way, there would be no life at all."

Dietrich remembered that Master Buridan had compared the world to a great clock that God has wound, and which swung now by its own instrumental causes.

"You are right, monster," Gregor said. "It is no comfort."

HELOÏSE KRENKERIN died the next day. Hans and Ulf carried her body to the church and laid it out on a bench that Joachim had prepared. Then Dietrich left them alone for the private rites that he had implicitely condoned. Afterward, in the parsonage, Hans held his flask up to the window.

"This many days only remain," he said, tracing the level with his fingertip. "I will not see you through to the end."

"But after the end, we will see each other again," Dietrich told him.

"Perhaps," the Krenkl allowed. He placed his flask carefully upon the shelf, then walked outside. Dietrich followed, and found him balanced upon the outcropping where he liked to perch. Dietrich lowered himself to the grass beside him. His legs complained and he rubbed his calf. Below them, the shadows were long from the setting sun, and the eastern sky had deepened already to cobalt. Hans extended his left arm. "Ulf," he said.

Dietrich followed the gesture to the weed-choked autumn field, where Ulf stood with his arms outstretched. His shadow ran like a knight's lance across the furrows, broken by the irregularity of the plants and the ground. "He makes the sign of the Crucified!"

Hans flapped his lips. "Perhaps he does. The Herr-from-the-sky is often whimsical. But see how he shows his neck to the sky. He invites the Swooper to take him. This was an old rite, practiced among Ulf 's folk on their far island in the Eastern Sea of Storms. Gottfried's folk and mine alike thought them foolish and vain, and Shepherd's folk tried to suppress them. Indeed, the rite has long passed out of use, even on the Great Isle; but in times of peril, a man may turn to the ways of his forefathers and stand exposed in an open field."

Hans unfolded from his perch, staggered, and nearly fell from the rock. Dietrich seized him by the arm, pulling him to safety. Hans laughed. "Bwah! There is an ignoble end! Better to be taken by Ulf 's Swooper than a clumsy tumble, though I would prefer a quiet death in my sleep. Ach! What is this?"

One of Manfred's loosed falcons had come to rest on Ulf 's outstretched arm! The bird sheered, and Dietrich and Hans heard its distant cry. But when Ulf did not provide the expected morsel, the bird spread its wings and soared into the sky once more, where it circled thrice before departing.

Hans fell to a sudden squat and hugged his knees, his side-jaws agape. In the far field, Ulf leapt into the air in the manner of Krenkish dance. Dietrich looked from one to the other in bewilderment.

Hans stood erect and brushed absently from his leather-hose the grass and dirt. "Ulf will take our baptism now," he said. "The Swooper has spared him. And if *It* can show mercy, why not swear fealty to the very Herr of mercy?"

"PASTOR, PASTOR!" It was little Atiulf, who had taken to following Klaus about and calling him Daddy. "Men! On the Oberreid road!"

It was the day after Ulf 's baptism, and Dietrich had been digging graves atop Church Hill with Klaus, Joachim, and a few other men. They joined the boy at the crest and Klaus fetched him up in his arms. "Perhaps they bring word that the pest has gone," the miller said.

Dietrich shook his head. The pest would never go. "By his cloak, it is the Markgraf 's herald, and a chaplain. Perhaps the bishop has sent a replacement for Father Rudolf."

"He'd be a fool to come here," Gregor suggested.

"Or overjoyed to leave Strassburg," Dietrich reminded him.

"We do not need him here, in any case," said Joachim.

But Dietrich had taken only a few steps down the hillside when the herald's horse reared and nearly overthrew him. The rider fought the reins as the terrified beast pawed the air and whinnied. A few paces behind him, the chaplain found his mount also fractious.

"Ach," said Gregor under his breath. "That's done it."

The two riders retreated into the pass between the hills before the herald wheeled his horse and, standing in the stirrups, tossed his right arm in what Dietrich mistook for the Krenkish gesture of dismissal. Then the shoulder of the hill cut them off from sight, and only a dust haze lingered to show where they had been.

They found Hans in the open space between the smithy and Gregor's stoneyard gazing down the high road toward Oberreid. "I thought to warn them off," he said, swaying slightly. "I had forgotten that I was not one of you. They saw me and . . ."

It was Klaus, of all people, who placed his hand on the Krenkl's shoulder and said, "But you *are* one of us, brother monster."

Gottfried stepped from the shadows of the clinic. "What matter if they saw? What can they do but release us from *this*? The one in the fancy cloak threw something in the dirt."

Gregor trotted down the road to retrieve it. Hans said, "It sorrows me to betray you, Dietrich. By us is motionlessness hard to see. I forgot myself and stilled. Habit. Forgive me." And so saying, he collapsed into the dust of the crossroads.

Klaus and Lueter Holzhacker carried the twitching body into the hospital and laid it on a pallet there. Gottfried, Beatke, and the other surviving Krenkl'n gathered round him. "He was sharing his portion with us," Gottfried said. "I did not learn of it until yesterday."

Dietrich stared at him. "He sacrificed himself, as the alchemist did?"

"Bwah-wah! Not as the alchemist did. Arnold thought the extra time would gain us the repairs. Well, he was not a man of the *elektonikos,* and who is to say he was wrong to hope? But Hans acted not from carnal hope, but from love of us who served him."

Gregor had come up with a parchment bound up in string. He handed it to Dietrich. "This is what the herald dropped."

Dietrich untied the string. "How long . . . ?" he asked Gottfried. The servant of the *elektronik* essence shrugged his shoulders as a man might. "Who can say? Heloïse went to the sky in but a few days; the Kratzer lingered for weeks. It is as with your pest."

"How reads the bill?" Joachim asked, and Dietrich pulled his spectacles from his scrip.

"If there be no priest among us," he announced when he had finished, "laymen are authorized to hear one another's confessions." He raised his head. "A miracle."

"What miracle," said Klaus. "That I should confess my sins to the mason, here? That *would* be a miracle."

"Na, Klaus," said Lueter. "I've heard you confess after a couple of steins of Walpurga's brew in you."

"Archdeacon Jarlsberg writes that there are no more priests to send."

"A miracle indeed," said Klaus.

"Half the benefices in the diocese are vacant—because their priests did not run off like Father Rudolf. They stayed with their flocks and died."

"Like you," said Klaus. And Dietrich laughed a little at the comment.

Gregor frowned. "Pastor isn't dead. He isn't even sick."

"Nor you, nor I," said Klaus. "Not yet."

DIETRICH SAT by Hans's pallet all day and slept there at night. They spoke of many things, he and the monster. Whether a vacuum existed. How there could be more than one world, since each would try to rush toward the center of the other. Whether the sky was a dome or a vast empty sea. Whether Master Peter's magnets could make a machine that would never stop, as he had claimed. All those matters of philosophy that had so delighted Hans in happier days. They spoke, too, of the Kratzer, and Dietrich was convinced more than ever that, if love had any meaning in the hidden hearts of the Krenkl, that Hans and the Kratzer had loved one another.

In the morning, the portcullis of the castle opened with a clatter of chains and Richart the schultheiss, with Wilifrid the clerk and a few others galloped furiously down Castle Hill and out the Bear Valley road. Shortly thereafter, the bell in the castle chapel tolled once. Dietrich waited, and waited; but there came no second stroke.

THAT AFTERNOON, the villagers held an irregular court under the linden and Dietrich asked the gathering which of them Ulf had found free of the small-lives. About half raised their hands, and Dietrich noted that they sat for the most part at a distance from their neighbors.

"You must leave Oberhochwald," he said. "If you stay, the small-lives will invade you, as well. Take also those whose fever has broken. When the pest has gone, you may return and set things aright once more."

"I'll not return," cried Jutte Feldmann. "This place is accursed! A place of demons and sorcery." There were mutters of approval, but some, like Gregor and Klaus, shook their heads and Melchior Metzger, grown suddenly old, sat on the grass with a grim look on his face.

"But, where would we go?" asked Jakob Becker. "The pest lies all about us. In the Swiss, so also in Vienna, in Freiburg, in Munich, in . . ."

Dietrich stopped him before he could enumerate the whole world. "Go south and east into the foothills," he said. "Shun all towns and villages. Build shelters in the forest, keep fires burning, and stay near the fires. Take flour or meal, so you will have bread. Joachim, you will go with them."

The young monk stared at him open-mouthed. "But . . . What do I know of the forest?"

"Lueter Holzhacker knows the forests. And Gerlach Jaeger has ranged about hunting deer and wolves." Jaeger, who had been hunkered down a little to the side of the group whittling on a limb, looked up and spat. "By m'self," he said, and resumed whittling.

Everyone looked at everyone else. Those whose blood harbored the small-lives, but who had not yet fallen ill, hung their heads, and a few stood and walked off. Gregor Mauer shrugged and looked at Klaus, who tossed his arm Krenkishly. "If Atiulf is hale," he suggested.

When the villagers had dispersed, Joachim followed Dietrich to the millpond, just above the sluiceway to Klaus's mill. The wheel turned in bright splashes of water, but the stones were silent, which meant the cam was disengaged. The mist cooled, and Dietrich welcomed the relief from the heat. Joachim faced the gurgling water where it jostled into the sluice, so that he and Dietrich stood with their backs to each other. For a time, the hissing water and the groaning wheel were the only sounds. Turning, Dietrich saw the young man staring at the bright, crisscrossed lines of sunlight that quartered the choppy stream. "What is wrong?" he asked.

"You send me away!"

"Because you are clean. Because you have a chance yet to live."

"But, you, also . . ."

Dietrich silenced him with a gesture. "It is my penance . . . for sins committed in my youth. I have nearly fifty years. How few I have to lose! You have not yet twenty-five, and many years more remain in service to God."

"So," the young man said bitterly. "You would deny me even the martyr's crown."

"I would give you the shepherd's staff!" Dietrich snapped. "Those folk will be filled with despair, with denial of God. Had I given you the easy task, I would keep you here!"

"But I, too, wish the glory!"

"What glory in changing bandages, in lancing pustules, in wiping up the shit and the vomit and the pus? *Herr Jesu Christus!* We are commanded all these things, but they are not *glorious.*"

Joachim had edged away from his diatribe. "No. No, you are wrong, Dietrich. It is the most glorious work of all, more glorious than plumed knights spitting men on their lances and bragging on their deeds."

Dietrich remembered a song the knights used to sing in the aftermath of the Armleder. *Peasants live like pigs/And have no sense for manners . . .* "No," he agreed, "the deeds of knights are not always so glorious, either." They had returned hate for hate, and abandoned all sense of that chivalry for which they had once been renowned—if that renown had ever been more than lies on the lips of minnesingers. Dietrich glanced toward Castle Hill. He had asked once of Joachim where he had been when the Armleder passed through. He had never asked Manfred.

"We have been found wanting," Joachim said. "The demons were our test, our triumph! Instead, most escaped unchristened. Our failure has brought God's punishment upon us."

"The pest is everywhere," Dietrich snapped, "in places that have never seen a Krenk."

"Each to his own sin," Joachim said. "To some, wealth. To others, usury. To others still, cruelty or rapaciousness. The pest strikes everywhere because sin is everywhere."

"And so God slays all, giving men no chance to repent? What of the Christ-taught love?"

Joachim's eyes turned dull and sullen. "The Father does this; not the Son. He of the Old Dispensation, *whose gaze is fire, whose hand is a thunderbolt and whose breath is the storm wind!*" Then, more quietly, "He is like any father angry with his children."

Dietrich said nothing and Joachim sat for a while longer. After a moment, the monk said, "I have never thanked you for taking me in."

"Monastic quarrels can be brutal."

"You were a monk once. Brother William called you 'Brother Angelus.' "

"I knew him at Paris. It was a sly gibe of his."

"He is one of us, a Spiritual. Were you?"

"Will cared naught for the Spirituals until the tribunal condemned his propositions. Michael and the others fled Avignon at the same time, and he threw in with them."

"They would have burned him."

"No, they would have made him rephrase his propositions. To Will, that was worse." Dietrich found a small smile in the jest. "One may say anything, if only it is framed as a hypothesis, *secundum imaginationem.* But Will holds his hypotheses as matters of fact. He argued Ludwig's case against the Pope, but to Ludwig he was a tool."

"Small wonder we are smitten."

"Many a good truth has been upheld by wicked men for their own purposes. And good men have caused much wickedness in their zealotry."

"The Armleder."

Dietrich hesitated. "That was one such case. There were good men among them." He fell silent, thinking of the fishwife and her boy in the Freiburg market.

"There was a leader among the Armleder," Joachim said slowly, "called 'Angelus'."

Dietrich was a long time silent. "That man is dead now," he said at last. "But through him I learned a terrible truth: that heresy *is* truth, *in extremis.* The proper object of the eye is light, but too much light blinds the eyes."

"So, you would compromise with the wicked, as the Conventuals do?"

"Jesus said the weeds would grow with the wheat until the Judgement," Dietrich answered, "so one finds both good men and bad in the Church. By our fruits we will be known, not by what name we have called ourselves. I have come to believe that there is more grace in becoming wheat than there is in pulling up weeds."

"So might a weed say, had it speech," said Joachim. "You split hairs."

"Better to split hairs than the heads beneath them."

Joachim rose from his rock. He skipped a stone across the millpond. "I will do as you ask."

THE NEXT day, four-score villagers gathered on the green under the linden, prepared to leave. They had tied their belongings into bundles, which they carried on their backs or in a sack on the end of a pole slung across their shoulder. Some had the stunned look of a calf at slaughter and stood unmoving in the press with their eyes cast down. Wives without husbands; husbands without wives. Parents without children; children without parents. Folk who had watched their neighbors shrivel and blacken into stinking corruption. A few had already started out alone on the road. Melchior Metzger went to Nickel Langermann, who lay on a pallet in the hospital, and embraced him one last time before Gottfried shooed him away. Langermann was too far in delerium to recognize the caress.

Gerlach Jaeger stood to the side and watched the assembly with no small displeasure. He was a short, thickset man with a wiry black beard and many years of the forest in his face. His clothing was rough and he carried several knives in his belt. His walking staff was a thick oak limb, trimmed and whittled to his pleasure. He stood now with both hands cupped over the top of it and his chin resting on his hands. Dietrich spoke to him.

"Will they fare well, do you guess?"

Jaeger hawked and spat. "No. But I'll do what I can. I'll train 'em up in makin' snares and traps, and there's one or two might know which way the bolt sits in the crossbow's groove. I see Holzhacker has his bow. And his axe. That's good. We'll need axes. Ach! We *don't* need a casket full of *klimbim*! Jutte Feldmann, what are ye thinkin'! We're goin' in the Lesser Wood and up the Feldberg. Who d'ye think'll carry that thing? Herr God in Heaven, pastor, I don't know what people have in their heads."

"They have grief and tragedy in their heads, hunter."

Jaeger grunted and said nothing for a time. Then he raised his head and took his staff in hand. "I guess I count myself lucky. I've no woman or kin to lose. That's luck, I s'pose. But the forest and the mountain, they won't care about grief, and you don't want to hie into th' wilderness with half a mind. What I meant is that they don't need to take everything with 'em. When the pest has gone, we'll come back and it will all be here waiting."

"I'll not be coming back," Volkmar Bauer snarled. "This place is accursed." And he spat for good measure. He was pale and unsteady yet, but stood among those leaving.

Others took up Volkmar's cry and some threw clods of dirt at Gottfried, who had come also to watch them go. "Demons!" some cried. "You brought this on us!" And the crowd growled and surged. Gottfried snapped his horny side-lips like a pair of scissors. Dietrich feared his choleric nature coming to the fore. Even in his weakened condition, Gottfried might slay a dozen attackers with his serrated forearms before sheer weight of numbers brought him down. Jaeger lifted his staff and brandished it. "I'll have order here!" he cried.

"Why did they stay when their countrymen left?" shouted Becker. "To show us our doom!"

"Silence!"

That was Joachim, employing his preacher's voice. He strode onto the green, threw back his cowl, and glared at them. "Sinners!" he told them. "Do you want to know why they stayed?" He gestured toward the Krenkl. "They stayed to *die!*" He let the words echo from the surrounding cottages and Klaus's mill. "*And* to give us succor! Who among you has not seen the sick comforted, or the dead buried by them? Who, indeed, has not been nursed by them, save by your own obstinancy? Now you are invited to a greater adventure than any minnesinger's invention. You are invited to be the New Israel, to pass a time in the wilderness, and possess as your reward the Promised Land. We will bring in the New Age! Unworthy, we are, but we will be purified by trials as we await the coming of John." Here he dropped his voice and the murmuring crowd fell silent to catch his words. "We will live apart for a time, while Peter leaves and the middle age passes away. There will be many trials; and some among us may be found wanting. We will experience privation and heat and hunger and perhaps the wrath of wild beasts. But it will strengthen us against *the day of our return!*"

There was a ragged, subdued cheer and a few amens, but Dietrich thought they were more cowed than convinced.

Jaeger took a breath. "Right, then. Now that everyone is here . . . Lütke! Jakob!" With a great deal of profanity and one or two swipes of his staff, he started his flock moving. " 'Children of Israel,' " he muttered.

Dietrich clapped him on the shoulder. "Those were also a fractious lot, I have read."

As the others filed past, Joachim came to Dietrich and embraced him. "Fare well," Dietrich told him. "Remember, listen to Gerlach."

The hunter, at the wooden bridge cried out, "Heaven, ass, and welkin-break!"

Joachim smiled wanly. "To the peril of my soul." The others had gone back to the village and the two were alone. Joachim looked back toward the village and a shadow seemed to pass across his features as he took in the mill and the oven, the mason's yard, the smithy, Burg Hochwald, St. Catherine's church. Then he brushed at his cheek and said, "I must hurry after," and shifted the blanket-bundle he wore around his shoulder. "Or I'll be left, and . . ." Dietrich reached out and pulled the monk's cowl up over his head.

"The day is hot. The sun can strike you down."

"Ja. Thank you. Dietrich . . . Try not to think so much."

Dietrich placed his palm on the other's cheek. "I love you, too, Joachim. Take care."

He stood on the green watching the monk depart; then he moved to the bridge to catch a final glimpse before they vanished between the shoulders of the autumn fields and the meadow. They bunched up there, naturally, where the way was narrow, and Dietrich smiled, imagining Gerlach's profanity. When there was nothing more to be seen, he returned to the hospital.

HE MOVED Hans that night out into the open so that the Krenk could gaze on the firmament. The evening was warm and moist, having the characteristics of air, being moved to that state from the corruption of fire, for the day had been hot and dry. Dietrich had brought his breviary and a candle to read by, and he was adjusting his spectacles when he realized that he did not know the day. He tried to count from the last feast of which he was certain, but the days were a blur, and his sleeping and waking had not always matched the circle of the heavens. He checked the positions of the stars, but he had not noted the sunset, nor had he an astrolabe.

"What seek you, friend Dietrich?" Hans said.

"The day."

"Bwah . . . You seek the day at night? Bwah-wah!"

"Friend grasshopper, I think you have discovered *synecdoche.* I meant the date, of course. The motions of the heavens could tell me, had I the skill at reading them. But I have not read the *Almagest* since many years, or ibn Qurra. I recall that the crystalline spheres impart a daily motion to the firmament, which is beyond the seventh heaven."

"Saturn, I think you called it."

"Doch. Beyond Saturn, the firmament of stars, and beyond that, the waters above the heavens, though in a form crystallized to ice."

"We, too, find a belt of ice bodies girdling each world-system. Though, of course, they turn on the hither side of the firmament, not the farther."

"So you have said, though I understand not what then keeps the ice water from seeking its natural place here in the center."

"Worm!" Hans replied. "Have I not told you that your image is wrong? The sun sits in the center; not the earth!"

Dietrich held his forefinger in post. "Did you not tell me that the firmament . . . What did you call it?"

"The horizon of the world."

"Ja, doch. You say its warmth is the remnant of the wondrous day of creation; and beyond it no one can see. Yet this horizon lies in every direction at the same distance, which any student of Euclid can tell you is the locus of a sphere. Therefore, the earth lies truly at the center of the world, *quod erat demonstrandum.*"

Dietrich smiled broadly at having determined successfully the question, but Hans stiffened and emitted an extended hiss. His arms flew up and across his body, presenting the serrated edges. *A protective gesture,* Dietrich thought. After a moment, the Krenkl's arms slowly relaxed, and Hans whispered, "Sometimes the dull ache sharpens like a knife."

"And I conduct a quodlibet while you suffer. Are there no more of your particular medicines?"

"No. Ulf needed it far more." Hans pawed with his left hand, seeking Dietrich.

"Move, twitch. I can barely see you. No, I would rather discourse on great questions. Unlikely, that either you or I have the answers, but it distracts a little from the pain."

Dawn was crawling up the Oberreid road. Dietrich rose. "Perhaps some willow bark tea, then. It eases head-pain among us, and may serve you also."

"Or kill me. Or it may contain the missing *protein.* Willow bark tea. . . . Was it among those things Arnold or the Kratzer tried? Wait, the *Heinzelmännchen* may have it in his memory." Hans chittered into his *mikrofoneh,* listened, then sighed. "Arnold tested it. It makes naught."

"Still, if it dulls the pain . . . Gregor?" He called to the mason, who sat by his eldest son on the other side of the smithy. "Have we any willow bark prepared?"

Gregor shook his head. "Theresia was stripping bark two days ago. Shall I fetch it?"

Dietrich dusted his robes. "I will." To Hans, he added, "Rest well. I'll be back with the potion."

"When I am dead," the Krenkl replied, "and Gottfried and Beatke drink of me in my memory, each will give his share to the other out of charity, and thus will the quantity double in size from being traded back and forth. Bwah-wa-wah!"

The jest escaped Dietrich, and he supposed his friend had developed a flaw in his weave. He crossed the road, waving to Seybke at work in his father's stoneyard. Carving tombstones. Dietrich had told the masons not to worry at the task, but Gregor had said, "What is the point of living if folk forget you when you're dead?"

Dietrich knocked on Theresia's doorjamb and received no answer. "Are you awake?" he called. "Have you any willow bark prepared?"

He knocked again and wondered if Theresia had gone to the Lesser Wood. But he pulled the string on the latch and opened the door.

Theresia stood barefoot in the middle of the dirt floor, wearing only her nightgown but crumpling and wringing a coverslut in her hands. When she saw Dietrich, she cried out. "What do you want! No!"

"I came to ask after willow bark. Excuse my intrusion." He backed away.

"What have you done to them?"

Dietrich stopped. Did she mean those who had left? Those who had died in the hospital?

"Don't hurt me!" Her face had turned red with anger, her jaw clenched tight.

"I would never hurt you, *schatzl.* You know that."

"You were with them! I saw you!"

Dietrich had just begun to parse her sentence, when she opened her mouth once more; only this time, rather than cries of fright, there issued forth a fountain of black vomit. He was close enough that some of it spattered him, and the rank of it quickly filled the room. Dietrich gagged.

"No, God!" he cried. "I forbid this!"

But God was not listening and Dietrich wondered madly if He, too, had fallen to the pest and His vast incorporeal essence, "infinitely extended without extent or dimension," was rotting even now in the endless void of the Empyrean sphere, beyond the crystalline heavens.

The fear and rage had fled from Theresia's countenance and she looked down at herself with astonishment. "Daddy? What's wrong, Daddy?"

Dietrich opened his arms to her and she staggered into them. "Here," he said. "You must lie down." He reached into his scrip and pulled out his cloth pocket of flowers and held it to his nose. But their essence had faded, or else the stink was too great.

He guided her to the bed, and thought as she leaned upon him that she had become already as light as a spirit. As it is the nature of earth to seek the center of the earth, so is it the nature of air to seek the heavens.

Gregor had come to the door of the cottage. "I heard you cry—Ach, Herr God in Heaven!"

Theresia turned to go to him. "Come, dear husband." But Dietrich held her firmly. "You must lie down."

"Ja, ja, I am so tired. Tell me a story, Daddy. Tell me about the giant and the dwarf."

"Gregor, bring my lance. Wash it with old wine and hold it in the fire, as Ulf showed us. Then hurry."

Gregor leaned against the jamb and ran a hand over his face. He looked up. "The lance. Ja, doch. So soon as possible." He hesitated. "Will she . . . ?"

"I don't know." Gregor left and Dietrich made Theresia lie down upon the straw. He arranged a blanket under her head as a pillow. "I must check for the pustules," he told her.

"Am I sick?"

"We'll see."

"It's the pest."

Dietrich said nothing, but lifted the sodden gown.

There it sat in her groin, great and black and swollen, like a malignant toad. It was larger than the one he had lanced on Everard. It could not have grown overnight. When the onset was rapid, the afflicted died quickly and quietly, without pustules. No, this had been growing for several days, if he was to judge by those he had seen on others.

Gregor rushed in and squatted beside him, first passing him the lance still warm from the fire, then taking Theresia's hand in his own. "*Schatzi,*" he said.

Theresia's eyes had closed. Now they opened and she gazed seriously into Dietrich's face. "Will I die?"

"Not yet. I need to lance your pustule. It will give great pain, and I have no more sponges."

Theresia smiled, and blood dripped from the corners of her mouth, reminding Dietrich of the stories of the Freudenstadt Werewolf. Gregor had found a cloth somewhere and he dabbed at the blood, trying to clean her, but more blood welled up with every dab. "I am afraid for her to open her mouth," he said tightly. "I think all her life will gush forth."

Dietrich climbed atop the woman and sat athwart her legs. "Gregor, hold her down by the arms and shoulder."

He reached toward the pustule in Theresia's crotch. When the point had but touched the tough, hard integument, Theresia shrieked, "*Sancta Maria Virgina, ora pro feminis!*" And her legs spasmed wildly, nearly unseating Dietrich. Gregor grimly held tight to her arms.

Dietrich pressed in with the point, thrusting a little to break the skin, as he had grown sadly accustomed to doing. *I am too late,* he thought. *The pustule is far advanced.* It was the size of an apple, and of a dark, malignant blue.

"She showed no sign of it yesterday," Gregor said. "I swear it."

Dietrich believed him. She had concealed the signs, afraid of being bedded among the demons. What sort of fear was it, he wondered, that could smother even the fear of ghastly death? The Lord had commanded, *be not afraid,* but men broke all His other commandments, why not that one?

The skin broke and a thick, foul, yellow ichor oozed forth, coloring her thighs and soaking into the straw ticking of the mattress. Theresia screamed and called on the Virgin again and again.

Dietrich found another pustule, much smaller, high up on her inner thigh. This, he lanced more swiftly and with a cloth squeezed out as much pus as he could. "Examine under her arms and on her chest," he told the mason.

Gregor nodded and pulled her gown up as far as he could. Theresia's cries had subsided into sobs. She said, "The other man was not so nice."

"What was that, *schatzi*? Pastor, what does she mean?"

Dietrich would not look at him. "She is delirious."

"He had a beard, too; but it was bright red. But Daddy made him go away." The blood ran down her chin as she talked and Gregor mopped after it without hope.

Dietrich remembered the man. His name had been Ezzo, and his beard had been red from his own blood, after Dietrich had slit his throat and pulled him off the girl.

"You are safe now," he told the girl, told the woman she had become. "Your husband is here."

"It hurts." Her eyes were clenched closed now.

There was one more pustule, under her right arm, as big as Dietrich's thumb. This was more difficult to lance, for when he came off her legs, they bent and tucked themselves up, as small children were wont to do when sleeping. Theresia hugged her knees. "It hurts," she said again.

"Why has God abandoned us?" Gregor asked.

Dietrich tried to pry Theresia's arm loose so he could lance the last pustule. He did not think it mattered. "God will never abandon us," he insisted, "but we may abandon God."

The mason swept his arm wide, relinquishing his grip on Theresia's shoulder. "Then where is He in all this?" he shouted. Theresia flinched at the bellow and he immediately took a more tender note and stroked her hair with his great stubby fingers.

Dietrich thought of all the reasoned arguments, of Aquinas and the other philosophers. He wondered how Joachim would have answered. Then he thought that Gregor did not need an answer, did not want an answer, or that the only answer was hope.

"Theresia, I need to cut the pustule under your arm."

She had opened her eyes. "Will I see God?"

"Ja. Doch. Gregor, look for some cooking oil."

"Cooking oil? Why?"

"I must anoint her. It is not too late."

Gregor blinked, as if anointing were a sudden and alien thing that had never been done before. Then he released Theresia and went to the other side of the cottage, near the hearth, and came back with a small flask. "I think this is oil."

Dietrich took it. "It will do." His lips moved in silent prayer as he blessed the oil. Then, wetting his thumb in it, he traced the sign of the cross on her forehead, then on her closed eyelids, praying, "*Illúmina óculos meos, ne umquam obdórmium in morte . . .*" From time to time, when Dietrich paused to recollect the proper words, Gregor would say, "Amen," through his tears.

He was nearly finished with the sacrament when Theresia coughed and a bolus of blood and vomit issued forth from her mouth. Dietrich thought, *the small-lives are in there. They will have gotten Gregor and me.* Yet this was not the first time he had been spattered; and Ulf, on his last inspection of Dietrich's blood, had pronounced it still clean.

But Ulf died many days ago.

When he had completed the rite, Dietrich set the oil aside—others would need it soon—and he took one of Theresia's hands in his own. It seemed a fragile thing, though the skin was rough and cracked. "Do you remember," he said, "when Fulk broke his finger and I taught you how to set it?" Her lips, when she smiled, were as red as berries. "I do not know which of the three of us was more frightened, you, I, or Fulk." To Gregor, he said, "I remember her first words. She was mute when I brought her here. We were out in the Lesser Wood searching for peony and other herbs and roots, and I was showing her where to find them when her foot became caught in the cleft of a fallen branch, and she said . . ."

"Help me," said Theresia and her hand clenched Dietrich's so tight as possible in her weakness. She coughed a little, and then a little more, and the coughing built until a great flood of vomit and blood poured from her, soaking her gown all the way to her waist. Dietrich reached around to turn her head so that she would not choke on the effluvium, but as he lifted it he knew, perhaps from that it was a little lighter than before, that his unbegotten daughter had died.

SOME LONG time afterward, he crossed the road to the hospital to tell Hans what had happened and found the Krenkl had died also in his absence. Dietrich knelt by the corpse and lifted the great, long, serrated arms and folded them across the mottled torso in an attitude of prayer. He could not close the eyes, of course, and they seemed still aglow, though that was only the rays of the declining sun out beyond the autumn fields reflecting through them like one of Theodoric's raindrops, and the shadow of a rainbow fell on Hans's cheeks.

· 9 ·

NOW
Tom

THE SUBCONSCIOUS is a wonderful thing. It never sleeps, no matter what the rest of the mind does. And it never stops thinking. No matter what the rest of the mind does.

Tom awoke in a cold sweat. *No, it's not possible!* It was absurd, ridiculous. But everything fit. It all fell into place. Or did it? Was it the answer to his dilemma, or a chimera that made sense only as a troubled dream?

He glanced at Sharon, who sprawled, fully clothed, beside him. She must have returned late from the lab and crashed. Usually, he woke when she entered the condo, no matter how late the hour or how deep his sleep; but he could not remember her coming in last night. She turned slightly and a smile sketched itself on her lips. Dreaming of chronons, no doubt.

He eased out of bed and tiptoed from the room, closing the door gently behind him. He seated himself at CLEODEINOS and called up the Eifelheim file. He carefully checked and cross-referenced each item, creating a relationship map. Information lay in the arrangement of facts, not in the facts themselves. Rearrange them in another configuration and—who knew?—their meaning could change utterly.

He put his facts into chronological order, placing undated items through context or through logical relationship, not always an easy task. Not only had the calendar been unreformed, but they had started years at different times. In the Empire, a Year of Our Lord started on the Feast of the Incarnation, while regnal years, like IV Ludovici, began on the civil new year day. It seemed screwy to Tom, but Judy had laughed and said, "*Render unto Caesar, Tom. Popes and emperors may have been trying to one-up each other for centuries, but no one ever forgot that they had different spheres of authority.*"

Which meant that everything from January 1 to March 25 of 1349 CE, in the modern reckoning, had been recorded as Anno Domini 1348.

He interpolated the dates when the Black Death had broken out in Basel and Freiburg, and any other contextual events on which he could find information. The record was spotty, incomplete. If the strangers had arrived in the fall, why had there been no rumors about sorcerors and demons in Oberhochwald for six months or more? He didn't really know when Dietrich had bought the wire; nor when the "travelers had determined to try for home." And how did Ockham fit in? The Pope had invited him to Avignon on 8 June 1349, but there was evidence he had left Munich earlier, just ahead of the Plague outbreak there. Nothing further was ever heard of him, and historians supposed he had died of the Plague along the way. His route would have taken him near Oberhochwald. Would he have stopped there to see "my friend, the *doctor seclusus*"? Had he brought the Plague with him from Munich? Had he died there?

Tom chewed on the tip of his lightpen. He envied physicists. The answers were always "in the back of the book." If the physicist were only persistent enough or clever enough, she could pry them loose from the universe. Cliologists were less fortunate. The facts themselves did not always survive; and those that did survived by luck, not importance. No amount of persistence could interpret a record that had perished in a long-ago fire. If you couldn't live with that—with the knowledge that the answers were *not* in the back of the book—best stay out of history altogether.

He studied his list and diagrams carefully, referring to the original documents from time to time to refresh his mind on the details. On a map, he checked the flight of the "Feldberg Demon" from St. Blasien "in the direction of the Feldberg." Oberhochwald lay in its path. In the end, he saw no other possible explanation. In fact, he wondered now why he hadn't seen it earlier. What had he told Sharon that day in the restaurant? Maybe the subconscious is smarter than we think.

Or maybe not. He leaned back in his chair and stared at the ceiling, pulling his lip. He couldn't see any obvious flaws in his reasoning; but what did that mean? Sometimes the obvious is only wishful thinking. He needed a second opinion. Someone on whose judgement—and discretion—he could rely. He copied his files and added a summary. When he looked at the old digital wall clock with its liquid crystal display, it was 03:20 hours. That meant 09:20 hours in Freiburg. He took a deep breath, hesitated, then, before he could have second thoughts, he downloaded all of it to my office, a quarter of a world away. It contained a single question: *Was glaubst du?* What's your guess?

TOM'S MESSAGE piqued my curiosity. I e-mailed that a reply would require several days' research, at least, and strolled off to the library at the Albert-Louis. There, I found some of the documents he had asked about and compared them to others he had sent. Then I searched out further documents and blew off the centuries and read them as well. Afterward in solitude, I smoked my heavy, carved, *schwarzwälder* pipe and in the tobacco smoke, I pondered. Dignity, we save for our old age; and what I had of it, I had earned. Yet, Tom was hardly the sort of man to leap to conclusions or to play a prank on a friend.

But a friend is a friend, and you may have noticed that he and I were *duzende.* We used "du" with each other, and that is no light thing.

So two days later, I scanned the documents I had found and compressed them and did all that wonderful stuff that modern technology allows; then I attached them to an e-mail. Cautiously—very cautiously—I outlined my conclusions. If Tom had the brains that God had given turnips, he could read between the lines as easily as on them. That is what "intelligence" means: *inter legere.*

"WHAT ARE you doing up so early?"

Tom started violently; his chair nearly rolled from under him. He caught himself on the edge of his desk and, when he looked around, he saw Sharon standing in the bedroom doorway, rubbing her eyes. "Don't sneak up on me that way!"

"Why, how *should* I sneak up on you? Besides, a Mack truck could sneak up on you, you were so intent on that printer." She yawned. "That's what woke me up. The printer."

She padded in her bare feet into the kitchen and turned on the teakettle. "Time to get up anyway," she called back over her shoulder. "What are you up to at this hour?"

Tom pulled the last sheet from the printer and scanned it quickly. He had been reading my message as it emerged. "I'm linked with Anton. We've been IM-ing for the past hour."

"Anton Zaengle? How is the old dear?"

"He's fine. He wants me to come to Freiburg." Tom flipped through the stack of printouts, riffling them with his thumb. "This is the bait to lure me there."

She poked her head around the kitchen archway. "Freiburg? Why?"

"I think he thinks what I think."

"Oh. Well, I'm glad you cleared that up."

"It would take too long," he said, "and sound absurd."

"That hasn't stopped you before." She wiped her hands on a dish towel and crossed the room, where she stood behind him, leaning with both her hands on his shoulders. "Tom, I'm a physicist, remember? Next to strange, charming quarks *nothing* sounds ridiculous."

Tom pulled on his lower lip. After a moment, he tossed the printouts into his desk basket. "Sharon, why would a medieval, backwoods priest need two hundred feet of copper wire?"

"Why . . . I don't know."

"Neither do I; but he ordered it specially made." He leaned forward and pulled a sheet from the stack. It was underlined heavily in red. "And during the summer of 1349, monks in a monastery near Oberhochwald heard thunder when there were no clouds in the sky." He put the sheet down. "And *peccatores Eifelheimensis,* the Sins of the Eifelheimers. Something Anton found. It denounces the heretical notion that there could be men with souls who were not descended from Adam."

Sharon shook her head. "I'm still asleep. I don't get it."

Tom was suprised to discover how reluctant he was to say his thoughts aloud. "All right," he said. "About seven hundred years ago, sentient beings from another world were stranded near Oberhochwald, in the Black Forest."

There. He'd said it. He held up a hand to forestall Sharon, whose mouth had dropped open. "Their vessel malfunctioned. I think it traveled through Nagy hypospace. They weren't killed, but it was enough to start a forest fire and injure some of them."

Sharon had found her voice. "Wait a minute, wait a minute. What *proof* . . ."

"Let me finish. Please." Tom gathered his thoughts and continued. "The aliens' sudden appearance out of nowhere and their physical features—yellow, bulging eyes, for example—frightened many of the villagers, who fled, spreading rumors of demons to the nearby towns. Others, including the village priest, Pastor Dietrich, saw that the aliens were creatures in need of help. Just to be safe, he obtained a carefully worded ruling from his bishop; something he could do in Latin without giving the show away.

"The aliens lived in Oberhochwald for many months. While Fra Joachim and others were accusing them of sorcery and demon worship, the villagers tried to help the aliens repair their damaged vessel. I should have seen that in the business with the copper wire. What possible use would that have been to earthly travelers? They also flew. Were they winged creatures? Did they have anti-gravity? Perhaps they had a way to harness that vacuum energy you talk about. In his letter, Pastor Dietrich carefully denied only that his guests flew by *supernatural* means."

He had run out of breath. He studied Sharon's face for a hint of her reaction.

"Go on," she said.

"The aliens were immune to the Plague—different biochemistry—and repaid the villagers' kindness by caring for them. At least some did. Others, I'm sure, had succumbed to apathy by then. Dietrich even converted a few. We have a record of at least one baptism. Johannes *Sterne*? Oh, he knew where his guests came from. He knew.

"The aliens, too, began to die. Not from Plague, but from the lack of some vital nutrient. That different biochemistry again. 'They eat, but take no nourishment' was how Dietrich put it. When his friend Hans died—this is a guess, now. When Hans finally died, Dietrich buried him in the churchyard and had a carving of his face put on the stone so that future generations would know. Only he didn't realize how many generations that would be; or that the village itself would vanish.

"The taboo? Easy. There really were 'demons' there. And shortly after Joachim cursed the place, it was struck by Plague. Impressive enough for superstitious peasants. Were the demons really dead, or just sleeping? Waiting for new victims? People shunned the place and passed the proscription on to their children. If you don't obey Mama, the flying devils will come and take you away. Shortly, Joachim's tag of *Teufelheim* was euphemised to *Eifelheim,* and the original name of Oberhochwald was gradually forgotten. All that was left was a custom of avoiding the location, vague folktales of flying monsters, and a gravestone with a face on it."

There it was. All out in the open now. A lot of it was surmise, inference. He had no primary sources on Brother Joachim, for example, but I had found him a memoir by an abbot at the Strassburg friary which quotes Joachim as saying, "The great failure at Oberhochwald brought the most terrible of curses on their heads, about which I had warned them repeatedly," which seemed clear enough evidence of his damnation.

SHE STARED at him, her head spinning. *Aliens?* she thought. *In medieval Germany?* It was fantastic, unbelievable. Was he serious? She listened as he described his evidence. His solution seemed more incredible than the original problem!

"And you think this scenario is true?" she asked when he had finished.

"Yes. And so does Anton." He showed her a note that had come with the printouts. "And he is nobody's fool."

She read the note quickly. "He doesn't come out and say so," she pointed out.

Tom grinned. "I said he was no fool."

"That's better left to you, I suppose. What I'd like to know is why you dragged Nagy space into it. If you're determined to ruin your own reputation, can't you leave mine out of it?"

Tom scowled. "Give me credit for a little sense," he said. "I'm saying this theory explains the facts very neatly. And, if it's true . . ." His voice trailed off.

If it's true . . . Sharon felt her heart quicken.

"I dragged Nagy space into the picture because neither Dietrich, nor anyone else, described a spaceship."

"How could they," she pointed out. "They had no concept of spaceships."

"Medieval people weren't stupid. They were having a technological revolution themselves. Camshafts and waterwheels and mechanical clocks. . . . They would have recognized a spaceship as a vehicle of some sort, even if they called it Elijah's chariot. But, no. Dietrich and Joachim and the Bull of 1377 all state that the aliens 'appeared.' Isn't that how you described hypospace travel the other day? A single stride covers great distances, was how you put it. No wonder Dietrich was so interested in seven league boots. And that's what Johann meant when he pointed at the stars and asked how he would ever find his way home again. Traveling the way he did, he would have had no idea which one was his own."

"Appeared. That's a lot to read into a single verb."

He slapped his stack of computer printouts with the flat of his hand. "It all ties together, though. Consilience, not deduction. No single strand of reasoning is enough to support the conclusion; but taken together . . . A prayer attributed to Johann says that there are eight secret ways to leave the Earth. How many dimensions in your 'hidden' hypospace?"

"Eight." The word came out reluctantly. Her blood hammered in her ears. *What if?*

"And the religious treatise attributed at third hand to Dietrich: to travel to other worlds you have to travel inside. You used almost those exact words. Your twelve-dimensional geometry became a 'Trinity of Trinities.' The writer mentioned 'times and places we cannot know, save by looking inside ourselves.'"

"But, that really was a religious treatise, wasn't it? I mean, the 'other worlds' were Heaven, Hell, and Earth, and 'traveling inside' meant searching one's soul."

"Ja doch. But the ideas weren't written down for seventy-five years. The writers took something they had heard at third or fourth hand and interpreted it according to some familiar paradigm. The rationalism of the Middle Ages was already giving way to the romantic mysticism of the Renaissance. Who knows what Dietrich himself understood when Johann tried to explain it to him? Here." He closed the flap on the manila folder and handed the entire package to her. "Read through it the way Anton did and see if it doesn't make sense."

She looked him in the eyes as she took the folder from him. *He really is serious,* she thought. Which, knowing Tom, could mean that he was unable to deal with the original problem's insolubility.

Or else, maybe his idea was not as crazy as it sounded.

Give him a fair chance. *He deserves that much before I call the men in the white suits.*

She went to her beanbag chair and slumped into it. She read the items slowly and carefully, relying on his English translations. Middle German was too hard to follow, and Latin was Greek to her. From the edge of her eye she could see Tom fidgeting.

Crazy, disconnected items. But a thread that ran through them, tying them together. She came at last to the treatise that Tom had shown her originally. She recognized the ugly, angular capital. Another illustration was the icon of the Order of St. Johan, which showed each person of the Trinity within small triangles set at the corners of a larger triangle. Curiously, the Holy Spirit was shown at the top. It was eerily similar to her own doodle of the polyverse.

When she finished, she closed her eyes and tried to see her way clear to the answer. She tried putting the puzzle pieces together as he had. If *this* went with *that* . . . Finally, she shook her head, seeing the trap that he had fallen into. "It's all circumstantial," she said at last. "No one comes right out and says anything about aliens or other planets." The teakettle began to whistle and she went to the kitchen to turn it off. She laid Tom's papers on the kitchen table, where she had dumped her own papers last night. She opened the cabinet above the sink and searched for a morning tea.

"Yes, they did," Tom insisted. He had followed her into the kitchen. "They did come right out and say so. In medieval terms and concepts. Oh, *we* can talk easily enough of planets orbiting stars; but they were just beginnning to realize that their own planet turned on its axis. 'World' meant . . . Well, it meant the 'polyverse.' And 'planet' meant 'stars that moved.' We can talk about multidimensional space-time-whatever continua.

But they couldn't. They were only just grappling with the concept of a continuum—they called it 'the intension and remission of forms'—and Buridan had only just formulated the first law of motion. They didn't have the words to define the words. Everything they learned from the starfarers was filtered through a *Weltanschauung* unequipped to handle it. Read Ockham someday; or Buridan or Aquinas. It's nearly impossible for us to make sense of them, because they envisioned things differently than we do."

"People are people," she said. "I'm not convinced." It occurred to her that she was not playing Devil's Advocate. It was Tom who was advocating devils. She wanted to share this Tom-like joke with him, but decided that it was not the right time for it. He was too deadly serious.

"Everything you have," she told him, "could be read another way. It's only when you put them all together that they seem to form a pattern. *But have you put them together right?* Do all your pieces even come from the same jigsaw puzzle? Why should there be any connection at all? Maybe the journal wasn't kept by your Pastor Dietrich. There might be other Oberhochwalds—in Bavaria, in Hesse, in Saxony. The 'upper village in the high woods.' My Lord, that must be as rare in southern Germany as Main Streets are in the Midwest." She held up a hand to forestall his objections, as he had done to her earlier. "No, I'm not mocking you. I'm just pointing out alternatives. Maybe the lightning flash really was a lightning flash, not an energy leak from a crippled hypospacecraft. Maybe Dietrich sheltered Chinese pilgrims, as you thought originally. Maybe Joachim was high on ergot when he thought he saw flying monsters. And copper wire must have other uses than repairing alien machines."

"What about the descriptions of the hidden, innner worlds and the Trinity of Trinities? Doesn't that sound like your hypospace?"

She shrugged. "Or it sounds like medieval theology. Physics and religion both sound like gibberish if you don't know the basic axioms." She poured the hot water into a teapot and let the brew steep. There was no room on the kitchen table, however. It was littered with papers. When she had dropped the folder there, some of the contents had skidded out. Tom's printouts were mixed with her own from the lab. Medieval manuscripts and circuit diagrams for chronon detectors. She tsk'ed at the mess and began to straighten it up. Tom stood in the doorway.

"Do you know what I find significant?" Tom said. "The way Dietrich referred to the aliens."

"If they were aliens, and not hallucinations."

"All right. *If* they were aliens. He always called them 'beings,' or 'creatures,' or 'my guests,' or 'travelers.' Never anything supernatural. Didn't Sagan once say that alien visitors would be careful not to be mistaken for gods or demons?"

She snorted. "Sagan was an optimist. The ability to cross space doesn't make anyone more ethical, any more than the ability to cross the ocean made the Europeans more ethical than the Indians." That page was Tom's, and that page. This page was hers. She put each into its proper folder. "I remember what he said *would* be convincing proof of alien visitors. It was in that book he wrote with Schlovski."

"What was that?"

"A set of plans for some sort of high-tech hardware." And that page was Tom's. And that was hers . . . No, wait. That wasn't a circuit diagram; it was Tom's illuminated capital. She froze suddenly, her throat tight. "Oh, my God!"

"What?" He jumped away from the wall. "What is it?"

"I don't believe it!" She grabbed the copy of the treatise and waved the illuminated capital in his face. "Look at it! Vines and leaves and trinities? That *is* a circuit diagram! Those are Josephson junctions! Tom . . . Hernando and I *built* this circuit only last week."

SHARON LEAFED through the papers until she found the diagram she wanted. She laid it side-by-side with the manuscript and studied the two together. Were they the same? The illumination was all twisted, like a real vine; not laid out geometrically. She tried to match the leaves and knots and grape clusters with the arcane nucleonic symbols. Only the connections in the drawing mattered, she told herself; not the length or shape of the vine-wires. Almost, it seemed to her. The two almost matched. Not quite, though.

"Garbled in transmission," she told Tom. Garbled, or was she the one now seeing things that she wanted to see? "That linkage is impossible—" She pointed to the capital. "And that is a shorted circuit. And those two components should be reversed. Or should they . . . ? Wait a minute." She traced the vines carefully with her fingers. "Not all the differences are garbled. This is a *generator,* not a detector. See there? And there? It's part of a generating circuit. It has to be. Part of their stargate. Damn!"

She had reached the bottom of the page.

"What is it?" he asked.

"Part is right. It's not complete." She frowned and left the kitchen, deep in thought. She reached her pillow sofa and dropped into it. She closed her eyes and began swinging through the jungle-gym lattice of her hypospace like an ur-hominid not yet out of the trees.

"This may sound weird," Tom announced, "but I feel oddly disappointed."

She opened her eyes and looked at him. He was studying the medieval circuit diagram. "Disappointed?" She couldn't believe he had said that. Disappointed? When they had just been given the stars?

"I mean, that they didn't leave a complete set of plans. Then you'd know what to do."

She stared back at him where he stood framed in the kitchen doorway. "But I already know the only thing that matters."

"What's that?"

"I know it can be done."

· 10 ·

NOW
Anton

I MET Tom and Judy at the Hauptbahnhof in Bismarckallee, where the magnetic train slid up from Frankfurt-am-Main. We took the Bertholdstrasse streetcar to Kaiser Josef Strasse and walked from there to the hotel on Gerberau. I pointed out the sights like the worst of tourist guides. Tom had seen it all before, of course; but it was new to Judy.

When we walked through the Schwaben Tor, she commented on its storybook appearance. This gate had been standing a century in the walls of the Old Town when Pastor Dietrich had befriended certain strangers. Nearby stood the Red Bear, which had been an inn already in that same era. The wind from the Höllental was cool, a sign that summer's end was near.

After settling them in their rooms, I took them to lunch at the Römischer Kaiser. We gave our full attention to the meal. To do otherwise in the Schwarzwald would have been a cardinal sin. No one on earth cooks like the Schwarzwälder; even our department store mannequins are portly. Not until the waiter had delivered our streussel did I allow the conversation to turn to business.

Tom wanted to leave for the Forest immediately. I could see the eagerness in him, but I told him we would wait for morning. "Why?" he wanted to know. "I want to see the site for myself." Judy waited patiently, saying nothing.

"Because Eifelheim is deep within the Forest," I said. "It will be a long drive and a hike, even if we can locate the site quickly. You will need a good night's sleep to recover from the jet lag." I took another bite of my streussel and set my fork down. "And another reason, my friends. Monsignor Lurm from the diocesan office will be joining us once he has received the bishop's permission. I have not, naturally, told him what we expect to find. Thus, he will be a valuable check on our preconceptions."

Tom and Judy glanced at each other. "What do you mean?" asked Tom. "Why do we need someone from the diocesan office?"

Sometimes my friend is a little slow. "It is a Catholic cemetery, *nicht wahr?* You did not come all this way only to look. Surely you will want to exhume the grave and see who, or what, is buried there. For that we need the permission."

"But . . ." Tom frowned. "That cemetery is seven hundred years old."

I shrugged. "What of it? Some things are eternal."

He sighed. "You're right. I suppose we must wait until morning then."

Americans are in too much of a hurry. A single fact is worth a volume of deductions. Best to plan carefully how to find that fact. Tom would have had us on the site sooner—but without a shovel.

WE DID do one thing first. I took them to the crypt in the Franziskanerkirche and showed them the mural of the grasshoppers in imitation of the *Last Supper.* The colors were faded and the paint chipped, and the figures had that odd appearance that those unused to Klimt or Picasso think unnatural.

Tom stood close and peered at them. "Do you suppose this is *them*?" I only shrugged. "Why are there only eight?" he wondered.

"I suppose to avoid a charge of blasphemy."

Judy said, "There are names under some of them."

That, I had not noticed on my previous visit. We gathered round and tried to read the corrupted letters. There had once been names under all, but the centuries had destroyed many of the letters, even entire names. One grasshopper wore the mantle of a Knight of the Hospital and was called—if we guessed the missing letters properly—Gottfried-Laurence. Another sat with its head tilted back and its arms outspread—in death? In prayer? That name began with the letter U, and must have been very short. Uwe, I thought, or Ulf. The one in the center, sharing out its bread, was "St. Jo—" and leaning on its breast was "-ea-ric-."

"Not your traditional names for the apostles," I commented.

But Tom made no answer. He could not take his eyes off the figure in the center.

MONSIGNOR LURM met us outside the hotel the next morning. He was a tall, gaunt man with a high forehead. Dressed in a faded bush jacket, only his collar revealed his calling.

"*Na, Anton, mein Alter,*" he said, waving some papers. "I have them. We must pay the proper respect and disturb nothing but the one grave. Personally, I think Bishop Arni will be more than happy to bury this Dracula nonsense." He looked at Tom and Judy. "That is something, isn't it? To bury it, we must dig it up!" He laughed.

I winced. Heinrich was a virtuous man, but his puns had earned him many years in Purgatory. I also felt guilty that I had deceived him regarding our intentions. "Permit me," I said. "This is my friend from America, Tom Schwoerin, and his assistant, Judy Cao. Monsignor Heinrich Lurm."

Heinrich pumped Tom's hand. "Dr. Schwoerin. It is to me a great pleasure. I much enjoyed your paper on the gene frequencies of the Swabian tribes. It greatly clarified the routes of their migrations. A good thing for you that my ancestors dropped their genes everywhere they went. Eh?"

Before Tom could respond to this latest *bon mot,* I interrupted. "Heinrich is an amateur archeologist. He has excavated several Swabian villages from before the *Völkerwanderung.*"

"You're *that* Heinrich Lurm? The pleasure is mine. I've read your reports, father. You're no amateur."

Heinrich flushed. "On the contrary, 'amateur' comes from the Latin *amare,* to love. I do archeology for love. I am not paid."

Heinrich had rented two Japanese pickup trucks. Two men with drooping moustaches waited beside them, talking quietly. There were picks, shovels, and other paraphernalia in the bed of the first truck. When the men saw us coming, they climbed into the bed of the second.

"I think there is an old logging road that will take us close to the site," Heinrich told me. "It cannot be too far a walk from there. I will drive the first truck. Anton, you take the second. *Fräulein* Cao," he turned to her. "You may ride with me. Since I am celibate, you will be safer than with these two old goats." He grinned at me, but I pretended not to notice.

WE TOOK the Schwarzwald-Hauptstrasse into the mountains, turning off at Kirchzarten. The road began climbing as we drove into the Zastiertal. I rolled the window down and let the cool mountain air blow into the cab. In the back, the workmen laughed. One of them began singing an old country song.

"Too bad that Sharon could not come," I said.

Tom looked at me briefly. Then he faced forward again. "She's working on another project. The one I told you about."

"*Ja.* The circuit diagram. That was the most remarkable thing of all. Never again will I look at a manuscript illumination in the same way. Think of it, Tom. Could you or I ever have recognized it for what it was, let alone what it meant? Pfaugh." I waved a hand. "Never. And Sharon. Would she ever have seen it? Medieval manuscripts. No, physicists do not do such things. Only because the two of you were together could it ever have happened the way it did. And if she had not thought of that comment of Sagan's just before she looked . . . ?"

Tom looked out the side window at the trees whipping past. "It was the wildest sort of coincidence. Who knows what else may be out there, lying in archives and libraries, unrecognized because the right people haven't looked at it in the right way? Things for which we've found safe, acceptable, *believable* explanations."

A few kilometers past Oberreid the road became rough and I paid all my attention to my driving. The Feldberg loomed high on our right. Shortly, the Monsignor honked and his arm jabbed out of the leading truck, pointing left. I saw the old logging road and honked to show that I understood. I pulled the floor shift to put us in four-wheel drive.

Heinrich drove like the lunatic he was. He seemed unaware that the road was no longer paved. Our truck bounced and shook as I followed him and I wondered if we would lose the two workmen clinging to the back. I silently praised the Japanese quality-control workers who had helped make our shock absorbers.

THE SUN was already high when we reached the area where Eifelheim had once stood. There was no sign of it. I had copies of the satellite images in my hand but, close up, everything looked different. Nature had reclaimed its own; and the trees had had seven centuries in which to grow and die and grow again. Tom bore a bewildered expression as he turned round and round. Where had the village green been? Where the church? We might have walked past the place entirely, except that the American soldiers who had stumbled upon the site had thoughtfully left behind their empty beer cans to mark it.

Heinrich took charge and the rest of us fell quickly into the roles of his assistants. But then he was a field man and we were not.

From among the equipment in his rucksack he took a GPS transceiver. Within moments he had pinpointed our location. He marked the map with a grease pencil, then pointed with it. "The church must be buried under a cruciform mound atop that small hill. The graveyard is most likely to the rear of the chancel; although it might also lie to the side."

We found the mound quickly enough and split into three teams, each searching the ground in a different direction from the chancel end. It was not long before one of the workmen, Augustus Mauer, found what might have been a headstone, smashed to rubble. We could not be sure. Perhaps they were natural rocks. We resumed our search.

JUDY FOUND the grave. I could see her off to my right when she stopped and stared down at the ground. She did not call out, but only stood quietly for a time. Then she crouched and I could no longer see her through the brush.

I glanced around, but no one else had noticed. They continued to pace slowly forward, searching the forest floor. I made my way across and found her kneeling next to a sunk and broken stone. Soil action had claimed the lower half of the stone, but it had sunk at such an angle that the face on it had been partially protected from the elements.

"Is this it?" I asked quietly.

She gasped and sucked in her breath. She turned and saw me and relaxed visibly. "Dr. Zaengle," she said. "You frightened me."

"I am sorry." I crouched beside her, my old bones protesting. I studied the face on the stone. It was worn, as only the breezes of seven centuries can wear. Its outlines were faded with time, obscure and barely visible. How had the soldiers ever noticed it? "Is it the grave?" I asked again.

She sighed. "I believe so. At least, it is the one that the soldiers found." She held up a cigarette butt to show how she knew. "The inscription is nearly illegible, and parts of the top are broken off; but see here? The letters? . . . HANNES STE . . ." She traced them with her fingers.

"Johannes Sterne," I said for her. "John from the Stars. The name he was baptized under." I looked around us. "Do you realize how many graves there must have been? And this is the one we find."

"I know. I'm scared."

"Scared? Of what?"

"When we dig him up. He won't be the right shape. He'll be something wrong."

I did not know how to answer her. Burgher or alien, whatever the shape, it would be wrong in one sense or another. "Gus found another headstone," I told her. "So did Heinrich. Both were smashed. Tom thinks that when the Plague swept through here the neighboring villagers came and destroyed the gravestones of the 'sorcerors.' Yet, this one—presumably the one that most frightened them—was not touched. Why?"

She shook her head. "There is so much we do not know, and never will know. Where did they come from? How many were there? Were they brave explorers or bewildered tourists? How did they and Dietrich establish communications? *What did they talk about, those last few months of life?*" Her face, when she turned it up to me, verged on tears.

"I imagine," I said as gently as I could, "that they talked of going home and the great things they would do when they got there."

"Yes," she said more quietly. "I suppose they would have. But those who could have told us are long dead."

I smiled. "We could hold a seance and ask them."

"*Don't say that!*" she hissed. Her fists, clenched tight, pressed on her thighs. "I've been reading their letters, their journals, their sermons. I have been inside their heads. They don't feel dead to me. Anton, *most of them were never buried!* Toward the end, who was left to turn the shovel? They must have lain on the ground and rotted. Pastor Dietrich was a good man. He deserved better than that." There were tears on her cheeks now. "As we were walking through the forest, I was frightened that I would meet them, still alive. Dietrich or Joachim or one of the villagers or—"

"Or something horrible."

She nodded silently.

"That's what frightens you, isn't it? You are a rational, secular, twenty-first-century woman, who knows absolutely that alien creatures would look different and smell different; and yet you would run screaming like any medieval peasant. You are afraid you would act as badly as Fra Joachim."

She smiled a faint, small smile. "You are almost right, Dr. Zaengle." She closed her eyes and sighed. "*Hay cu'ú giúp tôi. Cho toi su'c manh.* I am afraid I would not act as Pastor Dietrich did."

"He shames us all, child," I said. "He shames us all." I looked around at the tall oaks and the wildly beautiful mountain flowers—the woodmasters and butterheads—and listened to the rattle of the woopeckers. Perhaps Dietrich had had a fine burial, after all.

Judy took a deep breath and dried her tears. Then she said, "Let's tell the others."

HEINRICH GAVE directions for the dig. "After so long, the coffin will have disintegrated. Everything will be filled with clay. Dig until you find wood fragments; then we will switch to the trowels."

Gus and Sepp, the other workman, began their digging a little ways out from the grave. Because the remains would have sunk over the centuries, they would have to dig deep. They wanted the sides of the hole to slope inward so that they would not collapse. Both men were of old Breisgau families. Gus's folk had been stoneworkers for many generations; and Sepp Fischer was descended from a long line of fishermen along the River Dreisam.

It was already late afternoon when the digging began, but Heinrich had come prepared with gas mantles to work into the evening. There were also tents and bedrolls. "I would not want to try and find my way back in the dark," he said. "Remember Hänsel and Gretel."

It was only when the evening sun was setting that we discovered how the soldiers had discovered the face. The light streamed through a gap in the trees, stiking the stone and throwing the carving into sharp relief. Through some accident of weathering, it was only when lit from that angle, in the growing gloom of twilight, that the features stood out, as if it were a hologram projected into the stone. Gus and Sepp were bent over their shovels and did not notice; but Heinrich was stooped just beside it and, hearing Judy's gasp, turned and stared.

It was a mantis's face and it wasn't. The eyes were large and bulging and the stone carver had given them a hint of faceting, so that they sat like gemstones in the alien countenance. (Those eyes would have been yellow, I knew.) There were traces of lines that might have been antennae or whiskers or something else entirely. Instead of insectlike mandibles, there was a mouth of sorts; a caricature of human lips and chin. Judy grabbed my arm. I could feel her nails dig into my skin. Tom was tugging his lip. It was the face from the church crypt.

Heinrich paused and stared at the stone without speaking. It was obvious that this was no weathered distortion of a human face. It was a demon. Or something like a demon. Heinrich turned and looked at us, gauging our reactions. Already the sun had moved and the visage was fading. "I think," he said, "perhaps I should take a rubbing."

THE MOON was a ghost drifting through the treetops when Gus finally struck wood. The gas lanterns hissed and sputtered, embedding a shifting circle of brightness in the dark of the forest. Judy was kneeling by the edge of the hole, her eyes closed, sitting on her heels. I don't know if she was praying or sleeping. I could barely see the heads of the men in the pit.

Tom came and stood next to me. He held Heinrich's rubbing of the alien's face. *Hans,* I reminded myself. Not "the alien" but Johann Sterne, a person, someone who died a long time ago; far from home, in the company of strangers. What had he felt near the end, when all hope had been lost? What emotions had washed through that alien mind? Did my question even mean anything? Did strange enzymes coursing his blood play the role of adrenaline? Had he even had blood?

Tom pointed to the sky. "Full moon," he said. "Wrong time to dig up Dracula's grave." He tried to smile to show that he was joking. I tried to smile to show him that I knew. I shivered. It was cooler in the mountains than I had thought it would be.

Sepp called out and we all jerked like puppets. Judy came suddenly alert and leaned forward over the pit. Tom and I walked to the edge of the hole and looked in.

Sepp and Gus were standing to one side while Heinrich probed in the clay with a trowel. There was something shiny and smooth protruding from the earth. Pale. Not bone-white, but yellow and brown. He excavated around it and removed it, earth and all. Then he sat back on his haunches and scraped at it with a putty knife, cleaning it; his own face set as solidly as any carved in stone.

He knows, I thought.

A face emerged gradually from the embrace of the clay. Gus gasped and dropped his shovel. He crossed himself hastily three times. Sepp remained calm, watching with narrowed eyes. He nodded solemnly, as if he had always known the soil of Eifelheim would yield unearthly fruit.

It was a skull, and not a skull, and no earthly mind had ever sat within it. Soil chemistry had been at work on it, but our worms and bacteria had for their part found it unappetizing. The eyes were gone, of course, and two enormous sockets set on either side of the head gaped empty; but whatever had served him for skin was still largely intact. It was a mummy's head.

Heinrich held it out and Judy took it gingerly. Tom stood behind her, inspecting it over her shoulder. Heinrich climbed from the pit and sat on its edge with his feet dangling in the hole. He took his pipe from his pocket and lit it; though I noticed his hands trembled a bit with the match. "So, Anton. Now will you tell me what I have gotten into? I have a feeling Bishop Arni will not like it."

So I told him. Tom and Judy added the details. The mystery. The folktales. The hints and fragmentary evidence. Heinrich nodded as he listened and asked an occasional question. Tom's explanation of hypospace physics confused him, I think; but then he was getting it at second hand. I think Tom was confused as well. Sharon lived in a different world than we, an austere world and strangely beautiful; but one whose beauty we could at best only dimly grasp. Sharon had seen the likeness of a circuit in a manuscript illumination. Let it go at that. Her insight had given Tom the courage to test his intuition; and his intuition had sent her groping down a path that might one day give us the stars. Surely, God moves in mysterious ways.

Heinrich accepted it all quietly. How could he doubt when he had held the skull in his own hands? He looked out into the surrounding forest. "There will be the remainer of the skeleton, of course," he said, pointing into the grave with the stem of his pipe. "And of others as well. You say there were several of these beings? And out there?" The pipe stem swept the Black Forest. "Out there, what? Shards of metal or plastic, rotted or decomposed beneath the living soil." He sighed. "There is much work to be done. And don't forget the cries of fraud or hoax that will be raised. We will need to bring others up here; tell Bishop Arni and the university people."

"No!"

We all looked at Judy in surprise. She still held Johann's skull in her hands, and Gus, his initial fright over, was peering at it curiously, eyeball to eye socket. I was proud of the way our two workmen had reacted. Whatever was to come of all this, it boded well.

"You know what they'll do, don't you?" she said. "They'll dig him up and wire him together and hang him behind bulletproof plastic so tourists can gawk at him and children make nasty jokes and laugh. It isn't right. It isn't." When she shook her head her whole body shook.

"That's not true, Judy," Tom said, gently putting his hands on her shoulders. She twisted her head around and gazed up at him.

"Let them gawk and let them joke," he said. "Oh, we'll take measurements and holographs and chip off some cells for the biologists to wonder at. That much, *he* would have wanted. Then we'll make plaster casts and hang those. But him, we'll keep safe from harm and someday—when Sharon's work is done—someday we'll find out where he came from and take him home. Or our children's children will."

Heinrich nodded, his pipe sending filigrees of smoke toward the sky. Sepp still stood in the pit, leaning on his shovel. He had his hands folded over the top of the shaft, looking up where the stars shone through the canopy of trees; and his face was a mixture of wonder and anticipation the like of which I have never seen.

Oh happy posterity who will not experience such abysmal woe and will look upon our testimony as a fable.

—PETRARCH

HISTORICAL NOTES

I HAVE tried to depict the milieu of the mid-fourteenth-century Rhineland as accurately as possible, but that is difficult enough to do for early twenty-first-century America, let alone a time and place where the worldview was so different from our own categories of thought.

For one thing, they took Christianity seriously; in many ways, more seriously than modern Bible-thumpers. At the same time, they took it more matter-of-factly. It was Christendom, but the first stirrings of the nationalism that was to destroy it were being felt. At Crécy and elsewhere, it had begun to matter which nation or race you were.

Philosophers studied nature with virtually no intrusions by theologians who were themselves natural philosophers. Natural philosophy formed the basic undergraduate curriculum, along with logic and the "exact sciences" of mathematics, astronomy, optics, statics, and music. Art and humanities were not taught. Doctors of theology, medicine, and law had first to master this curriculum. Never before or since has such a large proportion of a population been educated so exclusively in logic, reason, and science.

Key was the concept of secondary causation: God had endowed material bodies with the ability to act upon one another *by their own natures*. Hence, "natural laws." If God made the entire world, then invoking God to explain the rainbow or magnetism or rectilinear motion added nothing to human understanding. Philosophers therefore sought natural explanations to natural phenomena. That a later century would invoke religion over a trivial matter of the earth's motion would likely have astonished them.

WITH TWO notable exceptions, the historical events and personages mentioned in the text were as described. The likeness of Margaret Maultasch, the Ugly Duchess of Tyrol, was used to portray the Queen of Hearts in *Alice in Wonderland*. The Markgraf Friedrich mentioned in the text was Friedrich III, who ruled in Baden, not his cousin, Friedrich IV, who ruled at the same time in Pforzheim. The months in which the Black Death struck various cities and regions were compiled by Peter Ravn Rasmussen in an atlas at www.scholiast.org/history/blackdeath/index.html.

Marshal Villars really did refuse to take his army through the Höllenthal, using the excuse quoted. The overthrow of the Strassburg town council and the Friday 13th massacre of the Jews were described in the *Chronicles of Strassburg*. Duke Albert and King Casimir did offer their realms as sanctuaries to the Jews, and the guild militias did assemble and defend the Jewish quarter of Regensburg. As in any age, there were wicked men and good. The story of the Feldberg Demon is recorded in the *Annals of St. Blasien*. The argument for natural rights of people against their prince was advanced by William of Ockham in his *Opus nonaginta dierum.* (And earlier, by Aquinas in *On Kingship.*) Ockham determined and incepted, but never took a doctorate. He was last heard of when he left Munich on 10 March 1349 to make his peace with the Pope. The date on his *Denkmal* in Munich is incorrect, as we know from documents that he was alive after that point.

The two major alterations to historical events are the Flagellant procession at Strassburg and the Storming of Falcon Rock. The Flagellants did not actually reach Strassburg until June of 1349 and the Papal Bull condemning the practice was not issued until 20 October of that same year, after the events of the story. I have moved both of them up to February to coincide with the Benfeld conference.

The Freiburger militias stormed and took Falcon Rock in 1389. I moved it up by forty years, to March of 1349 and had Manfred participate. The romantic *causus belli* was as described.

A minor alteration: Nicole d'Oresme did not write *De monete,* in which he enunciated Gresham's Law, until after the time of the story. There are a number of other small adjustments of this sort.

PHYSICS NOTES

THE MODEL that Sharon develops for the multiverse was slapped together and given a coat of paint many years ago for the novella "Eifelheim" (*Analog*, Nov., 1986) from which the "Now" portions of this book derive. Mohsen Janatpour, who now teaches at the College of San Mateo in California, was most helpful in this and Janatpour space was, and is, named in his honor.

Recently, variable light speed (VLS) theories have become a hot topic among cosmologists. One prominent advocate is João Magueijo, whose gossipy book *Faster Than the Speed of Light* is a good introduction, as well as an entertaining narrative of how physics actually gets done. I was pleased to read in his book that he considered the "Kaluza-Klein" model that Mohsen and I came up with back in the 1980s, though unsurprised to see him reject it. I decided to keep it, just because.

In all fairness, the historical decline in light speed really does seem due to changes in measurement methods. VLS theories address a change only in the aftermath of the Big Bang, as a way of getting around the kludge of inflaton fields. The inflaton, invoked simply to save the appearances of the theory and afterward allowed to disappear from the universe, would never have passed muster with Buridan, and Will Ockham would have howled about the needless multiplication of entities. VLS theories nicely resolve the "cosmological problems" using inherent feedback loops that homeostatically fine tune the universe. No new entities are needed.

When we last spoke, Mohsen and I discussed also the quantization of the redshift. Some physicists see it; others don't. Same data. One explanation for a quantized redshift is that time is quantized just as space is supposed to be. Since I had already invented the fictional chronon for the original "Eifelheim," the redshift business fits right in. If it's true, we may have to revise the universe, again.

A NOTE ON TERMS AND SOURCES

CERTAIN GERMAN terms, idioms, and turns of phrase employed from time to time have been written as if they were English: thus "gof " and "doodle" instead of *Gof* and *Dudl.* But for the most part, English equivalents have been used. So, Bear Valley and Stag's Leap instead of Bärental and Hirschsprung. Wiesen Valley instead of Wiesenthal. Birds like Waldlaubsänger and Eichelhäher are woodleafsingers and acorn-jays; flowers like Waldmeister are "woodmasters," and so forth.

The feudal and manorial systems were common across Western Europe although by the time of the story both had been breaking down for some time. The terminology is equally strange, whether German, French, English, or Latin. I have used the more familiar term unless there is good reason otherwise. So, *castle, manor, steward, dungeon* instead of *schloss, hof, verwalter,* or *bergfried.* Where the English term would have sounded "too English," the German was employed: *buteil, vogt, junker* instead of *heriot, reeve,* or *squire.* The German for a *joust* was *buhurdieren,* so I used the archaic English word, *bohorts.*

Manfred's speech on page 173 is adopted from the fourteenth-century biography of Don Pero Nino, *El Victorial* ("The Unconquered Knight,") by Gutierre Díaz de Gómez, one of his companions.

The description of Manfred girded for war on page 172 is adapted from the medieval epic, *Ruodlieb.*

Fr. Rudolf 's sermon on page 195 is from Peter of Blois, 1170. Max's complaint about sportsmanship on page 196 is likewise taken from life.

The story of Auberede and Rosamund on page 120, which took place in France, is recounted in Régine Pernod's *Those Terrible Middle Ages!* and combined with that of another peasant. That two medieval women serfs could own a house in town and go off there to live together may startle some.

The famous stink of Brun, brother to Otto, and the attendant bathing practices mentioned on page 194 are from the epic *Ruotger* and applied to Manfred's neigbor. We often read that people did not bathe in the Middle Ages, yet we have the evidence from *Ruotger* and also, more offhandedly, from the flagellants' oath not to bathe for the duration of their service. It would seem contrary to swear an oath to avoid something that one never did. More likely, in Transalpine Europe in a time before hot water heaters, bathing was a sometime thing.

"Falcon Song" on page 222 was modified and adapted from Franz H. Bäuml's *Medieval Civilization in Germany, 800–1273,* (Ancient Peoples and Places, v. 67).

Dietrich's discussion of the intension and remission of forms and the mean speed theorem on page 85 is adapted from William of Heytesbury's *Regule solvendi sophismata,* as quoted and discussed in Edward Grant's *The Foundations of Modern Science in the Middle Ages.*

The Latin honorifics bestowed on various philosophers have been translated. So Peter Aureoli, the *doctor facundus,* is "Doctor Eloquent" and Durandus, the *doctor modernis,* is "Doctor Modern." Will Ockham, who never completed his doctorate, was called the *venerabilis inceptor,* the "Old Inceptor." Inceptor was a "degree" short of the doctorate that endowed *ius ubique docendi,* the right to teach everywhere.